BOUND

BOOK TWO:
<u>SHADOWED SERIES</u>

Alyson Dawn

BOUND
Book Two of the Shadowed Series

Copyright © **2025** by **Alyson Dawn**

ISBN: 979-8-9996078-3-6

This is a work of fiction.
Names, characters, places, and incidents are products of the author's imagination or are used fictitiously. Any resemblance to actual persons, living or dead, events, or locales is entirely coincidental.

Cover design by Donnie Neuber
Interior formatting by Chapters at Dawn
Published by Chapters at Dawn

To the readers who've been told
they are *too* much, *too* wild,
and too impulsive.
May the shadows remind you
that your fire is never a flaw.
It's your magic.

Author's note:

Just a reminder that shadows are born in the absence of light. With that being said, this story tugs harder, cuts deeper, and asks more of its characters. As you start this journey, please know the shadows in this book are far less forgiving.

This book contains:
violence, blood, injury, death, emotional trauma, panic responses, references to sexual assault, child abuse, grief, sexually explicit scenes, and strong language.

Prologue

Black smoke curled from the rooftops like crooked fingers. Screams threaded through the narrow streets as steel clashed and glass shattered. Soldiers with polished helms and large blades swept through the outer quarter, bearing the silver-and-black banners of King Corvin. His cruel army had come without warning, attacking in the middle of the night.

The people of Myrth woke in a frenzy, fighting back with the only weapon they possessed: *shadows*. From alleyways and open courtyards, the Shadowborn emerged, men and women marked with ancient magic. Darkness shimmered in their eyes as their bodies bent the shadows to their will. Tendrils of black energy lashed from their limbs, slicing across armor and dragging enemies into momentary wells of darkness before striking.

Flames climbed higher from burning homes and shops as battle cries pushed the King's men back. The people of Myrth fought in unison, their shadows rising into walls of darkness that crashed down on the advancing soldiers. For a heartbeat, the tide truly shifted. Soldiers fell wide-eyed and panicked, as hope flickered.

Then, the alchemists came.

Released by the King's command, they moved like feral hounds, analyzing weak points. White masks hid their faces and large, reinforced bags clung to their backs. Curved tubes snaked from each pack to the nozzles in their hands. As they entered the battle, they twisted the valves, and a toxin spilled into the streets.

The gray-green vapor burst out with a hiss, curling downward as if pulled by its own weight. The moment it touched the Shadowborn, the fragile spark of hope with them died.

They collapsed instantly, the poison burning through their lungs. They clutched at their throats and eyes as their bodies writhed. The very power that had made them strong began to betray them, convulsing beneath their skin. Black veins spread across their bodies, angered by the poison. Some tried to vanish into the walls or cracks, but the toxin followed, seeping into every crevice.

A woman who once summoned blades from nothing fell to her knees, choking. A boy who wove illusions from darkness sobbed as he collapsed. Across every street and inside every home, Shadowborn fought for air and failed.

King Corvin watched the chaos unfold from atop a dark mare. He clutched his helmet in his hands, as his pale blonde hair whipped around him and his eyes swept over the dying city. The corners of his mouth lifted, and with each cry of agony, his smile stretched wider.

"Look at them," he said to the soldier beside him. "Fragile, just like their shadows. It's a shame their design was flawed. I could have saved them."

At the edge of the market square, where the toxin barely swirled, four cloaked figures gathered through the turmoil. The purple diamonds on their backs lined together as the last line of defense for Myrth. Celeste was the first to speak, addressing the others over the screams that echoed off the walls around them. "We do something, and we do it now!"

Idris eyed the area that surrounded them, his gaze landing on a small building away from the battle. "We have to be smart about our choice in order to save our people."

Muriel looked at him in disbelief as her eyes followed his gaze, "We are the only ones who can stop this! How dare we run."

Idris turned to her and then pointed to the structure in the cemetery. "This is bigger than our city, Muriel. What we do next decides the Shadowborns fate. If we fall here, with nothing in place, *everything* dies with us."

Kyron moved instinctively, following Idris's direction. The rest moved with him, even Muriel, who took a second to look around her as her shoulders fell in defeat. They slipped through the mayhem with purpose and determination.

Darting to the low building, they ducked inside, the door slamming shut behind them.

King Corvin noticed the movement and watched their escape. He tilted his head, considering pursuit, but then his gaze returned to the streets full of twitching, gasping bodies. Some were still trying to fight, all were failing.

The Shadowborn were dying and Myrth was falling.

1

The scent of iron and ash hit her first, sharp enough to drag her toward consciousness. A strange feeling followed, like crackling electricity under skin. It started at her fingers and toes, pulling her from the depths of the dark. The sensation climbed her limbs, the pulse strengthening along with her urge to wake up. Soon, the rippling current gained heat and then, it was as if fire had consumed her body. It converged at her chest and settled there, heavy and insistent.

Something called to her from within, urging her to open her eyes. She obeyed, blinking slowly.

Once.

Twice.

The third blink held and her eyes remained open. She stared up at the ceiling before slowly turning her head, letting the reality around her come into focus.

Bodies littered the floor. Some Hunters were whole with pieces carved out of them, others lay cracked and strewn across the stone. Her head began to throb as she lifted her gaze back to the dark above her. She tried to sit up, but a painfully familiar fire flared in her thigh, stopping her. That's when she heard *his* voice. It cut through the air with pained exhaustion, but it was unmistakingly his.

"Hey, feisty," Damien murmured from beside her. "Good to have you back."

She turned her head and found Damien on his knees. His tone was light, but his face was pale, too pale. The skin beneath his eyes was gray, the same tint that was now dulling his irises.

Her breath caught at the sight of him, and the blood that was smeared across his chest and neck. "Damien," she whispered.

Instinctively, she reached for him as another wave of white-hot pain ripped up her leg. She gasped and clutched her thigh to touch bare skin. In that particular area, where the pain was the most fierce, her pants had been torn away. As she moved her hand to the source of the pain, her fingers brushed against the outline of something; a shape that ran from just below her hip to halfway down her thigh. The skin there was hot, and the raised edges seemed familiar, resting exactly where her sheath had been.

Was it a dagger?

Yes. *Her dagger,* or rather, a perfect copy of it. An exact six-inch replica of her blade was embedded just under the surface of the skin on her thigh. Not metal this time, but a dark, intricate tattoo mimicking every edge and detail of the blade she once held. Even the purple gem was there, pulsing faintly. The only difference was a violet hue behind it.

5

Damien never looked away from her, he just watched her fingers as they trailed the mark. After a moment, she looked up and met his gaze. Pushing herself upright into a standing position, she ignored the pain it caused and focused on him. It took only seconds to register that something was wrong.

"Are you okay?" Blair asked, reaching a hand toward him.

Blake, lying a few feet away, stirred at her voice and groaned a response. "I mean, I'm alive but everything fucking hurts." He stretched with an exaggerated sigh and pressed a hand to his chest. His brow immediately furrowed as his fingers skimmed over torn cloth but found no open wounds. He stared down at his body, then looked up at Damien. "You can turn into a dark arch-angel thing *and* heal?!"

Damien didn't reply. He only gave a faint smile, one that didn't reach his eyes. His focus was still entirely locked on Blair and the hand she offered. His eyes skimmed over her, like he was memorizing every line of her face. His body trembled as he forced himself up, one arm bracing the wall behind him. He tried to stand, a slow and painful motion that ended the second his legs took any weight. He collapsed, a rough groan tearing out of him.

Blake moved fast, catching him under his arms. Blair was there half a second later, steadying his other side. She glanced at Blake, her eyes full of fear. Blake caught her expression and swept his gaze around the cavern. "We need to get to somewhere safe, preferably somewhere that's *not* collapsing around us." Blair nodded as Blake positioned Damien between them, taking most of his weight.

They moved out of the cavern slowly. Soon, they reached a smaller chamber off the hallway when Blake noticed Damien's breathing grow shallow.

"Hey," Blake muttered, tightening his grip. "Still with me?" There was no response as Damien's head slumped to the side, his eyes half-lidded.

"Damien?" Blake coaxed, easing him down to the cavern floor before kneeling and pressing two fingers to his friend's neck. Blake cursed under his breath as he watched sweat now bead along Damien's forehead. "His pulse is weak."

Blair's response was low and filled with terror. "How do we help him?"

Blake took a deep breath and then pulled Damien's arm around his shoulder, attempting to hoist him up. "I've seen this before. I think he's drained. We need to get him to a healer before his body gives out."

Blair took the other side of him, her gaze locked on the slight rise and fall of his chest.

Blake said nothing else as he searched for an exit. Suddenly, he stiffened, guiding them backwards toward the wall. "We have a problem."

Blair turned her head toward the hallway they came from, bracing herself. "Please tell me it's not more Hunters."

Blake stood still for a few seconds, his gaze scanning the dark that surrounded them. A cold chill swept the room as shadows began to materialize across the floor. A thin sheet of black crawled over the stone, weaving in slow, rippling waves.

Blair's eyes widened at the impending danger, and she looked over at Blake for any type of answer as to what was happening.

"We've got company. Don't be stupid," Blake muttered, pressing his back to the wall and setting Damien down deeper into the shadows.

Blair took position in front of them, with Blake soon joining, their eyes narrowing on the room's entrance. Moments later, movement stirred and a figure stepped through the darkness.

A man.

He was lean and powerful, with braids running over the top half off his head, the bottom shaved. His dark hair matched the shadows gliding across his tan skin. He wore no shirt, only a black tactical vest, a bow slung over one shoulder, and dark cargo pants that were tucked into scuffed boots. Shadows moved across his chest in waves.

A Shadowborn.

He stopped, lifted his head, and drew in a slow inhale through his nose, which was adorned with a silver piercing that hung from his septum. Chest full of air, he exhaled slowly and watched his shadows swirl across the floor. Then, he looked up, staring directly toward their hiding place, as if he had seen them the entire time.

A small grin curved his mouth.

"I'm not a Hunter. I'm here to help. So, option one is we sit here and *pretend* it's just me in this room," he said, voice calm. "Option two is that you come out, and I see if I can help the one who smells like he's dying."

Blake scoffed, lowering his chin as if in thought. Blair however, didn't need long. She stood and went to step toward the stranger.

Blake growled at her movement, throwing an arm out in front of her. "Blair, do not-"

She paused, looking at Blake, then at Damien. Her eyes filled with a silent plea as they stood there, staring at each other. Blake relented within a second and Blair turned back toward the man, continuing forward.

The stranger didn't move, only turned his head as Blair stepped out of the dark. He nodded in greeting, then glanced toward Blake's hiding place and smiled again. "Letting her be the brave one, huh?"

Blake sighed loudly and stepped out. Shooting a glare in Blair's direction, he moved only a few steps forward still shielding the barely-conscious Damien.

"I'm Kael," the man said, nodding as his shadows slithered up his legs and merged with the ones on his chest. "I-"

"What exactly can you do to help him?" Blair said quickly, a protective edge to her voice.

Kael met her gaze. "First, I want out of here. Preferably, in one piece." His eyes flicked to Blair, then Damien. "Whatever you fought is still here, and I want no part of it." His shadows rippled up his torso and across his shoulders as he waited for their reaction.

They stood in a tense standoff as the shadows settled and Kael inhaled deeply through his nose again. This time, he tapped his septum ring lightly. "We've got about ten minutes before more Hunters arrive."

Blair and Blake exchanged looks, weighing the options.

Finally, Kael stepped forward with a deep sigh. "Look, I was scouting the area. My tracking ability picked up something unusual, so I came to check it out. Anyone nearby would've sensed the power. You can believe me and come with me or I will leave alone. Either way, we need to move. *Now*."

Apprehension flashed across Blair's face. Kael paused slightly before continuing, "I have no reason to lie, but I'm serious when I say I'm getting out of here." He then turned and pointed east. "My people aren't far. You'll be safe there until you figure out your next move." He then motioned toward Damien, "That's how I can help him, by leading you there."

Blair immediately looked at Damien, his chest barely rising. Without hesitation, she turned toward Blake. "I vote yes."

"Are you *kidding* me?" Blake hissed. "We're just trusting hot, shirtless shadow-men now?" Blake didn't take his eyes off Kael. "Did you consider this might be a trap?"

"The hot shirtless guy has a name," Kael said dryly. "And you now have *eight* minutes before your *friends* arrive."

Blair knelt beside Damien again, brushing damp hair from his clammy forehead. Damien's eyes fluttered open. He weakly tried to lift an arm toward her but winced. Blake watched him for a moment, then shifted his gaze to the shadows slithering around Kael like loyal dogs. Blake's jaw flexed, then tightened, as his eyes focused behind the man in front of him. Sensing something beyond the cavern opening, his body went rigid. "He's not lying, Blair. I can feel them."

"So, we-" Blair breathed out as she bent and lifted Damien's arm over her shoulder, "trust the shirtless man or stay here to get torn apart."

"Fine," Blake muttered after a tense pause, glaring at Kael. "But I swear, if this is a cult or a death trap, I'm feeding you to Damien when he wakes up and he's not as nice as he looks."

Kael smirked. "Noted."

Blair shot Blake a thankful look as he grabbed Damien's other arm.

"Let's move," Blake said, groaning with the effort of supporting Damien.

They didn't stop until they cleared the cavern and tunnel system. The first breath outside the cavern hit them like a blessing. Cool, crisp, air filled their lungs as their eyes adjusted to the soft light. Time had not been a priority, but it was clear the battle had lasted through the night. The clouds overhead had begun to pale, not quite dawn, but close. A faint light now bled across the sky.

Blake and Blair carried Damien together, careful not to jostle him. He stirred occasionally, trying to walk on his own, only to stumble each time. His skin had gone pale, and his breaths were uneven. They walked until the cavern disappeared behind them and fatigue pulled at their legs.

Blake let out a frustrated growl as Damien's legs buckled for the third time. "We need to stop and give him a minute."

Blair nodded, motioning to a mossy patch near a large stone. They lowered Damien carefully onto the soft ground in front of it.

As Blair eased his arm off her shoulder, she crouched next to him and studied his features.

Blake turned then, his eyes sharp on Kael, who was watching them from under a low branch just a few feet away.

Blake's jaw tightened in irritation as he registered Kael's demeanor. "Hey tracker," Blake snapped, a vein bulging in his temple. "Anything *else* we should know? Like maybe what part of these woods you are going to kill us in?"

Kael's brows lifted, catching both the aggression and the glare. His face showed the faintest reaction, but he remained still and silent.

Blake's irritation spiked. "You should know, I'm not opposed to killing fellow Shadowborn." Blake said, voice steady as he straightened his posture. "And right now, I'm not exactly sure what you have to offer."

Kael exhaled slowly, a smirk on one side of his mouth. He stepped into the half-light, morning haze catching on the stitching of his vest. "I can tell you," Kael said slowly, lowering his chin at Damien, "that he's been shadow-drained."

Blair's eyes moved to Blake, who had said something similar. When he showed no signs of responding, she looked back to Kael. "What exactly does that mean?"

He tilted his head slightly, his gaze fixed on Damien. "It means his body is sick, drained of its own life force."

Blake still showed no reaction, so Blair pushed further, needing all the answers he could give her. "And you know that, how?"

Kael tapped his nose once, lightly. "Because I can smell it."

Blair blinked a few times, processing his words. "What?"

"I can smell everything," Kael said. "Not just physical ailments but emotion, magic, decay, energy. All of it leaves a trace. Most people never notice it, but I do." Kael paused, eyeing Damien up and down, "The air around him smells like rotted ash and death, a scent belonging to those whose shadows have left them."

Silence settled as Kael walked forward and knelt beside Damien and inhaled deeply again, frowning. "I'm guessing he burned through his reserve trying to keep one of you alive."

Blair's shoulders immediately slumped. "Yeah, something like that." She swallowed, inhaling before her next question. "How do we fix it?" she asked, voice taut. "How do we help him?"

Kael rose to his feet. "We can't help him here, consider it motivation to follow me."

Blake responded then, grabbing Kael's attention. "Where exactly is it that you are leading us?"

Kael folded his arms and looked Blake up and down. "Right now? Probably a spot to rest. If I don't return to our camp by midday, my companions will come looking. It's typically only as a precaution, but for your friends sake, it may be a blessing."

"The ones coming, are they trackers? Like you?" Blake asked.

"No," Kael replied. "Each of us specialize in something different. At least one of them can help stabilize him for the journey."

"*Journey?*" Blake asked again, a sarcastic edge in his tone.

Kael's eyes flicked between them. "My town is hidden in the mountains."

Blake was already shaking his head before Kael had finished his sentence. "The mountains?! That's at least a day's trip. Is there anything you can do for him *now*?"

Kael's expression didn't change. "No. His body's beyond empty. He's surviving on instinct, leftover adrenaline, and what little power his mind hasn't let go of yet."

Blair closed her eyes briefly. "How long can he last like that?"

"Not long," Kael said simply.

Silence hung between them again as morning edged closer. The shadows around them began to thin, but the cold air remained.

Blake crouched beside Damien again, brushing dirt from his sleeve. "Then we wait," he muttered. "And when your people come, they better be everything you promised."

Kael gave a single, solemn nod before smelling the air. "They will be."

2

Blair sat cross-legged on the moss, her fingers absentmindedly weaving through a patch of clover beside Damien. His chest rose and fell in shallow waves, his skin still pale. Sweat clung to his hairline and trailed slowly down his temples.

Blair watched the small droplets slide as she pressed the back of her hand to his forehead. The skin there was clammy, but he burned with a fever beneath it. It was at that point his body began to shake, which made Blake extremely uneasy. After about ten minutes of him pacing back and forth, Blair had finally convinced him to take a walk and find water. Casting a final glare toward Kael, Blake nodded and walked away.

Karl watched him leave from a few feet away as he sat on a fallen log. His chin lifted, and his nose tilted upward as he inhaled deeply, eyes half-closed. He stayed like that, as if entranced by the scents around him.

Blair's hand drifted across Damien's chest as she spoke softly towards Kael. "He's getting worse, isn't he?"

He paused mid-breath and opened his eyes slowly. Looking at her, he shook his head once.. "No. It may look that way but his smell would worsen."

She winced and lifted her hand above Damien's heart. "Right."

Kael's voice was neutral. "He's holding on. Barely, but he's steady."

She turned toward him, her hand still resting on Damien. "Have you ever had to trust a stranger before?"

Kael was still for a second before answering. "In this world, trust is a luxury we can't afford. We survive on instinct and nothing more." His eyes moved to the trees surrounding them. "If you're asking me that because you're worried, I would suggest listening to your gut. What does it say about me? About your situation?"

Blair's face showed no emotion but it was clear that several thoughts swirled behind her eyes. After a moment of internal debate, her shoulders relaxed slightly. "No sign of your companions?"

Kael shook his head. "Their scents haven't hit the wind yet, but they will soon."

Blair nodded, her eyes returning to Damien's face. *Just a little while longer.*

As if on cue, his eyes fluttered open and he tried to smile. She shifted closer, took his hand, and lifted it to her lips. Cautiously, she kissed his knuckles and whispered to him. "Hello."

Damien tried to smile again but only one side of his mouth lifted.

Blair pressed his palm to her cheek and relished in the small warmth she felt from him. Her eyes were frantic, unable to hide the fear twisting inside of her as she mentally screamed.

I wish I could do something, anything.

She tried to focus solely on him, as if sheer *will* could anchor him to this world. A tear fell down her cheek as her eyes moved to the unsteady rise and fall beneath her hands. "Listen," she whispered, shaking her head hard. "I don't have a fancy cottage to take you to or multiple healers to fix you. " Her voice cracked, raw and desperate. "But I'll help you. I just need a little time, okay? We're figuring it out." She leaned in closer, moving her forehead to his temple.

For a moment, everything went still. Then, with effort, Damien drew in a breath. Blair froze instantly, bracing for the worst. She watched as his lashes lifted and his eyes struggled to focus, like he was fighting his way back to her.

Another tear slid down her cheek, landing on his skin.

He drew in another trembling breath, his gaze flickering from her face to her exposed thigh. His fingertip brushed the raised mark. His touch was light, "You were marked because you deserve it," he whispered. "I knew it the first time I saw you."

Her breath broke on a shudder, and she squeezed his hand tightly between hers, desperate not to lose his touch.

"You can tell me all about it later." She swallowed hard as another tear fell. "After we get you to a healer."

Damien gave a faint smile as his eyes closed again. "I know you'll be safe now," he murmured. "I don't have to lose you."

A sob tore loose from Blair's chest. She closed her eyes, clutching his hand against her face, when suddenly, a blackness stirred between them. Wisps of shadow rose from the back of her hands, curling around his. The darkness pulsed and then expanded, before seeping slowly into his skin.

Damien inhaled sharply, as if instant relief had hit him. His chest expanded as his strength surged. More shadows appeared, swirling around their joined hands and then moving toward him, as if returning home. One by one, each strained muscle in his body relaxed as dark tendrils continued to pour into him. Blair sat frozen next to him, tears falling to her lap in quiet streams. The gray hue soon drained from his skin and natural color flooded his face and cheeks. The more shadows he collected, the more he came back to life.

After another deep, steady breath, he opened his eyes. With each blink, the murkiness receded from the crystal blue color. With his second inhale, something inside of him settled, just as his eyes drifted shut again.

Blair just watched, in awe. *Somehow, he was improving.*

"Blair," he murmured, the word like a prayer on his tongue.

19

She bent over him, pulling him into a tight embrace. Silent words of gratitude spilled from her lips as she willed every remaining shadow she had into him.

She looked up at Kael, who stood staring at them. His eyes were wide in astonishment and his arms were slack at his sides. For the first time, his demeanor was neither neutral or indifferent, he was genuinely in shock.

Incoming footsteps signaled Blake's return from the nearby stream. He carried wet strips of fabric and a canteen, his brows furrowed as he watched the ground in front of him. With his sleeves rolled up, Blair noticed the dried blood and dirt that caked his skin. His arm moved as he tossed one of the rags to Blair and then knelt beside Damien, raising the other rag to his forehead.

As his eyes landed on Damien, his jaw popped open in disbelief. In a mere second, his features shifted from bewilderment to relief. Blowing out a breath, he closed his mouth and shifted, sitting beside them. Shaking his head, his eyes moved between them, pausing on Damien and then the way Blair clung to him. His eyes then caught the faint shadows that lingered between their hands. Blake's mouth curved into a grin.

"Well," he drawled, "either I missed a miracle or you two just invented a very creative form of resuscitation."

Damien's eyes opened fully at the comment, steady and clear. He wrapped an arm around Blair, pulling her closer and pressing a kiss to the top of her head. She melted into him, relief flooding her system.

Kael remained where he had been, although he was no longer in shock. Now, he was just observing them.

Blake pulled his eyes away from the people beside him and turned his grin toward Kael. "So, Tracker, want to explain what I walked into? Because if *watching* is your thing, just know Damien gets real possessive."

Kael didn't return the grin, he didn't even acknowledge the joke. His attention lingered past Blake, on Blair. His eyes narrowed slightly, like he was trying to peel back her skin and see what lay underneath. Then he tilted his head, in fascination.

"When I found you," he said slowly, "there was a scent in the air. Not just shadow, not just power. Something older." His voice dropped lower. "I'd only heard of it in stories, so I assumed the scent was wrong." His eyes sharpened suddenly, recognition flashing in them. He looked directly at Blair. "But it was you, wasn't it?"

Blair's heart lurched as her eyes widened. She sat frozen, unable to answer his question. *She couldn't answer that question, she didn't know how.*

Damien's arm tightened around her, sensing the tension that flooded her body. A small silence stretched before Damien pushed himself upright and then stood. He stretched his back and legs, then addressed Kael. "That was me."

Once again, Kael failed to converse. He raised his eyes for a split second to meet Damiens before they landed back on Blair. Damien registered this, and took a protective step forward.

Blake snorted, breaking the tension. "You got that right. Who comes with built-in shadow wings?"

That stole Kael's interest and stopped Damien in his tracks. For the first time, Kael's body shifted as if he was actually interested in the conversation. He straightened his shoulders and turned toward Blake, who raised his eyebrows and nodded slowly.

Kael's reply was only two words. "That's interesting."

Blair rose and moved beside Damien. He slipped his arm around her shoulders and leaned into her. Immediately, she knew that was his body asking for help. Curling into his side, she wrapped her arms around him, and clasped her hands together to support him. To others, it was as if Blair needed the comfort.

Blake cleared his throat as he took a step toward them and nudged Damien with his elbow. "I guess that means my chance to steal Blair is gone, huh?" He gave Damien a sly smile. "Shame."

Blair snapped her head toward him. Damien, however, met Blake's gaze and smirked, shadows flickering at his feet as if in amusement. "Do you ever shut up?"

Kael didn't acknowledge any of their conversation. Instead, he turned his attention to a gust of wind that swept through the trees. Revelling in it, he moved his head back and forth slowly as his nostrils flared.

Damien's body twitched and he made a low, pained sound. Blair immediately pressed up against him, using her body weight as an added support. Even with the progress he had made, it was like his body hadn't caught up to his will.

"What exactly happened to you three to cause this? I don't smell regret or defeat." Kael said, gaze moving from Damien to Blake, before settling on Blair's tear-stained face.

Blake's grin appeared instantly, sharp and proud. "*Defeat?* Us? Absolutely not. Especially when we have a swift princess like Blair."

Blair's mouth fell open. "I am not a princ-"

Damien chuckled softly and the vibrations moved through her, stopping her from finishing the sentence.

Across them, Kael's lips twitched before he gave a single, understanding nod. "And what is the plan now?"

Blake glanced at Damien and then at Blair. No one spoke, not when they all knew there was no plan.

Kael didn't push for an answer, instead he straightened his legs and stretched out his arms. His expression then shifted toward the trees as he addressed them all. "My people are not far from here. I am sure once you have talked to our leaders, they will want you to stay. I say that's definitely safer than wandering around, especially while one of your Shadowborn is half-dead."

Turning back to the group, it was as if Kael was speaking directly to Blair now. "*You* need to think about the best option. Time is not a luxury you will find on the road."

It was then that Blair finally felt the weight from Kael's stare and her jaw clenched in anger. Her hands moved to Damien's shoulders as she spoke. "*We'll* decide

23

as a team what is safe. As for luxuries, I'd say we have none, considering we are currently wasting *time*."

Kael pushed himself off the stump underneath him, his eyes glinting with amusement as he turned his head north. "Wasting time on him, or *relying* on him?." He took in a long breath, then another, before he smiled, "They're close, all three of them, coming in from the north ridge. Half an hour out. One's carrying a mint salve that will Damien, along with rosemary oil."

Even though she was highly annoyed, Blair couldn't help but be slightly impressed. *That was one hell of a skill.*

Just as the thought entered her mind, Damien's shadows brushed against her. She looked down as they curled around her wrists and then vanished, reappearing on the other side.

Kael noticed, but said nothing. "Rest while you can. When they get here, we move."

They all nodded in understanding, settling into the silence around them.

Minutes passed, and just as their bodies actually began to relax, boots crunched through the forest around them. Kael mumbled something to himself before stepping away without a word.

Blake was the first to rise, his body antsy. When he spoke, it was clear that he was intrigued by what was coming. "Whoever they are, they're strong."

Damien and Blair looked at each other as they stood, moving their eyes to the tree line where Kael waited.

Three figures emerged from the dark just beyond the ridge, heading straight toward Kael.

First was a woman with blonde hair shaved on one side, the rest tied in a rough braid slung over her shoulder. A long scar ran down the right side of her face, disappearing beneath her jacket collar. Her eyes were a deep brown, almost black, nothing like Blair's. She wore patchwork grays and blacks, moving like someone who'd never been caught off-guard. Shadows rippled subtly along her jawline, crawling up her neck like veins. Her features held a sharp, stone-cut stillness. The corners of her mouth rested in a slight downturn that made her look perpetually angry, while her eyes were steady and unblinking. Her entire presence carried a weight, the kind that could silence an entire room without a word.

Behind her strode another woman, completely different in aesthetic. The first noticeable thing was her pale skin, which peeked out under swirling shadows. Half of her long black hair was pulled into a ponytail and the lower half draped down her back. She wore layers of black lace and leather which clung to her frame. Fishnet stockings covered her legs and fed into thigh-high boots. Rings covered every finger, thick kohl circled her eyes, and she radiated a sense of mourning. Whereas the first woman seemed angry, this one seemed detached.

The last person who appeared was a dark-skinned man with broad shoulders. His hair hung in thick heavy dreadlocks. They framed his face in bold lines, swaying as he walked. Each one had a metal bead at the end which caught the dim moonlight. The locks carried weight, not just in size but in a way that fed into his presence. The whole look gave him an untamed, powerful demeanor. His smile came easily, though his eyes remained sharp and thoughtful. He wore loose, layered desert-style garb in deep maroons and browns, designed for movement. His shadows danced lazily over his collarbone with each breath.

From just their appearance, Blake seemed to have been right. Each carried their own brand of power, of authority.

Kael greeted them with a simple nod. "About time."

The blonde woman scoffed. "Someone wandered off and left us a vague location to 'rescue him from'. Forgive us for not sprinting."

The man beside her chuckled. "We have supplies and a stretcher."

"Good, we'll need both," Kael said, nodding over his shoulder to Damien and Blair.

The pale woman shot Kael a look, then eyed the group. "I'm guessing they're the ones needing a rescue?"

Blake remained quiet as the strangers spoke, arms crossed tight over his chest. Blair watched too, then drew a steadying breath and stepped forward when their conversation faltered.

"Hi. I'm Blair," she said, gesturing to her companions, "This is Blake." Her hands then hesitated before motioning toward Damien, who was trying to support himself. "And that's Damien. He needs help, Kael said you could give it."

The blonde woman studied her, brows creasing, "Well, you have an interesting energy."

Blair hesitated, her hand instinctively drifting to her thigh.

The woman's eyes followed, widening slightly at the mark on her skin. "That's no small magic," she said, nodding toward the dagger.

"No wonder Kael took a liking to you," the long-haired man added, stepping up beside his companion with a large item strapped to his back.

Blair eyed the object, realizing it was the stretcher. She had never seen one like that, with a reinforced frame and shimmery black cloth.

Kael spoke, breaking her thoughts. "Damien's stable now, but he should still be checked."

The man in front of them nodded in response and swung the cot off his shoulder. "Let's see him."

They moved toward Damien, who sat resting against the stone. As they approached, he held his hand up. "I'm fine, just exhausted."

The woman in black was the first to kneel. "You don't get to decide that." She eyed his hand, and then slapped it away. Without another word, she placed a hand over his heart and closed her eyes.

Blake crouched beside her, gawking openly. "Are you always this mean? Not gonna lie, it's kind of what I look for in women."

She turned her head slightly and opened her eyes just enough to look at him from the corner, before ignoring him and closing them again.

Blake took this as an invitation to reach out and touch her. "Look, I'm only-"

The woman snapped her teeth at him, then focused back on Damien's chest.

Surprised, Blake fell back, landing in a sitting position on the ground. "You like to *bite*?! Oh perfect, so it's settled then. We're getting married."

The woman turned fully this time and glared, which made Blake squeal and grab his chest in excitement. She watched him for a second and then refocused on her hand as her fingers twitched. "He's stable, but we need to hurry. His body is fighting against itself."

Blair nodded, stepping in front of Blake. "Sorry about this one." She kicked him once and waited for him to move away before giving the woman a genuine smile, "I'd thank you, but I don't know your names yet."

The blonde woman across from them was the first to dip her chin in greeting. "Rhea"

The tall man next to her grinned and did a mock bow. "Adriel."

The woman in black lace stood last. When she spoke, her voice was low and smoky. "Marrow."

Blair's eyebrows rose slightly at the name. "Marrow?"

She shrugged as her eyes found Blair's, "It's fitting." The color in her eyes shifted slightly as she talked, different grays swirling into blue with black flakes. "It's what's left when everything else burns."

Shadowstepping back into Marrow's personal space, he smirked at her. "*That* name and *that* attitude? Yeah, this is gonna be fun." He winked at her, then looked toward the others. "Matter of fact, all of us Shadowborn together? Now *that* sounds like the best kind of fun."

Adriel cocked his head slightly and narrowed his eyebrows as he pulled the bag of supplies over. "I'm gonna pretend you didn't just say that." He then shook his head and began unfolding the stretcher. "Probably best if-"

"I've got it. I can walk," Damien groaned, trying to hide any notion of his pain.

Blair turned to the group as she slid her shoulder under Damien's."Kael mentioned your city. How far?"

Rhea quickly glanced at Kael before replying. "A day. Less if we move fast," Then, she looked at Adriel, dismissing the need for a cot. "It's near the eastern ravine. He can be fully healed there."

Blair nodded, straightening up and looking at Blake. "Then we'd better move."

3

The forest shifted as they entered the eastern groves. The deeper they went, the quieter everything became. Their footsteps were the only sound, echoing off thick trunks and broken branches.

Damien stayed silent, except for a few low groans he released whenever he became winded. The four strangers walked ahead, with Kael leading the group. Every few steps, he would pause to smell the air before moving on. His shadows explored the ground in front of him in ripples, as if they were finding scent trails only he could read.

They were halfway through a dense stretch of trees when a low growl shuddered through the air.

"Stop," Kael ordered instantly, throwing out a hand. Everyone froze.

Blair turned, her hand instinctively moving to her thigh, where the faint outline of the dagger turned hot. As she ran her fingers over it, she swore something shifted beneath her skin but before she could look, another loud growl tore through the trees.

"That sounds like trouble," Blake muttered, scanning the area.

Damien's grip tightened on Blair. What little shadows he had, sensed the danger and moved to circle around her.

Kael closed his eyes, nostrils flaring. "Pack of wolves. There's three of them and they're big."

"Easy," Rhea purred, flexing her hands. Blair watched as shadows slid down Rhea's arms, weaving into thick gauntlets of darkness.

"Probably deciding if Damien's worth dragging off," Kael murmured, his hand still raised for silence.

"They'll regret it," Adriel replied, rolling his eyes.

A snapping branch to the right was the only warning they received.

Three massive, hulking creatures burst toward them. Their forms were warped shapes, forged of muscle, fangs and shadow. Their fur gleamed like wet tar, and their eyes glowed hollow white. There was no life in them, only endless darkness within their body.

"They've been infused." Rhea muttered, as shadows snapped upward from her jaw. They moved fast, covering her face and crawling over her scalp and shoulders like armor. The next second they hardened into crescent shaped shields along her arms and torso. With a roar, she charged the first beast, and slammed her shadow-armored forearm straight into its gaping maw.

Adriel faced the second wolf, whispering in a language Blair didn't recognize. The shadows coiled around his collarbones and poured into his palms that ignited into ribbons of golden-black fire. With a flick of his wrist, two searing lashes of fire cracked through the air, slicing at the beast's legs and throat. The creature snarled once before collapsing, the shadows disintegrating.

The third lunged toward Blair but Damien was already in front of her. He raised an arm, unleashing a wave of darkness that blasted straight through the wolf's chest. Kael followed instantly, black whips bursting from his hands to ensnare the beast and drag it down. Another round of shadows surged from Kael's arms and chest, caging the wolf's muzzle in coils of black. He twisted sharply, and the shadows locked, slamming the creature into a tree with a bone-shaking crunch.

Blair watched in stunned awe as those around her swiftly neutralized the threat. *She had been there, in the caverns, when Blake and Damien had fought the Hunters. She had seen this magic.*

But this? This was something else entirely.
They moved in unison, they worked together.
This was her world now.

Another hot jab flared down her thigh, stronger than before. Her body tensed as if the mark had reacted to her thoughts, calling to something within her.

Damien noticed the change in her body immediately and he looked down at her, "You alright?"

She nodded quickly at him. "Yeah, I think so." She looked at the dead wolf and then Rhea. "What did you mean by *infused?*"

Rhea made a disgusted sound as she kicked her foot through the shadowed carcass. "Since the King has graciously decided to test shadows out, it's not just people he's experimenting on. He's been pushing boundaries."

Blake's head snapped up at that. "He still hasn't given up on shadow-infusion, huh?"

Rhea nodded, wiping blood from her neck. "You're lucky we weren't in the mountains yet. Here we've got space to fight back. Up there? Those things can get nasty."

They regrouped quickly, tightening their formation as they continued forward.

As they moved on, the trees around them grew tighter, then began to thin. The forest peeled back to reveal rock and tangled roots. The mountain pass loomed ahead of them like a sleeping giant. As they left the trees, a cold wind swept down from the peaks.

Rhea moved to the front, glancing at Kael "We need to watch our footing. I'll lead." Kael nodded and fell into step behind her. The rest of the group fell into line as they approached the mountain. The closer they got, the more Blair felt her thigh pulse underneath her skin. The sensation was insistent, like it was trying to somehow communicate. Lost in thoughts of what that could mean, she stumbled. Damien caught her elbow quickly with his free hand, almost falling himself.

Steadying her, he looked down. "Are you sure you're okay?"

"I don't know," she admitted, her eyes falling to her thigh. *She just needed to figure everything out, starting with what it was trying to tell her.*

"There," Kael said quietly, pointing to a large boulder in front of them.

The texture was darker than the others around it, nearly black. As they approached, a symbol appeared at its center, a shape that glowed with a purple iridescence, much like Blair's mark.

Blake stepped up next to Damien, nudging his arm. "I bet you a lap dance we're about to see something we've never seen before."

Blair and Damien looked at each other from the corner of their eyes, and Blair stifled her smile. She then shifted her eyes to the mystery in front of her. Pausing for a moment, she tilted her head at the familiar design. As she did so, the light that danced along its surface changed, especially toward the floor. It was as if the air at the bottom wavered.

Trailing her eyes back up, Blair realized there was a black sheen to the stone, almost as if it was coated in shadows. The more she looked at it, the more the surface almost pulsed with a variety of dark threads. As her mind caught up to what she was seeing, the dagger on her thigh stopped burning and warmed, almost comfortingly.

"Damien," she whispered in front of her. "I actually think Blake's right."

Just as she said that, Blake turned to them, his voice intense, almost as a warning. "I'm sensing *a lot* of shadows guys, more than I've felt in years."

Kael smiled at that, as he stepped up to the diamond. He raised an outstretched hand and conjured a wisp of shadows in his palm. The shadows unfurled instantly, rolling like living tendrils. He pressed his palm and the living wisps within it, directly into the symbol. The "boulder" reacted immediately, seeming to shudder. A shimmer rippled up from the floor to the air above it and then expanded, creating an opening in the dark wall. Through it, stood a city cloaked in a dark fog.

Walking through the barrier, they realized the darkness wasn't a fog but air thickened by shadows, tons of them. They cascaded around buildings and ran along the roads, all gleaming faintly in the dim light.

The space in front of them held tents that were built of dark fabrics, each stretched with curling runes that glimmered when shadows brushed them. Large structures rose in the distance, some tall and narrow, others short and long. Walkways of smooth blackstone wound through the city, glowing a faint purple beneath their boots.

"This is..." Damien murmured.

"Incredible," Blair finished.

They traveled deeper, swallowed by the city's darkness. Shadowborn were all around them, practicing their magic openly. Some wove smoke-like ribbons, others shaped shadows into creatures. They all practiced and trained without fear. Here, there was no reason to hide.

The thing that caught their attention most was the children. They laughed near the edges of the tents, their shadows forming animals that darted across the ground.

At the city's heart stood a towering obsidian statue that depicted a man in simple healer's robes. His palms were open and his expression was one filled with peace. Blair looked over the creation, noticing the detail that wound through his clothes and facial features. She then noticed a sign at the bottom and knelt to read the polished plaque.

A diamond, the same symbol from the "rock", was etched into its surface. She ran her fingers over the engraved lines. "What's that symbol?"

The group paused for a moment and together, they answered: "Safety."

"It's a good one to keep an eye out for. It marks safety for all Shadowborn," Kael said softly, "Four points for four founders." He took a moment to observe the large statue and then continued, "This is Idris, one of the first Shadowborn. He was a healer and a leader."

Blair stared up at the statue, her chest tight. There was something solemn in his expression, a calm strength that was carved into his features. There was no sign of arrogance and no fury. Just a certain presence that showed pure strength, even though it came off quiet.

"He bore the mark of Void, an ability that let him take others' shadows. As a healer, he used it to help balance the ones who needed it. As a leader, he used it to disarm his enemies." Kael continued. "But he did so, knowing it wasn't an easy choice. We remember him as we continue to build the foundation for what we are, what we stand for."

Blake crossed his arms, still staring at the statue. "Is this a sanctuary then?"

"No. A sanctuary hides," Kael corrected. "This place was built to endure." He then inhaled sharply and looked at Damien, whose shoulders had begun to fold. "He's fading again. The healer is just up ahead."

Everyone nodded.

Blair pulled her eyes away from the statue as she felt a tug from Damien's hand. She gave him a small smile as they followed Kael, who must have smelt the decline in Damien's reserve.

"We're almost there," Kael reassured, confirming Blair's suspicion that Damien was getting worse.

The path funneled them toward a large structure at the base of a hill. From where they walked, they could already see that it was different from an average building. The walls rippled faintly, shifting in and out of solidity. A green door marked the entrance, ordained with a shadowed healers symbol.

Blair stayed right beside Damien as they moved closer to it, one hand tightly in his and the other wrapped around his bicep. She watched as Kael knocked once and the door opened, instantly.

Golden light spilled out, carrying the scent of lavender. Blair's shoulders loosened at the comforting smell, a hint of safety settling into her chest. A tall woman in deep violet robes stood waiting. Her jade eyes filtered through the group and then paused on Damien. "Bring him in." She then turned and led them into her quarters.

Her dark red hair moved behind her as she walked. It was made of small braids threaded with bones, crystals, and flowers. Blair watched as each little item clacked against each other as the healer readied a chair.

Her thigh then warmed again. It was becoming a pattern, something about *this* place. She rubbed it in acknowledgment as her eyes looked over the room they were in. It was unlike anything she could have imagined. Like outside, shadows ran free. They hung from the walls, as if woven into the wallpaper. They lounged around bowls of dried herbs that lined the counters. Waves of darkness that continuously moved around them, not threatening or lurking, simply present.

Blair's attention was pulled away as the healer led Damien to a low, cushioned chair on one side of the room. She squatted down, positioning him quickly as her fingers moved in practiced gestures.

"My name is Mareya," she said softly, checking his pulse with gentle movements. "Hold still for me, please."

She set both palms above his chest and a low hum filled the space around them, as her shadows stirred awake. The air warped around her hands and black shadows pulsed over Damien, almost as a tool. A small silver symbol bloomed on her chin. The more she focused, the brighter it glowed as she moved her fingers across his ribs, and down his abdomen.

Her expression softened for a moment, and then her body went absolutely still as her eyes widened. The reaction was not one of fear, but almost recognition.

With a deep breath, she called to the shadows that hovered above him. They moved swiftly, weaving themselves into his skin, through his bone and blood.

"You-" she began, then cut herself off sharply. "are dangerously close to being drained of your shadows."

She continued poking and prodding him until her hand went still on his chest. "Mm." Then, her fingers pressed lightly against the sides of his temples, assessing deeper. "I hope whatever you burned your shadows out on, was worth it."

Damien shifted his gaze to Blair, offering a weak but certain smile. "Oh, it was."

Mareya kept moving around his body, assessing strength in different areas. "You can thank the deep well of shadows that reside within you. It may be the reason you survived this long." She put her hands on her knees then, and looked up at him. "Are you aware of just how much power you hold?"

Blake scoffed at that, "Yeah, he's aware."

Mareya nodded at Blake, then returned her attention to Damien. "You'll recover, slowly. Expect lethargy, confusion, and aching while your shadows rebuild." Mareya brought a hand up to her chin, her brows lifting slightly. "It's strange though, it's almost as if your shadows had a little jump start."

Damien watched her closely but didn't say anything. Ultimately, it was Blair who stepped forward. "It was me. I gave him some of mine."

Mareya's head snapped toward her "What do you mean you *gave* him shadows?"

Blair swallowed. "They moved on their own, but I think I ultimately sent them. Either way, it helped."

Mareya stared, stunned into silence as she raised her hand to rub a bone in one of her braids. "That shouldn't be possible and yet, it makes perfect sense."

Blake let out a dry snort from his place near the wall. "Nothing makes sense right now."

Mareya paused, then smiled. As she tilted her head back, a warm, rich laugh filled the room. "Well, you've got me there," she said, still smiling. "This place exists to defy what's possible. There's a good chunk of Shadowborn that don't even know these camps exist. Not yet, anyway. We want people to believe we were wiped out a long time ago and that our family has fallen."

She moved to a side table, pulling down jars and vials. Her hands moved deftly, grinding herbs with a dark-stone pestle and mixing them with a pale blue liquid which deepened into a violet as shadows rippled through it.

"This city has been my home for many years," Mareya confessed while she worked. "Protected by the combined abilities of those who remember the old ways." She then looked up, "I have traveled to all four camps over my time as a healer and I have to say, *I have never* seen darkness like yours, young man. Nor have I seen the ability to transfer shadows. Times are changing."

She handed Damien the elixir-filled cup, "Drink this. It will help your body catch up to your magic" she glanced at Blair, "It will help you produce more. If you combine that with what she gave you, you should feel better by morning."

Damien looked up at her with quiet gratitude. "Thank you."

Mareya smiled and patted his shoulder. "Rest, Shadowborn. Our kind was not meant to be weakened."

Whispering their thanks, they slipped out quietly into the cool air. Just in that short time, the light had dimmed, yet the sky above looked unchanged.

Immediately, Blair noticed Kael's group lounging outside the healer's quarters. It was only natural to assume they were there to watch the newcomers they had just brought in as a precaution. At first glance, that's what it seemed like, but the more Blair observed them, the more she noticed how comfortable they were, how it almost seemed like they were there genuinely to check in on Damien. Kael walked up and smelled him immediately, a pleased look crossing his facial features. He then began asking a few small questions about lodging and items needed. The rest stayed a few feet away, almost lounging, as if relaxed.

Strangely, their presence comforted her. As she realized this, the dagger on her thigh blossomed in warmth, the feeling radiating to her bones. Taking a deep breath, she looked up at the sky.

In SilverDawn, the sun had been bright, illuminating everything it touched. Blair thought *that* had been the prettiest thing to see, but that was no match compared to the sky above her now. It felt as though she'd stepped into a darkened snow globe, an enclosed sphere where light was dimmed and shadows drifted like glitter, settling and then swirling around her.

Rhea noticed her gaze and stepped to her side. "There's an ability here that dims sunlight," Rhea explained. "We get a bit of daylight at noon, but this is how it stays most of the time. We prefer it."

Another reason this world was remarkable.

Blair looked over at her and smiled, before returning her gaze to the sky. "I think I do too."

Rhea offered a small approving smile before returning to her companions. Blake immediately slid into Rhea's spot, propping his arm around her shoulders. "So, what now, princess?"

Blair didn't have time to reply before a shadow launched toward Blake and smacked him upside the head. Courtesy of Damien, who was still in conversation with Kael.

"Ow-okay!" He shouted to him, holding a hand up but stepping away from Blair.

With a small smile in Damien's direction, Blair answered Blake. "We focus on him first," she said. "Then, we'll figure it out."

4

Every tent they passed bore dark markings along the fabric, the woven material resembling living darkness. Though most were the same size and shape, each one was distinctly unique, as if they had been hand-made.

Stopping at a medium-sized tent, Rhea lifted the dark flap, "I assumed you'd want to stay together. This size will fit you nicely," she explained. Moving her hand to the similar sized tents, she spoke again, "The entire section here is our sleeping quarters." She then moved her hand and pointed farther beyond the tents, "behind you is the communal eating area, and training is to the east."

Blair peered into the threshold. The tent's interior unfolded like a space stitched from shadowed magic. It was easily four times larger than it should have been, with tall ceilings and lanterns hanging in each corner. Intrigued, she pulled back and looked at Rhea.

For the first time, a proud smile formed on Rhea's face. "Another ability we are lucky to have here."

As Rhea turned to leave, she paused, catching the grime that covered Blake's arms. "In case you're looking for a shower, there's some in the training area over there. I would suggest scrubbing." She gestured to the area she had shown before. "We'll be making a fire soon, if you want to join after."

Blake opened his mouth to respond and Blair placed a hand on his chest, nodding gently. "Thank you."

Rhea gave a small nod before vanishing into the shadows.

All three moved inside the tent, each one taking in a different aspect. The room inside was simple but clean. A large bunk bed rested against the far wall, with a dresser on each side. In the middle sat a round table that held a stack of extra blankets, each one woven from the same dark fabric as the tent. As Blair moved deeper inside, she studied the walls. Up close, they shifted and moved.

Blake gave a low whistle as his fingers grazed the fabric. "And I thought my ability was cool." He looked around, his eyes landing on the bed. Stepping forward, he patted the top bunk. "I call this one!"

Blair rolled her eyes, smiling before she caught the look of exhaustion in Damien's face. "Help me get Damien settled first, you man-child."

Mocking her slightly, Blake stepped toward the lower bed. Pulling the blanket down, he then took a pillow from his own bed and placed it next to the one Damien had before stepping out of the way. Blair then eased Damien onto the bed. Kneeling, she unlaced his boots and took them off, positioning his legs as he laid down. As soon as he fully laid down, his body relaxed and his expression softened.

"Go," Blair said softly, addressing Blake but brushing Damien's hair from his forehead. "Wash up and make some new friends at the fire but play nice."

"'Nice' is subjective," Blake grinned. "But I'll behave. *Probably*." With that, he ruffled her hair, moved to the dressers, and slipped out of the tent

Blair moved the back of her hand to Damien's forehead and smiled. *He was improving.* Pulling the blanket up to his shoulders, she watched his slow, steady breathing.

After a moment, she crawled into bed next to him, lying carefully on her side so she wouldn't disturb him. Her movements remained slow and deliberate. Silence settled between them, and she breathed deeply, content that he was finally resting. That is, until his voice came, quiet and raspy.

"Top three?"

Startled, she turned toward him. A tear slipped down her cheek before she could stop it, and she let out a shaky laugh. "Go to bed."

"I will. Just talk to me." he answered.

With a small sigh of defeat she smiled. "One," she began, softly. "I'm glad you're okay."

Damien turned his head and looked over at her as playfulness sparked in his eyes. "I'd be better if you were sitting on my face."

Blair chuckled at his weak tone and shook her head as his fingers brushed gently over hers.

"Two, I'm thankful for this place. I wasn't sure if it was the best move, following people we didn't know, but it feels right."

Damien nodded, eyes agreeing with her. "And three?"

"Three..." Her lips curled downward slightly as her voice cracked. "I have absolutely no idea what comes next."

Damien pulled her closer, the growing heat of his chest warming her side. He skimmed his lips along her temple. "Good thing you're not alone then, " he murmured.

She chuckled quietly as he kissed her forehead gently.

"How's your mark?" He asked, his hand moving to graze the dagger etched into her thigh.

"Honestly, I don't know how to answer that." She said, watching his fingers trace the lines. "Sometimes, I don't even feel it but other times, it's like it's trying to tell me something." She paused for a moment and then looked up at him. "You said I would be safe, that you didn't have to lose me. What did you mean by that?"

Damien smiled. "One of the only things I learned about the dagger was from my father. He told me that as long as I have it, I'm safe." He exhaled slowly and pulled her closer. "When you used it on yourself, you absorbed whatever it had. You were bound to it. You're a part of this world now, a part of us. I don't have to lose you."

"You were never going to lose me." she said quietly.

"We'll figure out what everything means. Give me tonight to recharge, and tomorrow we'll start."

Blair nodded into his shoulder, her thoughts spinning. He continued to hold her firmly until her body relaxed into him and soon the rhythm of his heartbeat was enough to lull her into a sense of calm. It took only minutes for him to follow, his breathing slowing until he drifted into sleep.

She stayed beside him, until her own restlessness rose. Carefully sliding away, she adjusted the blanket over him. Taking one last look at his peaceful face, she smiled faintly. This expression was so different from his normal guarded one.

Quietly, she moved to the dressers. Clothes had been one of the items that Damien had asked Kael for. As she opened the drawer, she realized her instincts had been right. This was where they were meant to be. Somehow, they had found a camp filled with people who were, at their core, *good*.

Blair looked over the filled drawers. There were towels, pajamas, and a variety of other garments for each of them. She mouthed a silent thank you before choosing her outfit. Closing the drawer, she glanced at Damien and moved to the opening of the tent. Stepping outside, she followed Rhea's direction to the showers.

The path led past the sleeping quarters and other random tents, toward a larger building. Looking around, she found a small bathing house. From the outside, it seemed like nothing special but to Blair, it was everything she needed.

Opening the door, she found white tile that led to four curtained stalls. They all surrounded a central steel post that split into diamond-shaped showerheads.

A table in the corner held small vials of soap, each labeled with a different scent. Blair picked one up and sniffed, a plume of cinnamon invading her senses. She wrinkled her nose and tried another, this time it was peony and lavender. *It smelled like home.* Smiling, she held it briefly before testing the last bottle, a mix of clove, vanilla, and something warm. Intrigued, she held onto the bottle as she readied for the shower.

Peeling off her torn clothes, her eyes lingered over the dried blood and scars that covered her body. Flashbacks from the fight filled her mind and she turned her hip, looking at her thigh. The dagger was still there, still glowing with a purple essence. Running her hand along her skin, she let out a quiet chuckle. Funny enough, it was like it had always been a part of her. The mark seemed almost natural, like the last puzzle piece she had been looking for. Now she just had to figure out the picture all the pieces made.

Stepping into a stall, she reached for the nozzle and turned it. Water hissed to life, already steaming hot.

She pulled back instantly, but soon, her body welcomed the warmth. As it cascaded over her, she imagined it washing away the past few days. Her fingers moved to her head, untangling the knots that had formed in her hair. As the last one slipped free, so did the tension that had anchored itself in her body.

She had peace for a few more moments before the calm dissolved. Anxiety crept in, pulling her thoughts back to Damien, who she had left, asleep in bed. She hurried through the last rinse as she scrubbed her skin, then stepped out and wrapped herself in a towel.

Dressing quickly, she pulled on the dark shorts and tank top she had chosen. Moving toward the door, she caught her reflection in the mirror. Same freckles like constellations. Same hazel eyes. Same chestnut hair. Yet she looked so different; the soft, dark fabric fit tighter now, revealing the lean muscle that had formed from travel and training.

Evening had cloaked the camp in a burnt orange light. Fires had come to life in her absence, their glow guiding her toward familiar laughter.

Blake's voice rose above the others, loud and unfiltered. "...so then she flips over and tells me to eat it, and of course I listened, because I'm a good boy..."

Blair paused for just a second, shaking her head as his voice faded back out. The group erupted in laughter for a second time just as Blair reached them. Adriel noticed her first, gesturing to the open spot beside him. "There's room here."

She sat, accepting a piece of fresh bread from him and receiving a nod of acknowledgment from Blake. The conversations continued around her until they started to fade and then the attention was turned on her. There were questions about where she came from, how she'd ended up here. She answered each one, learning names and hearing their own stories.

Then in a rare moment of silence, Rhea leaned forward, eyes narrowing toward Blair's thigh. "Do you know much about that?"

Blair's hand instinctively covered the mark. "I'm learning."

Adriel's voice came from next to her. "We can help with that." He then grabbed the bag at his feet and took out a leather-bound journal. Opening it, he flipped through the pages until his eyes landed on one in particular. He then turned toward Blair and held the book open in front of her.

Drawn in perfect inked lines was the dagger, *her* dagger. Every curve, every mark... *identical.*

"How do you have that?" she asked, eyes wide.

Before Adriel could answer, Rhea responded for him. "That's the dagger from our origin legends."

Adriel nodded. "The story of how Shadowborn saved themselves."

Rhea stood slowly, her gaze reverent. "May I touch it?"

Blair hesitated, uneasy but not afraid. She nodded. "Sure."

Rhea knelt and brushed her fingers over the dagger's hilt. Shadows spiraled up, curling around Blair's thigh like living ink. Everyone around the fire fell silent.

Rhea gasped as more shadows grew and drew back, eyes wide.

She then looked up at Blair and bowed her head. It was a small gesture but it made Blair uncomfortable.

"There's no need for that," Blair stammered.

"Yes, there is," Rhea said, her voice steady as she looked back at Blair. "Your mark means things are changing.

The look in Rhea's eyes was almost hopeful and as much as Blair wanted to deny everything, she couldn't take that from her. Instead, she just looked down at her mark. "And that might be true but for right now, I have no idea what that means. So, please don't look at me like that."

"You may not know *yet*," Rhea replied gently. "But you carry it all the same."

Blair didn't reply, she just looked at Rhea and then down at the fire that danced in front of her. "I think you're overestimating me."

"I didn't bow because of what you *think*," Rhea said, standing. "I bowed because I believe in what I *know*. That mark means I'm standing before something more ancient than the kingdoms, more dangerous than prophecy, and more powerful than any crown."

Blair's voice softened. "I know nothing of your prophecies and crowns."

"*Yet*," Rhea replied, prodding the fire as the group around them nodded in quiet agreement.

Blair exhaled quietly as Rhea looked over to her. "You don't have to know everything. That mark shows you have potential to change things. That's what matters."

Blair nodded her head once and stood. "I appreciate that. Thank you." Glancing over at Blake, she continued, "I think I'm heading to bed. You coming?"

He rose immediately, brushing crumbs off his lap. "Thanks for the food and the laughs," he said, then looked at Rhea. "For what it's worth, I believe in her too. I've seen what she can do already and she doesn't even know anything about it yet."

Blair narrowed her eyes at Blake before looking at the others. "Thanks for the hospitality," she added politely before turning away.

They walked in silence until Blair spoke, "Why'd you have to say that?"

"Because it's true," he said simply. "None of us know exactly what happened in that cavern, but you and Damien? You're meant for something bigger. I know it."

Blair didn't reply, she just walked the rest of the way in silence. Once they reached the tent, Blake opened the tent for her. "I'm gonna hit the showers one more time. I have some tension to release *away* from you two."

Blair scoffed and pushed him as she walked inside. The tent flap closed and the sound of his laughter followed him as he walked away.

Damien was exactly where she had left him, his body slightly turned as if he had reached for her. His color had fully returned and his breathing was normal. Blair laid next to him and then turned away, not wanting to disturb him. Instead, she tackled the whirlwind of thoughts in her head.

If Rhea was right, what does that mean? How would she fit into this world with power she doesn't know anything about?

With each word, her chest constricted more. Anxiety flooded her as the questions multiplied around the Shadowborn, their lore, and why *she* would end up with this dagger mark.

Just as her panic was about to reach its peak, Damien's arm came around her stomach and pulled her back, flush to his chest. His touch immediately stopped the storm and pulled her out of her headspace. The weight from his arm was an instant reminder of what was grounding her through this all. Little by little, her mindset shifted.

What if she was given this mark for a reason? What if she could figure it all out because she had him.

One by one, she replaced her previous thoughts with ones of hope within herself and the men that followed her. As her breathing calmed, her eyes became heavy and sleep soon found her.

5

Blair stirred as warmth soaked through the dark canvas around her. Opening her eyes, she found Damien still asleep next to her. Turning her head the opposite way, she noticed light had just begun to break through the woven shadows encasing the walls. She stretched her arm and draped it across Damien, shifting her body so her head now laid on his chest.

His heartbeat thudded steadily underneath her cheek, and when she shifted again, a deep hum came from him. One arm tightened around her back, and the other slipped down her side with a familiar mischief.

"Morning, beautiful," Damien muttered.

Before she could reply, he *rolled*, flipping her effortlessly so that she straddled him. In the next moment, his fingers went for her ribs.

"Don't!" she squealed, immediately knowing his plan.

"Too late." he grunted, tickling her mercilessly. His face broke into a crooked grin as she squealed louder and tried to squirm free. She slapped at his hands, laughing uncontrollably.

"Damien!" she shrieked.

From above them, Blake groaned. "Can we *not* turn this tent into an orgy before breakfast?"

Blair burst into another fit of laughter as Damien stilled and winked at her. He then looked up toward Blake's bunk, "Are you saying you wouldn't join?"

Blake's head popped over the side of the bunk, his eyes wide with excitement. "Are you being so for real right now?"

Blair rolled off Damien, still giggling. She was breathless and red-faced with a huge grin on her face. Damien chuckled and threw a pillow at Blake, "Over my dead body."

"Well, someone's recharged," Blair said, smoothing her hair.

"Eh, about eighty percent," he replied, standing with a grin. "But I'll fake the last twenty if it means I get to do *that again*."

Blake dropped from the top bunk, rubbing his eyes. "You two are nauseating. I love it. Can we eat now?"

"Please," Blair groaned, moving to the dresser to grab her clothes and boots.

They dressed quickly, pulling on light gear with reinforced fabric. The material was thin, clearly made for movement and combat. Blair wrapped her hair into a messy bun while Blake adjusted his coat, and Damien pulled on a fitted shirt that clung to his shoulders.

As they stepped outside, the cool morning air filled their lungs, laced with the scent of smoke and fresh bread.

Sunlight shimmered faintly through the ever-present haze of shadows that curled through the camp like mist.

Kael was already waiting next to a nearby tent, his arms crossed loosely over his chest.

Damien was the first to approach him. "Morning," Kael said in greeting, voice low and even. "You smell less dead."

Damien gave a shallow nod in response, but his eyes showed unmistakable apprehension as Kael continued on.

"Hope you're rested. The leader of our camp is requesting a meeting."

Blair exchanged a glance with Damien and Blake who nodded. "Lead the way."

They followed Kael down the winding camp path, past early risers warming their hands by small fires. The large tent near the fire pit from the night before loomed ahead, larger than any structure in the camp. Its sides were reinforced with stone, and deep shadow markings coiled along the canvas like veins.

Inside, the air shifted, becoming warmer. A long table sat at the center, and at its head, a man waited, standing as they entered.

Broad-shouldered and tall, the man's presence was immediate. He had tanned skin dusted with silver scars and eyes of rich onyx, a color that seemed to glimmer with something deeper. His hair was twisted back, streaked with silver, and tied with a thick cord. His tunic was loose, dark gray with a long sash trimmed in the same silver found in his hair.

He smiled as they approached, lighting up the entire tent with his energy.

"Well, damn," he boomed. "You three look far less like corpses than you did yesterday. I call that a good sign."

Blair blinked with surprise at the sheer power in his voice.

Kael nodded toward the man at the table. "This is Shiloh, my father, and the leader of this camp."

Shiloh stepped forward, shaking their hands with a grip that was firm, but not overwhelming. "Welcome! Sit. Sit!"

They obliged, each finding a chair. "Thanks for having us," Blair said, as she pulled hers out.

Shiloh laughed. "You think I'd let Kael drag strangers in without a reason? I know when the Veil stirs, girl. You didn't just stumble in. You were led."

He motioned with his hands, catching the attention of those standing in the corners. They immediately filed into a nearby door. "Eat. We can talk about everything after."

Within moments, the people who had left returned, their hands now full of different types of food. Blair noticed steaming bowls of root vegetables, fresh flatbread, and slices of something that tasted like honeyed fruit. Blake practically grabbed at them as they passed. Damien filled a plate quietly and began to eat as other things were set down. Even Blair couldn't deny her stomach's excitement from the food in front of her. She reached for everything that looked good.

Moments later, Rhea, Adriel, and Marrow entered and joined them, each offering a nod or smile. Rhea claimed the seat opposite of Blair, her keen eye darting up every so often to look at her.

After mostly everyone had cleared their plates, Shiloh stood and raised his hands. Shadows lightly rippled from his palms, almost smoke-like. They drifted into the air above the table and began to form shapes.

"I've summoned you here to tell you a story," Shiloh said, his voice quiet now, but commanding.

The shapes above them morphed, forming four figures, each cloaked in robes. Their features were indistinct but powerful.

"There were once four leaders who came together to create a kingdom. They forged a new way of life where shadow magic flourished and found a true home. It was where everything started for us."

The shadows shifted, showing the cloaked figures walking, offering food to citizens, and fixing things with their magic. Then, the shadows turned chaotic and Shiloh's voice dropped, filling with restrained anger. "The northern King heard of this thriving city and the people who dwelled there, the Shadowborn. He became jealous and wanted them, as well as the power they were known to harbor. Most of all, he wanted to use them as his personal weapons. He began to hunt them down, taking them out one by one until he learned enough to come for their home."

The shadows morphed again, showing a battle where the cloaked figures ran into a building. "Due to the knowledge the King had gathered, our people suffered greatly. Just as leaders should, those who led us made a decision to sacrifice their power- funneling it into a weapon capable of new life." He paused and so did the shadows, creating a dramatic effect before continuing, "There's a prophecy that speaks of that weapon," Shiloh went on, turning toward Blair. "That one day, someone would return with a mark not seen since its origin. A dagger, carved from Veilstone, capable of *unifying* our shadows and making us whole once more."

The shadows in the air shifted yet again, a dagger appearing now, its sharp edges wrapped in swirling darkness.

Blair's breath caught as she pulled her eyes away and looked at Damien. He was already staring at her, his eyes full of emotions she couldn't decipher. *He truly hadn't known.* She lifted her eyebrows at him slightly before finding another pair of eyes locked on her, *Rhea's.*

Shiloh noticed the exchange and gave a small smile. "I believe it's no coincidence one of you carries the mark of that blade," he said as the dagger evaporated into a diamond, one corner glowing faintly.

"This one is our city, modeled after Idris and the mark of Void." The other corners of the diamond lit as Shiloh explained the people they stood for; Celeste, Muriel, and Kyron. As soon as he was finished explaining, the shadows dissipated as quickly as they were formed.

Taking a deep breath, he faced Damien, Blair, and Blake. "I believe it is in your best interest to learn about each of those leaders and the marks they carried. I'm willing to bet you will need that guidance through your journey." He paused for a brief second before looking around the room. "You can start here with Idris's mark of Void and train until you can wield it. I think it's the best way to discover your potential."

Damien leaned forward, "Train how?"

Blair watched as Shiloh chuckled, lifting a brow at the young man. "A good question," he said. "One I would expect from her protector, but I don't have a simple answer for you." He turned back to Blair. "I think we see where you are and go from there. That is, if you're ready for it."

Blair nodded as she looked down and moved her hand to her thigh.

Damien exhaled and leaned back into his seat, grabbing her attention. "Free will, right Blair?" He then lifted bread to his mouth and took a bite before looking back at Shiloh. "I would say she needs time to think about it, but I would be lying." He glanced up again, a small smile spreading across his face as he looked over at Blair "Knowing her? She's already decided."

Blair grinned at him as her confidence grew. *An anchor, as always.* She sat straighter in her chair, and gave a small smile to Shiloh. "I'm in."

He clapped once, loud and sharp. "Excellent! We'll show you around after breakfast. You can begin with Kael and Rhea to see where you're at. The men can start with the

60

others. Each of our people specialize in something specific, they can help you in many ways." His eyes scanned each of them, as if showing them off. "Don't let their silence fool you, they are powerful."

Rhea grinned at that remark and Kael raised an eyebrow into a smirk.

Blair nodded at each of them as her gaze swept over them as well. Turning her head slowly toward Shiloh, she addressed him once more. "I have a question."

An approving smile grew on his face. "I'm sure you have many. Ask away."

"When we came here, we weren't just running from the King, but his men, his Hunters. Will they be able to find us here?"

Shiloh's shoulders and jaw tensed at the mention of them but a small smile stayed on his face. "The magic here is ancient, running so deep that only true Shadowborn or supporters that carry the mark of Myrth can enter. Those idiotic shells won't be able to find you here. Take all the time you need and when you prove ready, we'll figure out a way to find the next camp without any interference."

Blake, mid-bite, muttered around a mouthful of bread, "Okay, now I have a question. *Please* don't tell me there will be more running in this training. My strength lies in *other things*." He deepened his tone on the last two words, waggling his eyebrows at Marrow across from him.

Shiloh watched Marrow just stare at him, giving him no reaction. When Blake huffed in defeat, Shiloh chuckled again.

The table filled with conversation for a few more minutes as everyone took their last bites. Laughter echoed in uneven waves, bouncing off the canvas walls. Forks scraped against wooden bowls, and stories started to overlap.

Blair watched the people around her, her eyes swept from Blake to Marrow, and then Damien and Rhea. The last two in a deep conversation. "So you discovered your armor after getting mad at your cook?"

Rhea shrugged with exaggerated dignity. "I was six, and he burned my birthday cake, it felt personal."

"We all know he deserved the beatdown," Adriel chimed in next to them, snorting into his cup.

Shiloh observed it all from the front of the table. "You are all good people. The founders brought us together for a reason."

His words hung in the air as Blair thought about them. There was something unspoken here, a feeling she couldn't quite explain but could *feel*. Maybe it was the immediate kindness shared between the Shadowborn, or the bond she felt between them all. A strange pride filled her heart for a place she had barely found out about, as warmth spread along her thigh. The sensation was not an immediate flare, but a pulse, like a whispered confirmation of her comfort.

She stiffened for a fraction of a second, lowering her eyes to her thigh.

She couldn't see anything other than the intricate dagger on her skin but the warmth was undeniable, spreading like someone had laid a blanket across her lap.

Her heart rate rose slightly as she realized she wasn't imagining it. *It was reassurance.* A soft, wordless echo filled her chest and settled low in her belly. *You are where you are meant to be.* The realization struck with startling clarity, not because it was required, but because, for the first time in a long time, she felt like she actually *belonged.*

Damien and Blake had quickly become her home but being part of this, being among these people that had stories carved into their skin and strength wrapped in scars. This was no accident. Finding this place was the first step toward what came next.

Her eyes watered and she blinked away the emotions that were flooding into her.

Naturally, Damien sensed it, putting his hand on her thigh. "You okay?" He asked, his eyes narrowing with concern.

Smiling, she looked at him and laid her hand on top of his. "Yeah. Everything's good."

6

It wasn't much longer before everyone at the table had completely finished, besides Blake, who took every chance to cram more food into his mouth.

Shiloh eventually signaled the end of breakfast and motioned for everyone to go outside to the training arena. Kael and Rhea were the first to move, leading the others out of the tent. It was a short distance, but as they walked the path, the morning light began to reach the dark stone paths beneath their feet. Veils of shadow followed them, as they curled softly along buildings, chimneys, and clotheslines.

Another sight that Blair found breathtaking.

There were small groups of adults chatting as their children practiced their gifts. Even the smallest ones had shadows curling from their fingertips, stretching toward pebbles and rocks, trying to lift or toss them.

A girl no older than six let out a triumphant giggle as a stone rose shakily into the air before tumbling back to the ground.

Blake nudged Blair with his elbow. "Look at that one. Already better control than you."

Blair smirked and waved to the small child. "We'll see how funny you are when I take you down for the first time."

Damien chuckled beside them but didn't speak, he was busy observing the street in front of them. Blair watched him for a second, noticing how relaxed he seemed here. In SilverDawn, he always had his guard up, but here, he just simply existed.

Eventually, they reached the training ground where the smooth stoned pathway gave way to hardened earth. Ahead of them, was a large building with an open roof. The area next to the building was open, displaying a circular expanse of dirt and rock. In some spots, brush had been scorched and in others, it was evident there had been hundreds of training sessions layered upon each other.

Rhea and Kael each opened a door, welcoming everyone inside. As they did so, the towering steel doors creaked open. The building towered around them like the hollow shell of some forgotten titan, its walls made of stone. The floor stretched wide, designed to be an arena for many uses. No walls divided the space, but it was clearly split into four distinct corners.

Shiloh gave them time to take everything in before he addressed them, quieting the room. He raised his hand and pointed to the first area. To their immediate left, the floor was lined with mats and mirrors, a single bench and a large array of stretching bands were the only other things available. "This is the space we use for manifesting and concentration."

Blair nodded toward it, nudging Damien's bicep with her shoulder, "Look at that, now I have a corner to send you to when you start to get all broody."

A small smile twitched on his face as he nudged back, his eyes never leaving Shiloh who had now moved his hand, gesturing to a different corner.

This space seemed more challenging. An area that was clearly made to test many skills, the space provided a web of wood slats, hurdles, and ladders arranged in different drills. Rope anchors that were bolted to the floor snaked out in thick, coiled masses, while leather harnesses and rope hung like vines from tall metal frames.

"This corner is for agility. It trains the body to think and move fast." Shiloh explained.

This time, it was Blake who nudged into Damien. "Speed and footwork," Blake muttered, tilting his head. "I call that corner."

Blair stifled an eyeroll as Shiloh continued the tour. What came next was in the back left, a designated place for combat. Thicker padded mats covered the floor, bordered by low barriers. Heavy grain sacks swayed gently, suspended from chains that clinked softly with every shift of air. There were weapons too, wooden practice swords, training staffs, and dulled blades resting in racks.

"This is where you test your skills with combat. As you are now, I don't think you would last very long in the ring. You must start with strength."

Blair nodded, taking a deep breath in.

It was the final corner that made all of them pause as they walked up to it. There was no equipment within the space, just areas where the floor had been rubbed raw from scuffles. Thick wooden beams were embedded upright into the ground, wrapped in rope. Weighted sacks, waterlogged logs, and sand-filled barrels were piled nearby, each looking deceptively ordinary.

"This is the endurance pit." Shiloh said, his eyes full of pride.

"That looks like my own personal hell," Blake said quietly.

"That *looks* like discipline," Damien corrected.

They stood for a moment longer, each of them turning slowly as they looked at the entire space around them. One massive floor, four corners each presenting a different kind of challenge.

Shiloh motioned for Rhea and she moved to stand beside him. Using one hand, she swept her hair over her left shoulder and then crossed her arms. Beside her, Kael emerged. His energy was different as he nodded toward Blair, his shadows already coiling lazily at his wrists. Walking together toward the center of the room, they called for Blair to follow them.

Blair listened and stepped forward, even though her nerves were tingling. She had just picked up her foot to take another step when Damien caught her arm gently.

"Wait."

She turned with her brow raised in question.

He opened his mouth and then shut it, stepping forward and looking past her. His voice was low and calm as he addressed Shiloh. "She's never done this before," Damien said, his voice low but with a slight edge. "Go easy."

Easy? Blair looked up at him and pulled her arm back to her side. "I can do this."

Shiloh watched Blair's response before nodding at Damien. "I appreciate the insight." Then he looked to Blair, eyes locking with hers. "They will not be acting as your enemy today, their goal is to provoke you enough to cause a reaction, it's the best way to see what happens and where we need to start. We can use that to develop a plan for your needs and start a training plan in each specific area; manifestation, combat, agility, and endurance."

Blair nodded and walked forward, stopping when she was across from them. Rhea and Kael dipped their chin as she approached, their shadows already flickering around them.

Rhea's armor formed at her jaw and made its way down her body. Dark whips dropped from Kael's fingers as he wriggled them. Blair reached instinctively for her dagger. *Gone.* She swallowed in response

That's right, she didn't have one anymore. Her hands hovered at her sides instead, fingers twitching as her pulse picked up.

Shiloh's voice rang out behind her.

"Again, this is not a match. Rhea and Kael will not aim to harm, only provoke. Understand?"

Blair nodded.

His next word signaled the start. "Begin."

Kael was the first to move. He flicked his wrist, sending a crackling thread of shadow sailing past her head, not close enough to hit, but enough to make her flinch.

Blair spun on her heel to face him. "Really? Straight for the face?"

"Hey," Rhea called. "Don't talk. Focus on what you feel."

Rhea rushed next, fast and low, her dark armor gleaming as she lunged. Blair dodged left, barely missing a swipe.

Even that close to being struck, there was nothing. No shadows. No instinct. Just adrenaline.

Blair growled under her breath. "Any day now," she hissed at herself, willing something, *anything*, to rise.

Kael's whip lashed toward her ankles, making her stumble and fall to her knees. She immediately went to rise but Rhea ran behind her and struck the back of her shoulder, knocking her completely to the ground.

She took a breath and stood again, but Kael's whips took her out at the knees as soon as she straightened and this time, she landed on her back, the wind instantly knocked out of her.

The goal is to provoke, Shiloh's words repeated in her head as she fought to breathe.

Gaining her stance, heat flushed through her body as she tried to calm her rising anger. Her thigh stung as she tensed, sending a wave of pain through her leg. Rhea took advantage of the distraction and ran beside Blair, shoulder-checking her on the way. Blair's body tightened on impact, a dam breaking inside of her.

"Stop." Blair called out, fighting to unclench the muscles that had tightened on their own. She hunched over as a sound split through her, somewhere deep within. A cracking that was sharp, like glass breaking on a floor. Another crack followed, then another, until the noise became a chorus echoing inside her ribs, inside her skull, everywhere.

Next, came a heat that surged through her insides. A spark at first, then a molten river. Fire that wasn't burning her, but becoming her.

Her breath hitched as the warmth roared to life, rising from her chest and spilling into her limbs. A small pained groan escaped her lips as black shadows with a purple hue erupted from her spine.

Blair squeezed her eyes shut as she hunched her shoulders, her body visibly shaking. Shadows now coiled around her, first at her back, then her whole body. They thrashed in a wild and spastic manner before completely stilling, like they were assessing any potential danger she was in. After another moment, they *lunged.*

Kael's eyes widened as Blair's shadowed tendrils morphed, mimicking his whips. A large barrage came down on him, causing him to maneuver in order to dodge repeated strikes. One of the last ones struck his face. Rhea braced, raising both hands to her face as they moved to attack her as well. Using her armor to shield herself, the shadows ripped at the protection, forcing her to step back. She yelled in pain as her head was knocked to the side and a piece of her materialized shadow armor was viciously ripped away from her chin.

Blair forced her eyes open and gasped, stepping forward on shaky legs. "Wait, stop. I-I didn't mean-!"

But the shadows became more hostile, even as she tried to coax them back inside. They spun around her, faster and faster, driven not by control but by her raw and untethered emotion. The more her adrenaline rose, the more feral they became.

Another tendril shot out, this time aimed at Kael's head. He dodged, but barely. Rhea grunted as a coil lashed across her thigh, leaving an instant bruise.

Blair screamed, bringing her hands up to her head. "I can't stop it!"

Her yells were cut by a low, dominant voice. One that seemed to amplify over the chaos. "Everybody out."

A familiar presence lingered behind her as she felt a hand settle on her lower back.

Damien.

She didn't turn, didn't move, but she *felt* him.

Immediately, his fingers began to trace circles on her skin as his mouth moved next to her ear, "You're okay. You're in control. You're not alone."

She breathed deeply and repeated the words in her head as everyone looked at Shiloh for direction. He watched Blair with curiosity for just a second before nodding and leading everyone out of the arena. Blake was the last to step out, giving a brief salute to Damien as he closed the door.

The shadows *grew,* then shot towards Damien.

Just as they reached him, they paused. Lingering around him, they hovered, like smoke curling into itself. As his own shadows materialized, they moved together, finding comfort within each other's darkness.

As they calmed, she collapsed forward, panting. Her knees hit the dirt with a hard thud.

Damien knelt beside her, hands steady on her arms. "Let's go take a seat."

Blair nodded, lifting her hands up to him. Damien took them with a smile, hoisting her up and walking her toward the corner with mats and mirrors. Sitting on the small bench, the shadows swirled together around them.

He sat her down, and then stood at her back, looking at their reflection. Moving slowly, he raised his hand to her neck and moved her hair over, kissing the soft skin that was hidden there.

"You did it. You let them out." He said in-between kisses. "I need you to let them go again, Blair. Can you do that?"

A small moan slipped from her mouth as Damien wrapped his hand around the front of her throat, and pulled her head to the side, now licking the soft skin.

He paused only to whisper in her ear. "Show me your darkness, Blair. It's mine just as much as you are."

Blair's eyes remained shut as she leaned into his touch, the shadows already reacting to her heightened emotions.

"You're holding them in baby," Damien murmured against the shell of her ear. His fingers trailed up her spine before gliding back down slowly. "I want to see them."

Blair exhaled shakily. Then, her eyes opened.

Gone was the softness of hazel. In its place, was a void of black and purple swirls, like an endless pit that swallowed the light. Small webs crept from the corners of her eyes, like cracks made of ink. The mirror caught them both in perfect detail.

Damien, who had looked up at their reflection, was staring at her with an impressed and seductive smile. "There you are," he said, his lips curling into a pleased smile. "Gods, look at you."

Blair blinked slowly, the shadow-webbing at the corners of her eyes pulsing like it had a heartbeat of its own.

Damien's hand moved from around her throat to her shoulder, lifting her up off the bench. As she stood, his chin brushed against her ear and he spoke directly to her reflection.

"I know you're scared," he said, his voice a whisper, "But I need you to stop trying to battle it." He tilted his head slightly, eyes never leaving the mirror, "and wear it like a crown."

As if in response, her shadows suddenly snapped, one striking up toward the open sky, another whipping across the floor like dark rage. Blair flinched, panic rippling through her for just a moment.

Damien laughed as his shadows countered, softening the blow of hers. His chuckle grew louder as several shadows sprouted and tried to fight his for dominance. The sound was not cruel, but filled with a kind of wild joy. "Oh, *there* she is," he said playfully, grinning against her skin. "Careful, feisty. We wouldn't want to break all their fancy stuff."

The shadows battled for a few moments before curling inward like obedient hounds sensing their master's mood.

Blair glanced up at him in the mirror, as his hands trailed down her arms and then stopped at her waist. His fingers wrapped themselves in the fabric of her shirt before pulling it up and sliding it off. He moved slowly, gliding over her skin like he was savoring every second. He then moved to her waist, teasing his fingers just under the hem of her soft shorts.

Blair's heart spiked and her breathing quickened, her shadows reacting immediately.

"First thing to know is that they respond to you and every emotion you have." Damien murmured, pulling off her bottom layers and kicking one of her feet to the side. The motion caused her legs to spread apart. He pushed down on her lower back, inviting her to bend over the bench.

She responded, lowering herself down slowly, until her chest touched the bench. Skimming his hand down her curves, he rested it just at the entrance that was openly displayed in front of him. He waited there for a moment, before one of her shadows nudged him in, causing him to chuckle seductively.

The touch was not gentle or sweet. It was exactly what she needed.

The second he inserted another finger, Blair's shadows *exploded*, just like he wanted.

They shot outward with a thunderous pulse, tendrils of black lightning sending cracks up one of the mirrors. Damien didn't flinch, he focused solely on Blairs' facial expressions and what she liked best.

His own shadows rose in response, not with violence, but something *protective*. They wrapped around hers like arms in the dark, coiling around them as if to soothe them. Then the room blurred as their shadows wove into each other again- not in dominance, but unity. Her chaos and his control, a storm made of *them*.

Blair threw her head back, eyes wide and glowing black, her voice breaking. "Damien."

"Give it *all* to me," Damien said, his voice low and filled with need. "Every last part of you, including your shadows. Let me see your darkness, baby."

Blair moaned out as more black webs moved across her face.

Damien used his free hand to grab her jaw. "Look at yourself." He squeezed her cheeks, forcing her to watch her own reflection. "Look at how powerful you are, look at how goddamn beautiful you are."

With that, Damien pulled his fingers out, unbuttoned his pants and moved fully behind her. Lifting her hips, he glided inside in one swift motion, stretching her. "Gods, you're already so ready for me." Was the only thing he managed to growl out, as he tightened his grip on her skin.

His movements started slow but intensified quickly. Several whimpers escaped Blair, but Damien continued. "I want to hear it. So, tell me," he groaned as he slammed into her once again and then stopped, "tell me how good the shadows look on you."

Blair tried but her words came out in a jumbled mess, her sensitivity somehow higher.

"Say it." he commanded, fisting her hair and again forcing her to look at their reflection in the mirror, "You have to say it and accept this side of yourself. Stop being afraid of them. Control them like you control me Blair." With that, he moved with an unleashed ferocity.

A scream ripped from Blair's throat as she felt a warmth building in her core. Her words, still jumbled, fell from her mouth as the orgasm hit her. "Their mine. I-I want them." she half-screamed as an intense wave of pleasure tore through her.

Damien echoed her, groaning as he filled her.

It was only when her spasms had ceased, did he stop moving. Bending down, he kissed down her spine and pulled out. Securing his boxers, he walked to the racks on the wall and returned with a towel.

As he stepped beside her, he ran his fingers across her skin. "Feel better?" He asked, a little smug.

Blair looked up at him and nodded, smiling. The blacked webs gone and her eyes the normal hazel.

He began to clean her with the towel and then he stopped and looked her up and down. "I've always liked you riled up. I like it even more now that I can calm you down *properly*."

Blair smiled, pulling her clothes on and looking at herself in the mirror. The shadows were gone but it was almost like she could still feel them, right there at the surface.

"Will it always be like *that*?" she asked, turning her head toward Damien who had begun rubbing her thigh.

"You started as 'crazy wrapped in chaos', and then you went and added shadows to the mix... yes, our sex-life will always be that explosive." he said, his eyebrows raising, "Actually, that's how we will be dealing with the chaos within your mind from here on out."

Blair turned her eyes to her own reflection, blushing at how big her smile was.

Damien moved next to her. "Your shadows? They're not random. They're emotional echoes and they tend to flare when you feel, remember? Fear, anger, pain, sometimes even joy. That's why they can sometimes be challenging." He paused, clicking his tongue. "What happened earlier? That wasn't exactly you fighting your shadows, Blair. You were fighting *yourself* which caused fear and anxiety to overwhelm you. "

She dropped her gaze, almost ashamed, but something caught her eye, moving subtly along her skin.

A single tendril of darkness slithered from her forearm, gentle and slow. It surged forward, reaching for Damien. He watched and lowered his arm next to her. The shadow touched the inside of his wrist and then *circled.* Once, and then twice, like it was drawing a tether between them.

With his other hand, he pulled her head back and lowered his mouth down to hers. They shared a small kiss before looking back down at the shadows that still moved around their wrists. Blair watched as the shadow dissolved into his skin, coming out the other side and returning to her.

Damien chuckled, "Would you look at that."

Conjuring a few more small ones, he sent them to Blair. As they climbed up her chest, they sank into the skin of her throat. "Does this always happen?" she asked, bringing her hand up to where the shadows had disappeared.

"No, but I think it's how you were able to give them to me before." Damien sat next to her, and put his hand on her thigh. "When we were in the battle and you chose to use the dagger on yourself, your body rejected the shadow. Your skin started to crack and I knew what was coming, so I used my shadow to seal everything inside of you. I bound them to you, I bound myself, really. I think that's why we can share them, it has to be.

She finally looked up, her expression raw, open. "You bound yourself to me?"

"Give me the opportunity, and I will do it in every way possible." He said, lifting her hand and kissing the back of it. Damien gave her one last look, long and measured. "Are you ready to go back?"

Blair hesitated, then nodded.

"Alright," he said, standing. "Then let's head out before someone figures out why I needed to be alone to do that."

She smirked faintly, and he turned, already walking back toward their tent.

7

Walking back toward their tents, Damien led Blair by the hand, glancing at her often. "You know," he said, a slight edge of pride lacing his words, "I can help you with that anytime you need it."

"Is that so?" A content smile spread across her face for a moment before her steps faltered. "You've always spoken of your shadows as a hindrance, but what happened back there, what you said about me, you really meant that?"

Damien turned toward her, and grabbed her arms. His large hands wrapped around her biceps, squeezing them gently. "When I look at your shadows, I see power. I see strength that survived something it never should have. You never asked for it and yet, you carry them like they were always a part of you." He swallowed as his eyes hardened and his voice lowered. "When I look at mine, I see everything I lost. Everything I *did*, because of who I am. My shadows aren't power to me, they're a reminder of what I can't control. Or, *couldn't* until I met you." His hands moved from her arms down to her wrists before he intertwined his fingers with hers. "You're not the darkness, Blair. You're the light."

Blair's eyes watered as he looked at her, the sincerity in his voice stealing her breath. She couldn't speak, and even if that wasn't the case, she didn't know what to say. Instead, she answered his vulnerability by kissing him.

She lost herself in him then, pouring her light into all his cracked pieces. He accepted everything she gave, wrapping his hand around the back of her head. It wasn't until he pulled away that she knew her light was vital to him, to his healing.

As her forehead rested against his, she whispered the words that had been stolen earlier. "When I look at you, I just see you, Damien. Not your shadows or the darkness you think you have inside."

Damien closed his eyes at her words, as if her confession gave him a sense of relief.

A sound broke the moment between them just as Damien went back in to kiss her. It echoed around them, a laughter that came from the center of the tents. Blair pulled away from him, smiling at the darkness that was starting to infiltrate his eyes. "You hear that?" she asked.

Damien sighed, looking down at Blair's lips. "If Blake is cockblocking me from across camp, I'm going to skin him alive."

Blair pushed at him playfully, "No Damien, listen."

Sighing, he turned his head, catching a shadow that moved on the floor next to them. Another one appeared and she stepped toward it, maneuvering around a nearby tent.

Out of the corner of her eye, about thirty feet away, stood Blake. He hadn't noticed her, too busy shadow-stepping across the packed earth. He'd reappear for just a second before a flash of black fire would whizz past him. A grin stretched across his face, as he finally caught Blair's face and winked before disappearing again. Adriel moved into view, growling low in frustration as he hurled another wave of black fire across the space. It erupted from his palms like liquid night, flaring out toward Blake but ultimately missing, *again.*

"You'll have to aim better than that, Matchstick," Blake called, vanishing and reappearing behind Adriel in a blink.

Adriel spun, another coil of black flame spiraling into his palm. "Stop calling me that!"

"Ooh, not enough anger in your tone," Blake laughed, twisting just out of reach again. "You really need to work on your foreplay, or you'll burn out before we even get started."

Blair blinked, bringing her hand up to cover her mouth. Her eyes followed them, watching the fire arc dangerously close to the tents. "Blake is going to be the reason everything burns down."

From the shadows of a larger tent, Shiloh stepped forward, his expression calm. "As much as I love a little rivalry," he addressed, eyes flickering toward the battling men, "These tents are woven from shadowcloth, and I'd rather not test its limits against Adriel's mood swings."

As if on cue, Adriel flung another bolt of fire at Blake, this time it cracked across the dirt, leaving behind a burn mark. Blake appeared right behind him and licked his ear, missing a fist that immediately swung at him. He chuckled as he disappeared again, "There it is! There's the burning passion I crave baby."

Adriel snarled and turned, walking away from the apparent annoyance.

Blake laughed loudly at the personal win, spotting Blair and Damien as they fully stepped into the center. Without missing a beat, he called out to them, "Feel better, Blair?" He said, enthusiastically raising one eyebrow.

Blair's face flushed, her emotions landing somewhere between embarrassment and wanting to throw a dagger at him. Damien just snorted.

"Welcome back," Shiloh said smoothly, giving Blair a brief nod of acknowledgement, as if nothing out of the ordinary had happened. "Good timing. We're just finishing warm-ups."

Blair raised a brow and pointed to the scorch mark on the floor. "Is that what you call that?"

Shiloh's mouth twitched, almost a smile. "We'll be dividing your time here into training sessions. Each of our top Shadowborn will take you through their specialty. The amount of time you spend with them will depend on how much is needed in that area. Between the four of them, we have combat, agility, manifestation, and endurance. You'll train until your power surfaces in full. When it does, we'll know what you're capable of."

"Assuming we survive Adriel's temper tantrums," Blake muttered behind her, dusting ash off his sleeves.

Shiloh ignored him. "Starting tomorrow, I expect you to train until exhaustion. There is no doubt that your mark and the shadows that reside within you are powerful. We are going to help you connect with them, but first we need your body to be strong enough to withstand your full potential. If I may speak bluntly, the way you are now means it's only a matter of time before the power you have rips you apart. It's not going to be easy. Expect sessions that are intense and grueling, both physically and mentally. That's the only way shadow magic reveals itself. It comes alive under pressure, in discomfort. Are you ready for that?"

Blair met his gaze and gave a slow, steady nod.

"Good," Shiloh said. "So let's not waste today. I want you to take this time to explore the camp and rest. You'll need it."

As he turned and disappeared into the tents, Blake walked over to Damien.

"You do look better. Was it the walk, or... Damien's comforting *presence*?" Blake asked Blair, bumping into Damien's shoulder.

"Keep talking," Damien said dryly, his body staying still despite Blake's force, "and I'll teach Adriel how to aim better."

Blake held up his hands in surrender, grinning.

Blair shook her head at the two men, smiling to herself as they turned to find their tent.

They had just rounded a cluster of low tents that led to theirs when Blair paused. A soft sniffle reached her ears that was quiet, but unmistakable. Turning toward the sound, she found the source.

Just behind one of the supply carts, curled in the grass, was a girl, maybe seven or eight years old. With deep umber skin, her wide silver eyes were brimming with tears. Her arms were wrapped tightly around her knees, and flickering across her skin were small, shifting waves of darkness. Not shadows exactly, but what looked like black liquid moving just beneath the surface. They shimmered with anxiety, unpredictable and frightened.

She flinched as Blair approached.

"Hey. It's okay," Blair said gently, kneeling.

The girl didn't answer, just stared at her hands, where the black ripples kept moving."I can't make it calm down," she whispered.

Blair's heart cracked in her chest. "They're beautiful." Blair sat down next to her and watched the darkness move. "Maybe they won't calm down because they want to play?"

The girl remained silent, but her eyes lifted.

"You see this?" Blair asked, raising her arm slowly to focus on her shadows. They shimmered to life across her skin, coiling gently around her forearm. "Mine like to play too and sometimes you just need to say hi to them."

The girl stared, curiosity slowly pushing the fear out of her expression.

"It's not about controlling them, it's about accepting them," Blair said, her eyes rising to meet Damien's as she winked, returning her gaze to the little girl. "It's just new and new things can feel scary until we understand them… but this?" She moved her arm closer. "This is a part of you. Just like it's a part of all of us here." With that, Damien and Blake activated their shadows and the little girl smiled widely. Standing up to touch Blair's arm, her little fingers sank into the shadowy ripples, and for a moment, both their magic pulsed in unison.

The girl let out a long breath and smiled. Then, she ran off toward one of the tents, her shadows still flickering around her hands but no longer as out of control as they were when they found her.

Blair stood, brushing her knees off.

Behind her, Blake scoffed softly.

"What?" she asked, raising an eyebrow as they resumed walking.

He shook his head, smirking. "You make it look so damn *easy*. You just controlled them and it hasn't even been a couple days"

Blair laughed. "Maybe that's the problem. Maybe you have a hard time controlling them because you're all using pain and rage to call them."

Damien wrapped his arm around her shoulders and pulled her close, "There's my light."

"Ew. Stop being so gross." Blake muttered under his breath.

Blair let out a light laugh, feeling her confidence rise as they continued to walk.

They reached their tent and stepped inside. The woven shadowcloth walls greeted them, shimmering against the light leaking in.

As he kicked off his shoes, Blake clapped his hands together and stood in the middle of the room. "Alright everybody, Team Blake meeting time!"

The call echoed off the walls and fell.

Blair looked up at Damien who had begun to tape her hands, wrapping each knuckle that was red and swollen. Her brows furrowed just slightly as she turned to Blake with an expression that could best be described as blank skepticism.

"Team... *what*?" Blair asked.

"Team Blake," he repeated, clearly expecting drumroll or applause.

When the silence stretched, he added with a shrug, "We have to have some type of branding here and clearly my name is the best one."

Damien exchanged an unimpressed glance with Blair before his focus went back to her hands.

Blake held up both hands, unbothered. "Okay, okay. Fine. We can workshop it. Let's just go over what we know. Basically, we walked into a magical dome, force field thingy and away from our problems, *temporarily*."

Damien answered next, tapping Blair's hands to show he was finished. "We know we have training to focus on. We also know that there are different camps we're going to have to go to. Combine all of that, and we'll have the answers we need."

Blake made a groaning sound as he jumped up to the top bunk. "There's also four areas in the training area Blair's going to need to conquer. 'Each-"

Damien cut him off as Blake held his mouth open in protest, 'We. *We* need to conquer. I want eyes on her at all times but we will still need to keep up our training as well."

Blake popped his mouth closed and nodded a few times. "Fair. So, that means you're going to show them what you can *really* do, Mr. wingspan?" he asked, tilting his head in Damien's direction.

Damien looked back at him, his features concrete, "If it helps Blair, yes."

"Alrighty, so that's that. Now, each one of the areas is led by a different Shadowborn. I'm betting Rhea is in charge of the combat sector obviously, that scar on her face is no joke," Blake said as he stretched, talking toward the ceiling.

"Could Marrow be manifestation?" Blair asked Damien as she moved in close to his side and opened her palm to try and conjure a shadow. Damien watched her with a small smile before releasing one of his own. The shadow intertwined around her fingers before soaking into the skin of her palm. Her smile grew as she placed that palm on his cheek and the shadow returned to him. "She doesn't seem to fit into any of the others." She looked up at the wood beams that held the top bunk, raising her voice. "At least I'm assuming that, because she seems to manifest a brick wall between you and her," Blair added with a small giggle.

"Oh, just you wait, that wall will come down and I'm going to crack that beautiful girl open, literally and figuratively." Blake retorted, popping his head over the side and licking the air.

Damien kicked the platform that held Blake up as he looked at Blair. "That leaves Kael?"

Blair nodded. "And Adriel."

Damien clicked his tongue as he brought his left arm up behind him, laying it under his head. "The way Adriel moved earlier when Blake pissed him off, he's probably agility."

Blair nodded in agreement as Blake scoffed above them.

"So, Kael is endurance?" Blake yawned

"Maybe together, they can show me what it means to be one of you guys."

Damien looked at her. "No, they'll show you what it means to be *you*. You're different from the rest of us."

Blake agreed with a hummed "mhmm" from above. "Can we also talk about this camp? It's unreal."

A pause filled the space between them.

Then Blair sat up, looking down at Damien. "That's the goal, isn't it? To have *this*." she gestured to the tent walls, the laughter outside, the hum of peaceful energy, "A world where you don't have to hide. Where kids like that girl can grow up without being terrified of being put in a camp. Where you don't have to run from Hunters or kneel to a King who only wants you as a weapon."

Blake remained quiet for a moment before he answered, his voice flat. "Yeah, that would be a great life."

Damien looked up at her from where he lay on the bed. With a smile that reached his eyes, he agreed, "*Yes*, that's the goal. That's the world I want to create with you."

"Then that's our goal," Blair confirmed.

Damien pulled her down to kiss her slowly but stopped as Blake jumped from the top bunk, leaning into their space with one hand on the frame. "Then, what do you say we skip the naps and take today to look around and find people willing to help?"

8

The trio explored the camp at an easy pace, taking in everything around them. Every person they passed gave a friendly wave, regardless of what they were doing. The statue was the first thing they came across. The training grounds were next, filled with shouting instructors and other Shadowborn. After watching the session for a little bit, they turned toward a narrow path that ran through the tents. Following it, they found much larger, intricate tents with huge openings held up by shadows.

As they passed the first one, Blair caught motion from inside. She raised her arm, grabbing the men's attention. Angling her neck, Blair peered inside to find a woman sitting in front of a large, wooden device. Her concentration was on her hands, where her fingers moved in precise patterns pulling at different threads. At first, it looked rather normal, then Blake blinked and leaned in.

"Is she *spinning* shadows?" Blake asked under his breath, surprised.

They watched more closely. The woman's hands danced with ease, pulling shadow from the air itself. It stretched, thinned, and twisted into fine, silken threads that fed into a spinning wheel in front of her. The fabric she wove wasn't dull but glinted with hues of light. As her fingers moved, it shifted like liquid, patterned with subtle spirals and waves.

"That must be the shadowcloth Shiloh mentioned," Blair said quietly, awe in her voice.

"I bet they use this fabric for most things here," Damien added, running his fingers along the tent's outer wall. "An ability like that could be especially helpful."

A wave of curiosity hit Blair and she impulsively stepped inside the tent. The woman noticed immediately and looked up with sharp but kind eyes. Rimmed in orange hues, her brown eyes were soft. She had long silver streaks in her dark hair and her hands moved even as she spoke to Blair, "Hello lovely, are you new here?"

Blair responded right as two distinct presences appeared at her back. "Yeah. I'm Blair. This is Damien and Blake."

The woman nodded at each of the men individually and then inclined her head in greeting to Blair. "I'm Allesandra. It's nice to meet you."

"Your work is really incredible," Blair said, stepping closer to observe the folds of fabric that lay in different areas. "Are you creating things for the camp?"

Pausing the spinning wheel, Allesandra nodded and reached to a pile of fabric next to her. "I shadow weave most materials we use," she said. " Our tents, cloaks, even our shrouds for the dead."

"I've never seen anything like it." Blair said as she reached for the piece of fabric Allesandra offered her. Moving the fabric back and forth, the threads shimmered as if fortifying their layered darkness.

"Have you always been able to do this?" Damien asked, watching the fabric in Blair's hands.

Allesandra smiled, "My fondest memories were helping my mother weave. You see, I was the daughter of the seamstress for the kingdom and I went everywhere with her. That stopped once my abilities appeared, I had just turned seven. I tried to hide it and continue to help my mother, but the shadows would appear and mix with the silver threads. The king found out and soon forced my mother out, but kept me. We soon found out I could only produce so much on my own. Once I ran out, he became volatile and put me in a camp. That is, until Shiloh found me," Allesandra said. "Like he finds all of us *eventually*."

She paused and a small smile formed on her face. "Little did he know that when I'm around other Shadowborn, it charges my ability and my shadows refill. I was able to thrive here."

Blair touched the fabric gently. "I bet the camp appreciates you here, and everything you make for them."

Allesandra smiled, and her fingers began to weave again. "They do but it's not needed. This is my home and I will help in any way possible. You'll find your own way to give back. We all do."

They nodded, thanking her for her time as they left her in thoughtful silence. The three moved down the same path until a familiar clang of metal broke the quiet. As they rounded the corner, another large tent appeared. This one had an opening not held by shadows, but instead, was a large cut-out within the shadowed walls. Another hole was cut from the top, with curls of smoke pouring out.

A shadowed forge.

Damien was the one to pause this time, stopping in front of the tent to watch the work within. Inside, a man worked over an anvil, his body thick with sweat and soot. The steel he held glowed in a peculiar manner, catching all of their attention. Black veins of shadow crawled across the metal, flowing from his fingertips. As he struck it with his hammer, the armor gleamed with an unnatural sheen. Deep and dark, like obsidian polished to perfection.

"Okay," Blake said, impressed. "That's *actually* badass."

Damien watched, eyes focusing on the man who folded shadows into his plating. "He's not just coating it," Damien murmured, his voice low with interest. "He's imbuing it."

Blair glanced at Damien as he stared, noticing how his eyes never blinked, his concentration fully on the craft.

Damien spoke again, slowly. "I never thought about fortifying the weapons I made. I was always afraid if I did too much, it would give me away."

"Seems like you're not as smart as you think you are," Blake said, elbowing him.

Damien didn't reply or even acknowledge the jab. He simply watched the blacksmith continue to work.

Blake opened his mouth but Blair placed her hand on his arm and motioned to Damien, shaking her head. Blake closed his mouth, and leaned on the wall behind him, clearly trying to reign himself in.

They stood there for a few more minutes giving Damien time to observe. It was only when he pulled his eyes away and asked if they were ready, did they walk away.

Within the next few yards, the camp thinned. Trees edged the smaller tents here, and the rural area seemed more peaceful. In the center of a small clearing, a man sat surrounded by small, unusual tools. His shadows danced between his fingers and hovered above a wooden table, shaping objects with care.

He didn't look up when they approached, but a woman next to him turned, wiping her hands.

"Curious?" she asked, addressing them while the man's eyes stayed focused on what he was doing.

Blair replied for them, "A bit. It's amazing to see what everyone can do." She looked at the man, stepping closer, "What are you making?"

The woman smiled as she watched their interaction, but there was sadness in her eyes as she addressed Blair. "My husband doesn't speak."

Turning her head toward the woman, Blair took a step back. "Oh, I'm sorry."

The man looked up then and spoke to his wife, asking for a certain tool. His voice came out slurred and broken, shaped more by breath than sound.

She responded swiftly, handing him a small hammer.

Blake's body tensed and he stepped closer. With a cold, clipped tone he spoke. "Is his tongue missing?"

With a small sigh, the woman gave a slight nod and looked at Blake. "Thankfully, he has healed since coming here."

Blair's mouth dropped, shadows swirling at her feet. "Can I ask what happened?"

The woman nodded, "Our son was taken to a camp when his shadows formed. We were told he had a rare ability that would benefit the kingdom. My husband fought back and the Hunter that had come to collect him did not like how he was spoken to. As punishment, he cut out his tongue."

Damien's fists clenched as shadows swirled up his wrists and Blake folded his arms over his chest, unusually quiet.

The woman went on, her voice gentle, "Now we live our life here, where we no longer have to worry about things like that. "

Blair placed a hand over her chest. "I can't imagine that pain. I'm sorry about your son and what happened."

The woman just watched her husband work. "We all have scars. Some you see. Some you don't."

Blake and Damien each pulled a bag of coins from their pocket. Pouring the contents into one hand, they counted out a stack and offered it to the woman.

Blake spoke first, "I'd like a small knife, if you have one."

Damien asked for something that would be useful in sharpening a blade.

The woman's eyes rimmed with tears as she accepted their money and turned to relay the request to her husband. He responded with his hands and then moved around his items, picking up two different items carved from dark mahogany. As her husband handed the items to the men, he offered a small smile and mouthed the words "thank you". The wife then looked up at the sky, noting the time. Starting to gather their things, she looked up at them one more time. "It was nice meeting you. Thank you for your kindness."

As they went to leave, Blair stopped and turned back, embracing the woman in a hug. A look of shock crossed her face before she wrapped her arms around Blair, her shoulders relaxing the longer she held. Pulling away, the woman squeezed her shoulders and then turned back toward her husband who had packed up their things.

As the older couple filled their arms and walked down the path, the woman's shadows twisted around the man and items he carried. He leaned over and kissed her cheek as more spirals of soft darkness formed into a trail that followed them.

Blair watched them until they disappeared, a small smile forming on her mouth. *Even in the misery, there is still such beauty here.*

Behind them, a voice broke the quiet, "That's what our camp offers; healing."

They turned to see Rhea who was leaning against a tree with her arms crossed. Stepping toward them, she moved through a small patch of light that illuminated her scar, which stood out against her olive skin. Her eyes were still focused on where the couple had just disappeared. "It comes in different forms." She took another step forward, closing the space between them. "And sometimes, it benefits you to live through pain. It helps you see the true beauty in things."

Blair's eyes swept over Rhea's face, taking in the scar that seemed especially angry today. "You've obviously healed from certain things."

Blake looked from Blair to Rhea, his eyes slightly widening as if the vulnerability was making him uncomfortable.

Rhea nodded toward Blair. "Your observation is correct. Much like that couple, I had to endure certain experiences."

Damien's jaw clenched. "Was it also because of Hunter's?"

Rhea watched as a small animal scurried past her foot. "No. It was mainly because my parents weren't Shadowborn. They had no idea magic like this even existed until my powers manifested on my sixth birthday. My cake had been ruined and I threw a tantrum. They thought I had been possessed. 'A child of evil.' they said, so they tried to exorcise me."

Blair's mouth parted slightly, as her expression filled with horror. She swallowed, mind flashing to the night before when Rhea had mentioned this story previously.

"That's where my scar came from," Rhea continued. "They burned me. Tried to 'cleanse' me." Her voice didn't waver, but the weight of it was in her eyes. "Shiloh found me before they could finish."

Damien shifted his feet, repositioning the way he stood. "I'm beginning to understand a lot about Shiloh."

Rhea nodded as she straightened up. "This town is made from people who needed a new home, *all* of the camps are. It's here that I've learned to see the beauty within the darkness." She paused and then turned toward Blair. "Join me? I was just on my way to meet Marrow for lunch."

"Did you say Marrow? I'm in!" Blake replied, his mood changing instantly.

Rhea rolled her eyes and smiled, "We won't be eating with Shiloh in his quarters today. We'll be going to the actual dining area, I can show you the way."

Rhea turned and they followed her back down the path they'd taken.

The dining area was more structured than the rest of the camp. It was a real building, with shadow-forged beams and open windows. Inside, one whole wall had slotted openings that let you see into the kitchen. A sign was posted above each slot with a specific number. Through the openings, the group could see shadows moving in multiple ways to help with the meal distribution process. The cooks used them as extended hands to prepare food, shape flames, and stir pots.

The rest of the area was open seating, filled with round tables and chairs

Right now, only a few tables were occupied, including the one with Marrow. She sat with her back to them, the stark black of her hair contrasting the room as it spilled out of two buns high on her head. She turned before they had reached the table and looked them over before pulling the chair out next to her, in invitation.

Blake quickly took the seat next to her as the others chose their chairs.

"Hi," Blair said, sitting on the other side of her. "I hope you don't mind us eating with you." she added, kicking Blake under the table.

He made a muffled noise as her foot made contact. "Ou-yeah, I know you probably prefer the company of your gloom." Blake added.

Rhea laughed and slapped the table. "Gloom? That actually fits her ability quite nicely."

Marrow looked up at her and then at Blake slowly, as if assessing him. Her eyes focused on him for a moment and then widened. Realizing her reaction, a neutral mask fell over her face.

"Are we having a staring contest?" Blake said, leaning in on his elbow, and placing his chin in his palm.

Rhea, who seemed entertained by Blake's tenacity. Spoke between bites. " I would be careful with that one.

She is much stronger than she seems." Swallowing her food, she looked directly at Marrow. "Why don't you show them what you can do Mar. It's been a while since I tested myself against you."

Marrow raised one eyebrow to Rhea who had already braced in anticipation. One side of Marrow's mouth lifted into a smirk and within a few moments, shadows began to pour from her eyes. Rhea's posture changed instantly, along with her face. Her whole body froze as if held there, and her hands tensed, gripping the table.

"Rhea?" Blair breathed out, concerned.

"I'm f-fine," Rhea muttered through her clenched jaw. After a few more moments, Rhea sagged forward, panting as the shadows dispersed.

Marrow looked over at Blake. "Gloom doesn't begin to describe it. I surround the mind in the shadows that dwell within it. I manifest fears and show people the truth they try to run from, by creating illusions inside your head."

Everyone was speechless except Blake, who scoffed. "You're *amazing*."

A slight smile threatened to form on Marrow's face before she stood and walked away.

Rhea groaned and rubbed her temples. "Whatever you just envisioned, it's worse."

Blake leaned back in his chair, his eyes following Marrow. "Can't get much worse than what I've already seen."

Rhea rolled her eyes and looked at Blair, "I would suggest going to bed early. Shiloh seems easy-going but his work ethic is strong and he expects the same from those of us here."

Blair nodded in understanding, taking her first bite of the food set before her, a sandwich with a side of green beans. "Yeah, that actually sounds great. We just wanted to explore a little first before settling down for the night."

The rest of the conversation consisted of small talk and eating in pockets of quiet. When it was time to go, Rhea offered to show them around more but she was cut off by loud screaming that rose from the training arena. Shrugging, she excused herself and turned to head toward the chaos.

Blair looked over at Damien, "What do you say to exploring a little more?"

Damien squeezed her thigh under the table. " Let's do it."

All three of them gathered their things and stood, dropping their trash on the way out.

As if on cue, a group of younger Shadowborn came into view at a clearing to their right. They stood in a loose circle, murmuring to the shifting darkness that coiled beneath their feet. The shadows responded to them, stretching into dark shapes.

Blair leaned into Damien. "What do you think that is?"

"A shadow game," Damien said, stepping closer. "We played a similar one in the camp. It's a type of challenge. You have to try and protect yourself while going after one of the other players in front of you."

Blair's eyes lit up and Damien chuckled lightly before stepping toward the small crowd. As they approached, they witnessed the game begin. A girl with slate-gray eyes and black flower tattoos sent out two thick tendrils of shadows; One viciously thrashed, blocking two incoming attacks, while the second slid out and wrapped around an opponent's ankle. He had barely noticed it before it yanked him off the circle, forcing him to lose the game.

Each turn, someone attempted to eliminate the others by pushing, pulling, or maneuvering them off the circle. They continued to watch the various strengths between the children, some who had practiced certain skills. At the end, only one remained. The children then dispersed, running off to find other things to do.

It was barely evening when they made their way back to their sleeping quarters. When Blake motioned to their tent in question, Blair and Damien nodded in unison. It had barely been an hour before all three were changed and in bed.

9

Sunlight streamed through the high-arched windows, casting fractured shapes across the long banquet table where a single child sat. The chair he occupied was small, carved with delicate vines and silver leaf that curled along the arms. He wriggled in the space around him, the seat obviously too large for the blonde-headed boy who occupied it. His hair was pale and fine, and his face held a certain sadness.

A massive amount of food was organized in front of him, but he seemed to not care. His fork moved mechanically, pushing his food around in slow, aimless patterns. Occasionally, he raised a bite to his lips, but even then his jaw barely moved.

He looked out the window, beyond the glass panes where the courtyard was scattered with late-summer roses. A fountain murmured softly below, most of the sound muffled. Statues of past monarchs stood sentinel around the courtyard, their stone gazes cast forever downward. He watched out the window as the light changed from morning sun to evening glow.

This happened several more times, the light shifting and the table resetting, but the result never changed. He was always alone, like a still frame caught inside a living painting.

Blair watched from the shadows of the doorway, a growing weight in her chest. It wasn't long before she tried speaking to him.

"Hey…" she whispered. "Are you alright?"

The boy never replied, keeping his eyes on the food in front of him or the window. She moved closer and tried again, but louder this time, her voice echoing slightly against the high vaulted ceiling.

Still, there was nothing; no flinch, no reaction, no acknowledgment.

Confused, Blair turned slowly, taking in her surroundings. It was a royal castle, of that she was sure, but not one she recognized. The ceilings were arched, a picture painted across them. Tapestries lined the walls, blue trimmed in silver, their colors faded and edges frayed. They depicted grand battles and crowned kings, rivers of fire and towering cities. Above the hearth, there was a portrait; A family of two boys and their parents.

The changing days shifted to seasons, the environment outside changing with the food offered. The boy seemed to be changing too, his body growing slightly, as well as his hair.

Until one day, he vanished from the seat. The chair was left vacant, the plate still untouched. Blair looked *around for him but as she did so, the area around her became foggy and as she blinked, the castle was gone.*

Instead, she now stood at the doorway of a nursery. Her eyes adjusted to the gold wallpaper on the walls and the dust motes that drifted through the morning light that leaked in from the small windows. A woman sat in a chair inside the room, holding a bundle in her arms.

Blair stood there, dazed. Clasping her hands loosely in front of her, she watched the woman rock the child in her arms.

Her movements were slow as she moved in the carved wooden chair, its gentle creak the only sound besides her soft song. Her auburn hair fell in waves over her shoulder, catching the light in strands of copper and flame. The tune wasn't one Blair recognized, and the words she caught were in a foreign tongue.

As the melody deepened, the air shifted. Intricate symbols emerged on her skin, glowing silver runes that traced along the woman's arms and throat. The emblems continued to bloom as she sang. They shimmered with a quiet pulse each time her voice carried through the empty space around her. Her eyes, once a light blue, darkened slowly until they were pools of midnight.

Yet there was no fear in her expression, only love, as she gazed down at the baby. Moving the blanket down, her thumb traced lazy circles across the small face. The child cooed, eyes opening to reveal the same shade of crystal blue as the mother but these were pure and bright, untouched by shadow.

The woman gave another smile as every rune on her skin flared brighter. Her voice softened to a whisper as she finished the song. "Sleep, my son."

The door creaked behind Blair and she stepped aside as another woman entered, her steps slower but sure. Her silver-streaked hair was gathered at her nape, and wisdom lined her face in deep wrinkles.

"Grandmother," the woman murmured, looking up and dipping her head respectfully.

The older woman's eyes warmed as she approached the rocking chair, her presence commanding yet gentle. She moved next to them, resting a hand on the baby's small head. "He's perfect," she said, voice thick with quiet pride. "The shadows in him run deep already. Idris would be proud of his lineage." Her fingers brushed over his cheek, and runes came alive along her wrist. The baby's blue eyes flickered, though he could not yet understand what magic stirred within him.

The auburn-haired woman leaned her head against the back of the chair, as she nodded in agreement. Staring at the ceiling, her eyes were still black as night, but had a certain tenderness to them.

Blair didn't move, afraid to piece together what she was watching. The room glowed faintly, before going completely black and everything was gone.

10

The sun had barely begun to rise when Blake's scream shattered the quiet. His voice tore through the air like a whip, followed by the sound of bodies crashing.

Peeling her eyes open, Blair shot upright in her bed, waking Damien. By the time she scrambled out from under her blanket, Blake was already on top of Adriel, fists swinging in half-awake fury.

"You set my foot on fire, you fucking lunatic!"

Adriel, flat on his back, barely flinched. "What's wrong? I thought you liked that kind of foreplay, *baby*." he muttered, a smirk tugging at the corner of his mouth.

Blake drove his fist into the side of it.

Damien groaned, rolling out of bed. Pulling a shirt over his head, he handed clothes to Blair before turning to the two men wrestling on the floor.

"Enough," Damien said flatly, his voice a deep rumble in the tent. He flicked a hand lazily, and his shadows stretched between them. Blake was yanked backward mid-punch and Adriel was dragged to his feet, like two unruly children.

"*Really?*" Blake snapped, brushing dirt off his chest. "You couldn't have used your shadows a second ago when I was being charred alive."

"You're still whining," Damien said. "So clearly, you survived."

Blair snorted, despite her best efforts to keep a straight face.

Adriel rolled his shoulders with a wince. "Glad to see everyone's awake. I was sent to get you for your first day of training. I'll wait outside."

With that, he walked out of the tent, winking at Blake as he passed him. Blake raised his hand to punch him again, but Damien's shadow was quicker, stopping the swing mid-air.

Blake pulled on his pants, mumbling as he watched Adriel's figure outside the tent. Damien created a wall of shadow for Blair so she'd have some privacy, and within minutes they were ready to go.

The four of them arrived at the training arena to find Rhea, Marrow, and Kael already waiting for them. Adriel stepped forward and faced Blair, "I get you first." he said, "I was told to test your agility. The rules are simple for today. You dodge, or you burn."

Blair blinked. "That sounds more like a threat."

"Same difference," Adriel replied with a shrug. "Use your shadows to protect yourself or don't, but don't expect me to hold back."

Damien shifted beside her, clearly growing agitated. His dark eyes locked on Adriel with a look that could kill him. "I'm sure she'll be just fine, regardless of your effort." he said, his voice low.

Blake stepped beside Damien, "He's not as fast as he thinks he is, Blair. You'll be just fine."

Adriel raised his eyebrows and smiled.

Blair looked between the two men next to her and then back at Adriel. Stepping forward, she accepted his challenge before Damien had the chance to do something reckless. "I've got this," she said, then looked back up to the men behind her. "Go play somewhere else."

There was a small pause while Damien assessed his reply. His lips parted like he wanted to say more, but he swallowed it. With shadows stirring restlessly behind him, he chose to dismiss himself instead. "Call for me if you need me," he said quietly as he motioned for Blake to follow.

Blake listened but not before giving Adriel a rude gesture. "That's for my foot. Next time you burn it, I'll shove it so far up-"

"Blake!" Blair yelled, stopping him mid-sentence.

Blake sighed in response and moved off to spar with Damien, who was now across the arena.

Blair stepped into the training circle, shaking her head at the men she associated herself with.

"Ready?" Adriel asked, shadowy flames already flickering at his fingertips. She watched them before she answered, each one coiling in different ways, black and unnatural.

She had barely nodded before the first strike came. A fast lash of shadow fire seared across the ground, aimed at her legs. She leapt aside, barely dodging the singe of heat as it passed. Another strike came from behind, and she ducked, rolling across the earth.

Adriel moved like lightning, his hands cutting the air with growing ferocity. Shadow fire whirled and cracked around her, the air thick with its acrid scent. Blair's breath quickened, as her muscles started to burn.

She darted left, then screamed. A tongue of fire seared across her forearm, blistering her skin with white-hot pain. She stumbled, the scent of burned flesh catching in her throat.

She had barely looked up at Adriel, before she felt shadows at her back. A familiar veil of blackness fell between her and the next strike, absorbing the hit. As Blair followed the shadows, her eyes landed on Damien, who stood with his arms raised in a sparring position. His eyes had also found the shadows, the ones that moved across the floor from him to her.

As Damien's shadows moved up from the floor and wrapped around her, he gave her a small smile. That one moment awoke something inside of her and her mark flared to life. From her depths, a deeper form of shadow emerged out of her, creating a darker version that moved within his. The pain that came with it was bearable, and she tensed as more black tendrils moved around her. They mixed together, forming a haunting, ethereal purple energy that crackled through them.

Adriel froze mid-strike, eyes narrowing. "What is *that*?"

Blair didn't stop to ask. She barely looked before her instincts screamed at her to act. She reached inside herself, grabbed the power that pulsed there, and pushed.

Her shadow exploded forward, slamming into Adriel's chest with the force of a wall. He flew backward, hitting the dirt hard. A grunt escaped his lips as he rolled and landed face-down.

From across the arena, Blake howled with laughter as Adriel fell with an audible thud. "That's for my foot, asshole!" he called out, clapping his hands.

Adriel groaned from the ground, coughing dust. "I said *agility*, not *demolition*."

"You didn't say I couldn't hit back," Blair replied, chest heaving, the purple still flickering at her fingertips like embers refusing to die.

Adriel sat up, the breath still knocked out of him. He held up a finger, using his other hand to brush himself off with a wince. "I need a minute."

Damien stopped mid-strike as Blake shadowstepped away from him. Within the next second, he popped up right next to where Marrow was sitting "I'll take his place. Marrow! We're up!"

Marrow sat on a mat in the manifestation circle, perfectly still, with her legs crossed and hands resting on her knees. Her focus remained, as if she hadn't heard Blake's outburst, even though it was mere feet away.

Blake called out to her again, excitement written on his face. "C'mon. Agility is open for a minute, let's see what kind of gloom you got."

She still paid him no mind, not even opening her eyes.

He waved a hand in front of her face and squatted down. "Are you broken, or just ignoring me?"

There was a small, almost unnoticeable twitch in her eyebrow before her eyes flickered for a brief second and then opened fully. The whites vanished, consumed by black as her shadows surged out, then stopped. There was no reaction; no scream, no change in Blake.

Marrow's mouth popped open, and she simply stared at him.

Blake tilted his head. "Gotta say, not impressed."

Her shadows wavered for a moment and then faded. A strange expression crossed over her features, not of anger, or defiance, but confusion.

Marrow stared down at her hands, momentarily stunned. A low, antagonizing whistle drifted from Blake and her expression cracked, a new emotion taking over.

Blake, clearly amused, blinked and tilted his head. "Huh. That's disappointing. I was kinda hoping you would slam me against a wall."

Marrow's head snapped up at his words and her eyes narrowed. Without warning, she lunged.

Blake barely had time to laugh before her foot swept his legs out from under him, sending him crashing to the mat on his stomach with a hard *thud*. Before he could recover, she was on him; an elbow to his spine, a hand gripping the back of his neck and tightening until he hissed.

"Ohohoho," Blake wheezed into the mat, "How did you know I like it rough?"

He twisted under her, trying to use his weight to gain leverage, but she moved as if he was no challenge for her. Each movement flowed into the next, smooth and brutal. A sharp jab to the side of his stomach knocked the air from his lungs, and his smirk faltered as his breath left in a whoosh.

He hit the mat again as she flipped him, this time with a grunt that actually sounded pained.

Marrow straddled his chest, pinning both wrists with her knees and sliding her hands to his throat. Her breath came steady and her eyes were locked on him, cold and calculated.

Blake blinked up at her, dazed and grinning through the air cut-off. "I th-think I love you."

Marrow rolled her eyes and squeezed harder, as he opened his mouth again. "If you could j-just," he rasped, "Step on my neck."

Her hands loosened and she just stared at him, shaking her head in disbelief. Just as she went to climb off of him, she noticed him adjusting himself between his legs. Moving her eyes down to Blake's pants, her jaw dropped at the very obvious outline that protruded.

Blair, watching from the side, groaned Blake's name as Damien walked up and covered her eyes. Just before his hand fully blocked her line of sight, she saw Marrow turn back and look at her as if asking what to do.

"Just a little, Marrow?" Blake wheezed, raising his eyebrows despite being pinned to the floor. "I feel like I've earned it."

Marrow let go of his wrists with a short huff, not exactly a laugh or a sigh, and stood.

Blake stayed flat on his back, staring at the ceiling. One hand remained still, but the other moved in-between his legs, palming himself. "Yup," he muttered. "I definitely earned it."

Adriel, who had finally made it back to his feet and was brushing off his sleeves, glanced over. "She already won, now stop being an idiot."

Blake raised a finger as he went to sit up. "I think I won, seeing how I was seduced via blunt force trauma." He then stood, tucking himself into the waistband of his pants. "It wasn't that bad, *obviously* I liked it."

Damien, who was still shielding Blair, just shook his head at the whole situation, his shadows twitching in amused irritation.

Adriel looked from Blake to Blair, who now had her sight back. "Odd that it wasn't worse." Turning his head to Marrow, she narrowed her eyes slightly as if trying to tell him something. In response, Adriel's eyes lifted in amusement. "Seems your friend isn't affected by Marrow," he said to Blair, voice thoughtful. "Curious."

Then his expression sharpened as his eyes darted to Damien. "But I bet they're both not immune."

"Wait, what?" Blair asked, stepping forward.

But she wasn't fast enough.

Damien instantly dropped as Marrow locked eyes on him. Crumpling to his knees, his hands flew to his head. His brows furrowed, and a snarl escaped him.

Adriel reached out, grabbing Blair's arm as she moved toward him, but she shoved him off. Her mark reacted instantaneously to the danger, feeding off her emotions. A large wave of black and purple shadows erupted from her like a broken dam, lashing through the air at Marrow. As they did so, a jagged pattern formed on Blair's skin, surging from the dagger on her thigh. The more her shadows grew, the more the patterns spread.

Adriel yelled at Marrow to stop, but she already had her hands up as if she was no longer using her power.

Either way, it was too late.

Damien's shadows had also reacted, convulsing around him as Blair approached. Every tendril snapped out and upward as if electrified, then poured back into his body. His spine arched and the air around him crackled as vast, jagged wings burst from his back, made not of flesh but pure shadow. The veins of them pulsed faintly, shot through with silvery light. Black runes ignited across his arms and then faded into his skin as his head lifted. His eyes snapped open, a ring of silver around his blue.

Everyone watched as Blair stepped in front of him and placed both hands on his face. The chaotic shadows around him moved toward her, wrapping around her forearms, his body physically relaxing with her touch. She removed one hand and held it out. Multiple shadows of his circled her palm, and then dissolved into her skin. Blair looked up at him to find his demeanor calming. The more shadows she took, the more he relaxed.

She then called out, specifically to Kael. "You wanted to know about the power you felt." She looked over at him as the last shadows disappeared into her palm. "Now you know."

Adriel clicked his tongue, watching her with a mix of apprehension and fascination. "Mark of the Void sure looks good on you," he said. "Shiloh was right, it just needed a specific kind of push to come out and play."

Blair's shadows flared at those words before they calmed and moved along her skin, retreating. Slowly, the black mist that had filled the space disappeared into nothing. Damien's wings folded behind him, dissolving into threads of smoke that sank back into his spine.

From the edge, Shiloh's voice broke the silence as he stepped into the circle, stopping just a few feet away from Damien and Blair. He took in the shocked expressions of everyone before he inclined his head slightly toward Damien, the motion both respectful and deliberate. "You'll be training with me from now on."

Damien's jaw flexed, but he gave a single, silent nod as he continued to stare at Blair. His voice was low as he replied. "When do we start?"

Shiloh's smile sharpened. "*Now.* She goes with them, and you come with me."

Damien continued to hold Blair's gaze, even as the silver in his eyes dulled. "Are you good with that?," he asked, his voice sincere.

Blair scanned his face, making sure he was okay before answering. "I'll be fine."

Damien gave her a small smile before turning toward Blake. With one small gesture, it was as if a silent conversation took place between them. As Damien stepped away, Blake moved next to Blair.

Once Damien found his place next to Shiloh, he called out to Marrow, who was across the arena. "It's nice to see what you can really do though, Marrow."

Marrow's lips curled, unreadable. Perhaps amused or intrigued, either way it was more emotion than she had let show before.

Adriel's gaze locked with Blair's. "You've tapped into a piece of the dagger's power. The purple shadows are proof of that." He motioned toward her hand. "Obviously, your body reacted to help Damien, but I want you to try and activate it again. Just use what you felt earlier, or at least try."

Rhea walked in front of Blair this time, holding out her hand with shadows that danced above it. "I volunteer, let's see what you got."

Blair's shoulders began to tense but she looked over at Damien, who caught her eye as he walked away. She swallowed and placed her hand over Rhea's shadows. Blair closed her eyes, focusing on the rush of protection she felt, the urgency that had kick-started her adrenaline. It took a few moments, but the jagged black lines finally sprouted. Not enough to take over her body like before, but just enough for her palm to consume a small amount of shadows that Rhea offered. As the black wisps vanished, Rhea looked up at Blair proudly.

Blake came up behind Blair, resting his hand on her shoulder. "If I had feelings, I'd probably be feeling proud. It's disgusting, really."

Blair smiled up at him as he pulled her into a hug, releasing her to a keen Adriel who looked like he was deep in thought. Blair met Adriel's eyes as Blake relaxed next to her, his arm around her shoulders.

"Let's keep things going. Our goal is to keep it activated, and have it respond quicker."

11

Adriel stood before her, his hands behind his back, a sheer layer of sweat coating his body. "Again."

Blair exhaled slowly, letting her body loosen. It had been hours and she had just started to learn simpler ways to access her new skill. She closed her eyes and reached for the place of power that fueled her. She imagined the dagger and thought of Damien, which prompted a warmth beneath her skin that was almost familiar. Coiled in the muscles of her thigh, she felt it. When she focused harder, its pulse grew stronger, almost like a lifeline. The next step was to call to it. As it answered, she could feel the power crawling up her leg, torso, then chest.

This time, the heat reached above her elbow, and it caught her off guard.

"Don't force it," Adriel said, his voice cutting through the silence. "Just be ready when it comes."

She opened her eyes as purple light joined the jagged, lightning-like fractures that coated her skin. This design materialized almost every time she activated her power. Sometimes, the pattern was just a small area, but other times it flooded her body.

"Good," Adriel murmured. "Now hold it."

When she had first activated the mark this morning, it had taken her by surprise, almost like a reflex or emotional flare. Now, *the control* was the challenge. Holding it was like keeping fire in her lungs, not painful, but immediately draining.

She ground her heel into the dirt and shifted her stance, steadying herself.

Rhea walked past her, deliberately close, her own shadow brushing against Blair's.

"Take it," Adriel ordered. "From her."

Blair reached out, not with her hands, but with something deeper. The shadow responded instantly, peeling from Rhea's form and moving to Blair. At first, it curled up her arm, tangled with the purple markings there, and then vanished beneath her skin.

Rhea staggered slightly and arched her brow. "It's like being hollowed out. Not bad, though. Feels clean."

"You're not supposed to enjoy it," Marrow called from her corner of the arena, where she leaned lazily against a pillar, arms crossed.

Rhea looked over, as if surprised by Marrow's comment. Blair watched the interaction as she took another breath. Steadying herself, she prepared to take another charge of power.

"How long was I able to hold it?" she asked, voice tight.

Adriel watched her for a beat longer, then answered. "Thirty-seven seconds. Again."

She exhaled and let the power go. As she did so, the jagged lines dimmed and then receded.

This sequence repeated again and again. At first, Blair could only hold it for twenty seconds. Then thirty-five. Then nearly a full minute before her muscles shook and her chest tightened with the strain of channeling.

After a while, Rhea stepped out and Marrow replaced her. The difference in shadow energy was immediate, and Blair tilted her head as she realized why. Marrow's shadow had edges. When Blair pulled from her, they fought back, a writhing and resisting entity. Blair flinched when she first noticed, but held on. Marrow's grin deepened as though she knew it was a struggle.

"That's better," she said when Blair finally broke the link, panting. "If you can take from me, you can take from anything."

But it didn't prove enough. The Mark didn't truly *ignite*, not in the way it had when she faced real danger, real grief, like when Damien had been hurt.

Adriel realized it too. He stepped closer, voice lower now, almost gentle. "You're still thinking too much. Your mark doesn't care about logic, it responds to your *choice* and your *instinct*." He offered her a flask of water. "So, you're done for today."

Blair glanced up at the sky, surprised by how dim it had gotten. They'd trained past lunch, well into the edge of dinner.

"How long now?" she asked, her voice hoarse and her body exhausted.

Adriel gave a rare smile. "Just over two minutes."

Rhea gave a low whistle behind them. "That's a good place to start."

Blair rolled her eyes at them, but a weak grin spread across her face. Her body only seemed to drain more as she took a step toward the exit. She had just stepped outside when Rhea cleared her throat from behind her, "I'd like to be the one to escort you to the next camp when you're ready."

Blair turned her head to look at Rhea. "What?"

Rhea drew in a small breath. "I've been thinking a lot and I want to be a part of this. Whatever history this will be, I want to know what happens for myself."

Blair gave her a small smile and a slight nod, "I can understand that." she said, pulling her into a side hug. "Honestly, I'd love that. Sometimes the testosterone can be a little overwhelming." Blair squeezed tighter as Rhea kept rigid, and a small laugh escaped her. "Our men have sharp tongues, but you get used to it. If that doesn't happen, feel free to knock them around a little."

With that, Rhea gave a small smile and Blair took that as a personal victory, releasing her to walk toward the dining hall.

With each step, she thought about different parts of her day. What little training she had done had brought progress, but every inch of her body was angry. Knowing Rhea wanted to help was a small comfort, but one that also made her anxious. Then there was Damien, who had shown everyone his abilities.

All the thoughts bled from her as she approached a clearing near the edge of the trees. In the middle of the grass, she saw figures moving, the sounds of their impact and low grunts echoed around her.

As her vision focused in, she made out the forms of Shiloh and Damien. Both men seemed focused, circling each other as if trying to locate their opponents weak spots. Sweat slicked Damien's neck, his hair now plastered to his temples, while a single rune glowed faintly along his shoulder.

Neither of them seemed to be holding back.

Every strike from Shiloh was meant to provoke, not just test. He moved with the sharp precision of someone who knew exactly what he was doing. "Challenge yourself, Damien," he declared.

Damien's eyes darkened, but he stayed silent.

Shiloh smirked. "You'll never keep up with her, if *that's* your best."

The words angered Damien who reacted instantly, lunging with enough speed that Shiloh had to adjust his position several times to dodge. For a moment, it seemed like a game until Shiloh moved a fraction faster and drove a solid hit straight into Damien's side.

Damien staggered, his expression twisting in pain. Shadows rippled like water from his back, and with a sharp, echoing snap, a pair of wings unfurled.

Shiloh barely got an arm up before the wings opened wide. The force hit him like a gust from a storm, knocking him backward into the dirt. He lay there for a breath, eyes wide, then broke into a grin.

"Well," he said, pushing to his feet and brushing off his hands, "that's one way to prove me wrong."

Blair stepped out from the treeline as Shiloh's grin widened further. "This is good," he said, nodding toward Damien. "You should be training as much as she is."

Damien's wings flexed once before settling. He turned as Blair approached, the faintest smirk breaking through the tension. She reached for his hand and he gave it, wrapping her in a hug.

When he finally let her go, she looked up at him. "Hungry?"

"Starving." He answered, biting her lip. The shadows along his back shimmered once more before fading, wings dissolving into air. He laced his fingers through hers as they walked past Shiloh, toward the eating area.

Shiloh patted Damien's shoulder as he passed. "See you tomorrow."

As everyone gathered to receive their meal, the exhaustion was evident. Time in line, that was normally filled with conversation and banter, remained quiet as everyone decompressed. The dinner they received was simple; bread that was torn unevenly, with spiced lentils.

Moving to the table, they found Rhea already there with no food, just watching with a faint smile.

Blair nudged Damien's thigh gently with hers as she sat. "How did today go?"

He sat up and pulled his chair as close as he could to hers, placing his hand on her thigh before using the other one to take a bite. "It went well, feisty."

"Went *well?*" Blake mocked, sitting down and tossing a piece of crust at Damien, which bounced harmlessly off his arm. "Even I'm jealous of your wingspan there, buddy."

Blair laughed out loud as Damien rolled his eyes. Taking a page out of his own book, Blair leaned across the table toward Blake. "If you think that's impressive, you should see his-"

"*Okay!* Boundaries, Blair, boundaries." Blake yelled, jumping up to cover Marrow's ears, who had just sat down. "There are *ladies* present."

Blair stuck her tongue out at him before taking a few bites of her food.

Meals were eaten rather fast and soon the table was full of yawns and stretching limbs. Setting down his fork, Damien looked over at Blair. "It's getting late. You ready for bed?"

She looked up at him and nodded enthusiastically, before standing. She said goodbye to the others at the table and followed Damien out. Walking behind him, she took a moment to watch his back and the way his muscles moved through his shirt. She imagined how his wings formed, where the shadows actually attached. Blair was so enthralled with her thoughts, she didn't notice when Damien turned and went down a different path. Even as the temperature changed around her, she remained blissfully unaware.

The trail soon dipped, which caught her attention. Looking up, she realized the path opened into a hidden pocket of land. In front of them was a shallow pool that stretched beneath a crescent of trees. The water moved slowly with the wind, reflecting the colors of the sky like glass. Shadows flickered across the surface, swaying with the trees. It almost looked like a painting.

Blair exhaled, her voice quiet. "What is this place?"

"A place I stumbled on while out with Shiloh. It made me think of you," Damien said. "Figured we'd both need it, but if you're too tired, I understand."

She didn't even wait for him to finish before she was kicking off her boots with excitement. Looking up at him and shaking her head, she pushed her exhaustion to the back of her mind. *Tired? Don't know her.*

She then crossed her arms in front of her and lifted her top off. A playful look crossed her face as she then bent and slowly lowered her pants. He looked her up and down in approval, the whites of his eyes slightly darkening.

He followed her lead, stripping down and stepping into the shallow water with her. Immediately, her body jerked into him at the cold shock. Damien laughed as she shook, goosebumps now covering her skin. He moved behind her, placing his hands on her waist as she led them deeper into the water. The farther they got, the more he pulled her into him, creating warmth for her.

By the time they stopped, they were in the center of the pool. The water was now waist-deep, the floor full of smooth stones that laid beneath their feet. Blair sank into Damien's chest slowly, letting her head fall back to look up at him as she groaned from the comfort of the water on her sore limbs.

After a few moments of watching her, Damien pulled her into a standing position, his hands gently finding her shoulders. She didn't flinch or resist his direction. Instead, she let her head tip forward, relaxing even more as he began to work the muscles in her neck.

He was careful at first, using his strength with a firm, yet slow pressure. His thumbs pressed into the knots beneath her shoulder blades, drawing tension out of her spine. She didn't speak, only made approving sounds as the silence held around them.

"I want you to know," he said after a while, voice low and calm behind her. "You make me so damn proud."

Blair gave a tired huff. "Yeah?"

"Definitely."

She shrugged and whispered a reply, "I feel like I could be better."

Her words only made his grip adjust and move to the sides of her neck. His fingers found the base of her skull, and she melted a little further into the water. His mouth brushed her left ear, then moved down, gently kissing the side of her neck. His right hand moved up and stilled over her throat, his fingers spreading as he tapped the pulse in her neck.

It was quiet for a beat before she looked up and to the right, opening her throat to him more. He groaned in acceptance as his hands moved to roam her body. "It's like you don't even see it." he murmured, in a low, hushed tone. "You are, and always have been, too much, too wild, and too impulsive. But there is no way you could ever *be better*. You are perfect just like this." He kissed her jawline, beckoning her to look at him. "Did you know that?" he asked, kissing her lips as she turned to him. "Did you know that because of who you are I would pledge my soul to you. I would follow you anywhere in this world, without a second thought." He kissed her one more time, slowly.

With his words, a dark shadow rose from his chest and wrapped around her. The shadow tightened, then passed through her own chest before returning to him and funneling through one specific spot on his skin.

Blair turned, following the shadows as they seared a small crescent moon into his chest, almost like a brand, right above his heart. His eyes never left her, as if it was no surprise what was happening. He gave her a small smile as she looked down at the mark he now had. "This is me, Blair. I'm yours."

Bringing her hand up, she lightly touched the symbol with her fingers, expecting the skin to be warm. Instead, it was cool and rippled under her touch.

"What is that?" She asked, her fingers tracing the shape.

He looked down at his chest as he spoke, "As Shadowborn, we have the ability to create a shadow oath with someone. When we do this, we forge a bond with that person, pledging to them in some way." Damien then looked up, his eyes filled with sincerity. "I bound myself to you, for however long you'll have me."

Her fingers stilled and her eyes slowly raised to meet his. "Are you sure you can handle me for that long?" she asked with a small smile.

"Baby, you were never meant to be *handled*. You're meant to be worshipped, and protected. I'll give my life for that cause." Damien's eyes flickered with raw emotion as he spoke.

Without hesitation, Blair wrapped her arms around his neck, and kissed him deeply.

His body responded in reflex, his hands moving to her waist and pulling her flush to him. Grazing her sides, his fingers traveled up to pull off the only piece of fabric left that clung to her chest. In one fluid motion, he took it off and tossed it by her other clothes.

Focusing back on her, he kissed her cheek bone and then trailed his lips behind her ear. As he did so, their shadows released, intertwining and forming a thick veil of protection. Damien reached down, taking off the only clothing left between them. Hoisting her up by her thighs, he teased her mouth as he aligned himself between her legs. He pushed inside with one thrust and Blair let out a scream of pleasure before kissing him.

Damien moved slowly at first, staying in rhythm with the water that lapped at their bodies. Soon, his grip tightened and Blair knew his control was slipping. Running her hands through his hair, she pulled a low growl from her throat. She then turned his head, trailing a line of kisses down his neck to his chest, stopping on the insignia that now branded him. It glowed as he moved, almost as if showcasing his dedication to her.

Soon, the gentle motions turned into a feral desire, and passion exploded. With every thrust, his grip tightened around her legs. With every kiss, her nails drug across his back. The raw intensity sprouted shadows that clung to both of their bodies, heightening everything. Soon, they were both coming undone, wrapped in each other. Blair tried to scream as the wave of pleasure hit her, but he swallowed it, sealing it with another kiss as he forced her to ride through her body's tremors.

Soothing her, he used one hand to cradle her head to his chest as he moved out of the water. Just like in the hot springs, as she exited the water, his shadows moved instinctively to cover her exposed skin. Although this time, it formed into a black fabric that draped over her. Damien pulled on his pants and shirt while he watched the darkness move along her body. " See? I told you. They respect you."

She looked down and ran her finger along the darkness that covered her chest, as if attempting to feel it. Her finger moved right through it, as if nothing was there. She watched as the shadows seemed to cinch, creating a mold that looked like a dress. "Huh." She let out a quiet breath, as if amazed by what they could do.

The small walk back was filled with content quietness and the occasional yawn from Blair. By the time they reached their tent, she could barely hold her eyes open, so Damien swept her up in his arms as he stepped through the opening.

The soft snores from Blake filled the area around them as Damien laid her on the bed. He then walked over to the dresser and grabbed one of his shirts. Returning to Blair he pulled it over her head and repositioned her, sliding next to her in bed. His large body held hers tightly as he ran his finger in small circles over the dimple in her shoulder. "I meant every word," he breathed, fingers still moving. "You have me. My body, my soul, and my shadows."

He stayed like that, watching her sleep, until exhaustion pulled him under and the world faded to quiet.

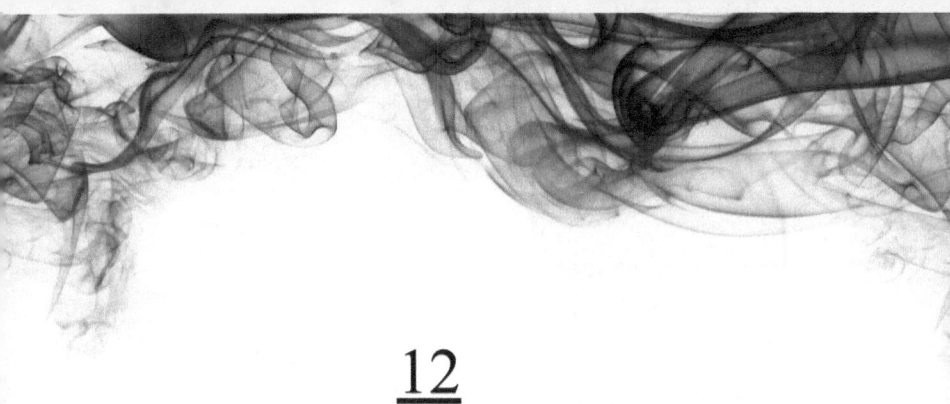

12

The next day was grueling, relentless, and exactly what Blair needed. The day began before sunrise, with Marrow there to collect everyone. Unlike Adriel, she was quiet and waited patiently while everyone woke and dressed.

On the way to the training grounds, she paused to let everyone grab a small bowl of oats, another luxury Adriel had forgotten the day prior. They ate on the way, dropping their bowls outside of the arena as they entered.

Walking in, Blair eyed Adriel, who was waiting for her. He gave Marrow a quick 'Thanks' before approaching Blair. "You activated the mark," he said. "But not with any real consistency. Today, that changes, and we aim to strengthen your body to match the power your mark can provide. We're going to focus on agility first and train until you can harness it at full potential. By the end of your time with me, you will be sharper and faster. In order to do this, we're working on your speed and control."

Blair nodded, swallowing her nerves as he explained they would be going outside today. Damien and Blake looked at her for confirmation before they left her side, and as she turned to follow Adriel, Damien gave her hand a gentle squeeze.

Within the first few minutes, Adriel had her running drills through the trees. Just physical movement first, with no attempt at activating the mark. She listened to him, dodging between trunks, leaping over roots, rolling beneath branches. Each time she landed wrong, he called her out. Each time she slowed, he pushed her harder.

"You're not as slow as I thought you were going to be," he snapped after she slipped and caught herself on a jagged rock. "But you *are* clumsy."

By midday, she had yet to see Damien or Blake, besides the occasional shadows that cascaded out of the top of the training area. Although she had thought of them a couple of times between Adriel's directions, her main focus stayed on her movements. It had only been a few hours and her limbs ached, a layer of sweat covering her whole body. Still, the mark on her thigh stayed dormant. This was her life over the next few days, different locations, but same grueling expectations.

It wasn't until the end of that week that she could activate her mark.

Adriel had looped a course of hanging ropes and spinning targets, an obstacle designed for failure. Blair knew that as soon as she saw it, but she tried anyway, and soon, she felt a shift. When she let her instincts lead, when she focused on movement rather than mastery, her body started responding differently.

Her movements were faster, almost light.

On a particularly sharp turn, as she jumped from one platform to another mid-air, the mark on her thigh flared. She landed hard, rolling to absorb the impact, and felt it. It wasn't painful, but almost like the warmth she had felt before, a comforting feeling.

The mark of Void shimmered just beneath her skin, motivating her to push herself further. Each one of her motions became deliberate and clean. She knew he had to have noticed, but Adriel didn't say a word. He just watched her and nodded as she passed him, blazing through the course.

The others came to watch the next day, a look of approval on each face. After that, they joined occasionally. Adriel would pair Blair with someone in sparring sessions and challenge her to activate the mark while fighting. Next came group agility drills where she would have to hold the mark or they would all be punished. *Blake hated those training sessions.*

At the end of the second week, Adriel didn't speak when she arrived at the training area. He simply pointed away from the building, into the surrounding woods, where a different course had been set.

As she approached, she knew this one was not like the others. There were no ropes or targets, only a series of stones scattered through the trees, some glowing faintly with silver etching. Blair narrowed her eyes at the large rocks. "Another challenge?" she asked, looking at Adriel.

Adriel nodded. "Activate the mark, then run. Touch each stone in order, while you keep it open. If you miss one, you start over."

She looked at the stones again, assessing the difficulty. After a few moments, she looked back at him. "Is there a time limit?"

He didn't confirm or deny. "You'll know if you fail."

That wasn't even close to an answer. Still, she breathed deep, closed her eyes, and let the power rise. This was a command she had now grown accustomed to. It came easier now, less a firestorm and more a surge. When it pulsed through her in response, she stepped forward and began.

The first stone glowed brightly when her fingers brushed it. She moved quickly, weaving between trees and leaping over uneven terrain. The mark gave her confidence but not immunity; she still had to choose each step and land each jump. She didn't stumble, didn't hesitate. One by one, she lit the stones as the black markings remained on her skin.

The final stone was high, embedded in the side of a jagged rock face. Blair didn't slow; she sprinted and jumped, fingers grazing the surface just long enough to ignite the rune.

Then she landed hard, but steady.

Behind her, the woods remained silent, unphased by her personal victory.

Adriel stepped into view then, arms crossed as usual, though his expression was different. His eyes held a hint of satisfaction.

"You're ready," he said.

Blair blinked. "For what?"

"For Marrow." He paused, then added, "She'll teach you manifestation. Her specialty comes in different forms, but now that you know how to activate it when moving, she'll teach you how to refine it and focus your intent."

Blair let a smile grow on her face.

"Do me a favor and don't let her coddle you. You've improved greatly but you need to keep pushing yourself."

"And if I don't?" she asked.

"Then you'll fail, and the Hunters- No, the King wins." he said simply, "But I don't think you will." he added, with a small smirk.

His words stayed with her as she walked inside the building and looked for Marrow, who sat in the manifestation corner. Blair locked eyes with Damien, before walking to her. Extra time with him had been limited lately. She was either teetering on exhaustion when with him, or he was out training with Shiloh.

Blair sat down on the mat, across from Marrow. Her attention was not totally on the task at hand, but instead, on Damien who was preparing to start the agility course. His arms crossed in front of him as he pulled his shirt up and over his head, discussing form with Adriel.

Marrow's hollow, crackling voice brought her attention back. "Your job with me is to learn how to center. The mark is not always a weapon you wield, it is however, always part of you, hidden in your roots. To reach it, you must create a safe space in your mind, one that is yours alone." Marrow crossed her legs and set her hands on top, palms up, as she continued, "Close your eyes."

Blair did as she was told, struggling against the mental image of Damien she had just summoned. The longer she sat, the longer her thoughts turned chaotic. Images played through her mind, first of Damien, then Hunters, Grei, the tavern, the past few weeks.

"Breathe," Marrow murmured, sensing her agitation.

Blair exhaled slowly, and as she did so, an image formed in her mind. *Silverdawn.* A small field she used to wander, tucked behind a ridge where the light always seemed to shine just a little more kindly. The ground was blanketed with soft, purple flowers. The scent there was always sweet. She stood there now, in her mind, barefoot in the blossoms.

Blair inhaled deeply, as if she could smell the florals around her.

"Good. Stay there and hold on." Marrow encouraged.

Blair's mind wavered as the image shifted. Shadows climbed from the trees around her and soon, she was cloaked in an eerie darkness. Physically, her heart raced, but Blair tried to breathe through it, digging her nails into her thighs.

In her mind, she heard a scream. A loud pitched wail full of terror from a small child. Another scream echoed around her, but this time it was Damien's voice. As that sound faded, the next one was her father, begging for help, for her to save him. The voices then started again, piling on top of each other in layers of sobs and gasps.

Marrow's voice broke through, "Focus through my ability, find something to ground you- so you can manifest the mark and pull those shadows into your void."

Blair tried to listen, but soon the voices doubled. One child turned into three, asking why she left them. Blake's screams soon accompanied Damien, both of them asking why she let them get hurt.

Deep in her chest, Blair felt a weight accumulate, an anxiety that forced her breathing to rise.

"If you do not focus, you will lose. Don't let the voices in your head win." Marrow encouraged.

Blair clung to those words, and slowly a small child formed in front of her in her mind. A small girl who was crying because she couldn't control her shadows. Blair watched herself lean down next to her, "You can control it, you just have to accept it." Her voice repeated it, louder this time, drawing out the negative voices in her head. Another voice took over, "*You are trying to battle it, when you should be wearing it like a crown.*" The voice took shape, and Damien was there, in her mind, helping her off the floor. Her hand was in his as it moved to collect the shadows around her. Slowly, they listened, funneling into Blair's skin.

Suddenly, it was like she could breathe, and Blair opened her eyes. A pulse in her thigh made her look down at her leg, which was covered in jagged black lines. Lines that covered her whole body.

She looked up and found Marrow with a small smile on her face. "So, it's him. He is your protector, your tank, the thing that grounds you." Blair smiled back and glanced over at Damien, who met her eyes almost immediately as he dodged Adriel's fire. A fast wink was all she got before he turned his body effortlessly to avoid being singed.

"Yeah, I guess he is."

Marrow nodded in approval. She closed her eyes soon after and centered herself. "We're going to go again. Ready yourself."

Blair nodded, rolling her head side to side before following the same steps, expecting the screams, but this time it was Hunters who came out, dragging a barely conscious Damien with them. They took turns beating him, torturing him in ways that made the screams so much worse. Blair tried to think of him again, calling on the healthy version, but Damien didn't come.

"Don't give up. You have to find another method." The words echoed around her as she watched Damien fight for his life. Blair tried everything, including the flowers, Blake's lighthearted laughter, and the books she loved to get lost in. *Nothing* worked, and the more time she took exploring options to help, the more Damien became a mangled mess right in front of her. Mentally, Blair dropped to her knees, a sob tearing from her throat. In her mind, she had convinced herself it was real. *It had to be real.*

She screamed.

Outside, she felt movement, but her mind wouldn't let go; it was stuck in a warped reality where she held Damien's lifeless body.

Hands gripped her as the shadows fell, and Blair opened her eyes to ice blue ones staring back at her.

"Damien?" she asked on a shallow breath.

"Hey, I'm right here." he reassured, grabbing her jaw. "It wasn't real."

Blair nodded, taking in his scent, leather and Teakwood.

Marrow cleared her throat beside them, "In order to help, I have to get her to push past her limits. It seems you are key to that."

Damien looked at Marrow for a brief second before turning back to Blair. His eyes intensified as he lifted her chin up, "You got this."

Blair nodded as he kissed her and moved back to his corner, where the others were waiting for him to continue training.

"You'll come across a lot of different abilities in this world, all trying to hurt or kill you. To be frank, I was holding mine back. You have to be ready for anything, including losing him." Marrow said. She extended her hand, fingers relaxed but purposeful. "Close your eyes.

Reach inside, deep into the shadows that coil in the corners of your mind. Find all your fears, your hidden doubts, your known pain. Do not resist them. Instead, find a place where you can be safe with them."

Blair shut her eyes tightly, her breath still uneven. At first, she felt nothing but cold silence, wrapped in Marrow's shadows. Then, beneath the surface of her thoughts, a whispering calm began to spread. Tentatively, she imagined it flowing through each shadow.

"Feel it," Marrow's voice was a low murmur, grounding. "This darkness is part of you. It is not your enemy. It is your shadow, your truth. Accept it and shape it. Mold it with your will. The mark you carry will help."

Blair clenched her fists and willed the darkness to bend. The inky substance responded, thickening, forming shapes that twisted and curled like ancient runes. Her breathing slowed and her heartbeat thudded steadily against her ribcage. Her hands opened, now a vacuum for the shadows around her. One small shadow swirled over her palm before disappearing beneath the skin. She felt it and opened her eyes.

This time, when she looked up, Marrow seemed content, relaxed even. "In order to master that manifestation, you must learn to hold the void itself. The void is silence, absence, and infinite potential all at once. It is strong, and you have to be able to control it."

Blair took a hesitant breath, inhaling sharply as though drawing in the mark itself. She felt something then, almost like an internal pull.

"Hold it," Marrow said.

Blair's chest tightened, but she obeyed. Slowly, she exhaled.

"Again," Marrow urged, "Inhale while focusing on the void, exhale to keep control."

Blair followed her direction, concentrating. The second breath was steadier, more fluid.

"When you manifest, you call on everything. You accept all pieces and welcome them," Marrow explained. "It is about holding everything at once; the darkness and the light, the void and the presence. If you sway too far to one side, the mark will wither. If you hold steady, it will awaken fully."

As Marrow explained further, Blair felt something pulse within her and then tighten. *The void.* Her dagger bloomed across her thigh, the threads of shadow curling from delicate patterns to jagged lines. Marrow's eyes gleamed as the mark of Void unfolded.

Marrow clicked her tongue. "It looks like you've got a good feel for it."

Blair stared at the marks. "I'm trying."

"Good, keep doing that because I'm going to push you harder now." Marrow replied, her tone flat.

The first change Blair noticed was Marrow implementing fragmented images into her mind. Blair watched as each one sharpened into focus. Suddenly, Blair was five years old, standing in the hallway of her old home. The lights flickered above her as something growled behind her. No matter how fast she ran, it never faded. She screamed, not out loud, but inwardly, a reflex she hadn't felt in years. Then she was back in the room, shaking.

Marrow didn't stop there, but she did give her some guidance. "Shadows are deadly, but you have more power. You'll learn to make a space where no shadow survives. If you fail, you'll be consumed, and not just here. Everywhere. Do it again."

So, Blair did. She went through five different mental situations, and then ten, and then fifteen, before she keeled over in exhaustion.

The second day when she returned, it was worse. Marrow didn't even let her prepare. She would speak softly, a hum or a whisper, and suddenly Blair was drowning in another nightmare. These ones had started with her fathers voice, but in a tone that was too eerie and hollow. He would whisper her name from behind a locked door with blood running upward instead of down. Her reflection would show in mirrors that had eyes that blinked when she didn't. Every time Blair tried to manifest a safe place, the shadows slipped through, like black ink spilling through the cracks in her subconscious.

However, by the end of day two, she could feel her mark trying to flare as her body reacted. The space she built in her mind always collapsed before the mark could actually help her.

"You're fighting with fear," Marrow said one evening when the sun had dipped into a dark evening color. There was no judgement in her words, only certainty.

"That's like using water to fight drowning. You need something deeper, something permanent."

Blair snapped at her. "And what is that supposed to be?"

But Marrow only raised an eyebrow and said, "Keep failing until you find it."

Within the next few days, Blair stopped trying to fight the nightmares as they came. Instead, she started observing them. When her limbs melted into ash or her mother's voice came from a mouth that wasn't hers, she watched. She catalogued the shape of her fear, the rhythms of it. Not to befriend it, but to understand its structure. When she felt the mark flaring, she tried to manifest it, and it began to react differently. Not as a shield or a wall, but as a tool to help.

One long inhale had been the key. Her focus broke through the chains as she watched her students being mauled. A strange sensation began in her thigh, and she pulled from it, sending it to the center of her chest. She imagined it as a place to store the mark, a place to contain the shadows that plagued her mind.

When Marrow changed the scene, and Blair was thrown into darkness, she didn't brace. She closed her eyes inside it, and soon, around her, light bloomed. It was small at first, barely enough to push the nightmare back an inch, but it held. The shadow hissed in response, and she knew she was onto something. In the next moments, her mother's voice turned to static, and the shadows started to disappear around her, clearing her mind. When most of them were gone, she opened her eyes to find Marrow staring back at her.

Marrow looked at her for a long moment, something unreadable flickering behind her eyes. "Again," was all she said.

Within that week, the nightmares Marrow created changed again. Blair would be mid-sentence or mid-breath and suddenly she'd be inside something impossible: walking across a bridge made of bones, sinking into a house where gravity bent sideways, facing herself in mirrors that spoke back, but each time, she created the space faster. A circle of warmth around her body. A dome of light that would move outward. A barrier she created that was not made of violence but of refusal. Her mark then responded like it had been waiting all along for her to find this place. Not a place she activated with brute force, but with intent. She didn't try to retaliate against the darkness, she simply gave the shadows nowhere to go.

On the last day, Marrow changed course again. She didn't start with a nightmare. Instead, she stood in the center of the room and stepped toward Blair herself, eyes pitch-black, mouth whispering things Blair couldn't understand. It wasn't an illusion this time but Marrow's full power. The shadows hit the inside of her mind with an extreme amount of pressure and dread. The space around her felt weighted with anxiety and fear. This feeling was so potent that it came in waves, assaulting her senses and putting her body into fight or flight mode.

Centering herself, she remembered the light around her. She breathed again, not desperately, but to ground herself. The warmth started in her spine this time, rising upward, and when it reached her hands, she shaped it. No shadows and no shield, just a sphere of absence. The shadows belonging to Marrow surged forward, then stopped along with their crippling magic. Blair then activated her mark and took in the shadows around her.

Marrow's voice spoke as the black receded from her eyes. "Well done, Blair. That was my full power." She stepped back and gave Blair a long, careful nod. "You've done it," she said simply.

Blair was shaking, but not from fear, but from an aftershock of Marrow's power. It was as if anything positive or hopeful in her body had been depleted. She shook her head, trying to understand, but another thought crossed her mind. "I can take in shadows through the Void now," she said quietly.

Marrow nodded. "You can indeed. Next, you'll learn how to fight them if their ability isn't a mental one but that's a trial for another day." She turned, walking toward the edge of the arena, and before she vanished into the dark shadows, she added, "You should be proud of yourself. You've survived not only your mind, but mine. That's more than most."

Blair remained sitting in the quiet that followed, the warmth still coiled inside her chest, pulsing steady like a heartbeat.

Fighting. That meant combat, and that meant Rhea.

She thought about this more as she started her walk back to the tent. That and the fact that for the first time in days, she felt like she wasn't just surviving her lessons, she was growing into them. Her steps quickened with anticipation, not just to rest, but because tonight, finally, she would have some time with Damien. No drills, no training, and no marks pulling at the edge of her mind. Just the quiet space they'd both carved out between chaos, where the world fell away and nothing mattered except being together.

As she neared the edge of the encampment, the familiar flicker of the lantern outside her tent welcomed her. She smiled to herself, brushing a loose strand of hair behind her ear. She pictured him, half-asleep with his boots kicked off and a smirk tugging at the corner of his mouth. He would probably even tease her for taking too long. A light chuckle left her as she pulled back the flap and stepped inside.

The tent was empty.

Her eyes went straight to the note that was propped neatly on the bed against a leather-bound book. The paper was folded once with her name scrawled across the top in his uneven hand. She unfolded it slowly, her heart dropping.

Hey Feisty.

Went out with the boys to refill the camp's supplies.

-Damien

Blair exhaled as disappointment stung her chest. She set the note down carefully, eyes lingering on the item next to it.

Of course he would help, she thought as she picked up the book. *It was one of the things she loved about him.*

That thought made her arm pause, the book hanging mid-air in front of her face. She blinked a few times, refusing to repeat it. Instead, she moved her attention to him. Damien never stayed still long. He was always offering to help, always stepping up before anyone asked. It was part of why she admired him. It was also part of why she missed him more than she ever said aloud.

"Be safe," she murmured to the paper, even though he was long gone. The tent felt quiet in a way she wasn't used to. Not completely silent, thanks to the distant crackle of fire from the camp's center, and the hum of conversation bleeding through the fabric walls but still, she felt lonely.

Blair tried to look at the positives as she repositioned herself on the edge of the bedroll, with the book. Letting herself sink into the worn blanket they shared, she opened it to the first page and found a familiar title. Not only was it one of her favorites, but it was filled with *annotations*. Damien had underlined, starred, and written messages in the margins for her.

A large smile broke across her face as she found a small note with an arrow to a paragraph on the second page. She laughed as she read aloud, hearing his voice in her head, "*Fuck that. I would never let you do this alone.*" She then skipped ahead to another page where he had crossed out 'veiny appendage' and wrote "*WHO SAYS THAT? Please don't ever call mine that.*"

A louder giggle escaped her, as her heart warmed with appreciation for him. She used her thumb to flip through the book. There were notations everywhere, like he had taken a careful amount of time to complete it.

She laid the book on her chest and hugged it, mentally promising herself she would read a chapter every night until she was able to read every last thought of his.

She winced as her body started to ache deep down in the muscle and bone. Training had stripped her raw these last couple weeks, and the idea of sleep was suddenly more tempting than anything else.

]Just for a second, she told herself. *Just to let her eyes rest.* The moment her head moved back, the moment she let herself give in, everything disappeared.

There was no slow descent. No drifting. Just one breath, then nothing. She opened her eyes to darkness. Not the kind that came from night or sleep or shade, but something vast and empty, something that pressed against her from all sides. She wasn't lying down anymore. She was standing, though she didn't remember rising. The ground beneath her felt like ash, soft and wrong beneath her feet. There was no tent around her. No firelight outside and no stars above her. Only the dark, sharp awareness that she was no longer in the safety of her tent.

13

The ground was cold beneath her bare feet. Looking up, she stood beneath a sky filled with storm clouds, wind snarling between the jagged cliffs around her. She blinked once, and then again, but the scene didn't fade. She looked around at the details surrounding her, everything was too sharp to be a dream.

Then, she saw them. Damien, Blake, Adriel, and Kael. Four silhouettes moving across the slope below her with weapons drawn, shadows shifting behind them. The wind carried shouts that seemed to echo around her. Blair's breath caught as she realized they were fighting. She stepped forward and tried to call out, but her voice broke soundlessly in the air. No one even attempted to turn and look her way. Her heart slammed against the inside of her chest as she realized the wind didn't twirl her hair like it did them.

She wasn't really standing there, only watching. Trapped in a moment she didn't understand. Below, two Hunters burst from behind the rocks, both cloaked in black fabric with the mark of the King. Their faces hidden beneath new masks marked with dark blue sigils. They were fast, inhumanly so, and they struck first. Damien moved with practiced instinct, parrying the first blow and driving his attacker back with a hard, sweeping strike. Thanks to his practice, runes manifested along his skin activating something within him. Blake flanked the second Hunter, shadows flashing on the ground as he drew him away from the others. Kael circled wide, his whips already coiling with defensive energy, while Adriel shouted sharp commands over the chaos. For a moment, they looked like they could hold their ground.

That is, until one of the Hunters summoned a wall of shadows and threw it against Damien with impossible speed. The shadows hit him, attacking the wings that had just manifested. As he fought them off, a black blade slashed across Damien's face in a clean, brutal line. Blood spilled instantly. Damien reeled back with his eyes wide, hand pressed to the wound as he staggered from the shadows that thrashed behind him. Blair screamed his name, but again, no sound came out. Her body tried to run to him, but her feet barely brushed the ground. She wasn't there. She couldn't help him.

As the Hunter raised his blade again, Kael didn't hesitate. He threw himself between them, catching the next strike across the meat of his shoulder with a grunt of pain. The blade hissed as it sank in, but Kael twisted, caught the hilt of the Hunter's weapon with his own, and drove him backward. A heartbeat later, Adriel was there, silent and lethal, his sword finding the weak point between the Hunter's armor plates and silencing him for good. Blair clutched at the air, trying to hold on to something real, anything, but there was no ground, nothing besides the pounding rhythm of fear in her chest.

Damien wiped blood from his cheek, and nodded once to Kael, who simply nodded back. He was already pressing cloth to his wound like it was nothing new.

Blair shifted her focus to the last Hunter who had been drawn to the far side. Blake fought with a casual grin, even as the Hunter lunged. "You've gotten slower, Renner," the Hunter taunted, voice rough beneath his mask.

Just for a moment, a smile flickered across Blake's face, but then he laughed, stepping back as if unconcerned. "Wrong guy," he said, spinning the short blade in his hand like it weighed nothing. "You must be thinking of someone else."

The Hunter tilted his head as he lunged, attacking Blake with ease. "Same eyes. Same voice. You don't forget someone like you."

Blake blocked, "Too bad the dead don't talk." he said, striking back.

The movement was sudden, one fluid motion that pushed the Hunter off balance and followed with a clean, sharp cut that dropped him to his knees. Blake twisted the blade once before yanking it free. The Hunter didn't rise again. "You're right, you don't forget." Blake added under his breath, too low for anyone else to hear.

Blair stared at him, shaken.

That name, Renner, rattled around in her head like a stone in a jar. It wasn't familiar to her, but the way Blake had responded told her enough, it was familiar to him.

153

Damien and the others walked up then, blood trailing down to his jaw. Motioning toward the ridge, he yelled out to them. "We need to move."

Kael took the point without a word. Adriel adjusted the bag on his shoulder with a grunt. Blake kicked one of the fallen Hunters once, just to be sure he was dead, before turning away. Blair followed after them, calling out again, louder this time. She shouted until her throat burned, until her legs gave out beneath her, and then she hit the earth with hands that passed through the dirt like smoke.

Damien didn't turn to help her, none of them did. She watched them disappear into the rocks, their silhouettes fading into the mist like shadows at the edge of sleep. Alone in the fading stormlight, Blair screamed again, but no one heard her, and the darkness began to pull her under again.

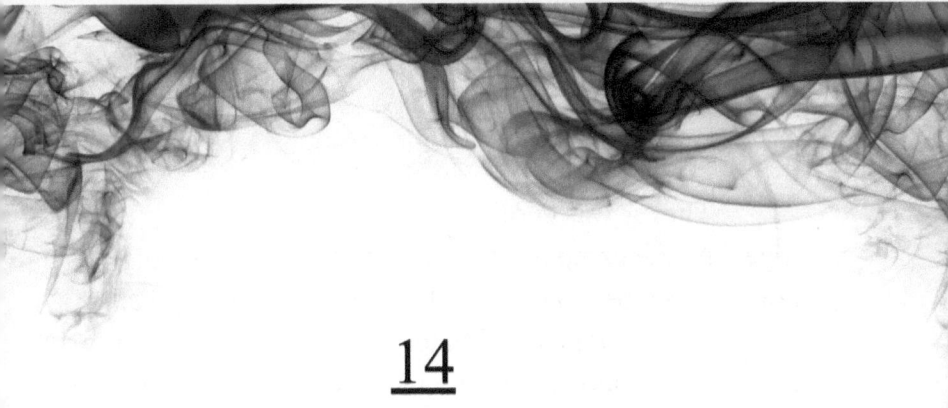

14

Blair woke with a gasp caught in her throat, her fingers clenching the bedroll like she'd been drowning. Her skin was damp with sweat, her heart hammering against her ribs as if trying to punch its way out. The tent around her was silent and still empty. For a moment, she didn't move. The echo of the vision, if that's what it was, still clung to her like smoke.

Damien's blood. Kael's grunt of pain. The name Renner.

All of it was still sharp and clear, like she'd just stepped out of the storm. She sat up slowly, glancing toward the table. Half of her had expected the note from Damien to be gone, but it was still there. The same white paper with the same handwriting.

She pulled her boots on, in silence; the weight in her stomach refusing to ease. The tent was too quiet, and it was starting to annoy her.

As she readied herself and braided her hair, no sound of footfalls or laughter came from outside. Just the usual buzz of early morning, and voices too far to make out. She tied her hair at the end, trying to shake the feeling pressing down on her shoulders as she stepped outside.

The air was cool, the sun not yet fully above the ridge, and the camp moved with the sluggish pace of morning routine. Blair made her way to the dining hall, grabbing a rough piece of flatbread and a boiled egg from the serving windows. She ate while standing, eyes scanning the space around her for familiar faces. There was still no sign of them. No Damien. No Kael. No Blake. Not even Adriel's quiet presence. Her fingers twitched as she turned and left, throwing the rest of the food in the trash.

The arena soon loomed ahead, and for the first time, she didn't want to go in it, not without knowing where everyone was. Convincing herself they would probably be here any minute, she stepped in and was greeted with emptiness. Only two figures stood near the center of the ring. Rhea, whose posture was relaxed but ready, and Marrow, with her arms folded. Neither looked surprised to see Blair. Neither seemed concerned that half the team hadn't returned. Blair approached, her nerves still sparking under her skin, and opened her mouth to speak, but Rhea just tilted her head, then looked past her.

Blair turned to find movement at the entrance and a sigh of relief escaped her as Damien entered. He wasn't exactly limping, but his steps were stiff and measured. A thick, angry line was cut across his cheek and temple. Blood had been smeared around it, dried now, but unmistakable. The sight of it stole the breath from her lungs. Behind him, Kael moved with one hand pressed to his shoulder, a cotton pad strapped down beneath his tunic which had already soaked through with blood. Adriel followed, his expression dark, his hands clean.

Blair's gaze jumped past them. *Where was Blake?*

Her chest tightened as she took a step forward.

"You have your own responsibilities," Rhea said, voice sharp and clear. Blair turned back just as a pair of training gloves hit her square in the chest. "Put those on. You're still expected to train."

"Where's Blake?" Blair asked, the words forcing themselves out. "He's not with them."

Rhea didn't blink. "Focus, Blair. That's not your concern right now."

Blair just stared at her for a moment before looking back at Damien, who hadn't looked up yet. The cut on his face followed the same path she'd seen in the vision, the exact same path. Her fingers clenched around the gloves.

The dream hadn't been a dream, and something had happened out there.

Rolling her eyes at the distraction, Rhea grabbed Blair's hands and wrapped her knuckles, positioning them in a defensive position. Then, she held her own hands up as targets and motioned for Blair to hit them.

Trying to find every shred of concentration she could, Blair pulled her eyes away from the men and struck. Although her hand was close to hitting the mark, her pinky knuckle grazed the side of Rhea's hand, which only annoyed her.

"You punch like a baby." Rhea's voice echoed through the training ring.

Blair dropped her stance. "I don't even know what that means. I just really need to-"

"It means," Rhea said, stepping in close and flicking Blair's elbow, "that this isn't how you throw a punch unless you want your wrist shattered."

The Shadowborn warrior moved behind her to adjust her shoulders and reposition her stance. "Feet shoulder-width and your hips need to be square. Don't even get me started on your noodle arms. You're not swatting flies, you're delivering intent."

After ten more minutes of basic form corrections and a few half-hearted jabs, Rhea clapped once and stepped back. "Enough theory. Time for you to fight. I hope you don't mind that I picked a special opponent."

Blair blinked. "Wait, what?"

From the other side of the room, Damien was heading straight for them. He cracked his neck, addressing Rhea but looking at Blair. "No holding back, right?" he said with a playful wink.

"No holding back," Rhea confirmed.

Blair barely had time to ask any questions before Damien struck. She dodged the first strike out of luck but the next one knocked her onto her back. He smiled as he stood over her. "Miss me, baby?"

She almost growled at him as she stood. "We need to talk." She managed to say before he was after her again.

She dodged, but he moved faster.

"Are you mad I left?" he asked, between throwing punches.

Noticing how easy it was to breathe through her movements, she silently thanked Adriel for starting with agility. "It's not," she started to say before ducking under a right hook, "about that."

He laughed out loud, as if his absence and injury meant nothing. "Is it the blood? I thought it would make me look more rugged."

With that comment, he swept his foot at her ankles. She fell hard, landing on her butt.

Taking a second to ground herself, she chose to save the questions for later. She needed to focus on what was happening now.

He managed to knock her down three more times before her reflexes gained momentum.

By the fifth attempt, she was able to block it fully. Then again. Her punches landed like feathers, but she was learning. She saw a grin flicker on Damien's face between blows, not mocking, but full of pride.

Rhea raised a brow. "Look at that. She's *not* glass."

After a few more rounds, Blair's movements were smoother, and she was able to predict Damien's attacks. After she blocked a few more, his method shifted, and he moved behind her to sweep her ankles.

Blair gasped as her knees hit the cold stone. She caught herself with her palms, but the blow rattled through her spine. Before she could push up, Damien was there, towering over her with his shadows at her back. The tendrils hovered above her, not touching, just close enough to let her feel the threat.

"Yield?" he asked, voice low.

She didn't look up. Instead, a smile curved her lips.

"You can," Blair slowly lifted her chin and tilted her head, eyes gleaming in the low light. "fuck all the way off."

His brows lifted, but he didn't have time to reply.

From beneath her, shadows erupted, catching him off guard. They twisted around her, coiling with intent at their target. Slipping across the stone, they grabbed at Damien's ankles before he could retreat. He cursed as he stumbled and was met by his own shadows. They swirled and yanked his arm back, dragging him down forcefully.

He landed hard on both knees in front of her, and she waited until he was bound completely by them before she slowly stood, a wicked grin forming on her mouth.

"Cheater," he muttered, struggling against the shadows that wrapped around his arms and chest.

Blair bent and brushed the dust from her knees. Straightening, she took a step forward and held his chin in her hand. "It's not cheating if they prefer to help me." she murmured, kissing his cheek as the shadows tightened around his torso, and his breath caught.

Rhea clapped loudly behind her and chuckled in disbelief. Some of the shadows dissipated, and others swarmed back to Damien. As he stood he scoffed as he watched the shadows recede back to him, "Traitors."

His attention then turned toward Blair, who was beaming from her win. Damien took one look at her and his eyes bled to black. Rhea noticed and swatted him away, announcing she was switching places with him.

Blair blew a kiss in his direction as Damien walked away, looking back over his shoulder with a hungry look in his eyes.

The energy shifted back to normal as Rhea began critiquing Blair over what she had done wrong. This continued as they practiced hand-to-hand combat.

"You need to move faster and think ahead of your opponent." Rhea declared, stepping around Blair and punching her in the kidney. "Not every fight is playful like the ones with your boyfriend."

Blair hissed in pain but turned, bracing for the next attack.

"Do not let your guard down, and put your left foot forward."

Blair stumbled but reset her stance. "I *had* it forward."

Rhea huffed. "No, you had it angled like it wasn't part of your body." Walking a slow menacing circle around Blair, she observed every angle. "Again."

Blair squeezed her fists. "I'm guessing you're not a fan of encouragement or positivity, huh?"

"I'm not a fan of wasting time." Rhea replied with a leveled glare, "so, *try again.*"

The more they moved, the more the air thickened with heat. Blair's shirt was now stuck to her back with sweat, and her thighs were starting to chafe. Regardless, she moved into position every time, chest tight with focus.

Rhea struck again without warning.

Blair blocked high, then low. As she moved again, she stumbled sideways, nearly tripping over her own foot for the second time.

"You *cannot* be serious." Rhea's voice cut through the silence like a whip. "You've got instincts. I'll give you that but your body's a goddamn liability."

"Hey." Blair winced. "I'm working on it."

"Well, work faster."

Rhea stepped in, quick and brutal, knocking Blair's block aside with sharp movements. Before Blair could react, she was on the ground, flat on her back, blinking up at the sun. She groaned as pain flared across her ribs. "Ow."

"*Liability*." Rhea said, crouching beside her.

Blair gave her the middle finger as she caught her breath.

Rhea smirked. "There we go. That's the spirit. Now *get up*."

Blair sat up with a grunt, dirt smeared across her face. She wiped it off with the back of her hand. "You know, for someone in charge of helping people grow, you're kind of a sadist."

"I'm not here to *help*," Rhea said. "I'm here to make sure you don't die because of something stupid." Rhea stood, arms crossed. "You want soft? Join a book club. You want to survive? Pick yourself up and keep going."

Blair stood, and shifted into position. Even as her legs started to shake, her eyes locked in. She even refused to flinch when Rhea raised her shadow coated fists. Instead, she moved into a defensive stance with her left foot forward and balanced. Her body was still awkward, but her core remained strong.

"Good," Rhea said. "Now, don't think. Just move and let it happen."

Rhea pivoted, coming from a different angle.

This time, Blair blocked the first strike cleanly, then the second. Her counter came a breath too late, but it *came*. She slipped and nearly lost her balance, but recovered by instinct.

Rhea's brow twitched. She didn't say anything, but her strikes came down harder.

Their skin and leather smacked together as Blair grew more confident, blocking hits and trying to land her own. Blair was far from winning, but she hadn't fallen again.

When they finally broke apart, Blair was gasping. But grinning like a maniac. "Still think I'm a lost cause?"

Rhea walked over to the water canteen and leaned against it. "Not a lost cause, I'd say more along the lines of an inconvenient project."

Blair shrugged, shaking out her arms as a smile formed on her face. "I'll take it."

Rhea raised an eyebrow, "But you're not done."

Blair's smile dropped. "That wasn't the last round?"

"Nope." Rhea responded, with a small smile before she took a drink.

Blair groaned in response as Rhea tossed her a water flask. Blair caught it with two hands, nearly dropped it, then recovered.

"Fast brain, slow feet," Rhea said. "Your coordination's still trash, but you're learning faster than I expected."

Blair watched Rhea move as she swallowed down water. She walked back to the center of the yard and motioned with both hands for Blair to join her. "One more round. First one to drop loses."

Blair gawked at her and dropped her shoulders. "I already dropped like six times today. Can we just say you win?"

Positioning herself to strike, Rhea responded with a shrug, "Maybe just stop dropping then."

Blair tensed and her muscles screamed. She had never put her body through anything like this, but somehow it made her fight harder. With a rush of courage, she stepped forward, causing Rhea to nod approvingly. "Now fight me like you mean it."

Blair fought hard and fast, throwing everything she could into her moves. By the time the sparring was done, the light outside had receded. That meant today's training had gone for most of the day, but she felt good. *Exhausted*, but good.

Rhea, who was now covered in sweat as well, put her hand on Blair's shoulder. "You don't give up and you learn well. I see why you were chosen to bear the mark."

With that, Rhea crossed the room and headed out the door of the arena.

Just as she left, Damien entered the building, a bandage now wrapped around his bicep and bruises started to form alongside the cut on his cheek.

"Back for round two?" Blair asked, her eyebrows rising with each step he took.

A large smile covered his face as he spun her before kissing her, "If you want me on my knees, you just have to ask."

Blair rolled her eyes before grabbing his hand and pulling him to one of the benches. She sat first with one leg over each side, staring straight at him. "What happened while you were gone? Are you okay?" Blair asked, running a finger over the cut on his face.

"I'm fine. It turns out the Hunters never stopped looking for us and the King is pretty mad that he can't find us. He has some new tricks up his sleeve now but it wasn't anything we couldn't handle." His hand cupped hers, "It's already healing."

Blair nodded as she remembered the masks the Hunter's had worn. She took a deep breath in, deciding not to say anything until she had more information.

"Does the name Renner mean anything to you?" Blair asked, watching for any changes in his demeanor.

Damien brought his head back and forth as if scanning the files in his mind. "Nope. Why do you ask?"

Blair bit her tongue. "Just wondering."

Damien lightly grabbed her chin and kissed her forehead. "I promise we are good. *I am good.* Supplies were secured and we're back. I'll give you more notice if I have to leave next time, yeah?"

Blair nodded as they stood together and walked to the dining hall which seemed to be pretty full. As they entered, she scanned the crowd for Blake. He still wasn't there.

Finding an open slot, they received their serving of stew and bread before taking it to their table. Setting it down, she looked around one more time. "Have you seen Blake?"

Damien shook his head as he fell into his chair, the bread already in his mouth. "My guess is he's messing with Adriel somewhere, maybe checking in on Kael."

"Or Marrow," Blair added, sitting down as well, "She's not here either."

A small smirk passed over Damien's features before he turned his full attention to his food, "Not our business."

Blair looked up from her stew. "If he acts like a five year old" she mumbled, shoveling spoonfuls of the stew in her mouth, "I get to treat him like a five year old." She moaned as the warm broth filled her throat. "This is delicious."

The grin returned to Damien's face as he set his spoon down, eyeing Blair. "You like it, huh?"

Blair nodded, tipping back the bowl to finish the last bits of the liquid inside.

Damien watched her until her dish was empty and she stood, for seconds. "I'm glad you liked it, because it was *bison* stew."

Blair's face blanched as she looked down at her bowl and then at him, her eyes wide.

Damien outright laughed, "Just don't think about it too hard and you'll be fine."

Trying to control the gag reflex that had kicked in, Blair counted to ten in her head.

Damien laughed harder, offering his bowl to her. "You've eaten meat since being here. You're going to be okay."

Blair shook her head, attempting to change the subject. "Can we go back to that one area with the water soon?" she asked, squeezing her eyes shut and envisioning everything besides a Bison.

Damien's smile turned wicked, "I will *take* you anywhere you want."

Blair opened her eyes just as Blake plopped himself in the spot next to her, his eyes glued to Marrow who had also just entered.

"I'm this close," he said, raising his fingers in a pinched way, "to cracking *that* wide open."

Blair stared at him for a moment before groaning in disgust and shoving him with her shoulder, "Gross. Is that where you've been?"

Blake shrugged, laughing as he stood to get his dinner.

Damien stood as well, just as Shiloh entered the hall. He shook hands with the Shadowborn guard at the door and then headed towards their table, his eyes set on Blair. "I've heard good things about your training. Let's keep it up."

Blair nodded and as Shiloh walked away, Damien took her hand, leading her out of the hall. They walked together, their shadows entwining around their arms.

The sun had almost set once they were settled and although the shower sounded amazing, Blair's body refused to move. Damien sensed that, gathering blankets and pillows for her.

"Are you building a pillow fort?" Blair asked, a sarcastic curve to her lips.

"No, It's our nest." he chuckled as he laid beside her, "Now shut up and get over here." He opened his arms and she crawled to him, laying on his chest.

Looking up at him, she smiled faintly at the line on his face, the one that was already almost completely healed.

Both of them fell asleep within ten minutes.

15

Blair's first day of endurance training started the next morning. She quickly kissed Damien on the cheek and changed into light clothes, imagining a day full of running. The sun had barely climbed over the tree line when she walked up to join Kael in the training arena. She stood at the edge of the circle, not exactly sure what to expect.

Kael stretched and lifted his nose to the air, "You smell nervous."

Blair followed his movements with her eyes, "Endurance isn't *exactly* my favorite."

Kael let out a small chuckle before switching sides, "Can't imagine why." He brought his arm over his head to stretch the muscles in his back and motioned for her to do the same.

She complied as he started to talk again, "My training with you will be short. Although I've heard that you have come close to mastering some techniques. Unlike Marrow's, my teaching lies inside your body, not your mind" He bent, stretching different back muscles. Blair began to follow his movements. "You smell weak in some areas and I want to improve that. The fastest way to do this is by cardio. It will strengthen your heart, muscles, and all the smaller areas."

Blair popped her head up, "I smell weak?"

Kael gave another light chuckle before walking past her and tapping the top of her head as he walked by. "Let's go."

Reluctantly, she followed him. She was surprised at how manageable the first run felt. Just a few laps, paced at a comfortable jog. Her legs moved easily, her lungs didn't burn, and there was even a tiny flicker of pride in her chest when she reached the end, not winded. Kael had watched her the whole time, and Blake had even shown up half way through, like he had nowhere else to be. That, or Damien had sent him to check on her.

"Nice form," Blake said, handing her a water bottle. "Don't let the *coach* fool you. Day one is always a lie, it gets worse after."

Blair laughed, thinking he was exaggerating, but he wasn't.

The next day, the pace picked up. Kael demanded a longer distance with fewer breaks. By the third day, her calves screamed after every session. The only advantage was she was sleeping harder at night, but woke up sorer than ever.

When the next morning came, Blake was there, waiting for her. As she walked up, he pulled himself off the wall he was leaning on. "You're tensing your shoulders when you run, that's why your body is so sore."

Blair halted just a few feet short of him. "Excuse me?"

He shrugged and then bent to stretch his legs. "I'm tired of hearing you ask Damien to rub them, so I thought I would help."

"I'm sorry, am I missing something?" Blair stepped closer, eyeing him with suspicion. "You're going to *run* with me? He who hates running?"

Blake looked up with a small grin and moved into yet another position to stretch. "Loosen up. You're wasting energy."

Blair stared at him for a few moments, waiting for an explanation, but he just cracked his neck before gesturing for her to start the run.

Within a few minutes, they found a steady rhythm and fell in sync. Every now and then Blake would bump into her, telling her to relax or watch her breathing. After the third time, she scoffed in annoyance to which he laughed. "Just move your body, stop thinking so hard about it."

"Coming from the man who's done this his whole life," she grunted, accompanying her words with an eye roll this time.

He smirked. "Not my *whole* life. Lucky for you though, I'll be joining you every day moving forward."

That made Blair stop in her tracks. She blinked a few times before looking at him. He paid no attention to her reaction, jogging in place.

"Really?" she asked, taking a step and falling back into her jog.

"Give a special thanks to your boyfriend, turns out he pulled a few strings because he doesn't exactly trust *everyone* with his precious marked cargo."

"But what happens with *your* training?" Blair asked, mentally searching for a reason he would endure this.

"It turns out you're not the only one improving." He said, a cocky smile on his face. "I've been working on shadowstepping since you've *abandoned* us. I'm managing three and a half miles now, so that seemed sufficient enough to be given babysitting duty. It's not all bad though, I was promised extra time with a certain pristine, gothic creature." he said as he bumped into her side again, almost pushing her off the trail.

"No way," she said quickly and pushed him back, and then with a light laugh she added. "I mean, *thanks.*"

Having Blake run beside her made the miles less unbearable. His presence was steady, his stride easy. He didn't talk unless she wanted him to, and sometimes just knowing someone else was there made it easier to keep going.

But that wasn't the only reason she was thankful he was there. She planned on doing more than just running during this time. She'd convinced herself that she would use this as an opportunity to ask him the questions that had been burning in the back of her mind. Questions she didn't seem to be brave enough to ask with everyone else around. There were things she needed to understand.

172

She had decided this the first day he had shown up. Rehearsing as she ran, the questions racked her mind. *Who is Renner? What did the guard mean?*

Unfortunately, asking those questions meant that she would have to explain *how* she knew that, which she didn't think she was ready for. So, the words never left her mouth. The silence stretched, and she filled it with small talk instead.

By the third day of running with Blake, she realized she'd wasted every opportunity so far. He was right there, right in front of her. There were no distractions, no place to run... and still, she said nothing. Every time she opened her mouth, something pulled her back. A beat of hesitation, a fear of saying the wrong thing, or worse, the chance of hearing something she wasn't ready for.

On the fifth day, he was the one who started the conversation. "You're quiet today," Blake said as they slowed to a walk between tents.

"Just tired," she mumbled, wiping sweat from her brow. "My muscles are mad at me."

He gave her a sideways glance. "You're doing better than you think, kid."

"Kid?" She mocked, but he picked up pace again, jogging with obnoxious ease.

The next time he opened his mouth, it was because she had started to struggle. "You know, most people breathe *in* and *out*. Meanwhile, you're doing something new and innovative, like dying."

"Shut up, Blake," Blair wheezed.

"I'm just saying," was his only reply.

Despite herself, Blair laughed, nearly tripping on a root. She caught herself, her stride evening out. The pain in her calves didn't disappear, but it blurred into the background as Blake kept talking nonsense beside her.

By the end of the five-mile run, Blair was still gasping for air but she didn't stop once. That felt like a victory, especially because her insides were on fire. Kael then made them do different exercises that raised their heart rate just to slow them again.

His training style was different from any of the others. He didn't yell like Rhea or evoke like Marrow, he just expected. He set the rules and you did them.

After the run, they were outside the training arena, dripping sweat, red-faced, and standing in front of a line of weighted poles stuck into the ground like blunt spears. Each had a different color band painted around the top; White, blue, red, and black.

Kael pointed to the black-banded one. "Carry it."

Blair stepped forward before Blake could say anything. She wrapped both hands around the rough wood and heaved it up. It was heavier than it looked. The weight shocked her arms, shoulders screaming as she settled it across her back.

"Five laps," Kael said. "No breaks."

The first lap was tolerable. The second hurt. By the third, Blair's legs were shaking. Sweat blurred her vision, and her arms felt like they were being torn from their sockets.

"Still standing?" Blake asked, somewhere beside her.

"Barely," she gasped.

"Good. Because I think my arms have entered a new evolutionary phase. They've detached and they're living their own lives now."

She snorted. "Tell them to carry the damn pole."

Lap four was worse. That was when her vision tunneled and her breath came in harsh, shallow gasps. She stumbled often, but didn't fall.

Kael watched like a silent mountain, his eyes flinty. When they dropped the poles at the finish, Blair didn't collapse, but it was close. She braced her hands on her knees, heart jackhammering.

"You done?" Kael asked.

She looked up, surprised. "Wasn't that it?"

"Endurance isn't just about how long you can run or how much you can lift," he said. "It's about what you do *after* you think you're done."

He pointed to the sand pit. "Push-ups. Drop once, start over."

Blair opened her mouth to protest but Blake beat her to it. His voice raspy and exhausted, "Okay, now *this* feels personal."

Blair bent, her arms already jelly. Her core trembled with every inch of movement. Sand clung to her sweat-slicked skin, and her breath came out in spurts.

Blake was still beside her, somehow managing to sweat *and* smirk at the same time.

175

"So, when do we get to the fun part?" he panted.

"This *is* the fun part," Blair ground out.

"Oh good. I was worried the hallucinations wouldn't kick in until set two."

Kael crouched beside them suddenly, watching Blair's form. "Elbows in. Core tight."

She adjusted, biting back a groan. Everything burned. Her arms, her shoulders, her pride.

"You're not weak," Kael said, quiet but firm. "But you need to stop treating fatigue like a stop sign."

Blair gritted her teeth, her eyebrows coming together in irritation. "What is it then?"

Kael rose to his feet. "It's a lie."

An hour later, she found herself lying on the mats inside of the arena. She could barely move, each muscle twisting with aftershocks in her arms and legs.

Blake flopped down beside her, groaning like he'd just survived a siege.

"That was absolutely horrible," he said, laying next to her.

All she could manage was a quick, "Yup."

He groaned as he rolled over to his stomach. "I'm going to sleep for at least a week."

"You won't sleep just yet," Kael's voice cut in as he stood over them, with his arms crossed. "We have two more exercises."

Blake groaned louder. "You're not a man. You're a demon in a tactical vest."

Kael just looked at Blake for a moment before replying to him. "Well, the demon is done with you anyway." he said, as he stepped closer to Blair. "However, you and I will keep going. *You'll* draw from me using the void. I want you to successfully *hold it*, while moving. More so, I want you to hold it while fighting *and* tired."

She blinked up at him, her mouth hanging open in disbelief. "I can't do that."

Kael's eyes glinted as he crouched down next to her and looked down at her exposed thigh. He reached out, placing two fingers to her skin, tracing the object. "You can pull from it more than you are."

Blair pulled back from his touch but he grabbed her thigh forcefully, examining her skin and bending to smell it.

Blake's face twisted into a look of pure rage as he sat up, pushing Kael back. "Hey, don't you know that princess over here is precious cargo? I think you should look up the phrase 'personal space'?"

With a sly smile, Kael looked straight at Blake before brushing his thumb over the mark again. "I'm just testing something." Kael slowly explained, his eyes glued to Blake. He squeezed her thigh tightly and then slapped it before standing and backing up, ushering Blair to join him. Blair just looked up at him with an irritated glare

"Don't touch me without permission" Blair said loudly, as she stood and pushed into his shoulder. After a moment, Kael bowed his head in an apology.

Keeping his eyes on her, Blake watched her settle into position before he made a slight nod at her and shadowstepped out of the building.

Blair squared her shoulders and took a long breath in through her nose as she concentrated on Kael. A sly smile spread across his face as he brought his arms up. "I'm willing to bet the mark manifested as a dagger for a reason. Try pulling from it and see what happens."

Blair narrowed her eyes, "*What*?"

His smile grew, "You heard me. Think of the dagger itself and try pulling from it." Internally rolling her eyes, she closed them and thought of the grounding tips Marrow had given her. She thought of the SilverDawn flowers, and her Mark flared to life, as did the jagged black lines portraying the void.

As she opened her eyes, Kael was right in front of her. A black wall of shadows stood behind him, like a tidal wave. "You smell scared. Unsure. Work on that and pull from the dagger." A small pulse shimmered through the shadowed whips behind him and then he released them. Blair gasped as they moved around her.

This had to be Kael's power at full power. Her muscles trembled as she braced, pulled, and pushed. Her knees nearly buckled as Kael's voice barked, "Try to cut them." A moment of silence before he yelled again, "Now!"

She forced her feet into motion. At first, her body tried to resist but the shadows inside of her sensed danger.

Every movement felt like she was wading through a hurricane made of tar, thanks to her exhaustion.

She focused on the void first, targeting a single thread of shadow and pulling it into her. Her pace faltered but Kael noticed.

"Don't stop," he called out.

So, she pushed harder and the shadows inside her responded, creating a vortex that took in everything around her. Even as she continued to move, it continued to collect his whips, one by one. Sweat began to form around her hairline as she then focused on her second task.

Zoning in on the actual dagger itself, she rested her hand on it and pulled up, a web of shadows following her palm and extending from her skin. As she took hold of the manifestation, she brought it up in front of her face. There, in her hand was a dagger made of shadows. She barely had enough time to register it, before Kael pushed more shadows at her.

"Thatta girl, I smell your curiosity. Figure out what it is." he said around her, his voice echoing in the shadows as they became more rampant. Her arms felt like iron and her legs like stone but she dodged left, rolled over gravel, spun up, and struck the air with the dagger that held firm in her grip.

"You're strong," he said, stepping around her somewhere in the wall of shadow. "Figure out *how* strong Blair."

Kael laughed and lifted his hand, pushing even more shadows around her.

Blair screamed as one slammed into her chest, crackling like thunder. Her knees hit the ground. The Mark *roared* in response, black jagged tendrils lashing out of her skin like writhing ink.

"Hold them," Kael said. "*Hold them off* and use the dagger."

"You mean throw?" She managed to grit out as she clenched her fist around the dagger, her arms starting to shake. Her heart was pounding so fast it felt like it would crack her ribs. The dark threads tried to swallow her again but she clamped down, not with magic but with *will*. She forced the void to take them as she flipped the dagger in her palm, its weight identical to the one she practiced with so many times. She rose to her feet slowly, the Mark pulsing in rhythm with her breath.

Kael's eyes narrowed at her, his face pleased.

With a slight shift of her hand, she threw the dagger at him. He twisted, moving while the shadows swirled around him. The solidified shadow blade whistled past his ear.

She moved her hand to her thigh, repeating the steps and another shadowed dagger was produced. She threw it again while simultaneously taking in what shadows she could, through the void.

Kael noticed her improvement and stopped. The wall of black slowly thinned and then vanished all at once. A small veil of black wisps was the only thing left in the air.

"Impressive," Kael said, raising his hand to shake hers.

Before her hand could touch his, a figure emerged from beside them, throwing a left hook straight into Kael's throat. He dropped instantaneously, sucking in what air he could.

Damien stood over him, black veins across his skin. Blake was behind him, making a low whistling sound as he shook his head slowly.

"Don't ever touch her again." Damien growled, taking Blair's hand and stepping in front of her. Shadows raced down his arm, circling her wrist and soaking into her skin.

Blair took a sharp breath as she looked over at Damien, who was staring at Kael with his eyebrows furrowed. More shadows moved between them, feeding back and forth.

A loud chuckle caused everyone to turn, and Shiloh walked in. "I was coming to make sure everyone was headed to dinner but I guess I missed the show." Shiloh joked, his eyes moving from Kael, who was still hunched on the floor, to Damien, who had now turned completely.

Then, his eyes locked onto Blair and Damien's hands. More specifically, on the shadows that wove back and forth between their skin. "Huh, I wasn't aware you were bound to each other."

Blair looked straight at him. "It was a pledge."

Shiloh looked over at Damien, who stood still. "A shadow oath is different from what this is. The ability to share shadows means you do not only have his oath. Being bound to someone isn't just emotional, it's elemental for the Shadowborn. It means the essence of what you are-your magic, your will, your *existence*, knows the other person, recognizes them like they were always meant to be there. Your shadow is able to transfer because it doesn't see you as two separate people anymore."

Damien looked at Blair from the corner of his eye as she glanced down at the merged shadows, her voice softer now. "So what does that mean for us?"

Shiloh gave the faintest smile, something flickering behind his eyes. "It means you don't get to walk away clean. Not from each other. Not from whatever this is. Even if you tried, your core would remember. Your shadow would still reach for the other." He brushed Kael off and then addressed him, "More importantly, it means *you* don't get in between them, yes?"

Kael nodded, holding his neck with one hand. "That wasn't my plan sir. I was only teaching her."

"Good." Shiloh nodded toward him before turning to the others, "Now that that's settled, let's get dinner."

Everyone gave a shallow nod in return and followed Shiloh out.

Damien held her hand tightly as they walked, his stance too straight and tense. She squeezed it gently as she thought of all the ways she could help him with his tension. A memory flashed in her mind then, of him biting her because of Blake. A small blush fell over her cheeks and she spent the rest of the walk replaying that night and the small scar that now lived on her skin.

The eating hall was dim, lit only by the warm flicker of the overhead lanterns. Everyone sat at different tables, the plates full of nothing fancy. On each one, there was a slab of dark meat, slathered in some kind of gravy, along with rice, and steamed greens. Aesthetically, the small piles of food on the plates weren't exactly appealing, but the smell immediately surrounded them as they entered.

Marrow sat with Rhea, eating with slow movements and mechanical efficiency. Blake sat beside her, eyes fixed ahead, fork moving fast and precise. Across from them, Blair kept her gaze low, half-glancing at Damien every now and then.

There was no conversation, no clinking of glasses or laughter. The area around them filled with the soft scrape of utensils against trays and the occasional shuffle of a boot against the stone floor. This carried on the whole dinner, which lasted less than ten minutes. When the last tray was pushed forward and the hum of chewing quieted, Marrow stood.

"Showers are open," she said, voice low but clear. "I suggest we all take advantage." On the last word, her eyes found Blake and lingered for a split second, which caused his eyes to light up.

Rhea was first to her feet, already untying the band from her hair as she left the hall. Blair followed her with a small nod, and Marrow was soon right behind her. They moved in rotations, taking just a few minutes to scrub the dirt and sweat off their bodies, with Blair being last.

It wasn't long before the girls were done, the area smelling faintly of soap. They returned to the hall where the men were waiting. Damien disappeared first, quiet as always. Then Adriel, towel slung over his shoulder. Blake followed, eyes scanning the area before he went. Kael was last, trailing behind like he always did, humming something barely audible under his breath. By the time the last person had washed, everyone was on their way to the sleeping quarters.

When Blair, Blake, and Damien got there, the room was barely lit, the late sun sending slivers of light across the walls. The compound was quiet now, mostly everyone settled and getting ready for bed.

Blair lay on her side, one hand tucked under her cheek, the other resting close to Damien's. He was stretched out beside her, arm behind his head, staring up at Blake's bed like he could see through it.

"You didn't have to hit Kael today," she said, voice barely above a whisper.

Damien snorted softly, not bothering to hide his annoyance. "He didn't *have* to touch you. That's my job Blair, anyone who thinks otherwise can have their neck snapped for all I care. "

Blair turned her head slightly, giving him a look that was more shock than amusement. "That's a little dramatic."

He shrugged, the motion subtle under the blanket.

Blair laughed lightly, her chest warming at his possessiveness. "Be nice."

"No." Damien replied, eyes still on the ceiling, like it was that simple.

Blair let out a quiet laugh, her forehead brushing his collarbone as she settled against him. " I've been thinking about something a lot."

"What's that?" he asked as he yawned.

"I feel like I barely see you around. Are you always training with Shiloh?" She asked quietly, her finger tracing over the mark on his chest.

"I'm everywhere." he said with a smile.

"Damien." she retorted, slapping his chest.

He sighed deeply. "I'm never *not* with Shiloh. That man's one mission is to break me into my final form."

Blair lifted her head slightly and looked up at him, "And how is that going?"

"It's going well." Damien said, "But you need to focus on what *you're* doing. I'm just here for the ride."

They didn't say anything else after that, sleep finding them fast.

16

    The rest of the week passed in a rhythm that felt more like survival than routine. Days were now set in rotations between Rhea, Adriel, Marrow, and Kael; each of them reiterating what they had taught her. Marrow focused on control, precision, and grace. Kael pushed endurance and adaptability, forcing Blair to think while her body begged for rest. Adriel demanded raw execution, strength over finesse. When it came to Rhea, she just tried to break her in any way she could. Blair learned the most from her and the refusal to let her slip even once.

    There were no easy days and no leniency.

    The training didn't slow, not once, not even when her arms trembled from overuse or when her head spun from trying to understand the mark that lived just under her skin.

    But as she pushed herself, the mark of void grew stronger, just like she did.

    When she first started, it was like a flicker. Brief and unstable, the power danced at her fingertips but never stayed long enough for her to grasp it. Then, slowly, it began to obey. Not just awaken, but listen. By the end of the second month, she could call it, she could hold it, she could aim it, and she could use it on almost anyone.

Even Shiloh raised an eyebrow when he came to watch her. He didn't say anything of course, but Blair noticed the slight change in his demeanor, he was proud.

She didn't comment on it, didn't ask for recognition.

The next evening when drills had ended and shadows had begun to stretch across the camp, everyone gathered. Amongst the small crowd, Alessandra appeared.

She didn't speak at first, just approached Blair as the rest of the camp bustled around her. Her cloak trailed behind her as she held a wrapped package in black velvet.

"Blair," Alessandra said softly, voice carrying despite the quiet. "This is for you."

Blair looked at her and then at the item in her arms as she unfolded the cloth.

Inside was a bodice, sleek and shaped to her form, made from shadowcloth. Purple stitching traced the edges in elegant sweeping patterns, delicate, but strong. Underneath that, was a matching pair of pants with diamonds cut out along the sides, meant to showcase her mark.

"For your progress," Alessandra said, holding the garments out with both hands. "For your survival as you travel, and for your place in the Shadowborn."

Then, without warning, she bowed.

It wasn't deep but it was sincere, and the action sparked those around her. One by one, everyone followed, bowing their heads in respect to her potential. Even the four leaders, who had spent their time training her, bowed in recognition. Rhea looked at her as she did so, her eyes full of a fierce and loyal fire. Blake pressed a fist to his chest, and Damien, Damien bowed last, slow and certain.

Blair didn't move for a second. She just stared at the gift, at the people around her. For the first time, the weight of the unknown didn't feel heavy, it felt secure.

Then, finally, she reached out and took the bodice in her hands. The fabric was cool and light-weight, one that she would proudly wear. "Thank you," she said as those around her straightened.

Shiloh joined the crowd then, placing his hand on Alessandra's shoulder for a brief second. He turned his attention toward Blair, Damien, and Blake. His towering silhouette was sharp against the soft glow of the campfires scattered beyond.

"I think it's time to continue your journey," Shiloh said, his voice steady but carrying through the crowd. "Volunteers have been arranged to travel with you. Some possess abilities meant for camouflage and concealment, skills that will come in handy."

He paused, scanning the faces around him.

Rhea stepped forward. She moved with a calm certainty, closing the distance between herself and Blair until they stood side by side. "I'm going with them," Rhea said simply.

Shiloh blinked, a flicker of surprise crossing his features. Then, with a slow nod, he gave his approval. "Very well."

Before the words had fully settled, Marrow rose from her place beside Blake and stepped forward as well. She stood next to Rhea, the resolve in her eyes unmistakable. "I'm going too."

Shiloh's gaze swept to Kael and Adriel. The two exchanged a brief look before nodding in unison and stepping forward together, joining Rhea and Marrow. Shiloh just stood, nodding to each one of them, as if he had expected nothing less.

Blake followed his gaze and frowned, a look of concern tightening his features. "Not to kill the family vibe here," he said, voice firm. "But how do we know you stand with us, and not just because of the mark she carries?"

Rhea met Blake's gaze steadily. "It is the same thing." She looked at Blair then, and continued, "I've watched her here, watched how she has grown, and learned of the soul that resides in her. I believe in her for not only what she carries, but for who she is."

Without hesitation, Rhea raised her hand, with her palm up. "I pledge myself to you," she said, voice strong. "I give myself to you as armor. I will act as a comrade and a protector. I will also put my beliefs in you as a leader."

Blair looked down at Rhea's hand before glancing briefly at Damien. He answered her silent question with a brief reassuring nod. Blair's heart swelled with pride as she placed her hand on Rhea's. "I will be your friend and your guide. I will direct us to the best of my ability and I will continue to push myself while doing so."

At the touch of their hands, shadows stirred near their feet and rose. Dark tendrils, silky and alive, traveled up and curled around their linked arms. They stretched and spun before moving to Rhea's wrist and then Blair's.

As they slowly receded, a small shield marked Rhea and on Blair, a star had formed in the same spot, filled with a swirling black. Symbols on each of them that showcased their new bond.

Marrow cleared her throat then, moving to stand next to Rhea, who smiled as she felt her presence.

Marrow's voice was calm as she raised her own hand in offering, "I pledge myself to you as well Blair. I give myself as a comrade and protector.

Blair's eyes widened and a small smile formed on her mouth as she looked between the two women in front of her. She nodded slightly as she held out her own hand, repeating the same words. Swirling shadows soon encased their locked hands, marking them both.

Before pulling away, Marrow gave a quick glance toward Blake who had been watching them intently. He made no comment, only shrugged in contentment.

Shiloh's voice filled the space around them. "Does that give you enough confidence in them, Shadowborn?" He asked, looking at Blake, whose eyes were now locked on Marrow.

Blake nodded, "For two, yes."

Blair looked at the two women beside her, no longer just comrades, but a united front, bound together by beliefs and hope. Damien stepped up beside her, the mark he himself had, lightly peeking out from under his shirt. "We'll rest tonight and head out in the morning."

The Shadowborn nodded in agreement before splitting ways, Marrow's eyes hung on Blake a few moments before she walked away. Blake's gaze followed her until she was out of sight, then he turned to Blair and Damien, "I'll be late coming home. Don't leave the light on." He took a couple steps and then turned around, "Sick ink by the way. *You're welcome.*"

With that, he was gone.

Blair's eyebrows rose in curiosity as she watched Blake follow the path Marrow had taken.

Damien nudged his shoulder into her, "So, pledging myself wasn't enough? You had to go and recruit a small army?" he said, a playful tone in his voice.

"Honestly, I don't even know what just happened." Blair said, leaning up against the wall behind her. "I only knew what was going on because you had already claimed me."

"*Claimed* you? I like the sound of that." he growled as he pushed into her space. She gasped as if shocked before she swatted him away, only to pull him back to her in the next second. "I'm only a little jealous they got a pledge back."

She swatted at him and gave him a look that reiterated the fact she still had no idea what was going on.

"Top three?" he spoke into her hair as he pulled her into his chest.

She shook her head, as if she didn't want to answer.

He hugged her tighter, shaking her. "Come on feisty, tell me."

"I'm still just trying to figure this all out." she explained, squeezing her arms around him and burying her face in his chest.

Damien took a deep breath in. "You know, I used to think the same thing. Toward the end, the camp got pretty bad. I would lay awake at night listening to others scream and I would fight the idea that everything happened for a reason. I never let myself think that there was some grand design behind the camps and the darkness. Most of the time, it all felt random and cruel, like we were being punished for being born." He shook his head slightly. "But now I see it. I feel it, in ways I can't explain." He turned her fully toward him. "I wish I would have approached you as soon as I saw you in SilverDawn. I'm sorry I didn't find you sooner, it would have given you more time to figure it all out."

"Damien.." Blair's heart warmed at the unexpected, vulnerable words and she hugged him close.

"I wish I'd given you the dagger the moment you asked for help. I wish I would have listened to those voices sooner, the ones that told me the dagger belonged with you.

I knew it the first time I saw you. I just knew, and even then, I still waited. I shouldn't have."

He leaned forward, his lips hovering above hers.

"No matter what happens as we figure this out, this is how it was meant to be. You were always meant to have it. To have this. "He broke eye contact to gesture to the space around them, "That's something you don't need to figure out. You're the hope."

Blair stared at him, not sure if the pain in her chest was because it was threatening to burst or if it was from the weight in his words, maybe both.

"I can't fix my past. I can't figure out why things happened the way they did." Damien smiled faintly, "But I can figure it out for you. I can fix the future for you, and I will."

His words weren't just a promise, it was a vow; One that ripped out the heart she thought she had and stitched together a new one, one that beat for him.

She tried to respond, the first attempt coming out as air. The second attempt wasn't much better, her words a broken whisper. "I don't think you understand what you just did."

He smirked as he kissed her jawline. "I'm just doing my job."

She let out a short laugh and shifted, letting her hand fall to her thigh out of habit. Her fingers curled as if gripping the hilt of a sheathed dagger and even though there was nothing there, the mark answered her motion.

From the shadows beneath her palm, a blade formed. As she pulled it up, a sleek, dark, shard of shadow showed itself.

Damien's brows lifted, pride shining behind his grin. "Damn. Maybe I really don't know what I just did." He leaned back casually, hands bracing behind him. "What are you going to do with that?"

Blair's smile twisted. Without answering, she rose in one fluid motion, stepped lightly to the side, and threw.

The shadow blade cut through the air like lightning.

Before it could strike, a wall of darkness grew in front of it, courtesy of Damien. The weapon sank into it and disappeared like a stone into deep water.

Damien laughed as he took a step away from her.

"Oh, that's how it is?" She moved her hand again, another dagger forming from the air. "You think your pretty words will make me go easy on you?"

"Maybe," he said, circling her now, shadows flickering around his boots like smoke. "I definitely won't make it easy."

They clashed, another shadowed blade meeting his conjured one in a spark of dark energy. He guided her arm, corrected her stance with a tilt of her wrist, all while grinning like he was barely trying.

"You're dropping your left shoulder," he said.

She adjusted as she slashed toward him.

"Better," he allowed, ducking under one of her punches. "Still predictable, though."

"I hate you," she muttered.

"Lies. You love me."

She lunged and missed. His shadows danced around her legs, curling up her calves and her hips. Each one teasing and distracting her.

"Stop doing that," she snapped.

"Doing what?" he said innocently, appearing behind her in a swirl of night.

She turned a second too late, a flustered look on her face. Her mark flared as a pulse of jagged black lines exploded from her skin, clearing his shadows in a burst of force. The world around her quieted and there he was.

She didn't give a warning as she tackled him. They hit the ground in a tangle of limbs and laughter. Damien let out a winded oof, but he was grinning even as she rolled on top of him.

"You tackled me?" he laughed. "That's cheating."

"Says the guy who fondled me with shadows." Blair teased as she stared down at him, hair falling out of her ponytail and across her shoulder. One hand was on his chest and the other clutched the dagger. His chest rose beneath her as their eyes locked.

"You're impossible," she whispered.

"And you're dangerous," he murmured back.

Then, a tone quieter, she responded "Good."

She rolled her hips slightly, her weight shifting just enough to make him react. Damien inhaled slightly, the faintest twitch in his jaw as shadows threatened to take over his eyes. She grinned at the victory. Even more so as she felt something move underneath her.

A hard shape, pressing against her inner thigh where their hips met.

Her brow furrowed playfully as she rocked her hips again, "What is that?" she asked.

Damien arched a brow, trying to fight the shadows threatening to take over. "You'll have to be more specific." he said in a husky voice, picking up his hips to meet her movements.

Blair leaned back just enough to slide a hand down in between her legs, to the side of his thigh. Her fingers gripped his outline which sent shudders down his body.

The movement made Blair smile again, one that grew wider as he grabbed her hips. "I've seen raw power before. I've seen it commanded as the one in control. I've fought under people who thought strength came from fear and from force." He looked into her eyes, as he moved against her again. "But you move the world differently."

She held his gaze, her new heart beating a little faster.

"You make people want to follow you. Not because you demand it, but because you inspire it. I saw it with the children you taught before, I see it now in the way you carry everything."

"Damien, I-"

"I'm not finished," he whispered, sitting up and pulling her into his lap. His voice was low now, softer than she'd ever heard it. "You amaze me, Blair."

His hand reached out, brushing a strand of hair from her face. His fingers lingered at her jaw, tracing it with the kind of care that made him everything to her.

He leaned in, and his lips slowly found hers. Her hands rose to his shoulders, holding him like she needed to anchor herself.

She was breathless when he pulled away, "I've fought for so many people who never deserved it," he said, his forehead resting gently against hers. "But if there's anyone in this world worth kneeling for, it's you." He then grabbed her thighs and rolled her, landing on top of her. She giggled from the movement and he kissed her again, passionate and rough.

Their shadows bloomed, moving around them in a screen of black. He stood then, pulling her up and against him. "You have five minutes to get to the tent or everyone will see what's going to happen."

She squealed and pushed away from him, running through the paths. For a moment, she thought about hiding but then remembered how easy it was for him to find her. Instead, she moved as fast as she could.

She made it inside half a second before him. He barreled in and grabbed her, kissing her again. Starting at her jaw, he moved up the side of her neck and she melted into him with every touch. His hands gripped her thighs and she jumped into his arms.

"You're so fucking perfect." he whispered, kissing her behind the ear, "And you're mine."

Growling at the last word, he laid her on the bed and began pulling off her clothes as his black bled into his eyes "You never denied it earlier…" he said, pausing when she lay completely naked in front of him. His eyes roamed over her body and his nostrils flared, "that you love me."

He pulled his own clothes off, "You want to know the truth Blair?", he said, positioning himself between her legs and aligning to her entrance.

"I love the smell of you," he said, pushing inside of her with one hard thrust. A gasp ripped from her throat as he kept talking."'I love the red in your hair when the sunlight hits it." he says again, picking up speed. "I love your mouth, and the feisty shit that comes out of it."

Blair tried to talk, to reciprocate, but Damien kissed her, stealing her breath. He only stopped when he continued on, "I love your smile." He said as he kissed her again. He then pulled out of her, emanating a whine from her lips. "I love your legs, and what's between them.' He knelt down to kiss her, lightly swirling his tongue over her. She relaxed her legs, as he moved to lick the inside of her thighs, his beard leaving a wet trail on her skin.

Soon, his lips were back to hers. "I love the way you taste." he said slowly.

Blair wrapped her arms around his neck and pulled him into another kiss, pausing to look him in the eyes. "I love you more, Damien."

Five simple words was all it took for him to turn completely feral. His shadows exploded out, licking her skin. They groped her chest and moved down her body, where he met them. Finding her clit, they worked together tracing it and circling the nerves. Blair moaned loudly as he and his shadows did the work of multiple people.

Fighting through her body's tremors, she spoke to him. "I give myself to you Damien, in whatever way you'll have me. I give you every piece of me. The light, the dark, and everything in between." The shadows of her oath arose, a light illuminating the middle of them, just like before, with Damien.

It ran over her body to him, where he stayed focused in-between her legs. The shadows then gathered and coiled on her chest, in the exact spot of his. He noticed and growled, pulling the bundle of darkness down to her foot, placing it back down on her skin.

"I want it here," he snarled, "I want you to remember no matter how far you go, how far you rise, you will never stand alone. I will always be here to ground you."

Her eyes involuntarily rolled at that, as if his words applied pressure just where she needed it, right along his shadows. Everything she felt was suddenly heightened, especially as the shadows dug into her skin and radiated a pain so deep, it swirled to make pleasure. It was as if the bond hollowed a piece of her out to give to him. It was a good pain, one that she reveled in.

A hand took over for his mouth, claiming her. It was only a few moments before he was coaxing the first orgasm out of her, a scream ripping from her throat. He didn't stop, even as she tried to slow him down, to have him pause through her convulsions. Instead, he removed his fingers and filled her.

Together, they climbed higher, as the shadows played, building her up and then stopping. Blair's body wound tighter and tighter. Soon, her body tensed more than it had before and Damien chuckled wickedly, as he finally let her release. An unintelligible sound filled the tent and Damien soon followed her release a few moments later.

They laid panting, wrapped in each other's arms, basking in the swirling shadows that circled them.

Damien looked over at Blair who seemed spent of energy. He laughed at her as he moved to grab clothes for both of them. Walking back to the bed, he pulled her up by her wrist into a sitting position. Placing the shirt above her head, he pulled it down, and kissed her gently. She then stood as he knelt, lifting up her legs one by one to place them in her shorts. Blair looked down at him with a smile plastered across her face, her cheeks flushed from her body's release.

They said nothing as they laid back down. Damien pulled her close, wrapping his arm around her. Blair slowly traced his arm with her fingers, triggering goosebumps across his skin. She watched as they ran over the prominent veins that ran along his forearm, the arm that brought her such comfort and safety. She fell asleep in his grasp, as her mind drifted away.

17

The room was bathed in an amber glow, the only light coming from flickering bulbs that hung over the beds. Not beds, but gurneys. Plain, metal cots on wheels that were all empty, except one.

Blair stood motionless, blinking into the darkness around her. The air was thick here, as if she was underground. She could just make out the bare, dark gray walls around her. Her gaze then drifted to the beds which were adorned with white cloth sheets and random buckles with chains attached to them.

She didn't know what this place was, nor what was around her. She did, however, know that she couldn't move, not really. Looking down, her bare feet were planted on the cold stone at the edge of the room. As she fought to make her body budge, she noticed movement on one of the beds.

Across the room, beneath the harsh yellow light, was a boy.

His blonde hair was matted with sweat, and he wore only shorts. His skin wasn't just pale, it was a sickly, translucent shade that made quite a contrast with the wires that surrounded him. There were dozens of them protruding from his ribs, shoulders, and neck. Their metal glinted like veins made of steel. Thick needles jabbed into both arms, and from them, oozed a black sludge.

Every time the fluid surged forward, his body spasmed violently. Muscles in his arms, chest, and legs jerked as his back arched. His eyes, almost closed, flickered open in a blaze of agony. Then, a scream ripped across the walls.

She wasn't just witnessing pain. This was something else entirely.

"Stop," Blair whispered, her hands covering her mouth in horror. Her voice felt trapped in her throat, muted by the nightmare in front of her. She tried to move closer to help him as his agonizing screams rose. She again pleaded with her legs to take just one step, but her limbs wouldn't obey. Something invisible held her in place, and she stood there listening, as the boy screamed again and again.

The sludge was coming faster now, gurgling through the tubes in surges, invading his body. It poured from his ears in oily rivulets, dripping to the floor where it hissed against the stone.

His skin began to change. It stretched and warped, like it was making room for something else. As his body swelled, joints bent in unnatural angles. The wires disappeared beneath his swelling form, as if being swallowed whole. The boy's face contorted and his jaw elongated as his teeth pushed forward like needles. Last, his eyes blackened.

With what energy he had left, his screams had turned to whines. The rawness and fragility of the sound broke Blair. The tone wasn't human anymore and continued to worsen until his body settled and he grew quiet.

Blair gasped at the sight, her heart breaking for the child. She would give anything to help him.

It was like a nightmare she couldn't wake up from. Her heart pounded and her skin became clammy, just as a headache pulsed in her temples. Somewhere distant, she heard someone calling her name. In the next second, she felt hands on her shoulders, but her body in the dream kept convulsing, twitching as if the darkness she'd witnessed was bleeding into her.

"Blair!" the voice cut sharper through the dream now, urgent.

Her eyes opened, and it was like she surfaced from black water. She sucked in a breath as her voice released a horrified scream. Her body was completely tense, and all of her muscles were locked. Damien's face hovered over hers, his eyes wide with fear, and his hands still gripping her shoulders.

She tried to speak, but her throat felt scorched.

He let go instantly, flinching back with a breathless curse as his eyes roamed her body. Looking down, she saw it then; the reason for his reaction.

Her skin was glowing.

Dozens, no hundreds, of small, black geometric patterns shimmered across her arms, collarbone, and neck.

Each pulsing faintly with a purple light and each connected to the intricate brand on her thigh.

"It's another power," Damien whispered, eyes wide.

Blair stared down, still dazed, still seeing the boy. The table was engraved in her mind, along with the sludge forced inside of him. Her fingers twitched reflexively as if trying to claw the image away.

He reached for her again, slowly this time. "Whatever that was, it wasn't real."

Blair didn't respond, her ears still filled with the screams. *He was wrong. That had to have been real.* She closed her eyes but that didn't help, the child's face burned into the backs of her eyes.

For a few minutes she just sat there, silent. Her body curled into the tangled sheets, listening to Damien's voice as he talked about different things to calm her down. His voice stayed soft and calm.

She didn't stop him, even though it barely did anything. She didn't tell him about the way the boy's screams had cracked something inside her. Mostly, she didn't mention that she felt like she knew him, somehow.

As Damien's voice finally started to soften her anxiety, Blair's fingers brushed over one of the patterns on her thigh. It was warm but fading, the purple color transferring back to her skin tone.

"I've got you, Blair." he said, his hand moving across her thigh. "We're going to figure this all out."

She looked up with a sad smile, motioning for him to lay with her. "I know we will."

Damien lay down on his back, pulling her to his chest. Asher hazelnut hair draped across him, he slowly ran his fingers through it as he held her close with his other hand.

It felt like hours before she was finally able to fall asleep, thanks to his constant reassurance.

18

By the time the morning sun peeked over the edges of the trees, the Shadowborn were ready to depart. Blair stood at the front, exhaustion etched beneath her features. Damien flanked her, with Blake on the other side. The remaining four stood in formation behind them. The town had gathered to say goodbye, bringing various gifts for the road. Due to everyone's generosity, all supplies had been stocked. Each of their bags were full of special items woven from shadow, warm clothes and different kinds of food.

Shiloh approached first, his eyes landing on each one as he shook their hands and addressed them. Stepping back, he looked at the four from his camp, specifically Marrow and Rhea. "Follow your oath, protect her." With that, he waved his hand and the outer shadows wavered, lifting to allow them out.

Mist clung low beneath the trees as the Shadowborn moved in silence. Each one stepped out ready, with their packs slung, and their cloaks drawn tight against the lingering chill. Kaythorn Pines lay ahead, the second camp.

Kael led with his head low, nostrils flaring subtly with every step.

"There's something about three miles ahead," he muttered. "Metal and burned oil, but it's not moving."

Blake peeled away to his left, eyes narrowing. "No shadows," he confirmed. "Whatever it is, it's dead or waiting."

Adriel stepped forward next, raising his hand. A subtle crackle of heat shimmered off his skin as the plants thickening the path shriveled, blackening into ash. "And just like that," Adriel smirked, "it's easier to walk."

"Easier?" Blake scoffed. "You'll call attention to us that way."

"Oh, sorry," Adriel snapped, brushing ash from his sleeves. "Do you want me to leave the thorned bushes for you to handle?"

"Sure," Blake said coolly. "I'll show you how a real man handles business."

Adriel shot him a glare, lips already curling with a retort.

"That's enough," Rhea cut in, voice low but firm. "Save that for the things that want to kill us, not each other."

Adriel rolled his eyes and walked ahead. Blake shrugged, falling back. The forest changed as they moved deeper, the paths in front of them becoming quieter and thicker.

Blair walked near the middle, her fingers skimming the mark on her thigh.

"So, do we know how long until the next camp?" she asked.

Adriel, still smoldering from the interaction with Blake, answered without turning around. "It's not an exact spot."

Blair frowned. "What do you mean?"

Adriel eyed her over his shoulder, voice hollow, almost distant. "These kinds of places each hide in their own way. If they want to be found, we'll find them. It's all a matter of when and how. We were just told to go to the Pines."

Blair raised an eyebrow but said nothing more. She kept walking as her boots crunched over the dead leaves beneath her. Her eyes lifted as Blake veered off toward Marrow.

"You know," Blake said, sidling up to her, "You look like someone who could use some company."

Marrow didn't even blink. "You talk like someone who's trying too hard."

"Ouch," Blake winced. "But also, fair."

Marrow cracked the barest smile before shaking her head, but Blake stayed beside her, his eyes roaming over her frequently.

The rest of the group stayed quiet as the hike continued. By midday, the forest was no longer just a forest. Thick trees and groves gave way to winding thickets of silverleaf and hollow-barked thornwood. The undergrowth thickened, and the trees leaned in, crowding the path.

Still, the Shadowborn pressed on.

The sun arced high and then dipped low, but no one asked for lunch. No one complained; there was a kind of momentum to their pace now. It tugged at their bones and pushed their boots forward. By the time they reached the edge of a narrow creek wrapped in roots like skeletal fingers, dusk had begun to settle in. They made camp without speaking, the space between them filled with tired glances and the soft rustle of packs being opened.

Kael found a mossy stump and sat with his back straight, chewing slowly on dried meat. Blake sprawled on a patch of rock, tearing into a dense ration bar with all the enthusiasm of someone chewing bark. Adriel muttered to himself as he warmed his portion with a flick of his fingers. Blair stared into the fire she'd helped build, the flickering light playing off her thoughtful expression.

And then something shifted around them.

Kael froze, meat halfway to his mouth. Blake sat up quickly, eyes locked beyond the tree line.

Damien also noticed it. His hand wrapped around a blade of shadow that had materialized within his grasp. He moved in one swift motion, standing between the group and the dark beyond the fire's reach.

"Something's coming," Kael muttered, voice low. "The smell is wrong, like iron and blood."

Blake's voice was tight. "It's a Phantom."

They all stood and waited.

The fire crackled quietly. Then, from between the trees, a figure emerged. A man, broad-shouldered, draped in worn leathers that blended too well with the underbrush, stepped into view. A longbow hung casually over one shoulder and a wicked hunting knife gleamed at his hip. His smile was too wide, too pleased.

"Well, would you look at this," he chuckled, spreading his arms. "All the prey in one place. Didn't think I would find so many together, but here you are."

No one answered but their response was apparent. Every step he took closer was matched by a step forward from the group, Rhea with her exposed armor, Damien with his dark sword already positioned, and Adriel's fingers glowing faintly.

Then the Phantom's gaze landed on Blake and he tilted his head, as if in recognition. "You."

With no warning, Blake vanished, stepping into his own shadow. A blur of darkness snapped forward, and in the blink of an eye, the Phantom crumpled to the ground, his neck twisted at an unnatural angle.

It was only a second later when Blake reappeared, stepping back from the body with a frown. "How was he even that close." he asked no one in particular, his voice sharp.

Kael stepped forward, crouching over the body. He sniffed once, twice, then stood. "He was alone, there was no one else with him." Kael then paused, and looked at Blake. "Why do you smell nervous?" Taking a step forward, he cocked his head slightly and stopped. "It was almost as if he recognized you, could that be why?"

Blake took a large step toward him, his demeanor turning cold. "I'm nervous because we were so late in realizing he was here." His voice rose then, laced with anger. "What if next time it is five of them or ten, and we get ambushed? Someone should have caught it sooner." Blake then took an audible breath and moved away from Kael, forcing his body to relax. "And yeah, he probably did know me. I've run into a lot of them throughout the years and I'm not exactly good friends with any of them."

Damien opened his hand and the blade he had wielded, dissipated. "None of us are friends with them and I agree with Blake, we need to be more aware, especially those who have the ability to sense them. We double the watch tonight."

Blake agreed, and everyone else nodded, except Kael who watched Blake carefully.

When they sat again by the fire, no one instantly reached for their food. They all stared into the flames, lost in their own thoughts. Eventually, cans of vegetables and beans were passed around and everyone took their own serving before passing it to the person next to them.

After that, tents went up and a schedule was set. The Shadowborn would monitor in shifts of two, switching every three hours.

Most of them stayed up through the first shift anyway, sitting around a small, smoldering fire. Everyone, except Blair and Rhea who were having a small sparring lesson in an open space that was close. That continued until

211

the next shift, where Rhea took over watch and Blair went to lay down.

Damien had the tent secure by the time she arrived to climb in. He looked over her body as if checking her for any injuries and then pulled her into him, muttering a quick goodnight. It wasn't long before both had fallen asleep, only to be awoken at the next time they were needed.

No other Hunters appeared through the night but the tension continued through the morning as they packed up and set out to finish their travels.

Heading in the same direction, everyone seemed more alert, especially when the terrain started to shift. Craggy hills gave way to long stretches of sun-cracked earth. Dust clung to their boots as the group walked in silence.

Blake, who was walking near the middle of the pack, finally exhaled a dramatic sigh and spun halfway around. Walking backward, he addressed the Shadowborn around him.

"Alright. This silence is killing me." He spread his arms. "Who's up for a game?"

Damien didn't even look at him, his eyes set on the trail in front of him. "I prefer silence."

Blake pouted towards Damien. "You didn't even hear my idea."

Damien gave no reaction. "Still no."

Blair tried not to respond as she grinned silently and continued to walk.

"Rhea?" Blake offered with an exaggerated grin. "What about you?"

"Hard pass."

Kael shook his head as Blake turned his attention to him.

Sighing he turned his body the other way, "Adriel?"

"The answer is no."

"Wow, okay." Blake turned to Marrow, his last chance of hope in a sea of rejection. "Looks like it's just you, Marrow."

She didn't break her stride, even as the dust kicked up around her feet with each step. Her voice was low, flat, and carried no emotion. "Fine."

Blake perked up. "Finally! Thank you. Alright, here's the question: if you had to be stuck in a room with one of us for a week, right? No food, no sleep, just conversation. Who would it be?"

Marrow paused for a beat. "I think I'd rather just not be in the room."

Everyone glanced back at her. Blake just cocked his head. "That wasn't one of the options."

She turned her head slightly, just enough to face him. Her expression didn't change. "You're annoying."

Blake laughed. "If you think I'm annoying, you should have met my brother."

As he spoke, Adriel, who was walking just ahead of him, held back a thin branch to clear the path. "Oh goodie, there's *another* one of you somewhere?" He waited just long enough for Blake to approach, then let go. The branch snapped forward with a loud whip of sound.

Blake had expected that, vanishing mid-step. A ripple of black mist marked the space he'd just occupied. The next moment, he reappeared at the front of the group with a grin, eyebrows raised in triumph.

Marrow shrugged, her eyes finding Blakes, "I don't know, two sounds kinda fun."

Blake's jaw popped open as he shadow-stepped next to her.

Damien and Blair chuckled together, finally breaking the silence. It was then that even Rhea cracked a brief smile. Blair caught it and smiled back slightly before something moved in the corner of her eye. She stopped walking and briefly scanned the area. A shadow, long and snake-like, slithered along the ground. It was unnatural, a black shape independent of any light source.

Blair stepped toward it, intrigued. "What is that?" she murmured, catching Rhea's attention.

Rhea turned, following the shadowed movement with her eyes. Her body tensed as if sensing danger, the start of black armor reflecting alongside her jaw. "I'm not sure."

Blair moved forward again, and the shadow darted away at a quick and sharp speed.

Rhea's brows furrowed as she watched the shadow with Blair. "There's something not right about that."

The others slowed, then turned, and joined next to the two women.

The shadow stopped just ahead of them, as if teasing them, coaxing them to come closer. It stayed there for a moment, shifting and pooling like spilled black water. Without thinking, Blair took a step toward it. Noticing it didn't dart away, she took another step. As she did, the shadow moved underneath her foot, creating a veiled hole for her to step into. Blair vanished in a mere second.

19

"Blair!" Damien shouted, rushing forward toward the blackness, just in time to disappear as well.

Rhea followed instantaneously, which triggered all of them to step in.

Blake looked down at the shadow and then up at Marrow. "Ladies first?"

Marrow narrowed her eyes at him for a brief second before giving him an eyeroll and stepping through. "Such a baby."

Blake let out an insulted scoff as he watched her disappear. Shaking his head, he followed, vanishing into the dark along with the other Shadowborn.

They hit the ground hard, only a few of them fast enough to conjure shadows to break their fall. The air around them kicked up as black dust flew when they landed. The ground was soft, almost ash-like. They stood in what looked like a barren desert, if it could be called that. There was black sand everywhere around them, creating a ground that shimmered like powdered coal. The sky above was an endless stretch of stars that pulsed with an eerie light.

Blair was the first to move through the space. She immediately scanned the horizon and the rest of the area that surrounded them. Stretching her eyes as far as they would go in the darkness, she spotted a figure who was walking toward them. A woman, by the looks of it, who was moving slow and steady.

She was tall, nestled in a flowing robe of gray silk that hung tight to her body. Although her hair was pinned up, everything else was mostly hidden by a veil that hung over half her face. The silver lace laid across her cheeks, down to her shoulders. She stopped in front of the group, her gray eyes landing on Blair. She then spoke in a voice that was low and quiet, but carried strength.

"Only women may enter the camp of Muriel, Master of the Veil."

Damien stepped forward, scowling. "I'm sorry, what?"

The veiled woman repeated her words, voice exactly the same: "Only women may enter the camp of Muriel, Master of the Veil. The others must stay here, outside of our city. It is law."

Blake whistled as he looked around at the others. "Did I just hear what I think I did? *Only* women? That means-"

Damien cut him off abruptly. "*Only* women? Where are the men expected to go?"

The veiled woman paid no mind to Blake but did acknowledge Damien, answering him as she pointed to the area around them. "Here. We will bring supplies as needed, for however long the women stay."

Damien let out a harsh laugh. "Absolutely fucking not. If she goes in, I go in."

The woman nodded and turned to leave, excusing herself from the conversation.

Blair watched her walk for a moment before yelling out, "Wait!"

This made the woman pause. Knowing she could only have seconds to convince him, Blair turned toward Damien. "I have to follow her."

Damien gave her a sharp look. "We don't even know-"

"I have to go, Damien." She looked around at the others, suddenly aware of the oaths that some of them held to her, and then her eyes met Damien's again. "I need to see what's in there. Besides, I won't be alone."

Damien went to argue, but as if on cue, Rhea and Marrow stepped up behind Blair. Rhea's mark seemed to brighten, enhanced by the words she spoke. "I've got her Damien."

Damien exhaled through his nose, his eyes flickering to the shield that now adorned Rhea's skin. Taking a deep breath in, Damien gave a single nod.

Kael audibly inhaled as the air around them seemed to thicken with apprehension. Stepping up beside Damien, he laid his hand on his shoulder. "Fear? That's a new scent from you."

Before Damien's shadows could react, Blake immediately knocked his hand off, pushing him away from Damien. "Has anyone ever told you that you're a pretty weird dude? *No one* wants to be smelled like that. Learn some manners," he sneered. Blake shook his head a few times at Kael before he crossed his arms and looked at Damien and then Blair. "We'll wait here. I'll keep the big guy from freaking out, if you keep gloombug close to you."

A victorious smile spread across Blair's face and she nodded in agreement and turned on her heel.

"I *don't* like that." Marrow said flatly as she followed Blair, walking toward the veiled woman.

"That makes me love it even more." Blake yelled after her.

Blair was just about to look back, to offer a sign of confidence that everything was going to be okay, when Damien called out to her. "Come back to me tonight or I'll come looking for you."

Rhea rolled her eyes and pulled Blair beside her as she directed them toward the woman waiting for them. Once they approached, the woman spun and led them over the mounds of black sand.

The woman in front of them stayed at a slow pace. Each of her footprints leaving a dent in the vast, dark desert. For a moment, it was like there was nowhere to go, besides farther into the darkness, but just as they crossed between two large dunes, a camp came into view.

One, that was very different from the last.

Trees sprouted from the darkness beneath them. They were not trees in any true sense, but tall figures of compacted black sand. Their surfaces were smooth and glasslike, their roots disappearing into the dunes. Some leaned as if tired, others curved and twisted like sculptures. From their branches hung the dwellings of the veiled people, thin tents spun of grey and purple silk that rippled gently in the breeze.

Around the edges of the city, tall pillars marked the boundary. They were made of the same black sand as the trees, standing like silent sentinels against the massive dunes. Each pillar bore a piece of silk at the top, stitched with a purple diamond. *Safety.*

There was no main source of light anywhere, just scattered orbs that were randomly placed around the area. They glowed and hovered mid-air, like broken pieces of moonlight.

When it came to the inhabitants of the town, it was very clear that they were all indeed, women. Each one wore a different gray dress and laced veil. Some veils were simple and covered just their mouths, others were adorned with complicated patterns. Some eyes lifted as they passed, others deliberately looked down or walked the other way.

Above them, the blackness continued to pulse, as if the sky and the orbs of light were connected, surging together. The rhythm increased as they reached the heart of the camp, a round clearing surrounded by a separate inner-layer of pillars wrapped in silks. As they approached, they found another woman standing in its center.

Her veil was lighter than the others, close to the color white. The fabric was speckled with different shadows that shifted into runes. Her presence was calm, yet fierce. Blair immediately knew, without a doubt, that this must be the leader. As they approached, she watched them from underneath her veil. Once they were in front of her, she addressed them, her voice low but strong.

"I am Lailah," she said, gathering the bottom of her dress in her hands and bowing slightly. "Welcome, bearers of change. You must have many questions for me."

Blair stepped forward and held out her hand out, unsure how to bow, or if she even should. "My name is Blair. These are my comrades, Rhea and Marrow."

Lailah dipped her head in acknowledgment and then her eyes locked on the dagger marked on Blair's thigh. "It begins again." She whispered, almost under her breath. She turned her body away, motioning for them to follow her as she led them into another open space. Fires flickered in bowls around them now, casting long shadows against the columns that surrounded them in a wide semi-circle. The veiled woman moved to the middle and sat down on a folded piece of white fabric. Blair joined, taking a seat across from her, as did Marrow, but Rhea remained standing.

"What begins again?" Blair asked, lowering herself to the floor.

Lailah adjusted her veil, revealing a jawline marked with faint runes that matched the fabric that covered her face. The symbols began to glow just as her veil fell back into place.

"Long ago, we were hunted," she began. "Not for anything we did but for what we carried inside us. A gift from the world-before, misunderstood by kings and scholars alike. They feared us because we could hide what must be hidden, protect what must be preserved. We call it the Veil, it lets us conceal the truth from those around us." She looked around at the pillars that surrounded them, "When the world burned from the king, we veiled ourselves and used our power to preserve our people. We have stayed this way, waiting for our time to begin again."

Blair held her gaze which made the woman smile faintly under her veil, "Our job *now* is to prepare *you*."

Rhea looked down, assessing Blair and what her next move might be. Deciding to trust her instincts, Blair crossed her legs to signify that she was comfortable. "The symbols on your face and veil, what are they from?"

There was no pause as Lailah answered, just raw honesty. "Our four leaders had unmatched power and Muriel found a way to use these symbols. They let us enhance our abilities, using each other's magic to boost our own."

Blair nodded in understanding, her head still moving as she asked the next question, "And why only women?"

"It wasn't always this way," Lailah began. "Once, there were veils of every age, thousands spread across the kingdom."

That information stunned Blair. *That many?*

"But history eventually forgot them," Lailah continued. "Because so few survived." Lailah's eyes lowered as she continued. "It was quickly learned that men who wielded the Veil's power used it for the wrong reasons. Women, treasure, and sometimes even land, were all hidden. In turn, it amplified aggression, dominance, and wrath."

It was Marrow now, who adjusted her legs for extended comfort.

Lailah watched before addressing Blair again. "But this will change, I've seen it in the Loom. You will learn how to wield your mark and we will help with that."

"So it was you, then? The shadow that brought us here?" Blair asked.

Lailah nodded, her veil folding in multiple laces and then straightening out. "You already have our ability. You need help molding and transferring it." Lailah explained, "We will practice that, along with other things."

Blair looked over at Rhea and Marrow, who both watched her with intent.

In such a short time it was odd how much she knew she could trust them. Very similar to the fact she knew she could trust these camps.

Lailah rose, "I would like to show you something in order for you to understand."

Blair stood along with her and walked behind her as she turned toward a central tent, unlike any other in the camp. Its entrance shimmered faintly with black sand that ran up and down the seams, "The Loom awaits."

Rhea looked at Blair for confirmation and as she nodded, Rhea stepped in front of her, taking the lead. Inside the tent, the air was thick. Tiered white candles flickered around a circular basin in the center, filled not with water, but something else. Inside, was an endlessly swirling liquid, forming brief images before collapsing again.

Lailah moved her petite hand, gesturing for them to step closer.

"The Loom of the Veil is not made of thread or cloth. It is memory and history alike."

She raised her hands, and the liquid in the basin surged upward, forming a tower of shifting images. There were cities burning, a masked woman shielding children, and soldiers blinded by a wave of black mist.

"These are the echoes of the Veil. Past bearers who all reveled in celebrations and defeats."

"And you're showing us this *because*-?" Rhea asked.

Lailah peered at her with a knowing gaze. "Because the pattern is beginning again. The mark does not awaken without reason. The world outside this valley has turned violent and desperate. You will soon see that for yourselves. The most important thing to know is the mark you carry is not new," the woman continued. "It is old. Older than the kingdoms you know. Every bearer leaves something behind and it is woven into the Loom. A thread of them, a glimpse of importance."

She gestured to the basin. "Yours will one day join them, but for now, just watch."

Blair knelt, the cold from the stone seeping into her bones. She looked down into the basin and the smoke stilled.

Then it moved, not like fog but like a living thing drawing breath. From the depths of the basin, a shape began to form. A tall figure cloaked in gray was running through a burning city. Her mark shimmered bright across her shoulder as runes flooded her skin. She suddenly turned into a building and placed a child into a hidden wall. He was wrapped in a blanket, his blue eyes wet with tears. As the mother stretched her hand out, shadows erupted behind her body, blanketing the path behind her. Soldiers chasing her vanished into the dark and did not come out.

Then, just as suddenly, the image unraveled and more followed.

This time it was not a random woman but Blair. Not her as she was now, but her with everyone around her, standing at the edge of a castle. She was facing a figure in black armor as her shadows riled around her. Behind her, Marrow was screaming.

Blair recoiled and the image dissolved.

"What was that?" she asked, voice rough.

Lailah answered without looking away. "A thread that is tied to you and those around you. The loom remembers but also sometimes warns."

Blair stared at the basin, the contents now still once more. "Why show me this?"

"Because you are not the first to carry the Veil," the woman said. "And you will not be the last. However, you are the only one who can choose what your thread will be." She turned then as another woman approached, her veil shorter than the others with a gradient color of black fading to gray. Waving her hand, a shadow manifested much like the one that had brought them here.

Lailah looked down at it before returning her gaze to Blair. "I will send someone to collect you tomorrow. I want you to sit with what you've learned today and we will begin veiling first thing in the morning."

Marrow was the first to walk toward it. She looked at Rhea as she stepped into it and Rhea moved beside Blair.

Looking down at it, she turned to Lailah. "Thank you. I appreciate the knowledge and insight you have given us."

Lailah nodded and stepped toward her, giving her a hug. "I have no doubt that you are weaved for greatness."

With that, Blair pulled away and stepped through the darkness. Releasing her shadow a moment later, she was able to stop herself before she hit the ground.

"You literally had mere seconds before Damien was about to explode." Blake yelled to her, "and it hadn't even been that long!"

Blake's voice was a small comfort as Blair looked up at the men who had been waiting for them. Damien's eyes were glued to her, like usual, analyzing her body for any harm.

Blair walked straight toward him, grabbed his face, and kissed him deeply, forcing him to relax.

<u>20</u>

It wasn't long after Blair sat cross-legged next to Damien, that his hand slipped to her waist and drew her gently onto his lap. She didn't resist. She could still feel his unease about the situation they were in. The air between them was quiet, yet comfortable.

Rhea and Adriel were off to the left, locked in practice. Their arms were locked in defensive blocks, as their bodies moved in mirrored precision. Their hits broke through the silence every few moments, and against the crackle of the fire. Across from them, Marrow sat close to Kael, who was bent over the ground, sifting through the black sand. Every now and then he brought a handful close to his face, smelling it, murmuring to himself.

Blair tilted her head toward Damien. "How did you even manage to set this up so fast?" she asked, her voice low but edged with awe.

Damien's mouth curved faintly. "The sand helps," he said. "It remembers shapes if you press it right. The tents hold steady if you anchor them near the denser patches."

Blair smiled at yet another ability he possessed, resourcefulness. Her eyes then wandered back to the fire, its center glowing white-hot. "Today went well," she said, her tone softening. "We met Lailah, the leader. She showed me connections to the ones who have wielded the Veil before. She has this thing called a Loom. I used it to see memories or maybe visions, they all kinda blended together. After I was done, she explained the images as threads that ran through time."

He tilted his head slightly, curious. "Huh. What did you see?"

"They all moved so fast but I think I saw myself facing someone. Before that, I saw a woman and a child, who seemed to be fighting to get away from something."

Damien's brow furrowed. "A child? That seems pretty vague."

She nodded slowly. "A boy wrapped in a blanket, he was being hidden-" Her gaze lifted to meet his, and her next words caught in her throat. A sudden realization settled like a stone in her chest.

The blue was the same.

The hair was the same.

The firelight painted shadows across his face, but nothing could dull that look in his eyes, the same one she had seen in the loom.

Damien sensed the change in her. "Being hidden by what?"

Blair turned her gaze back to the fire, her thoughts spinning. She watched the sparks rise and vanish into the air before she spoke again. "Can I ask you a weird question?"

Damien's arms tightened slightly around her, pulling her closer. His reply was quiet, but steady. "You can ask me anything."

Blair hesitated, then asked, "Tell me about your mother?"

For a heartbeat, his whole body went still. His arms remained around her, but his breath hitched slightly.

She felt it, even though he hid it well. "You don't have to talk about it," she added softly.

He shook his head. "It's alright." His voice was rough around the edges. "I don't remember a lot before the camps but I do remember my father, or the things he did for me. I remember exploring with him and stories he told me every night. My mother died when I was young, before the camp, before everything."

Blair turned slightly, just enough to see the flicker of memory cross his face. "I'm sorry," she whispered.

Damien looked away, toward the others. He watched for a moment as they laughed together. A flare in the fire illuminated his face, the blue in his eyes seeming endless. "I don't know anything else about them," he said. "I only learned what a family was, because of you."

Blair's chest tightened at his words. She understood that completely. Not trusting her voice to answer, she leaned more into him, her head now resting under his chin. He wrapped his arms tighter as her mind repeated through the vision she had seen and if her instinct could yet again, be right.

Blair took a deep breath in before spilling the thought rattling around in her head. "I think the child might have been you Damien. I think the Loom was trying to show me your connection."

Damien didn't respond at first, as if he was thinking over his words carefully. "Meeting you was the best surprise I could have gotten. Whether it's the Loom or your mark that allows you glimpses of past and present, I don't want to know anything. I just want to live the life I have now, with you. I don't want to ask questions about things I'll never have answers to or worry about things yet to come." He waited a few moments before continuing, "Does that make sense?"

Blair moved her hands to his sides and hugged him. She could only imagine how much he had struggled in his life, how the camps had affected him. "Yeah, it does," she answered, nestling herself into his chest.

The others around them excused themselves and moved away in groups.

After a few moments, Damien spoke again as he filled his chest with air. "I know you have to go back to the camp. I realize it's the best plan and as much as I hate to admit it, I trust Rhea and Marrow with you."

Blair smiled automatically at his words. "I trust them too." She then turned slightly to look up at him. "What's the plan for when I'm gone?"

Damien scoffed at her before kissing the end of her nose. "Training, strategizing, keeping the boys from killing each other." His tone changed then, to a more serious one. "Don't worry about this side of things. I want you to stay focused on what you need to do over there."

She nodded, her eyes expressing her gratitude as she settled back into him. They sat like that for a long time, the sounds around them dying down and the flame almost flickering out. The fire pit was now just a residual heat, its light a warm, pulsing heart against the sweep of black sand that surrounded them.

Blair was still on Damien's lap when the others began to reappear. Rhea and Adriel walked side by side, their bodies sweaty from training. Behind them came Marrow and Blake, and Kael trailed last, still dusted with the faint shimmer of the sand he had spent hours studying.

"Thought you'd all gone to sleep," Blair said as they approached.

Rhea grinned faintly. "No, just enjoying the environment, figure we'd get a few more moments of this warmth before bed."

One by one, they sat around the pit.

Damien leaned forward, cradling Blair as he repositioned himself to see everyone. His eyes landed on Marrow and Rhea, "Blair is going back to the camp tomorrow, I'm assuming you will be joining her."

Marrow inclined her head. "As Rhea already said, we've got her."

Rhea's eyebrows furrowed, as if insulted. She lifted her arm and turned her wrist so the firelight washed over her skin. There, the mark of her shield shimmered. "It's literally written on me. She won't go anywhere alone."

Damien's eyes softened just slightly, though his posture didn't. "Good," he said. "I just needed to hear it again."

The group fell silent for some time. Eventually, Blake leaned back on his hands, staring up at the stars. "Feels strange," he murmured, "to have a plan that doesn't involve running or fighting."

Adriel smirked faintly as he stood. "Give it time."

Everyone followed his lead, standing and moving to their tents. Blake quietly slipped in behind Marrow as she retreated into hers. Adriel, Kael, and Rhea found their own. Blake and Damien were the last to enter their tent.

They laid down over their blanket, the sand forming to their bodies as they got comfortable. Once in position, Blair yawned and Damien chuckled. Wrapping his hand around her waist, he pulled her back to him and started to rub her earlobe. He kissed the back of her head and whispered 'good night' just as her eyes closed.

When Blair's eyes opened, the first thing she felt was the cold. She was standing on a large pale stone, and in front of her was a house.

Its windows glowed dimly with candlelight, the soft flicker of flames dancing against the walls inside. The structure looked old but lived-in. There were wooden beams, whitewashed walls, and the faint smell of smoke curling through the night air. Blair took a step forward, her hand brushing against the rough bark of a tree beside her.

It was then. That she realized she was dreaming again.

Her awareness sharpened as if the world had been drawn in charcoal, every detail darker, sharper, and more deliberate. Through the nearest window, she could see movement. A woman darted back and forth, pulling things from shelves and shoving them into a bag. Her hands trembled as she did so, her face pale and drawn. A man stood beside her, helping her, though his movements were slower. It seemed like he was trying to calm her, though fear was etched into the set of his shoulders.

"They know," the woman said, her voice low but frantic. "They found the link to my lineage. They're coming."

The man shook his head, as if he didn't want to believe it. "You don't know that for certain."

"Yes, I do!" she snapped, spinning toward him. Her eyes glistened with unshed tears, and in them, Blair saw something familiar, something that made her heart skip. "They'll come for me, and when they do, they won't stop there. You know what that means."

He swallowed hard, glancing toward the door. "Then we'll run," he said finally. "We've done it before. We'll do it again."

She moved closer, gripping his arm. "Promise me," she said. "If anything happens, if they find us, you take care of Damien." The name fell from her lips like a wound reopening. "Promise me."

The man's face softened. He lifted a trembling hand and cupped her cheek. "We'll keep him safe," he whispered. "I promise."

For a moment, the world seemed to still.

Damien.

Her eyes flicked toward the back of the house, where a small bed sat near the corner. There, under a thin blanket, a toddler slept soundly, reddish-brown curls against the pillow, one small hand curled around a stuffed animal.

The door to the bedroom opened and the man walked in. He lifted the boy carefully, whispering something soft and reassuring as the child stirred. The woman moved to the door, her breathing sharp, her hands trembling more as she reached for the handle.

Right before she stepped out, she paused. Her shadow stretched long across the floor, and with a flick of her fingers, it moved. The shadows in the room came alive. Stretching and twisting, they rose up like living things. The furniture shook, objects fell, and the shelves splintered. The entire house began to come apart, consumed by darkness that was not flame but void. The woman didn't look back. She took her husband's arm, the child clutched against his chest, and together they stepped into the night.

The door closed behind them and the lights went out.

Blair stood frozen, watching their silhouettes fade into the darkness.

Then, all at once, the dream fractured.

The house, the sand, the cold, all of it shattered into black glass, and Blair gasped awake beneath the tent canopy, the echo of that name still burning in her mind.

Damien.

She looked over at him, and she knew.

Blake had been right from the beginning, Damien was a descendant of the original four.

21

The morning came fast. There was no sunrise to mark the edge between night and day, only a soft thinning of the darkness around them. The black sand shimmered faintly beneath them as Blair, Rhea, and Marrow waited at the edge of the camp. The air was cool, still holding the hush of early morning, and the wind brushed gently against the tents they were leaving behind.

They didn't have to wait long. From beyond the dunes, a figure soon emerged, her steps still slow and measured. Like the others who carried the Veil, this woman was draped in silk, but she seemed to be different. Her veil flowed nearly to the ground, brushing through the black sand with every step.

The woman stopped a few paces from them. As she spoke, her voice was rich. "I am here to collect you for Lailah."

Marrow nodded silently.

"Come," she said simply, turning back toward the dunes. "They are waiting."

It wasn't long before they arrived, the black pillars of the settlement coming into view.

Lailah was waiting for them just inside the boundary, hands clasped before her. Her expression was warm, but her eyes were sharp.

"Welcome back," she said as she greeted each one. "Come. We have much to do today."

She led them through the winding rows of silk tents until they reached the grounds they were at the day before. Today, the space had changed: no fabric on the ground, but instead, there were tables and chairs.

Motioning to sit, Lailah turned to Blair. "You've had time to process yesterday," she said softly. "Tell me what you think."

Blair hesitated, glancing at Rhea and Marrow from the corner of her eye. Rhea's expression was cautious, Marrow's as still as the sand itself. Finally, she spoke. "I think," she said slowly, "that the veil was protected because it is easily connected to everything. I think it's safe to assume truths can be veiled, too. Even by those closest to you."

For a moment, Lailah's eyes lingered on her, as though she heard more than Blair said aloud. Then, a faint smile curved her lips.

"Truths," she said, "*and* memories. Because sometimes, it's best not to know some things."

The echo of Damien's words struck Blair like a quiet chord. The resemblance of the conversation was too much to ignore, but before she could question it, Lailah was already moving.

She crossed to a long table near the wall. Upon it,

lay a scatter of objects that ranged in sizes. There was a small black stone, a length of silver thread, a simple wooden cup, a folded blanket, and a few unremarkable trinkets.

"Today," Lailah said, "we begin working with the Veil itself. You've seen what it can do; how it binds, conceals, and protects. To wield it properly, you must learn to visualize before you command."

She placed a hand on the table. "Each of these items carries weight. Some of them are greater, some less. Your task is to cover them with the Veil, to draw them into shadow. You will not just hide them, you will *cast* darkness over them. There is a difference."

Blair nodded as she walked up to her table. Drawing in a breath, she steadied herself and reached for one of them, the smallest one. She focused on the black stone, remembering Lailah's voice, remembering how the Veil had looked in the loom, alive and breathing, endless.

But nothing happened.

The stone stayed exactly as it was, gleaming dully on the table. Blair tried again. Once, twice, a third time. Each attempt left her chest tighter, her head heavier.

Lailah's voice was gentle but firm. "You're trying to grasp it," she said. "You cannot hold the Veil. You can only *invite* it."

Blair closed her eyes and tried to imagine inviting something unseen, something vast, but her frustration got the better of her. When she opened them again, the stone was yet again unchanged, and Lailah was watching her quietly.

After several more tries, Lailah attempted a different approach. She came to stand beside her, resting a hand lightly on her shoulder. "You'll find your way into it," she said softly. "Sometimes the Veil doesn't answer until it knows what you're asking."

Blair nodded, though her chest ached with the weight of failure and the memory of blue eyes she had seen in her dream.

"I want you to think of a memory you wish you didn't have. One filled with fear, agony, or anger." Lailah explained.

Blair's mind reeled but soon she pulled one up from the depths, a night where her father had emptied multiple bottles of alcohol and had become violent.

As she looked up, Lailah recognized that she had one. "Do you wish to forget it?"

After only a mere moment, Blair nodded.

Lailah smiled slightly before asking Blair to close her eyes. "I want you to envision the veil washing over the memory, hiding it from your mind's existence. Watch how it falls over the image, how it molds to the edges."

Blair did so, finding it slightly easier to fulfill this exercise. It only took a few minutes for darkness to leak over the vision. As it did so, her mark warmed, faint swirls of black igniting around it. A few minutes later, she blinked her eyes open and the swirls faded.

Lailah watched her for a moment before speaking, "Do you remember it?"

Blair looked at the ground before raising her eyes to Lailah again, "No. It's gone."

Lailah clapped her hands softly. "This is the Mark of the Veil. When used correctly, it can help in many ways. I am sure you can figure out just how badly it would be if someone could just veil others memories. It runs even deeper than that as well. Emotions, decisions, anything can be veiled."

Rhea shifted in her seat, as if hearing the veils potential made her uncomfortable.

Lailah continued, "It is interesting that you connected with that training more than the physical one."

Blair looked over at Marrow who was already looking at her. "I have been trained in manifestation and shadows within the mind already."

"Ah." Lailah exclaimed, acknowledging Marrow. "You have done good work with her."

Marrow dipped her head slightly as a thank you.

Lailah moved to the table again and picked up the rock. "I want you to apply the same thinking. Form the darkness around the rock, just like the memory."

Blair took the rock from her open hand and squeezed it gently. Taking her time, she recalled the training with Marrow and pulled from that. A small gasp broke her concentration as she opened her eyes to find Rhea smiling at her. Looking down, she caught the rock flicker back to life in her hand. She had done it, if only for a mere second.

Lailah embraced her quickly, before conjuring up a shadow at her feet, signifying her release for the day. "I look forward to what you do tomorrow."

Blair smiled as she stepped through the shadow, and back to her camp. Like before, she caught herself just as she was about to hit the sand.

Rhea and Marrow were soon behind her as she approached the men, her hand still gripping the rock.

As they got closer, Rhea scoffed out loud at what unfolded in front of them.

Over a makeshift table, Blake and Adriel were in the middle of an arm-wrestling match. Their eyes were glued on each other as Damien stood beside them. His eyes met Blair's with a smirk as he yelled. "Go."

The two men battled back and forth, pulling and pushing their weight. Growls and snarls filled the space until Blake managed to summon just enough strength to win. He jumped up and did an obnoxious dance as Blair stepped up beside Damien.

"What is this?" she laughed.

"This is *me* keeping the boys from killing each other." he explained, motioning between the two. He then used his hand to grab her and kiss her. "How was your day beautiful?"

She smiled up at him, her eyes bright. Testing herself, she placed the rock in her pocket and focused on Damien's finger, soon the tip of his pinky vanished.

"Introducing the mark of the Veil." Blair announced quietly to him.

Damien looked at his hand, turning it slightly. As he did so, the connection broke and his pinky reappeared. "That's amazing, but also unsettling. Where does it go?"

Blair followed his eyes to his fingers, "It's there, just veiled from the eye."

Blake walked over then, having watched everything. He stood and let out a low whistle. "And I thought *I* was cool winning an arm-wrestling match." He flashed a grin. "Remind me never to piss you off."

Blair pushed into him with a smile as they moved to create a fire and make dinner. A crate had been delivered to the men earlier in the day, full of fresh fruit, a loaf of bread, and meat.

Blair sat near the fire as Adriel helped it grow. Marrow worked on the food, using a large bowl to combine cumin and other herbs.

As they ate, the boys told of their day. Kael began a half-finished story about nearly getting swallowed by the dunes. Damien ended up interrupting him three times to correct the details. "You tripped, Kael, the sand didn't eat you." Soon they were all laughing hard enough that the sounds mixed into each other.

When the laughter died down, Blake leaned over his bowl and shot Marrow a teasing grin. "You know," he said, his tone casual but his eyes bright, "for someone who talks so little, I find you the most interesting person here."

Marrow stilled, spoon hovering halfway to her mouth. "Is that supposed to be a compliment?"

"It's supposed to be a hint," he replied smoothly, his lips curving. "You should talk more. Maybe start with what kind of man you are looking for."

Rhea groaned, throwing her hands up. "Here we go."

Blair laughed into her drink, watching the scene unfold as Marrow shifted slightly but didn't look away. "I like the relentless ones, the ones that don't give up."

Blake only shrugged, his grin widening. "*That*, I can be."

The group laughed again, Rhea tossing a small piece of bread at Blake. "You're shameless."

"And proud of it," Blake said, catching the bread midair before eating it triumphantly. "Especially if that helps me win *her* over."

As the noise settled, Rhea leaned back, her gaze shifting toward Blair. "You did well today."

Blair looked at her as if caught off guard. "Thank you."

"No, really." Rhea's voice deepened slightly, carrying that rare note of sincerity. "You are growing every day."

Blair felt pride rise in her chest. "I'm trying."

"That's the point," Rhea said firmly. "You're not trying to just consume everything and gain power. You are learning first."

For a moment, Blair didn't know what to say. She smiled instead, a small and sincere gesture. "Coming from you, I'll take that as the highest praise."

Rhea smirked. "Good. You should."

Blair felt the weight of those words settle deep in her. Rhea didn't hand out approval easily, it was something you earned, piece by piece. Hearing it from her meant more than she wanted to admit aloud.

Around them, the conversation picked up again. Adriel started to argue with Blake about whether shadows could be used to cheat at cards, Marrow quietly finishing her stew as if pretending not to listen. The fire crackled, the night deepened, and warmth and laughter surrounded them.

When the meal was done, Rhea rose and stretched. "We'll have to be up before sunrise again," she said, half to herself, half to the group.

The woman agreed, standing to go to their tents.

Blair had barely ducked inside when Damien was at her back. She turned, expecting him to urge her to sleep, but his eyes were black and pinned to her. "I need you."

Blair chucked softly, then undressed, slowly. She lay back and opened her legs, sliding her fingers to the spot between her thighs. He didn't move, but shadows were now at his feet, pulsing.

Blair played with herself for a moment before she gave him a coy smile. When she spoke, the words were a command. "Then eat."

Immediately, Damien dropped to his knees, his shadows lashing out to hold her thighs open.

245

There was no tasting, no slow movements.

Damien found that one specific spot that sent spasms down her whole body, then he devoured her.

Blair gripped his hair as she lifted her hips against his mouth, drawing a growl from him. His shadows worked with him, one skimming over her skin to squeeze her chest, another entered her just as he quickened his tongue on that one spot that drove her wild.

Blair drowned in the pleasure that his darkness brought. Black webs formed across her fingers as they gripped the back of his head. Her shadows responded to her need, tugging at his pants and releasing him from the fabric that confined him. As her first climax built, her shadows gripped and stroked him. He moaned into her as she shattered on his mouth. She tried to pull away but he refused, and kept eating as her legs convulsed. She cried out in protest but he was fast to cover her mouth, along with the tent walls, to swallow their sounds.

Damien never let up, even going as far as lifting his face to scold her. "Tell your shadows to stop. When I cum, it will be inside of you."

Reluctantly, she obeyed and her shadows retreated. "Good girl," he mumbled as he went back to her, his face and chest glistening.

Six more times, release tore through her, and Damien never faltered. It was on the last one that her muffled scream was his undoing and he pushed inside of her just as he exploded.

Blair could barely move, she could barely speak, as he wiped her clean. He then moved to his own body, cleaning her off of him before laying next to her.

She barely heard him as her body succumbed to sleep.

"I'm proud of you too."

22

For the next week, they settled into a familiar schedule.

Each morning began the same. Rhea was outside of her tent first, twisting her hair back with steady hands. Blair emerged next, fully refreshed due to Damien completely exhausting her. Last was always Marrow, who came out of her tent with messy hair and Blake whining for her to come back.

Every time they were summoned, it was a different woman with a different veil. Regardless, every day they were led across the dunes where Lailah was always waiting for them.

Blair's lessons began small, just like the rock. Lailah spent a large part in the beginning explaining each object and how to cover it. She moved through the objects on the table. First, it was another pebble, then a thread, finally a folded scrap of parchment. Even though it seemed like such a small task, the first few days were full of frustration. The Veil would mask things only for them to flicker back. Fortunately, Lailah was patient and Blair learned to persevere through each setback.

By the third day, she managed to pull a thin layer of shadow across the small stone, holding it for only seconds before it wavered and dissolved. Still, the length of success set something on fire inside of her.

While she trained, Rhea and Marrow grew comfortable enough to take turns and leave to help elsewhere in the city. Blair sometimes caught glimpses of them through the columns around her. Once, it was Rhea using her strength and armor to bind fractured structures of black sand into solid form. Another time, Marrow was just sitting with a veiled woman who needed help measuring silk.

By the fifth day, her lessons changed. Lailah brought her a small knife, its blade carved from dull stone.

"Try," she said simply.

Blair closed her eyes and reached out. Focusing on the sense she had begun to recognize as her link to the Veil. She invited it closer, not as a force, but as a presence.

The dagger shimmered. Its surface darkened as the edges blurred into the air. For a heartbeat, it vanished completely, swallowed by the Veil.

When Blair opened her eyes, Lailah was smiling. "You see?" she said softly. "It's starting to answer you."

At the end of the week, Blair could cover the knife, the rocks, and even a folded cloak with fluid precision. Every time she held it a little longer, it began to feel less like effort and more like a natural extension of her will.

Blair grew stronger every day, and by the seventh morning, she no longer hesitated when Lailah called her forward. The Veil came easily now, wrapping and unfurling like an old friend.

This was put to the test when Lailah called a woman over to them. She came out from a tent that was close to their training area. As she approached, Blair realized the woman was younger than her and had a veil that was frayed at the end.

Lailah introduced her as Scarlett, and took her hand as she approached.

Scarlett's eyes stayed glued to the ground as Lailah spoke to Blair. "Scarlett was involved with one of the men we spoke about when you first came. He was vile and became angry when he was told no. He used his power to take what he wanted anyway."

Blair swallowed, understanding the weight of what Scarlett had endured.

Lailah paused then, squeezing Scarlett's hand and lowering her voice. "She wants you to veil the memory."

Blair's eyes widened at this request and then settled on Scarlett who looked up for the first time. A small, meek voice came from under her veil as one tear fell down her cheek. "Please."

Blair's thigh lit up with different sensations, helping her burn away all doubt. She stepped up to Scarlett and held out her hand. The young girl responded, placing her own petite palm in Blair's.

Closing her eyes, Blair asked every fiber of her being to help with this. She then spoke to Scarlett, "I need you to think about it one more time. That's it, just one more." Blair said, with a reassuring squeeze of her hand. Another small tear fell as Scarlett nodded slightly.

Blair tried to remain calm as she closed her eyes again. Soon, an image materialized in her mind. It was blurry at first, but then it sharpened. A large-framed man was above her, covered in sweat and body odor. His voice slurred as he spit venomous words at her as he took off his belt and wrapped it around her wrists. His weight was heavy, and a fear of what was coming swept over her, even as she continued to try and fight him off. She knew there was no escaping as her legs were forced open and a sharp pain flooded her senses.

Blair heard a sob tear from Scarlett which caused her to focus even harder. One by one, she encouraged each and every shadow to flood his face, the pain, and the experience. She watched as they filled in every crack and corner of this memory, leaving no trace of what had happened. Within a few moments, the image was lost to a sea of darkness and she knew it was done. Opening her eyes, Blair could see that not only had Scarlett already physically relaxed, but her eyes were a shade brighter than they were before.

Blair squeezed her hand as Lailah looked down at her. "Do you remember Stoic?"

Scarlett shook her head gently. "Who?"

Lailah smiled as her eyes slightly watered. "Nevermind, I must be confused."

Scarlett shrugged and gave a small smile before turning to Blair. "It was nice to meet you."

Blair stepped forward, giving her a small hug. Behind them, Lailah watched, a small tear of her own falling on her veil.

As Scarlett excused herself, Blair watched as she walked away, her entire energy lifted. When Blair turned back, Lailah held a small box in her hand, one she had unveiled. She opened it and produced three bracelets.

They were small but woven together from black leather. Lailah handed one to each of the women around her. One to Blair, one to Rhea, and one to Marrow. She then closed the box and looked at them all. "Like the threads of these bracelets, your story is tied to many. As you leave here, please remember that your strength grows through these bonds, and without them, you will unravel."

For the last time, a puddle of darkness moved across the ground, appearing beside them. Blair kept her eyes on the bracelet as she slid it on, then brought them back up to Lailah and smiled. "I came here seeking help but you changed me more than you know. I am especially thankful that your destiny was woven into mine."

To that, Lailah hugged each of them.

They dropped into the camp, just in time for dinner.

Blake's voice carried over the black sand. "Is it almost ready?."

"Just cut the vegetables," Damien yelled. His eyes then lifted to meet Blair, who had appeared out of the darkness. Tossing Blake a bundle of herbs, he mumbled to him and moved towards her, "and wash your hands."

Marrow immediately stepped in beside Blake to help him while Rhea silently sparked flint to create flames. Soon it was crackling, and warmth began to fill the space around them as they ate.

Blair hadn't spoken much since they returned but as she brought her spoon up to her mouth, the flickering light caught on the bracelet that was now on her wrist.

Damien's eyes moved to it. "That's new."

Blair paused, fingers brushing over the gift as she nodded. She swallowed another bite of dinner before looking up at him. "Lailah gave it to me." She inclined her head to the other women across from them. "We all got one."

Her smile then faltered as she thought of Scarlett. As respectfully as she could, she explained how she was able to help her, gaining the attention from the others around the fire. Rhea and Marrow looked down and a silence fell around them. Blair's heart cracked a second time for the small woman.

Adriel cleared his throat which caused Blair to look over at him. His posture seemed almost awkwardly straight, as if rigid. His eyes were slightly widened, as he stood and stepped closer to Blair, stopping just beside her. As he spoke, his voice was raw and quiet.

"Many women will never have the chance you gave her. So, they spend their life trying to forget, *like my sister*." The last few words left his mouth as a whisper. "This world is lucky to have you, as are we." When he looked up, his eyes were filled with a dull sadness. "I didn't understand how it was coming so easy for you, but now I know it's because you are meant for great things."

Blair just watched him, not sure what to say.

He inhaled before extending his arm out toward her, his next words a declaration. "I pledge myself as your aid, in all things you may command."

Blair froze. "Adriel. You'd bind yourself to me?"

"Yes, for *her*. I wish she would have had someone like you. For that reason, I want to stay with you, to create a chain of protection for anyone who needs it. I'm sorry it took me so long to figure that out."

Without a second thought, she stood and took his hand. A dark current surged between them, tendrils of living shadow coiling around their wrists. When the wall of darkness receded, both bore new marks.

On Blair's wrist, was another small black star, faintly luminous. Adriel's was a chain linked together, encircling a steady flame.

He bowed his head. The faint glow of the flame catching the sharp line of his jaw. "Thank you," he whispered.

Blair looked around the circle and then down at her bracelet. "No, thank you," addressing not only Adriel but the other people around her, "for choosing to be here."

She looked at each of them, her gaze steady. " I'm learning everything I can and pushing myself every day to become someone worthy of this mark."

Kael looked down at his bowl as his voice answered Blair's. "They have given their oaths because they already believe that. We wouldn't risk our shadows otherwise."

Blair looked over at him as she repeated his words. "Risk your shadows?"

Rhea was the one to answer, explaining it, "Those who break the pledge lose their shadows. It is the cost of going against something so precious" she said, voice low and sure, "So, you need to understand, we made the pact because we believe in what you are doing, regardless of the reason. It is not just a small gesture to us. This moment. This group. You. This is the beginning of everything." She looked around, lips tight with emotion. "We've spent our lives waiting for something to *matter*, and this matters."

No one spoke as Blair absorbed Rhea's words.

It was a short time before everyone moved to clean up and shifts were agreed upon without fuss. Rhea, Kael, and Adriel headed to their tents. Damien stood last, helping Blair clean the last remaining things before leading her to their tent.

Inside, Blair lowered to the bedroll, eyes already half-closed as Damien pulled a blanket over them both.

As she settled, Rhea's words and Scarlett's face appeared in her mind. "Do you ever wonder if we were all meant to find each other?"

Damien didn't answer right away. He shifted closer, brushing a hand down her arm. "No." She stilled as he continued, "I don't wonder," he said softly. "I know."

Relief loosened her shoulders as he smiled at her. As if on cue, her body relaxed into his. "Good," she whispered.

Sleep tugged at her gently and as she closed her eyes, the warmth of his body next to hers calmed her nervous system. It was only minutes before everything melted into darkness.

She was surrounded by women in veils. Blair watched them as they all moved, completing different tasks. One was preparing salve, one was braiding another's hair, all busy in some way. The environment then shifted and she stood at the Loom, the familiar black liquid stretching and growing.

Before it, a woman knelt; Lailah.

Her voice was soft as she spoke to the Loom like it was alive. "She doubts, yes, but they do not bend her shape and that's where power begins."

Lailah paused and lifted her head, as if sensing something. Slowly, she turned her body and looked right at Blair, across the dream. She pulled off her veil then, exposing her lower face. Black veins split across her skin, like shattered porcelain. She smiled again at Blair as she spoke directly to her. "I'm grateful for our time together. Let me reintroduce myself as a friend. I am Lailah, leader to the ones broken by the world's darkness. We come here when we have been shattered by it, but you... you are not meant to break. Go north, Blair. The rest will follow."

Blair woke with a quiet breath and Lailah's face burned into her mind. There was no panic, but a realization that Lailah had trusted her.

She sat up slowly, the blanket she shared with Damien sliding down her arms.

Go north.

A simple direction but now their whole plan.

She turned toward Damien and smiled. He was deep asleep, his beard indented from where she had been laying. His jaw was slack, hair a mess, but utterly peaceful in a way she only got to see at night. She leaned in and pressed a kiss to his cheek.

He murmured something incoherent, and she smiled again before deciding to take a minute outside.

The air was cool on her skin and the fire they had eaten around had burned low to glowing embers. She was staring at the fading colors when there was a sound to her right. Her hand siped her thigh, forming a shadowed dagger. She turned-

Blake lay unbothered by a nearby tent. The pulsing sky illuminated his body and the figure that was underneath him. Laying on his stomach, his face was buried between Marrow's thighs. Blair tried to pull her eyes away as shadows moved up Marrow's body. They settled around her neck, tightening as she writhed beneath him. In the next moment, her hands pulled at Blake's hair as her body convulsed and she arched her back in pleasure, whimpering.

Blake looked up at that moment and moved his tongue slowly upward until his entire face was exposed. He grinned toward Blair, his chin dripping with Marrow's release. He winked once as he licked his lips, and then lowered his mouth back down.

Blair's face flamed and she spun on her heel, covering her face and stepping back inside her tent. As she entered, she yelled at herself for not walking away, knowing Blake would have plenty to say about it. *That idiot.*

Slipping in next to Damien, he moved just enough to pull her to his chest. She laughed silently at herself and the whole situation she had just encountered before she relaxed under the blanket and curled against Damien.

23

Blair blinked awake, a sheer film of sweat covering her body. The darkness around her was warm as it filtered in through the open tent flap. Damien was already up and outside, she could see him on the other side of the fabric opening. He was bent over, lacing his boots a couple feet away from where she lay, giving orders to the others. She shifted, angling herself to see beyond the opening. Adriel was standing next to Damien, zipping his bags shut while Blake was helping Marrow disassemble her things.

Rolling to her side, Blair stood and quickly changed, blinking away the last remnants of sleep. She then gathered the blankets they had slept with, folded them, and stepped out. Damien spotted her immediately and in-between giving direction, he grabbed her as she tried to walk away, making her squeal.

Blake looked over, groaning in annoyance.

Damien smacked him upside the back of the head with one of his shadows as Blair cleared her throat, lifting her voice. "I see you have already started."

Kael made a sound that was almost a scoff, "We started two hours ago."

Blair shot Damien a look, as if in question, but he only responded with a small shrug. She sighed, pushing him away before moving in tandem with the others. Together, they worked to clear their space and pack everything up.

An hour later, a broad shadow opened in the middle of camp.

"Our ticket home?" Blake asked, tossing his and Marrow's bag over his shoulder.

Kael stepped forward, bending down to inhale. "It smells of forest."

Damien looked at Blair, who watched the dark circle grow. Grabbing what he could, he nodded to her before stepping through. She watched as his body disappeared and moved to follow, the rest joining in after her.

In a blink, they went from desert to forest. This time, they landed gently on dirt and grass, surrounded by familiar trees made of average bark.

Everyone exhaled at once.

Marrow moved first, approaching a bush filled with berries. "Let's grab a snack and discuss what's next." she suggested, running her hands over the coarse leaves.

Damien dropped his bags and walked over to Marrow. "Sounds good to me." He then stood next to her, plucking a few ripe berries off the bush before returning to Blair and offered her one. She looked down, smiling at the familiar fruit. It was a round, blueish-purple Crescent berry, one that he had tried for the first time with her. She looked up at him with a knowing smile and popped it into her mouth.

A few others like Adriel and Blake, gathered some as well. Rhea and Kael were the only ones who used that time to reorganize their belongings.

As Rhea finished, she looked over the group. "Alright. What are we thinking? If we go east there's a valley route-"

"No," Blair answered, popping the very last berry into her mouth.

Everyone looked up as she chewed. "We're heading north."

Blair stood slowly, brushing the stems she had pulled off from her lap.

There was a slight pause and then Rhea tilted her head, just slightly, in question.

Blair braced herself for pushback. She readied her tongue for debate, or skepticism, or outright refusal but when none came, she stood a little straighter.

Rhea gave a slow nod and looked out past the trees. Adjusting her cloak. "North it is. Let's get ready then."

Blake approached Blair from behind. "You really thought we'd argue with you?" Blake asked rhetorically as he stepped up next to her. His voice dipped low as he leaned into her. "I bet you could tell me exactly what my breath smells like right now. I'll give you one clue, cracked *wide open.*"

Blair shoved him with a horrified laugh. "What is *wrong* with you?"

"Everything." Blake cackled before wandering over to Marrow, who was stretching. Blair watched as Blake leaned in and said something that made Marrow's cheeks flush red. She gave him a shove, just like Blair had, which Blake took as an invitation to tickle her.

Blair couldn't help the smile curling on her lips as she watched them.

Damien appeared at her side, placing his arm around her shoulders. He stood there for a moment, watching them as well. "Maybe she can help calm him," he said, almost hopeful.

Blair snorted, turning her body into him. "I would bet my life that *no one* can do that."

After finding a small stream to fill water canteens, the group readied for their journey. Packs were tightened, weapons were checked and boots were laced. As they gathered at the edge of the trees, Blair's gaze turned north, and they started walking.

The path curved through a narrow forest and scattered hills swallowed by moss. Sometimes, a trail guided them, other times they carved their own. They moved fast but carefully, weary of their surroundings.

Around midday, Kael's head shot to the side as he inhaled deeply, his eyes rolling back with the strength of the smell. "We are close to people. They are grilling vegetables and charred fruits."

Rhea looked at him as if his actions never bothered her. "Could it be a town?"

Inhaling one more time, he nodded. "A small one."

Rhea looked at Blair and then Damien, "It would be smart to stop for supplies."

"And food," Marrow added, "We don't know how far the next town is."

"I agree, but we don't exactly look like common townsfolk." Adriel added, pointing to the bags and weapons.

Blair looked over their supplies and then at the ground for a moment, as if contemplating something. "Let me try something."

She closed her eyes and pictured each item in her mind. Slowly, she imagined the veil covering each and every one of them. As she did so, spiraled wisps crept over her skin and moved to the bags on their backs. Shadows coiled each one, before covering them completely When she opened her eyes, it was as if they were not holding anything at all. They looked like average, tired travelers.

Blake turned in a slow circle, letting out a low scoff. "Huh, not bad princess."

Blair narrowed her eyes at him but appreciated the compliment.

Soon after, the trees parted, and a small town emerged in the distance. Narrow buildings lay one each side of the opening, made from brick. The dirt road between them signaled the start of the town. As they entered, they swept the area. The largest building in the space was a general store, its faded sign swinging lazily above a porch. Second, was a tavern that sat squat and square, leaning slightly to one side. Beside it, a blacksmith sat quiet on a stool, a small booth next to him carrying tools to sharpen blades.

Kael had been right when he described the town as 'small'. This was everything, a few buildings and scattered people in-between. The only other feature being a small well that marked the center of the town, mimicking SilverDawns fountain. It was small with a cracked stone base and a rope that creaked whenever the wind moved it.

Besides the one or two people stationed at each building, there were no others around. This place seemed like an area to stop and refill supplies before the road pulled you onward again.

Blake looked around with a look of bewilderment. "This is it?"

Kael nodded, sniffing toward the tavern, finding the source of the food smell. "There are a total of ten people."

Footsteps from behind them caught their attention and a small man made of lean muscle waved as he approached, his brown eyes warm and kind. "Welcome to Harlow. Are you looking for anything specific?"

Blair looked around the area. "Harlow? I've never heard of that."

The man smiled, as if he knew his town was a glorified secret. "Most haven't, it's not on any maps."

Blair nodded in understanding, returning to his original question. "We aren't looking for anything specific. Thank you, though. We just figured we'd stop in as we passed."

The man nodded before giving a brief explanation of each building, some having dual purposes. Each one, a mini version of something you'd find in another town. After he was done, he bowed to them and returned to his station.

Damien watched him leave and then looked around. "This should be a fast run."

Agreeing, they broke into pairs. Rhea and Kael moved toward the tavern with the goal to stock up on different types of preserved foods. Marrow and Blake filled water flasks and stopped at the apothecary for any salves for common dangers. Damien and Blair passed the Blacksmith, where Damien paused for a moment and then groaned, moving to talk to him.

"Do you have any small blades?" Damien asked, eyeing the small set up.

The blacksmith was a big man with thick arms covered in different scars. He squinted at Damien, then stood and bent down. "Depends what you mean by small," he said, as he dug around different items. "Knife? Dagger? Are you looking to gut a fish, or take down a bear?"

Damien replied just as the Blacksmith stopped moving and looked up, waiting for an answer. "Something quick. Concealable."

The blacksmith scratched his beard before crouching back down. "Not much call for that kind of steel these days. Folks want blades they can show off." He pulled up a few worn knives and a rusted hunting dagger, laying them out one by one on the table next to him. They all seemed dull and ordinary.

Damien's expression didn't change, but the blacksmith must've caught something in his eyes, a hint of disappointment, because he hesitated. Then he reached down again, deeper this time, rummaging within another pile.

"Wait," he muttered. "There's one more, now that I think about it."

He drew out a small blade, sheathed in black leather, its hilt wrapped tight in cord. "This one isn't selling for that exact reason," the blacksmith said, turning it in his hand. "Traded off a traveler months back. Never seen metal like it. Cuts cleaner than it should."

Damien took it, testing the weight. He slid the blade half free, catching a glimpse of its mirrored surface. It gleamed dark and silver at once.

"Perfect," he murmured.

The blacksmith nodded, the corners of his mouth lifting just a little. "Didn't think anyone'd want such a strange thing. Guess it was waitin' for the right hand."

Damien handed over a few coins, silent again.

When they left the stand, Blair watched him with curiosity. "For someone who can conjure them whenever he wants, why would you *buy* one?"

Damien's reply was quiet but short. He cast a glance toward the far edge of the market, where Blake's laugh carried faintly from one of the buildings. "Veil it. I don't want Blake seeing."

Blair's grin widened. "Oh, It's for your boyfriend. Got it."

His narrowed eyes only made her smile grow as she mentally focused on the knife in his hands. It was gone in mere moments and even though it looked like he was moving air, he placed the knife in the back of his pants.

"There," she said proudly. "You're welcome."

By sunset, they were done and the supplies they had gathered had been organized into their packs.

The rations held them over for the next few days as they traveled without any real direction. They kept north, walking relentlessly, hoping for something that might help guide them. A strange quiet settled over the group as darkness fell, broken only by their footsteps.

Blair walked ahead of the rest, just behind Rhea. Silent and focused, she was straining for any type of inner voice. As she walked, Lailah's words replayed over and over in her mind. She knew this was the right thing to do, but her nerves still twisted with how long it had been.

A few steps behind her, Kael drifted closer to Damien. "Mind if I have a word?"

Damien didn't break stride, only flicked a glance toward him. He nodded once, permitting the conversation.

Kael's voice lowered, "We've passed that ridge twice now and the same smells keep coming back, like we're walking in circles."

Damien's jaw flexed. When he spoke, his words were steady. "She leads us. If you have questions, ask her." The weight behind his tone was unmistakable. "Whatever she decides is what we go with. If that means we walk ten miles, we walk ten miles, even if it *is* in circles. If you have an issue with that, figure it out now."

Kael stared ahead as his nostrils flared. Damien didn't look at him as he continued, "She's learning, not guessing. There's a reason behind the things she does. I'm assuming you haven't smelt anything too concerning."

Kael opened his mouth, then closed it again. Whatever argument that was still within him dissolved in the hush that followed.

Eventually, Kael took Rhea's place and Damien stepped up to Blair, brushing his shoulder against hers in a quiet reassurance. She glanced at him and her face softened slightly before turning back toward the path.

They continued until they found a small clearing suitable for rest. Tents were pitched and a fire soon crackled to life, breathing smoke into the stars that illuminated the sky above them.

Blair sat between Damien's legs, knees drawn up and her hand wrapped around a tin mug of lukewarm tea. The others were scattered in varying stages of rest, some speaking in low voices, others content with the silence.

"Alright," Blake announced suddenly, springing to his feet with a grin. "Time for another little game."

Blair narrowed her eyes. "What kind of game?"

He gave an exaggerated bow. "Throw your shadow daggers at me."

She stared at him in disbelief. "You want me to throw knives at you?"

"Calm down," he said, waving a hand. "You won't be able to hit me. Rules are simple. You miss, I win. You hit me, you win."

Damien glanced up, faint amusement tugging at his expression. "What does she get if she wins?"

Blake grinned wider. "Anything she wants. Come on, fearless leader. Let's show them what real skill is."

There was a brief pause. Then, to everyone's surprise, Blair stood, and rolled her shoulders. "Alright, try not to cry when I cut you."

All members of the group stirred, rising from their seats to watch. Blake shifted into a loose, cocky stance. Blair's hand shimmered as a blade of shadow formed in her grip. In a sharp notion, she hurled the first dagger.

Blake vanished in a blink, reappearing ten paces to the left.

"Too slow!" he taunted.

Two more daggers formed instantly, one landed high, the other low. Blake dodged both.

"Time to actually try," Blair said, already shaping the next blade between her fingers.

They went several rounds. Each throw was met with a shadowstep and Blake appearing in different patches of brush or dirt. The others smiled at the show, even Marrow who heckled him every time he stumbled or reappeared in a bush. Rhea cracked a smile when one dagger shaved the side of his shirt.

He looked down, just as the next dagger flew through the air with deadly precision, opening a shallow line on Blake's cheek.

He froze. "Okay. Alright. You win."

Blair smirked and tossed the last dagger into the dirt where it fizzled out.

"Thanks for the confidence boost," she said, returning to the fire. "I win. Now pay up."

Annoyed, Blake wiped his cheek. "Is my blood not enough for you?" "What more could the princess want?"

Blair formed a smaller shadow dagger and twirled it in the air. "She wants a secret."

The others, who had just settled back around the fire, listened intently. Blake stood with his eyebrows raised and cocked his head to one side. "A secret?"

"You said whatever the *princess* wants." Blair reminded, pointing her blade at him in warning.

He swore under his breath. "Fine. I am nothing but a man of my word."

24

Blake sighed dramatically. "Alright. One time, when I was nine, I swallowed a spider, and it came up through my nose." He then rubbed his hands together as if he had fulfilled his duty.

"Blake." Blair said, narrowing her eyes at him.

He cracked a grin at her in response. "Okay, okay." The humor faded from his face as he leaned forward, elbows on his knees. "My brother and I used to sneak out past curfew to watch the stars. We climbed the roof of our house and nearly broke our necks doing it. He asked me why some were so bright. I told him that only babies could see the light and the older you got, the more they dimmed." A faint smile tugged at his mouth for a moment before it slipped. His gaze then drifted toward the flames, unfocused. His jaw tightened and then he blinked hard a few times.

Marrow shifted next to him, clearing her throat. "I entered the Void camp because Shiloh found me after there was an incident in my town." She took a small breath to which Blake put his hand on her thigh. "My powers awoke during my first nightmare, one that I accidentally portrayed to those around me. Everyone thought they were still dreaming but they were really just stuck in the hallucinations my fear had created." Her eyes lowered to the floor as she continued, "They tore each other apart while I screamed for them to stop. I didn't mean to cast anything. I didn't even know I could."

Everyone was quiet for a moment as they watched her.

"Shiloh and Kael found me sitting in the center of it all. Everyone was dead by that point. I didn't even know what was real until he put his cloak around me." She straightened her spine, as if strengthening herself from the inside. "He took me back to his camp and taught me how to control it, to manifest on purpose. That's my secret."

Kael smiled softly at her. "Your's is tragic, mine is just weird."

Marrow elbowed him, and he chuckled. "Shiloh wasn't my father. I spent most of my childhood running from the King and his poisoned scent." He wrinkled his nose like the thought disgusted him. "I found the camp right before I turned thirteen. I stumbled upon the forcefield after finding a new scent I had never experienced. It smelled like home, like safety. I stayed there for two days before they finally accepted me. Honestly, I think Shiloh only did it because I wouldn't stop sniffing around."

Rhea snorted. "That tracks."

Kael nudged her next. "You're up."

She rolled her eyes. "They know my secret."

He stared pointedly until she looked over at him and groaned. "Fine." She let out a loud sigh before beginning. "I was raised in a wealthy household where our faces were widely recognized. We were well known within large circles, who taught about the divine nature. I grew up quickly realizing that any type of weakness meant a stain on our name." She exhaled through her nose. "On my sixth birthday, the family cook burned my cake."

Blair remembered this part; Rhea had told it before.

"And I cried," Rhea said simply. "I mean, I was six and heartbroken. My sadness manifested as shields." She gestured to her chin, where a faint sheen glinted under the firelight. "To my family, who had never known shadows to exist, I was evil. A curse; something to be cleansed. They consulted within their circles and decided fire was the best option, to burn away the sin." Rhea's mouth twitched, not into a smile but something colder. "I was held down by our maids while my father poured gasoline on me." She then paused for a moment. "Funny enough," Rhea added quietly, "it was Adriel's flame that put mine out."

At that, Adriel stood, the shadows around him flickering as if drawn toward her grief. He placed a steady hand on her shoulder. "I guess that leaves me then."

Bringing his hand up, a black flame grew out of it. "My fire erupted the day my town was attacked by the King," he said, voice deep. "Hunters searched it, looking for Shadowborn. I was too young to help so I had to watch as they beat my family and friends." He paused then, squeezing Rhea's shoulder who nodded up to him. "I thought the worst had passed, until two Hunters made me watch as they took turns with my sister without her permission."

Damien's shadows spread silently below him, swirling around on the ground in angry coils.

Adriel noticed out of the corner of his eye but continued talking. "They ended up staying behind to enjoy their fun as the King moved on to the town beside us. I exploded into flames and burnt them to the ground as they begged for mercy," he said flatly, letting the flames move up his arm. "But nothing undid that day. Things got better when Shiloh found me after I was caught committing arson," he continued. "He knew I was broken." His gaze shifted to Blair then. "I left with him immediately and I've never looked back."

Blair gave him a small, grateful smile before scanning the others. "You guys are all amazing and have lived through so much."

Rhea shifted, clearly uncomfortable. "If nothing happens by morning, I think we need to make a plan Blair, a real one."

Blair nodded. "We'll regroup at dawn." She watched as Rhea turned away. "Thanks for telling us your story Rhea." Rhea paused and gave a short nod before continuing.

Damien rose next. "I'll take the first watch once I get her to bed." He held his hand out to Blair. She took it and stood.

The air grew colder as they walked away from the fire. Inside their tent, Blair sat at the edge of her bedroll, staring into the dark.

Damien settled beside her.

"They've all been through so much." After a second, her voice dropped low. "What if I'm leading them the wrong way?" She looked at him, shadows softening her features. "Those people believe in me, even after the personal hells they went through. I'm starting to think I'm letting them down. You heard Kael earlier."

He squeezed her leg as he spoke. "You're not letting them down. They wouldn't even be here if it wasn't for you."

She sighed before looking at him. "What if the shadows made a mistake?"

"They didn't." He leaned closer, voice low. "Each of us has a different strength. I'll keep reminding you of yours, until you believe it. You were meant for this. You were meant to be the light for them Blair. A group of *Shadowborn* just talked about their darkest secrets because you make them want to be better, just like you want to be better." He then looked at her in a way that seemed like he was baring his soul to her. " That's who you are and because of that, I'd follow you without the shadows, without the mark, without anything else."

Blair said nothing as she moved, giving Damien several small kisses as she fought back tears. After a moment of him holding her, they laid down together. "So, the knife is for Blake?"

He sighed, like he was irritated with himself for being nice. "Yeah, I want to imbue it for him. I was going to try some methods during my shifts."

Blake's laughter drifted from the fire, likely at Adriel's expense. Rhea's voice followed, lighter than it had been in days.

"Look at you, being so nice." Blair yawned as her eyes fluttered closed, the sound outside filling her with happiness. Soon, her breaths were long and deep.

Damien watched her for a few more moments before tucking the blanket in around her and leaving to start his watch.

<u>25</u>

Blair woke to a calm stillness.

She lay beneath the thin blanket, just listening. The movement around her consisted of layered sounds. At first it was just the soft rustle of leaves, then the clinking of metal. After another moment, she registered the faint rise and fall of the voices of her team. They were all awake, which meant they were probably waiting for her *again*.

She sat up, rubbing a hand over her face. Yet another night had passed with no vision, and no help of any kind. She'd hoped for some scrap of reassurance, some hint of the next step, and yet, the dagger remained silent, its usual heat and hum, dormant. It was as if the mark was waiting for her to figure it out herself. Although the more she thought about it, it didn't feel like abandonment, it felt like a test.

She stretched and stood. *You're not always going to be led*, she thought. *Sometimes you'll have to choose to move anyway.*

She dressed in practiced motions, fingers tugging at buckles, tightening straps, tying her boots with a final, firm knot. She took a steadying breath as she readied herself for the day.

One more day, she decided, the small voice inside more of a gut instinct than feeling. *She would just need to convince the others.*

Blair stepped out of the tent and shielded her eyes. The clearing had been washed over with pale light and everyone seemed to move a little lighter than the day before.

Blake was crouched near Marrow, tossing jokes at her. To his disdain, her features never budged.

"Are you sure this one has feelings?" Blake asked dramatically, noticing Blair, "I think she may be defective."

"She is definitely defective if she puts up with you," Kael muttered. "She has patience, I'll give her that, but I'm surprised she hasn't hit you yet," he continued, flipping something in a pan over the fire. "That's what I'm looking forward to."

Marrow gave Kael a smile, which made Blake scoff.

Damien and Rhea shared a flat rock, both sharpening blades in companionable silence. Sparks flared briefly as their hands moved in unison.

As Blair approached, Damien looked up at her. "Morning."

The others around echoed it, in their own ways.

Blair kissed Damien's cheek and waved to the rest of them. "Smells good," she said, nodding to Kael and the pan he held.

"Smells burnt and stale, but it'll be edible," Kael replied.

"Barely," Adriel added, gathering plates.

They ate quickly in a loose circle. The food was warm, but definitely burnt. Blair chuckled as the men described it as a root mash with something Kael claimed was "forest spice."

As the last bites were taken and the fire slowly died down, all eyes turned to Blair.

Looking at Damien first, her head turned to the others. "We will travel one more day."

Kael tensed, just slightly. There was no challenge in his movement, but Blair still noticed. "I know we're tired and it feels like we're chasing nothing, but I need one more day," she said. "We keep our path. If we find nothing by dusk, we stop and make a new plan, a different direction."

There was a pause, a moment where silence balanced on the edge of decision.

Then Damien gave a single nod.

"Sounds fair," Adriel said, already accepting the plan.

Kael gave the faintest sigh but rose with the others. "One more day."

Blake saluted with a fork, tilting his head toward the pale woman beside him. "If we die, I better get a smile before my eyes close."

Marrow looked at him from the corner of her eye, and took another bite.

They packed with practiced speed, tightening bedrolls and adjusting bags. They set out a few minutes later, boots meeting dirt, as they started down the trail.

Rhea led the way, her braid swinging as she stepped over a fallen log. Kael followed in silence, pausing now and then to smell toward the trees around him. Behind them trailed Blair, Marrow, and Adriel, voices low.

Damien walked near the back with Blake. Everything was quiet between them until he reached for his belt.

Blake noticed, eyes narrowing slightly. "What's that?"

Damien didn't answer. Instead, he extended the gift out.

Blake slowed, brow furrowed. "You're giving me something?"

Damien's gaze flicked up, then back to the path.

Blake reached out, hesitating for a fraction of a second before taking it. The moment his fingers closed around the hilt, shadows rippled across the blade like smoke. They twisted and breathed along the edge, wrapping it in darkness.

Blake stopped dead.

"What-" His voice caught. He looked at the weapon, then at Damien. His usual grin was gone, replaced by something raw and unguarded. "How did you do this?"

Damien shrugged, eyes still fixed forward. "It was something to keep me busy during the night shifts."

"Are you serious?" Blake's tone cracked between disbelief and awe. "You imbued it?"

"Mm." Damien's response was almost bored, but there was the faintest twitch at the corner of his mouth. "Don't make a big deal of it."

Blake stared at him, still not moving. "You can't just hand me something like this and say 'don't make a big deal.' Do you even see-?"

Damien finally looked over at him. "Thanks for protecting her."

Blake's mouth fell open, but no words came. For once, he was completely speechless and his eyes filled with different emotions.

Rhea called from ahead, "You two coming? Or do you need to pitch a tent for some alone time."

Blake turned to her. "*Actually*, Marrow might just have some competition now." He looked down again at the blade, still glowing faintly in his hand. When he looked back up, Damien was already walking away, shoulders relaxed, shadows licking faintly at his boots.

Blake jogged to catch up, still holding the weapon like it might vanish if he let it go. "You know," he said after a moment, voice quieter now, "I don't really- I don't know what to say."

"Good," Damien murmured. "Just stop talking then."

Blake laughed softly, "You're a bastard."

By the afternoon, the early-morning confidence had thinned and Blair started to doubt herself. Right as she convinced herself to make a different plan, the forest opened onto a lake. Pines ringed the shore and a waterfall spilled from a rocky cliff on the opposite side, pushing waves up on the thin beach that surrounded it.

Blake whooped, dumped his gear, and impulsively dove in. "Gods, that's good!" he shouted out as he emerged. "Come on, Marrow! You're missing it!"

Marrow didn't move. "Missing what, exactly?"

"The best damn part of being alive!" Blake grinned, sweeping his arm through the water in a dramatic arc.

Marrow rolled her eyes but a small smile betrayed her, one she hid as she turned away from him. In one motion, she stripped the black dress that clung to her body. Stepping in, the water rose to her knees, then her hips, and then she vanished beneath it completely, resurfacing with a sharp inhale.

Blake caught her at the waist as she came up, spinning her around. She shrieked, splashing at him. "Put me down, idiot!"

"You say that," he teased, "but I can hear the joy in your voice!"

His laughter carried across the clearing, up to the others who had yet to join.

Rhea crouched, watching the water for potential danger. After a few moments, she looked back at the others on the beach. "We can take some time here. The water is clean."

Kael was the first to approach, his sharp eyes scanning the edges before he crouched down. "That means it's safe enough for me." He reached forward, and wafted the air above the water up to his nose. "Moss, newts, and trout," he murmured, unfastening his boots.

Beside him, Rhea followed suit, rolling her pants up to her knees. As the water washed over her ankles, she inhaled softly.

"It's warm," she said, almost surprised. "Didn't expect that."

At the edge of the sand behind her, Blair sat down on the bank. Pulling her arms up to rest on her knees, she watched the ripples of sunlight on the water's surface. As Blake and Marrow battled, she smiled.

Damien stood behind her, arms folded. "You know, you could join them." Blair let out a soft scoff as she internally debated it. "Come on, let go a little." he coaxed, slightly pushing his knee into her back.

Blair looked up at him, his smile settling her thoughts. She then shifted and looked out to those around her. Rhea's feet were still in the shallows with Kael beside her. Marrow splashed Blake hard enough to make him choke, which made her outright laugh and snort. A look of pure joy rose on Blake's face as he dove for her again, squealing like an excited child.

"Fine." Blair sighed, wanting to be part of the fun. "But you come with me."

"I'd expect nothing less," he said, offering his hand.

He didn't say anything as she stepped them closer to the water. Even kept quiet as she dropped her shorts and lifted her tank top above her head. He followed her moves, and stripped down to his trousers.

She smiled faintly as they stepped in together. "Not bad." she admitted.

Damien crouched. "Told you," he said, running his fingers through the water.

Adriel appeared then, shedding his coat and rolling up his sleeves. He knelt by the shallows, cupping water into his hands and pouring it over his face. A sigh left him, long and genuine. "It's nice to finally feel clean."

Blair went to agree with him but a shout stole her attention.

"Adriel! You're next!" Blake yelled in warning.

Adriel barely had time to react before a wall of water hit him square in the chest, soaking him instantly. For the first time, Adriel laughed at the attack, a real laugh, low and rare.

Kael just shook his head, murmuring, "Children."

Blair waded deeper, the water stroking her skin, everywhere except the Mark which seemed to be heat for the first time in days. She thought she even felt the area around the dagger begin to pulse.

Something dark shimmered below the surface, next to her. A plume of black that was soft and slow, emerging from the lake floor. Trusting her gut, she dragged her hand across the surface and the water reacted. The murky black substance started to disperse, coiling around her hand and fanning outward in a ripple. It moved from her to Damien and soon, the entire lake started to darken. As it reached them, Blake stopped moving and Rhea called out, halting them from moving.

As the darkness covered the whole lake, bubbles started to form. In random small areas across the lake, the water started to boil. At first the water simply churned, as if agitated but then it sprayed as human-shaped forms rose from the turmoil, cloaked in darkness. A total of six figures rose from the surface of the water and moved toward the Shadowborn.

As if they had been together their whole lives, the Shadowborn stepped into formation around Blair. Rhea's armor, along with a wall of shadow from Damien, created a defensive barrier around them all.

Blair watched the figures approach. With each step they took, her dagger pulsed. *That was no coincidence, not when it had acted like this at each camp.* "Hold," she said, barely above a breath. Everyone around her heard, and obeyed.

Giving Damien a small glance, Blair stepped around the people protecting her and toward the giants. Up close, it was obvious they were not human. Their forms shifted and moved as if made my shadows. There was no solid base for them. Instead, they were formed by many layers of darkness that folded over each other, always moving. They were completely still as she took another step.

She stood directly in front of one now, watching it carefully. Slowly, it looked down at her and then bent to bow to her. As Blair felt Damien reach her side, she looked at the other dark figures. One by one they followed, before turning and wading toward the waterfall. As they neared, the dark water that spilt over, separated, revealing a cavern.

Blair moved without thinking, just like Damien knew she would. They walked together until the bottom of the lake fell away, and then they swam. Rhea looked to Adriel who understood her expression. Tossing bags and clothes over to her, Kael grabbed some and brought up the rear. They joined the others, supplies above their heads.

Under the fall, the pool of water eventually shallowed and led them into a cave. Blair broke the surface first, stepping onto the cool ground. Damien emerged beside her as Blake and Marrow came next. Rhea and Kael set the bags down and threw clothes to their owners.

The space behind the waterfall was vast. Black granite covered the walls, veined with purple crystal shards. It was a massive area that was entirely lit by torches.

Damien wrung his shirt, and pulled it on, as he looked around. Blair did the same as she twisted her hair up. Each of them scanning, as they shouldered their packs and moved deeper.

Blair nodded as her eyes fell on shadowed figures gathered at the back, the same ones that had led them here. She grabbed Damien's attention, nudging him. The passage funneled them deeper, the veins twisting and turning. The small space was illuminated entirely by a purple glow, much like the one behind her dagger mark. It wasn't long before the space opened into something close to a cathedral, built by time, instead of hands. The top opened to the sky, the ridges covered in vines that fell from the roof. Along the edges of the room, Blair could just make out the figures of more shadows, along with another cluster that guarded a narrow doorway.

As they fully entered the room, a line of them parted and a man stepped from the dark. His skin was rough, as if he had seen many battles. A short silver beard framed his mouth, and though his expression rested somewhere between weariness and curiosity, there was no mistaking the sharpness in his gaze. He moved with a fluid grace, dressed in black cloth woven with thread that seemed to shimmer like the purple on the walls. His face was strong, almost ageless.

"She who seeks the night," he said, his voice low. "You've come at last." He then looked at each of them and greeted them, calling them by name.

Rhea stepped forward, armor whispering into place. "How do you know who we are?"

He smiled faintly. "I've known you were coming for some time now. I'm lucky enough to learn many things from my *friends*." Gesturing with his hand, he pointed around the room to the dark figures. "They mainly act as my guardians but they can also explore and bring back valuable information."

With that, one of the largest ones stepped up next to him. At about ten feet, this shadow had more defined human features than the rest. His face was round with high cheek bones and deep eyes. Defined muscles covered his body and as Blair looked closer, she could almost make out small features such as a ring on his finger.

"I'm Malrik." The man next to the shadow continued, his gaze finding Blair. "And these are my shadows. Please think of them as my extensions, they will not harm you."

Damien scoffed, his eyes scanning the figures that outnumbered them. "And you just expect us to believe that?"

"Well," Malrik looked around the room before nodding in the direction of Blair, "I expect her too."

Damien turned his head, waiting for some kind of direction from Blair. She released a deep sigh right as her thigh began to throb. Dipping her chin, she nodded slightly, signaling her approval. One by one, Malrik's guardians disappeared into his own shadow that spread across the floor. "Why don't we start by letting me show you around?"

Blair had chosen to listen to her mark but she also knew how important it was that she was smart about it. Stepping back, she created room for Rhea and Damien to move in front of her. As they did so, they nodded to Malrik who led them through the doorway.

Beyond the initial room, there was a small chamber that branched into separate halls. Malrik took an immediate left into a large domed room where more purple veins cascaded down the walls. Several beds occupied the space along with a few dressers, much like a bunker.

"If you choose to stay, this is where you'll sleep. I have other rooms as well, once you are comfortable enough to split up. I would suggest dropping your belongings until you decide."

Kael heaved his bag over his shoulder and stepped up to Malrik. With as much air as he could inhale, he smelt him, swiveling his head in front of his chest. Clicking his tongue, he moved around the room, inhaling the fabric on the beds and in wood on the dressers. Once done, he nodded at Rhea who moved to claim a bed. The others followed suit.

Blair shimmied her bag off and placed it on the orange, cloth sheets that were closest to her. Running her hand over the bed, she felt the weight of Damien's bag next to hers.

Throwing his bag across the room, Blake stretched across the farthest bed, cuddling the blankets like he was already familiar with it. Rhea was the only one who remained standing, quietly setting her bag on the bed that was left.

"I want you all to become familiar with the area and the shadows that dwell here. As I said before, they are an extension of me. They do my bidding and follow my will, which means they will never approach you unless I have sent them. Their presence is purely a defense, not a danger." Blair nodded slightly as Malrik ran his gaze over the others, checking for their understanding.

As they grouped together and stepped out to follow him, one shadow reappeared next to him. This one was short and stockier.

Blair imagined them hidden, watching and waiting.

He had mentioned that they knew information from collecting it. Had these things really been following them the whole time?

That seemed impossible, especially since Kael and Blake hadn't mentioned anything.

As if he had guessed her thoughts, Malrik took a moment to explain more about the shadows. "What you are witnessing is the ability to raise shadows using the mark of Night. I do not carry that gift, but the shadows around me were activated because of it. Whether it is someone else's shadow or your own, it lets you extend yourself and your power. It is a rare power that only some can control but if you learn how, you gain untraceable shadows."

Moving down the hallways, Malrik pointed out the other bedrooms, a kitchen, and what amounted to underground showers. The floorplan was much like a maze with each path leading to a different room.

After showing them everything, he encouraged them to explore on their own before leaving them to decide.

Adriel was the first to speak. "You trust this, Blair?

Blair looked at Kael and then back at Adriel, giving him a small smile. "In this world, trust is a luxury we can't afford. We survive on instinct and nothing more. The mark was telling me to listen, so I did."

Rhea gave a small smile and turned back toward their room. "That's good enough for me. I'm headed back to the room, I'm sure we'll have lots of time to get lost in here."

Adriel and Kael gave a quick nod before running after Rhea.

Blake looked over at Marrow and grabbed her hand as he ventured down another hallway. "Let's go on an adventure, bug."

Blair looked over at Damien who gestured to the opposite hallway. Blair smiled and took his hand, as they started their exploration.

They had found supply closets, pantries, and extra rooms where old boxes were stored. From the surface, it seemed like Malrik had nothing to hide, not even weapons.

A few small rooms later, they walked into a large stone chamber where someone sat cross-legged on a stone dais, eyes fixed on the faint glow of purple veins tracing the walls.

Blair sighed and called to Malrik, who looked over at them. "I want to know more about the Mark of Night."

.

26

Malrik chuckled softly. "I knew it wouldn't be too long."

Blair raised her eyebrow as he hopped off the stone and gestured for her to sit next to it. Blair did so, as Damien positioned himself against the wall.

Fixing her eyes ahead on Malrik, she stilled her body, besides the occasional glance to Damien.

"You're here because of the Mark of Night. The gift of extending yourself and your power, like I explained earlier. As challenging as it can be, I'd like to teach you if you are open to it."

Blair's reply was quick. "I am. I'd like to learn everything there is to know."

A small shadow drifted from Damien to Blair, in reassurance.

Malrik watched as it formed around her ankle and slid up her leg. "You see, our shadows tend to have a will of their own, almost like a personality." He looked over at Damien. "Much like your need to protect her, your shadows feel that also."

Damien turned to Blair. "So, that can either be a good or bad thing for you. Your shadows came from the dagger, which means they will either mimic the original four or forge a new personality that is like yours. Maybe that's why they've been easier for you to control all along."

Malrik remained silent for a moment before speaking directly to Damien. "Is the darkness hard for *you* to carry?"

Damien's gaze flicked up to Malrik but he didn't respond.

After a moment, Malrik nodded slowly. "That makes sense. Most who bear it lose themselves long before your age."

Blair frowned and looked back and forth between the two men. "Bear what? Shadows?"

Malrik didn't answer her directly, instead his eyes remained on Damien. "*His* type of shadows, yes."

Damien hesitated as his jaw tensed. "I have no more trouble than anyone else with this gift."

Malrik gave a soft, humorless smile. "You cannot lump those who have shadows together. They all hunger in their own way. You can leash them, yes, but they'll always pull toward what they're made for." His voice lowered. "Especially for those tied to the lineage of Idris."

The name hung in the air like a heavy weight.

Blair looked between them one more time before resting her eyes on Damien. She had already known this, or *guessed* it, because of the dream. She also had *already* tried bringing it up to him.

Damien had yet to say anything but somehow, Malrik understood his expression. "You didn't know? The mark of void runs through your bloodline. It's what makes your darkness restless."

Damien's shoulders stiffened, but he didn't look away. "You're mistaken.".

"My shadows had already guessed, but the moment you showed up here, I knew." Malrik leaned forward slightly, his tone still gentle but unrelenting. "Your shadows move as if they are alive. Are they trying to devour?"

Blair's lips parted as she turned toward Damien who refused to answer. The shadows along his arms coiled slowly, curling over his skin as his emotions rose.

Malrik's gaze softened as he watched the swirling blackness expand over Damien. "Perhaps they don't crave to take, but create? I hear you manifest things."

Blair inhaled, realization dawning. She whispered, "Damien," as her eyes flicked to his hands and the variety of items his shadows had formed.

Damien's expression faltered, the faintest sign of realization that it could potentially be true. He looked down at his arms where the shadows had begun to twist tighter, as if listening. "That doesn't mean-"

"It means what you want it too," Malrik said softly. "I am only letting you know."

For a long moment, no one spoke, as time was given to process. Finally, Damien exhaled and lowered his gaze. The shadows on his skin pulsed once, then receded.

His voice was steady but detached. "Even if what you say has truth, I would rather only focus on Blair."

Malrik tilted his head. "You would deny claiming your blood? Your title?"

"I would do anything I needed to, for *her*," Damien replied, eyes shifting toward Blair. "That's all that matters now."

Blair didn't look away as his eyes held hers, the tether they held unbreakable.

Malrik nodded slowly, the faintest glimmer of respect in his expression. "Then we'll speak of it no further." He turned to Blair, "What would you like to learn first?"

Blair placed her hand on Damien's thigh. "Anything I need to know before we start?"

"From the very beginning, it is vital that you think of them as part of you. They are not a separate entity, but something that can be voluntarily freed. You have to trust them." He lowered his hand and closed his eyes. "That will be the first thing I have you do, just listen to them and understand who they are."

Determined to jumpstart the process, Blair willed herself to reach inside and feel the presence of her shadows. Both Malrik and Damien sat quietly, allowing her to attempt the process. Minutes soon turned into an hour and yet still, there was no connection, or at least not the one Malrik described.

The more she sat, the more the voices in her head multiplied. She tried to pull from the strategies Marrow had taught her, but it wasn't long before she just couldn't sit still. The silence felt like a weight pressing down, and the empty space between her and her shadow seemed to mock her.

"There's nothing there, at all," she muttered as she finally opened her eyes.

Just as she was about to close her eyes again and push harder, Malrik's voice cut through her frustration. "We have plenty of time to develop this, there is no need to rush." With that piece of reassurance, he stood.

"But I need to-"

"No," Malrik interrupted gently. "Forcing it now will only push it further away. Your shadow is part of you, yes, but you need to remember that it responds to patience and presence, not desperation."

Blair swallowed her next word, rubbing her tired hands over her face. "Tomorrow?" she asked quietly.

Malrik nodded. "Yes. Rest now. Let your mind and spirit settle."

She offered a reluctant nod, standing slowly. She looked up at Damien who said nothing but followed her and Malrik out of the room. "I'm still proud of you." he whispered, as they moved out of the space.

"I'm proud of *you*," Blair said back, "You handled all of that Idris stuff well."

Damien shook his head slightly, "No, I handle *you* well." His words dismissing the topic, yet again.

As they walked, Blair eyed the darkened forms that seemed to live in every corner. "I can't imagine what it takes to control all of these."

With those words, Malrik stopped and turned toward her, his expression shifted into one filled with sadness. "These shadows you see are not mine, but I do not control them. I call them extensions, but they are the shadows from my people." He turned, looking at them one by one. "I led them into a situation we could not win. They fell, but their shadows attached themselves to me so that I could survive."

"A shadow oath?" Adriel's voice broke through the quiet, approaching them from the other side of the hallway.

Malrik shook his head slowly. "No. I believe it was a choice made after death. A bond forged in loss that was sealed because of the Mark of Night."

Blair watched as his expression darkened from the memory. "The process to learn will take control and strength. I have no doubt you can do it." Blair nodded as he continued, "These two are my personal guards. They will be assigned to you during your stay."

"Is there a need for that?" Damien asked, eyeing the shadows behind Blair.

"I think it's reasonable to say that nothing is completely safe. I would rather be proactive and have measures in place." Malrik replied.

Blair gave a quick 'thank you' before the shadows slipped behind her and blended into her own that was flickering on the ground.

Blair and Damien soon excused themselves, leading Adriel back to the room. Blair crossed the threshold first, her eyes scanning over the others that occupied it.

Blake dropped onto his bed with a groan and Kael leaned against the cold wall, arms folded. "We shouldn't get comfortable yet."

Damien was silent, lowering himself onto the edge of bed. Looking up, he gave Blair a look.

Blair sat next to him, looking at Kael. "Malrik is going to train me. My guess is we will be here for a little while."

Rhea nodded. "The bunker's reinforced. Plus, he has food stores that should last."

A faint movement caught Blair's attention. From beneath the heavy steel door, a stream of darkness began to pool across the floor. It slithered forward, coiling until it rose, and took on a vague, humanoid form.

Blake's hand went instinctively to his blade before Blair raised a hand to stop him. "It's really hard to believe these things are *friendly*," he muttered.

The shadow turned, stretching one arm toward the hallway and gestured toward it.

Blair stood up. "I think it wants to take us somewhere."

Adriel eyed it with suspicion, "For once, I have to agree with pretty boy over there, I don't love this."

As each of them stood and gathered together, Blake elbowed Marrow and whispered. "Did you hear that? He thinks I'm pretty. You better do something about that."

Marrow simply shook her head and walked right past them and up to Blair.

Without another word, the group moved as one through the twisting tunnels as they followed.

At last, the corridor opened into the underground kitchen. The air smelled inside faintly of dust and herbs. The shadow slipped beneath the far counter, then vanished, as Malrik stepped out.

"Hungry?"

27

Malrik moved easily around the small, stone room. His hands were steady as he prepared a simple meal over a low flame. The scent of roasted root vegetables and fresh herbs filled the air.

Blair, Damien, and the others had settled at a rough-hewn wooden table in the center of the room, which Malrik had slowly started to fill with food.

Rhea looked over the plates cautiously, even after Kael had checked them. Damien watched and picked up a plate first, filling it with different items. After his first bite, the others followed.

It didn't take long for everyone to finish. The meal was not one meant for long discussions, just a simple form of hospitality from Malrik.

Surprisingly, his shadows also showed this, as Rhea stood to dispose of her plate. Walking out from the walls, two walked around the table, taking dirty plates from the Shadowborn's hands. Another one moved quickly to clean the mess from cooking. The Shadowborn just watched in fascination.

In between his last bites, Malrik looked up from the table. "I told you, they will bring no harm."

After the food was cleared and the shadows had dispersed, the group said goodnight to Malrik and made their way to their room.

Everyone settled in quietly, except for Blake, who yelled almost instantly as he walked into the room that housed their beds. Marrow's items had been moved to Rhea's, which caused an immediate dramatic outburst from him. Grabbing her things, he tossed them back with his.

"I'm not sharing my bed with you." Marrow said, leveling a look at him.

"I'm sorry that you think you have a choice," Blake shot back with a sly grin, "now get your pasty ass over here." He lay on the bed, pulling her down by the wrist. Her body fought against him for just a few moments before she surrendered and cuddled into him.

Blair watched the events unfold with a small smile as Damien sat beside her. The others paid no mind to the two and the cat and mouse chase that was ensuing. Lanterns were blown out and soon, the room fell into a thick darkness.

Blair counted the minutes until she heard soft snores from multiple people. Yet, her eyes remained wide open, tracing the shapes she could barely make out of the darkness. She remained still, hoping sleep would find her but as hard as she tried, it refused to come.

About thirty minutes later, she felt the bed shift beside her as Damien pulled her closer, his breath warm against her ear.

"Can't sleep?" he whispered.

Blair shook her head silently, heart fluttering.

A soft smile touched his lips as he brushed his mouth against her ear. "That's something I can definitely help with. Follow me."

She fought him as he tried to roll out of the bed. "Damien, we can't just-"

"Oh, really?" he teased, pulling her out of bed and into the hallway. He moved down the hall, leading her by the hand, and entered an empty room off to the side. Closing the door behind them, he kissed her as her back hit the wall. She turned her head as he moved down her neck, and her eyes rolled in anticipation. His fingers then brushed lightly against her thigh, like a gentle question. "Are you sure we can't?"

A flicker of movement in the corner reminded Blair of how many shadows were hidden here, including the two that now followed her. "Malrik has eyes everywhere."

Damien's voice was low, and filled with need. "Then let him watch."

That was all it took. Without hesitation, Blair parted her legs, welcoming his touch. His rough hand traced her thighs before moving in between them. He used one finger to trace her over shorts before he moved them over and ran his finger against her most sensitive part. A small gasp broke from her lips as Damien slid his hand over her mouth."Shhh."

Starting in small circles, the intimacy was almost too much, and her body shuddered with warmth as heat began to coil low. He moved slowly at first and then faster, building anticipation and making her bud swell with need. Once he got her close, her body would brace but then he would stop abruptly, causing a stifled whimper.

Kissing her cheek, he moved his mouth back to her ear. "I love those goddamn sounds."

Her body felt it, a tightening low in her belly. As if he knew, he picked up speed, coaxing the orgasm out of her as she came on his fingers. As it hit, her legs gave out and shadows formed, bracing her against the wall as she shook. A mischievous smile flashed on his face, as he moved his mouth to hers and grazed her lips. "When I know for sure that no one's watching, I'm going to worship you." With that, he raised his fingers to his mouth and sucked them.

He then kissed her slowly, gripping her thighs. "As soon as I have that chance, I'm going to take it, but for right now, we're going back to the room and you're going to go to sleep."

Blair whimpered into his mouth as he kissed her again. A low growl formed in his throat. "I swear to every god out there, if you don't turn around and walk away from me right now, I'm going to get on my knees right now."

Blair squealed as Damien grabbed her hips and turned her, pushing his full erection into her backside. She giggled and started to run back to the room.

As they settled back into bed, she could feel how much that release had helped ease her. "Go to sleep, feisty."

It wasn't long until she obeyed, falling asleep with a mischievous smile on her face.

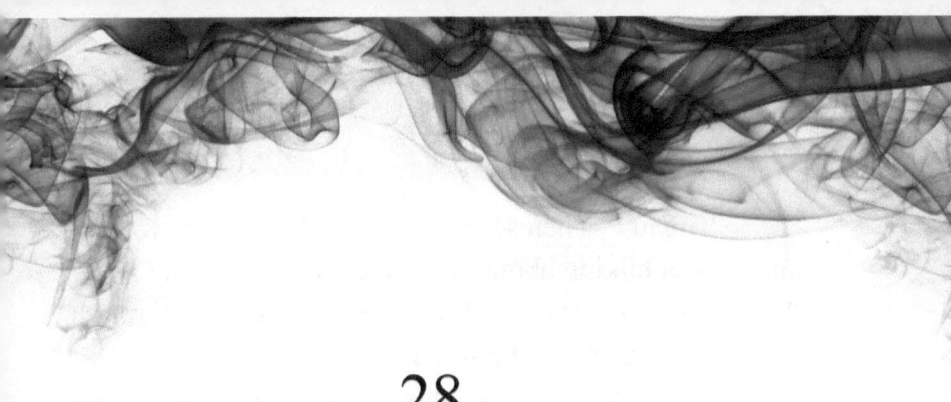

28

The room was silent as Blair sat on the cool floor, her palms resting gently on her knees. It was day one of training and the room they were in was dark, aside from the purple pulse of light from the cracks in the walls. Across from her was Malrik. He sat unmoving, his eyes closed in deep focus. It had been this way most of the morning.

After finally putting some trust in Malrik, Damien had dropped her off first thing, and then left with Blake. Since the first camp, they had made time to train with each other. Finding areas where Damien could continue to push his boundaries with his shadows and transformation. The last thing Blair had learned was that he could now call on his wings willingly, without them being formed by a strong emotion.

She was proud of him and the way he worked hard, but selfishly, she always felt better when he was with her. Without him, everything seemed dull.

She peeked one eye open as her mind, yet again, wandered away from the task at hand.

"Close your eyes," Malrik said softly. "You have to begin with quiet."

Blair let her out a small sigh before she tried again.

"Breathe. Then search and find the shadow within you. I'm not talking about the power that you hold. I'm asking you to find its actual form. You must listen through the quiet and the space between you."

Blair inhaled deeply, pushing down the noise in her mind. Her thoughts were everywhere all the time, and that was a problem. *What does this power mean? What happens if I'm not what they think?* She dug beneath it all, pushing past the fear and noise until there was a small flicker of something.

There, past everything in her mind was a faint and wispy presence. It was small, but it was *there*.

"I see something," she whispered.

Malrik's eyes opened, glowing faintly in the low light. "Describe it."

"It's not a shape exactly, it's fuzzy. Almost like a ripple in the air or an electric current. It's not moving, it's just watching."

`A slow nod came from him, as if he understood what she was describing. "Good. That's the shadow presenting itself to you."

Blair blinked her eyes open, surprised to realize she had been holding her breath.

"Now we move on to step two." Malrik said, standing.

Blair followed him to a wide ring of ash drawn on the floor. At the center of the ring, a single candle burned with purple flame.

"You seem to struggle with drowning everything out. We need to get that under control. This is a power drawn by intention, and that's exactly where your problem is. I want you to walk the circle and focus on one thing as you watch the flame. Between the movement and the visual stimulation, you should be able to still the thoughts."

Blair looked from him to the candle, and then to the ring. As strange as it was, she wasn't here to judge, she was here to learn. This process probably helped with a lot of different things.

She paused and realized that was the whole point of this, *stillness*. Taking a deep breath, she stepped into the ring.

For two hours, she walked. Her mind wandered countless times as she followed the line, her focus shattering with each step. Every time she thought she was close, her feet stumbled or her thoughts veered.

Eventually, she came to a halt with a groan.

"I suck at this."

"Well, you're not exactly failing," Malrik said calmly. "But you are resisting. The more you fight this, the more you will be blocked by it. You have to free space in your mind."

"Easy," she muttered.

Malrik cracked a faint smile, the first she'd seen that was genuine.

"You're frustrated," he said. "So talk. Ask what you need to, as you walk."

Blair stood straighter, brushing her hair off her damp forehead as she started walking again. "Do you ever get tired of being alone with them?"

A pause, and then an answer. "Yes," he admitted. "I miss the people they were. Like this, they're more like walking memories."

She tilted her head and focused. "Do you talk to them?"

"Sometimes," he answered, watching her.

"How long have you been here?" she asked, feeling her mind start to zone in on the task at hand.

Malrik didn't speak at first, as if the answer had weight. "A while. I think the mark of Night led my shadows here because this was once Shadowborn territory." Malrik explained

Blair nodded and then paused, her feet stopping beneath her. "This used to belong to them?"

Malrik nodded again, "We are close to where they fell. Their kingdom lies just a few miles west in ruin."

Absorbing his quiet honesty, she envisioned what it would look like now. How it must have looked in its prime.

It was then that she realized he had been right, by asking questions, her mind had become calm and still. Thoughts were no longer buzzing in her head, only intent. The shadow inside of her responded, showing a fraction more of itself, its edges sharpening in her mind.

A smile tugged at her mouth, and Malrik gave a knowing smile.

Malrik then pushed her further. The challenge had her back on the floor, calling forth her shadow while remaining absolutely silent.

She genuinely tried her best, but before long, her frustration returned and cracked into soft laughter.

"Something funny?" Malrik asked.

"No, not really," Blair said, grinning. "I just find it interesting that *this* is what I'm struggling with," she paused, tilting her head at him, "Different training. Different camps. Yet, I fail at my own mind."

As she closed her eyes again, she searched for the presence she knew was there somewhere. Concentrating even harder, the silhouette appeared and eventually darkened, staying there for a few minutes.

Malrik was content with that. The goal had been to focus and connect, which she was able to do. With that, she was dismissed from training for the day.

The exercises had seemed simple, or so it seemed. Blair was mentally exhausted and she hadn't accomplished much, at least not by measurable standards.

But when she looked at Malrik, he wasn't disappointed.

"Today went well," he said simply. "You saw it. That's enough for day one. We want to take this slow and build your connection. Tomorrow brings bigger things."

Blair exhaled, nodding. "Okay."

He gave her a knowing look, "I mean that. No exercises when you're not with me. Give your mind and shadow time to rest."

She reluctantly agreed and left the training chamber. Walking down the narrow hallway, she decided to head to the showers. After a few more steps, something tugged at her attention. Her mark pulsed, and a small quiet pull within her, told her to go toward the cavern entrance, where the sound of the waterfall echoed.

Blair listened, pivoting and heading in that direction. Soon, she entered the large space, the air cool and damp. She sat near the edge of the water for a moment, staring at the shimmering protection that marked the cave's entrance.

Closing her eyes, she listened to the fall's constant rhythm. Watching the water was soothing, as her eyes followed the different layers that cascaded down. Following one stream in particular, she noticed a slight movement on the other side, outside of the cavern.

Her eyes snapped open, and she adjusted her position to try and make out the figures just beyond the falls. Across the shore, there were people, not Malrik's shadow forms, but actual people.

Three of them, cloaked and slow-moving. They stopped and turned in circles as if they were looking for something. She watched as one raised a hand and a wisp of shadow curled from their palm and sank into the ground.

Blair stood sharply.

Hunters. She could *feel* it.

A quiet presence stepped up beside her, and she didn't need to look to know it was Malrik. His gaze was locked on the figures outside as well.

"My shadows found them earlier while we were practicing," he said calmly. "They're circling the lake, almost as if they know we are hidden here."

Her breath hitched. "Will they be able to get in?"

"No," he said, voice like iron. "They'll try, but I have many shadows in place."

Blair didn't relax at those words, not fully, but she trusted him.

The two continued to watch and after some time, the Hunters turned and vanished back into the trees, their shadows melting behind them.

Malrik sighed, turning toward Blair. "It may not be my place to say this but one of your people disappears quite often. Were you aware?"

The hair on the back of Blair's neck stood up and a knot formed in her throat.

"I did not allow my shadows to follow him once he stepped into one of his own but it happens often, even here."

Stepping into shadows? He was talking about Blake.

Blair swallowed the lump, hoping he was wrong. "Who is it?"

Malrik's next words erased all doubt. "The one with no filter. He leaves at night and is sometimes gone a few hours before returning." He exhaled one more time before he glanced over at her.

Replying with a short nod, she stared back at the water as he turned and returned to where he had come from.

Blair watched him go before walking a different path to the showers. A path that was filled with internal screaming. *Blake!? Where the hell was he going?* The questions kept running circles in her mind, continuing even when she found her destination.

It was a small room, like a closet. There was about three feet of space where you could undress and then you stepped under one spout that hung from the ceiling.

Stripping her clothes, she turned the faucet on and begged her mark to give her any insight about what was happening. There was no answer from within, only her body quietly thanking her as the hot water hit her skin. Unfortunately, this had re-tangled her thoughts.

After she was done, she headed for the kitchen, where the others had already gathered around the table. Damien was in the middle of a conversation with Kael but noticed her immediately. Walking up to the table, she slid into the seat next to him. Continuing his sentence, he welcomed her by sliding his arm around the back of her chair.

She looked down at the plate of food waiting for her, courtesy of Damien, or more likely Malrik. A steaming baked potato was in the middle, with green vegetables surrounding it. A combination of spices filled her nose as the aroma hit her, but her stomach anxiously twisted.

Instead of eating, her eyes drifted between Damien and Kael as they talked about their day. She then turned to Blake, who was shoveling food into his mouth.

"Did you sense any shadows earlier?" she asked, nudging his elbow.

With a mouth full of food, he glanced over at her. "No?"

She didn't respond as peas fell from his mouth onto the plate he was leaning over. She didn't reply as she leaned back in her chair."

Blake frowned at her as if sensing her mood. "What-" he then paused, shook his head and stood, moving to a counter that Malrik had set sweets on.

Blair was on her feet immediately, even after Damien protested behind her. She approached Blake swiftly, calling out as she stepped to his side.

"Are you shadow-stepping out at night?" Blair asked as she watched him spoon more food onto his plate. His hands froze for a split second.

"What do you mean?" he asked, looking at her.

She sighed, giving him a pointed look. "Where are you going, Blake?" she asked, stepping closer.

He laughed at her attempt to be intimidating. "I'm not going anywhere, Blair."

Blair placed her hand over his plate as he picked up a cinnamon roll. She looked up at him and raised her eyebrows.

Staring at her, he eventually sighed in defeat and put his hand down. "The basic answer is that I just need to step away and clear my mind sometimes. You know? I get stressed out and I just need a minute." He took a deep breath and placed his palms next to his tray. "The deeper answer is I pretend I'm good enough for Marrow and that we'll settle down some day, so I look for land that she would enjoy." He lifted his head and locked eyes with Blair, his green eyes bright.

A small sigh of relief left her. "Why didn't you just say something?"

Blake looked at the ground for a split second, like he was battling himself. In the next blink, he picked his tray up and gave Blair a coy smile. "How 'bout this, *mom*. I'll let you know next time I leave. I promise to be safe and not talk to strangers." With that, he walked away and headed back to the table.

Blair watched him as he sat down and jumped into a conversation with Damien, who glanced past him and gave her a questioning look. Blair took a deep breath and headed back to the group. As she stood behind her chair, Damien looked over at her. "Not hungry?" he said gently, grabbing her plate.

Blair shook her head. "Thank you, though."

Damien stood as a shadow grabbed the stack of dishes from the table. "Let's go get some rest."

Blair nodded at him, and then looked at Blake who seemed to be avoiding her. She took Damien's outstretched hand and they began their walk back to the room.

The steps were full of silence, which prompted Damien to look at her occasionally. He didn't push or ask any questions, just tightened his grip on her hand.

Once inside the empty room, Blair sat on the bed and intertwined her hands, fidgeting with her fingers.

Damien closed the door and leaned against it with his arms crossed. "Okay, either I'm hallucinating or you're the quietest I've ever seen you. What's going on?"

She looked up at him and sighed at the blue eyes that seemed to catch everything, especially when it came to her. "I saw Hunters outside the waterfall earlier. I think they know we're here."

His soft expression hardened, brow furrowing in quiet alarm.

"I'm afraid I'm not going to be able to handle the Mark of Night."

He stepped toward her slowly. "Is there more?"

"Yes." She hesitated but then answered with a smile when she looked up at him. "I love you."

The tightness in his face instantly disappeared as he stepped forward and moved into her, forcing her to lay on her back. "Hold on, say that last part again."

She looked up at him and cracked a small smile as she whispered it again. "I love y-."

His lips crashed into hers, fierce and warm. He pulled away only to move his mouth to her cheeks, her jaw, her forehead. Each rapid kiss ignited a giggle from her as she tried to defend herself. Soon, she was full-on laughing, the tension in her chest breaking.

He pulled away and watched her as she gasped for air. "There she is," he muttered with a crooked grin. "That's better."

Blair turned toward him, her eyes soft and her face flushed.

He shrugged as he poked her in the side. "Now that you're actually here with me, let's talk through everything. First, how many were there?" Damien asked as he moved beside her, with one arm tucked behind his head. The other now under Blair's head.

She was curled toward him, her cheek against his chest as her fingers idly traced a pattern on the fabric of his shirt. "Three."

Damien inhaled deeply and his chest rose. "That doesn't sound like a coincidence"

She nodded into his body.

Lifting her head slightly, she looked at him. "I didn't recognize them, but they were too close. They weren't just passing through Damien, they were looking for us."

Damien was silent for a long moment, his hand tightening gently at her side. "Where exactly were they?"

"Near the water."

He let out another breath, this one slow. "And they didn't find anything?"

"No, even Malrik confirmed that." She paused, then added, more reluctantly, "But there's something else."

Damien shifted slightly, "What?"

Blair had to force the word out of her mouth. "Blake."

His face shifted, as if confused. "Blake?"

Now it was Blair's turn to take a deep breath in. "I know how it sounds, but something's off with him."

"I think it's safe to say, every day brings something new for us. That can be a lot for some people." Damien said slowly.

Blair bit the inside of her lip but remained quiet.

"As far as the Mark of Night, you mastered the other forms rather quickly." Damien continued, "Your progress has been rapidly increasing. It sounds like you're just expecting a lot from yourself. Which is okay, just remember to give yourself some grace."

Unaware of how tight they had been, Blair's shoulders loosened as he continued, "This one's harder. It's not just power anymore, it's control and precision." He tapped her sternum lightly with two fingers. "You'll get it."

She exhaled slowly, letting herself melt back into his chest."Yeah?"

"Yeah."

They lay in silence for a while after that, even as the others returned. He never said anything more as he held her, his fingers tracing the skin of her arms. When she could feel sleep coming, she looked up at him and kissed him once, slow and certain.

He chuckled against her lips. "There we go," he murmured. "Now, let's get you to sleep."

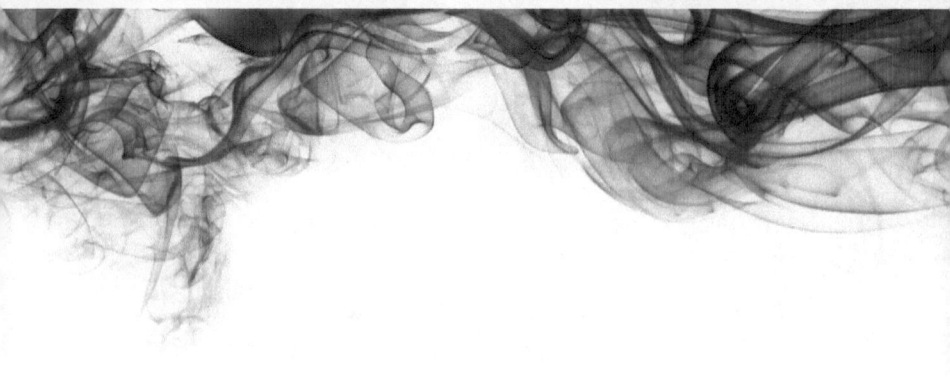

29

The morning brought a comforting, grounding silence. Her body felt light, and surprisingly rested. There was no tension in her chest, and no residual shiver from dreams she couldn't explain. *Maybe she didn't miss them as much as she thought.*

She glanced up at the stone ceiling for a moment, then turned her head toward Damien. His arm was still underneath her, his face relaxed. She smiled, leaned forward, and pressed a kiss to the corner of his mouth.

He stirred just slightly, murmuring her name before falling back into a deeper rest.

Sliding from the bed quietly, she stretched, then padded across the room and did a quick count of those sprawled across their beds. Everyone was here, including Blake, who was half-off the mattress.

Blair grabbed a change of clothes from the dresser and quickly pulled them on. Then, she pulled her hair back into a low tie and made her way down the corridors.

Navigating it rather easily, she entered the training chamber. Malrik wasn't on the floor like the day before.

Instead, he sat in a tall-backed chair in the corner, his hands clasped before him.

As she entered, he sat up, stretching his back. "You slept well."

She nodded. "I did."

"That's good." His eyes briefly moved to the shadows coiled in the edges of the room. "Could mean the mark is beginning to regulate your mind's energy," he then shrugged and added, "Or it could be because of *other reasons*."

Blair tried to hide her smile. "A bit of both, probably."

Shaking his head slightly, he stood. "I'd like to give you an update on what we saw earlier. The Hunters did not return to the beach last night. My shadows report they're still close, but they haven't attempted to cross the threshold."

"Why would that be?" she asked, voice quiet.

"Cautious, maybe? Perhaps they are waiting for an opportunity?" He stepped closer. "With that being said, let's move into business. *Today's* task is more difficult than yesterday's. It's not one that you do physically, but mentally and spiritually."

Blair rotated her head. "How much more difficult?"

"You're going to let your shadow take over."

She froze, with her neck bent as she looked at him sideways. "I'm sorry. Did you just say *take over*?"

"Yes," Malrik confirmed. "A shadow needs to know that you trust it. In return, it will trust you. Today, you'll offer it to your body, temporarily. It's step two in the binding process."

"Whelp, that sounds like fun." Blair said, her eyebrows raised in caution.

He gestured to the stone at the center of the room. "Sit. You won't be alone during this, so don't get in your head. I'll be here the entire time."

Blair hesitated, then moved and sat cross-legged, her palms open on her knees.

"Close your eyes," Malrik directed, his voice low and sure. "You have to talk to it as you would a friend. It is important that you are genuine and speak with intent."

Even though she knew this part was vital, she still felt a bit ridiculous. What he wanted was almost like speaking to herself in the dark. She wondered where to start, how she could connect genuinely with this thing that lived inside of her.

She started off small. In her mind, she began talking about random pieces of her life and her journey. She explained Damien, and the others that she had met along the way.

After a few minutes of this, the dark wisp materialized. At first, just a swirl in the distance of her mind, curious and cautious. Then it grew larger and stronger the more she talked. Despite her best efforts, it kept its distance, growing but not moving.

So, she tried a different tactic, *speaking with intent.*

"I want us to work together."

For the first time, the swirl pulsed faintly in response, as if it liked the idea.

Blair settled in, knowing this was the key to making slow progress. She inhaled, imagining herself sitting in the center of a vast void with her legs crossed. There was no ground and no ceiling, just dim nothingness. Taking a second, she imagined the purple flowers from SilverDawn, the ones she had loved so much. They fluttered down around her and she picked one up, holding in her open palm.

"I would say I'm not afraid of you, but that would be a lie," she confessed. "I'm probably as nervous as you are and if you want me to be honest; the truth is I know I can't do this without you."

Minutes passed and then the presence in her mind grew closer, as if wanting to know more. She took that as a sign to keep going and focused on the message she was trying to deliver. The more she spoke, the more she could feel it moving.

Soon, a large black shadow hovered next to her. Not just a black mass, but a huge, swirling storm of darkness threaded with vibrant, pulsing veins of purple. It loomed over her shoulder but didn't strike, it just *watched*.

She was so close.

Choosing to be bold, she pushed down all her walls, baring her true self to the thing inside of her.

"This might sound pathetic but I question if I'm worth any of this. I know what people think of me and what they *need* me to be." She looked over just as the shadow flashed with a brilliant purple. "But I'm just Blair, and sometimes Blair doesn't feel like enough."

She didn't move, even as her pulse quickened. After another moment, she carefully extended a hand toward it. It flinched at first but then accepted her touch. Tendrils of shadow swirled into her palm.

"You have to show me I'm wrong. Please prove to me this wasn't a mistake. If you can do that," she whispered, "I'll stop doubting. I'll trust it. I'll trust us."

The shadows lifted, brushing her cheek like a soft fingertip, an answer without a voice.

"Okay. Then I'm yours, I'm all in."

The shadow next to her tightened once, gently.

It was an acceptance.

In the real world, Blair's body jerked in her seat.

Malrik stood instantly at her side "Blair?" he called cautiously.

Her eyes opened, but they were no longer hazel. They swirled in a black and violet galaxy.

She didn't speak or blink, because it wasn't truly her. The shadow was there, in her place. Not just inside her, but *looking through her.* It turned her head slowly, scanning the chamber. One hand flexed experimentally, testing her body for any retaliation. After a moment, it settled, almost content.

The shadow seemed pleased.

Then, her eyes closed again, and when she reopened them, they were hers. A warm hazel looked up at Malrik, whose gaze was steady but wide.

Malrik clapped once. The sound cracked through the chamber like a spark. "Well done," he said. "That was step two."

Blair let out a shaky breath, adrenaline fading from her limbs. "I didn't think it would be so big."

"That's the power within you, your potential. Blair, it's important to know the mark didn't just give you this, it *built* upon what was already there. The shadow you saw within you is what you could be. Tomorrow, you'll try again, and this time, you'll learn to move with it."

Blair nodded, a warm flare of hope settling in her chest. *The shadow had confirmed everything. There was no more room for doubting, this is who she was meant to be.*

She looked at Malrik with a new sense of confidence. "I'm looking forward to it." She then thanked him and walked out to the dim corridor.

With each step, her body thrummed with the excitement she had just experienced. The emotions running through her weren't frantic, but more like a door had just been unlocked. Embracing her shadows was one thing, but building an actual connection with them was another.

Rounding the corner toward another hall, she nearly collided with a figure leaning casually against the wall.

"Oh!" Blair startled. "Marrow?"

The dark-haired woman stood with her arms crossed, eyes flicking toward Blair with what looked like a hint of surprise. "Didn't expect you back so soon."

Blair smirked, crossing her arms to match as Marrow's eyes swept the hallway. "Didn't expect you to be standing around, waiting for someone."

Marrow's brows rose and her pale cheeks turned a light shade of pink. "I'm not."

"Oh? You're not? Not even for a reckless, infuriating whirlwind of green eyes and charm?" Blair asked, lifting one eyebrow.

"Don't look at me like that." Marrow scoffed, pushing off the wall. "I only tolerate him because I have no choice."

"*Mhmm*," Blair said, drawing out the sound like a tease. "Tolerating him is one thing, trying to hide the fact you guys can't be apart is another. We're not blind Marrow, and he's not exactly nonchalant about things. "

"He's really not." Marrow said, her voice low as if mimicking a growl.

Blair tilted her head like she could see through every one of Marrow's words.

Marrow sputtered, then exhaled sharply, rubbing her palms down her arms. "It's not what you think."

Blair fell into step beside her as they started walking back toward the kitchen. "Do explain."

Marrow didn't answer right away, but eventually her steps slowed and then came to a stop. Blair waited patiently beside her as she gathered her thoughts.

"I've never really been able to get close to people," Marrow said finally, her voice quieter than usual. "Not without hurting them. The last time I let anyone in like that,

324

they all-" Marrow swallowed and took a few moments before trying again. "I just can't get close to people, it's not in the cards for me."

Blair's teasing expression softened as Marrow allowed her guard to fall.

She continued talking with her eyes straight ahead. "My ability, it's really just glorified sorrow and grief. It comes out in different ways and can affect those around me. If I use it for too long, or if someone's too emotionally open they end up drowning in my darkness. Not literally, but emotionally. I've seen people break because of what I carry. Because of *who* I am."

Blair stayed silent but reached for her hand. Marrow flinched but accepted the comfort.

"I tried to keep people at a distance after my family. I knew it was easier and safer for everyone, but then Blake showed up." She trailed off, exhaling again as another hint of pink rose in her cheeks. "He doesn't even *feel* it. I've activated my power a dozen times around him, and it's like it bounces right off."

Blair chuckled softly. "That sounds like him."

"It sounds like a problem, Blair." Marrow snapped before a smile formed, soft and unsure. "It's bad. I can actually *breathe* when he's around. I don't have to pull back or shield him. It's actually irritating, I don't even find him *annoying* anymore." she said with a small sigh, like she was finally admitting it out loud, or even just to herself.

Blair bumped her shoulder lightly with a small smile. "You like him."

"I like," Marrow admitted, "not feeling like I'm a bomb waiting to go off."

They rounded the corner into the dining space, voices echoing off the walls.

Blake, who was already at the table, caught sight of them immediately and let out a low whistle.

"Love those shoes, Marrow!" he called across the room with a grin. "Will you step on my neck with them later?"

Marrow stopped, cheeks *fully* red now.

Blair turned to her with a smug smile. "Man, it's a good thing he doesn't annoy you anymore, huh?"

Marrow rolled her eyes at Blair, who shrugged and laughed. She shot Blake a glare that held absolutely no heat and made her way over to a chair.

Blair followed a step behind, watching Blake's eyes follow Marrow the entire way.

"She's gonna kill you one day," Blair said under her breath as she approached him.

"Then let me die between her legs," Blake replied in passing.

Blair snorted and moved next to Damien. He held a bowl of food out to her as she settled.

"You look different," he said, smiling. "Something happen?"

She took the food and leaned up to kiss him lightly. "Yeah, it turns out I'm finally figuring things out. My shadow took control, even if it was just for a minute."

Damien gave her a sideways glance, like the news almost made him uncomfortable. Before he responded, she added, "Malrik was there watching the whole time."

Damien's face softened and he nodded. "I'd still like to be with you next time."

"We can arrange that." she said with a little grin.

Blair took a bite and nodded as conversation branched between them into different subjects. After a while things settled and Blair looked around at the Shadowborn that surrounded her. "Do you know the kingdom that belonged to the Shadowborn is close?"

With her words, many stilled, including Blake.

Rhea set down her fork. "It would make sense."

Damien noticed Blake who seemed to be clenching his jaw. "Have you been there before?"

Blake looked up at him, and then at Marrow before replying. "Yeah, I've seen it once or twice through my travels."

A shudder ran through Kael's body, "I bet it smells delightful."

Blake looked over at him but remained silent, as if he had disassociated for a moment.

Adriel filled in the silence, "Once we are done here, we'll go there. Blake can take us."

Blake didn't respond, filling his mouth with another bite before motioning for the shadows who now waited at the edges of the table to help clean.

After dinner was the time everyone took to decompress or explore. Now that all of them had become comfortable, the evenings were everyone's downtime, some even moving into other rooms.

Most of the time, Blair and Damien would just retreat to their bed and she would read his notes from her book while he laid next to her and explained them. She had just finished the last chapter when she closed it and looked over at him. "Do you think we'll actually go to their kingdom?"

Damien made a small sound as he drew her closer, both of them too exhausted to finish the conversation. When she fell asleep, there were no dreams.

<u>30</u>

The training room was colder today, even with the whole team watching from the edges.

Blair stood in the center of the stone chamber, arms folded tightly across her chest as she watched Malrik pace. The air had a charge to it, like the cave itself was holding its breath.

Last night, she had slept better than she had in weeks, no dreams and no weight in her chest.

Malrik stopped pacing and turned to face her.

"Today is step three," he said. "You've invited the shadow. You've let it in. Now, you have to *move* with it, outside of yourself."

Blair raised an eyebrow. "You mean like, let it walk around?"

He nodded. "Exactly."

She squinted. "Are you sure I'm ready for that?"

Malrik's lips twitched, not quite a smile. "We'll see if you can handle it."

Her skepticism lingered as he spoke, but she nodded anyway. "Alright. Let's do it."

She took a breath and lowered herself into a seated position. Her fingers brushed the cool floor, grounding herself as she closed her eyes and searched inward. This time, it was almost immediate. The presence of her shadow moved internally, as if it had been waiting. The darkness acted familiar now, like a loyal animal not quite tamed.

Remembering that it was her friend, she called out to it. "You wanna try something new today?" she asked silently. "I'd like to show you all those people I told you about."

For a moment, there was nothing.

But then, a swirl of energy flickered in the edges of her mind and a low vibration filled her chest.

In the chamber, Malrik watched closely, sensing the shift in the air, as did Damien.

The shadow inside Blair wavered. Then, a storm emerged beside her, thrashing wildly. A pulse of purple ran through the darkness, like veins of lightning in a stormcloud. The lightning began to shape, until it was a towering figure. No face. No eyes. Just a being of silent power standing next to her.

Malrik's mouth opened, along with everyone else's. "By the void…" he muttered, barely audible.

Blair opened her eyes slowly. She didn't need to look beside her, she *felt* it there, standing next to her like a dark reflection.

That wasn't the only thing that had appeared, a thick black line ran through her leg. Sprouting from the top and bottom of her dagger, the vertical darkness traveled the length of her entire leg.

She stood up and the shadow stood with her.

She gestured to each person in front of her and introduced them, and then walked over to Damien.

The shadow moved with her, mirroring her steps like a protective guardian, even as she stopped. "This is Damien, the guy we talked about."

The shadow didn't move but then slightly bowed its head. With every moment that passed, the shadow grew calmer, its edges softening and its movements less rigid.

Behind her, Malrik whispered instructions. "Create distance and see what it does."

Blair turned toward it, tapping Damien's hand. "I'd like you to stay with him for a minute, okay. Trust him, like you trust me. He's safe." With that, she walked the opposite way, across the room. The shadow listened, flickering slightly but remaining still. It watched her the whole way, awaiting more instructions.

Blair let out a slow breath then walked back toward it. This time, her shadow didn't wait. It moved with her as she walked along the edges of the room.

"Damn," Blake muttered under his breath, grinning.

Adriel let out a low whistle of appreciation.

Kael smelled the air, "It smells strong, stronger than I was expecting."

Blair turned toward the group of Shadowborn, the shadow pivoting half a second later, like a late echo. Pushing the boundaries a little bit, she stopped directly in front of them. "I'm going to ask you to trust them too. They are my family."

Each of them slowly stepped toward the shadow. Kael even reached out to touch it which caused another small ripple through it.

Rhea seemed the most stunned, as if she couldn't believe it. "You did this," she said, turning to Blair. "In this short amount of time?"

Malrik stepped forward, eyes moving between Blair and the manifestation beside her. "Yes, she has. But I bet she can do more."

Blair's head snapped. "What?

Malrik smiled like he had every belief in the world in her. "Keep the shadow out and activate another mark."

Blair had a hard time processing his words, hesitating at the request. She had built her confidence but that didn't just sound hard, it sounded brutal.

The shadow alone took everything she had to hold steady and layering another ability on top, meant channeling two forces at once.

Still, she nodded, recalling the conversation with her darkness."I'll try."

She turned her palm upward, unclasping the leather bracelet on her wrist. Running her fingers over it, she closed her eyes and steadied her breathing. A flicker of heat ran up her thigh. A heartbeat later, audible gasps filled the chamber as the mark of Veil activated down her leg, merging with the line that was already there.

She opened her eyes, checking to see if the shadow was still there. It stood silent and unwavering. Murmurs spread as she lifted her hand to show an empty palm, the bracelet gone from sight.

"Again," Damien said, voice quiet but firm. "Another one."

Blair swallowed, her stamina thinning. Once more, she reached inward

"Rhea, produce shadows." Blair requested. Her breath hitched as a second energy surged through her legs, the Mark of Void blooming on top of the others. The room tilted slightly as Blair focused on the shadows that curled from Rhea's arm.

Blair lifted her palm toward them. The shadows drifted slowly, then absorbed into her skin.

One second, then two.

Then the connection faltered and snapped.

The shadows whipped back to Rhea, the bracelet suddenly flickered back into view, and the shadowed form dissipated just as Blair's knees buckled.

Damien caught her before she fully collapsed, his hand gripping her arm.

Blair looked up, chest still heaving. "I almost had it."

"You did have it," Malrik said, stepping forward.

Blair couldn't help the smile tugging at her lips. Everything hurt, but she had done it, even if it was only for a few seconds.

"You're ahead of schedule," Malrik announced.

"At this rate, you'll surpass Damien," Blake scoffed, glancing at him.

"She already has." Damien muttered, eyes fixed on the space where the shadow had vanished.

"You'll train with me at dawn and dusk," Malrik continued. "Midday, Damien will run you through form transitions. At night, you'll rest."

Blair looked at Damien, who nodded, and then she looked back at Malrik.

"You're close, Blair. Closer than anyone has any right to be this soon," Malrik said, "so let's keep going. Full force."

"Okay." Blair said, her voice strong.

31

The first morning nearly broke her.

Malrik didn't speak much during this final form of training, only barked instructions with the weight of iron. "Center. Ground. Again."

Blair followed every time, her body mirroring his movements. She sat with him in the cold dirt until her legs were numb, trying to hold all three marks without letting one spill over. Sometimes she would take too much shadow from him, and the objects she tried to veil would flicker. Other times the shadow wouldn't appear at all, as if offended by her attempts.

At dusk, she was trembling.

"You're starting to think too much again," Malrik growled. "Instinct, Blair. Your power isn't meant to wait for permission."

She gritted her teeth, trying again. The bracelet disappeared and she pulled shadows from around her as her shadowed guardian walked to the other side of the room and dissolved.

Malrik's only response was, "Again."

This continued for days, the intensity upping even more the day Malrik added Damien to the sessions.

On this particular morning, Damien took her through motion drills in the cave, forcing her to run full-speed combat forms while keeping the shadow active behind her. Every time she was told to veil something, the shadow behind her flickered. Every time she moved too fast, she couldn't siphon the shadows that Damien offered.

Damien watched her as she gasped for breath. "You can do this. Remember who you are."

It was the fourth morning that she started to remember that.

Malrik and Damien watched with the same hopeful, intense eyes. No part of the routine had changed but when Blair closed her eyes this time, she didn't try to control anything. She relinquished everything to the shadow within her.

She simply let herself fall into the background. With that, the power flowed and three marks activated. As she held it, the shadow clung to her, pushing her to keep going. So, she did.

By the fifth day, her endurance had doubled. She could now hold all three marks for a few minutes before something buckled. She could move with the shadow active, and her thigh was often covered in all three marks. She'd even managed to have the Shadow fight alongside her.

"You're not battling it anymore," Malrik observed during one of their sparring sessions. Damien nodded in agreement next to them. She knew it was true, the shadow had grown, taking more space in her mind and pushing out the thoughts that normally swirled there. The marks now lived in her like pieces that fit together.

The real test of that, came that night.

Malrik had said there would be a final test, something she hadn't expected. She assumed it would be some kind of duel or simulation, maybe a group challenge but it wasn't.

He brought her into an old arena, deeper than most of the hallways they had called home for the past month. Inside this specific area was a stone chamber.

"You'll be locked in," he said, stepping back from the massive gate. "You don't leave until you can hold all three marks, under *real* pressure."

"What kind of pressure?" she asked slowly.

Malrik gave a grim smile. "You'll see."

The gate slammed shut as she entered the space. The lights dimmed around her, not completely, but enough to throw everything into an uneasy darkness.

Then the illusions began, courtesy of Marrow.

Children hid in the corners, trembling in fear when figures stepped out of the dark. Shadow creatures, born of light-bending magic and soundless rage. They didn't speak to her, but they also didn't hesitate before charging at the kids. Blair reacted on instinct, creating multiple shadowed daggers to throw. As she did so, a mark of black tendrils moved across her skin, allowing her to take away some of the shadowed forms. The mark then combined with two others. Blair veiled the children, having them vanish in thin air while a shadowed figure detached from her and stood over them, ready to defend them as she would. She attacked then, dodging the first two creatures with a blur of motion. The third slammed into her chest, knocking her backward and the veil protecting the children flickered out.

No.

She pushed herself up, with an ambition that burned from the inside-out. She called on all three marks at once, calling them by name.

Void.

Veil.

Night.

They surged through her, working together to create purple shadows that flared behind her. She danced around the other creature, a blur of power and focus. The shadow fighting at her back in tandem with every strike she made. She was faster than she'd ever been, shadows dancing like armor around her, her guardian helping her by forming blades, shields, and claws.

Not once did she break. She held them, even as minutes passed. Then, it went even longer and just as the illusion faded, she looked around with an absolute look of victory.

That is, until, the gate creaked open and revealed two Enforcers.

Her eyes narrowed in recognition of what was happening. This was it, this was the last challenge. If she won this, it was over. Blair moved through the dark training chamber with smooth, practiced steps, her breathing calm, her mind focused.

Immediately she knew Marrow was giving it her all, these images showed no imperfections. They weren't blurry, they didn't shimmer with that telltale distortion of a projection. These were solid, and worse, she felt the pull of their power, both cloaked in deep shadow magic.

Her mind flicked to action before doubt could sink in. She reached inward, and pulled, again igniting the purple burst of shadows. The nearest Enforcer raised his hand, sending a whip of shadow hurtling toward her. She opened herself to it and absorbed it almost instantly. The black tendrils vanished into her chest with a hiss, the darkness feeding her like breath. The man staggered as he watched and the other lunged forward.

"Not this time," Blair hissed, stepping into the attack as her shadowed double swung from behind her, sweeping low and tripping the second Hunter clean off his feet. She moved like a storm, her shadow dancing in sync. Every strike of her shadowed daggers mirrored by her double's. In this fight, there were no reactions, just pure instinct and adrenaline.

A scream ripped through the air and Blair froze. The sound wasn't part of the illusion. It was real and raw, bouncing off the walls surrounding her. The air around her shimmered and the floor beneath her cracked. A jagged ripple ran through the stone like this reality was something that had just been split open.

Blair stepped back, watching most of Marrow's illusion disappear. Everything except the shadows faded, the shadows that belonged to the men in front of her.

They came at her harder, angry. Her shadow intercepted one while she blocked the other. Her breath picked up with each movement. Something wasn't right.

No.

No.

This wasn't just a simulation.

It was *real.*

Her eyes widened as her thoughts became words she spoke out loud. "You're here."

Her shadow activated, fueled by her fear. The Void burst across her skin as she lashed out, forcing one Enforcer back as she devoured his shadows. A dark form moved along her side, diving into the other one like a predator.

That's when the door exploded behind her. Stone and shadow flew everywhere as Damien burst through, covered in blood and fury, his shadowed wings encasing his body like armor. He didn't hesitate and with a single lunge, and a sweep of his blade, a Phantom behind him dropped without a sound.

"We have to GO!" he shouted, grabbing her by the arm.

Blair turned just in time to see her shadow impale the second Enforcer through the ribs, then she ran.

They pounded up the hallway, Damien half-pulling her. Her eyes caught flashes of her surroundings as they moved, it was all a blur of shadowed movement. Just as they emerged into the cavern, she saw the true chaos around her.

The entire area was under siege by a small army of Hunters.

They were everywhere. Almost all of them engaged with someone, battling. In some places, blood stained the black walls, speckled across the purple veins. In other areas, furniture lay broken and walls were cracked.

Malrik stood at the far end of the great chamber, surrounded by his own small army of shadows. They had morphed from people into monstrous things that moved quickly, tearing into the intruders. Blair's body instinctively shifted toward him, ready to help, just as another Enforcer manifested a chain with a scythe-blade attached to it. Blair threw a shadowed dagger, forcing the weapon to drop. That was all she had time before Damien continued to pull her.

"Move!" Damien barked, shoving her forward.

They met together with the others by the water, forming a defensive line. Working in tandem, they drove against them with a small but vicious force, taking a large portion of them down. All the training together came out at this moment. Blair dodged an incoming strike by spinning under a Hunters arm. Marrow had to weave three times to prevent being impaled by flying shadow weapons. Damien moved swiftly, the runes on his skin pulsing.

The entire area was pure chaos. The torches on the walls lit the underground lake, which was now strewn with bodies of Enforcers, half-disintegrated.

As they fought, Malrik's voice echoed through the stone, "Get out! Now! There are more coming!"

Kael tried to shout back but his voice vanished into the noise. Instead, he partnered with Adriel, who swept through two more Enforcer's with black fire. Black blood hit the floor in streaks that hissed.

A group of Enforcers noticed the Shadowborn's victory and rushed them. Damien's answer was a shadowburst from his wings that shattered the torchlight, plunging the cavern into blackness. In that dark that now consumed them, the Shadowborn became relentless.

Screams rose and broke against the stone walls. *This* was something Blair had not prepared for. She could see nothing but movement, shadows gliding and colliding. When her vision finally adjusted, she realized the Hunters were losing ground.

They knew this too. A large one in the back threw his head up and whistled, a high-pitch sound that carried through the cavern.

A strange noise came in response.

It started low, rumbling through the hallways just as the Phantoms Malrik had warned them about, stepped into the battlefield.

The sound then changed to a high-pitched howl that rang through the open tunnels. The fighting stopped for half a breath as everyone readied themselves for what was coming. Another howl joined the first.

Blake froze mid-swing. "Please tell me that's not-"

Before he could finish, they poured in.

From the narrow tunnels beyond the main cavern came creatures born entirely of shadow, massive dark wolves, their forms dripping dark tendrils that bled into the floor. They ran silent but hit like a storm, barreling through the Shadowborn with a fury that shook the ground.

The first tore through Malrik's shadowed army, ripping through their throats. The second leapt beside Blair, attaching itself to Adriel, who screamed in agony. Another went after Damien, attempting to shred his shadowed wings. Damien grabbed it and snapped it in half, the shadows releasing and funneling into his body, just as three more lunged for him.

"GO!" Rhea screamed at Blair, Damien, and Blake. "We'll handle it!"

But Blair refused to listen as she noticed Adriel, who writhed on the floor. As another wolf targeted him, she lifted her hand to consume its shadow.

Blake grabbed her wrist immediately. "You're not about to die when there is so much still coming."

She locked eyes with him. For once, he wasn't exuding cockiness, his eyes were glossy. He was afraid. The tone of his voice snapped Blair out of her headspace, and she turned back toward the water.

His gaze flicked from Blair to Marrow, who was fighting off two Enforcers that had approached her from different sides. Blake snarled in anger and activated his shadow, first wrapping his arm around Blair's waist and then grabbing the collar of Damien's shirt.

The ground surged beneath them as the world shifted. In just a mere second, they were transported. One moment, Blake was beside them apologizing and then the next moment, there was silence.

Blair and Damien landed hard on rocky ground. A different cave, one that was empty. There was only cool air and the moon above. As Blair's heartbeat slowed, she realized that was the only sound around them. She gasped, stumbling forward and then turned back toward where they had come from. There was nothing there but a stone wall.

Blake had Shadowstepped them out and then left them. There was no way to go back.

No Adriel or Kael.

No Rhea or Marrow.

No Blake.

There was no one there besides her and Damien.

<u>32</u>

The sound of their arrival faded too fast, leaving them in silence.

Blair's legs threatened to give out, as she took a step, her boots hitting a chunk of uneven stone. Her heartbeat filled her ears as she focused on her breathing.

Damien stood completely still for a breath, then another, before he erupted. A roar tore from his chest as he spun toward the wall, slamming his fists into the stone. The cave shook and cracks splintered across the rock like spiderwebs. His shadows lashed out from him in wild streaks of darkness, tendrils that carved deep into the stone around him.

Blair flinched on instinct, but a dome of dark energy flared around her, cast by Damien even through his rage. The fury seemed to consume him entirely. She had never seen him like this. It was nothing like the calculating look that she'd seen in his eyes before, but something deeper. This was from an emotion that dragged him through his past, into grief and guilt he couldn't hide.

Blair stayed where she was for a long moment, watching him, tears streaming down her face. When she could no longer bear the sight, she sank to the cold floor, arms loose around her knees.

Damien kept hitting the wall, again and again. His knuckles tore on impact, blood smearing the stone with every strike. His breathing turned ragged as he continued, finding comfort in the pain. The shadows around him soon lost their shape, no longer blades, just raw fury.

Then, all at once, he stopped.

He turned to face her, his chest heaving, his hands trembling. Bracing himself against the cracked wall, he bowed his head as blood dripped from his fists and spattered against the jagged stone.

The forcefield around her dropped and she slowly stood. The adrenaline had worn off and her limbs were sore and stiff but what hurt the most was the broken look in his eyes.

She walked to him without speaking, placing a hand gently on his chest. She didn't ask if he was okay, nor did she speak with empty comfort. Instead, she reached down, grabbed the hem of her shirt, and tore off a strip of cloth. She carefully took his left hand and wrapped it gently.

Damien didn't move, didn't even blink, his eyes staring past her. His jaw was clenched, shadows still flickering at his shoulders like angry embers. She moved to his right hand then, wrapping the bloody knuckles in silence.

When she was done, she crouched near a patch of dry stone and gathered some splinters and old moss from the cracks in the wall. She used them to spark a small fire with two stones.

As it caught, warmth filled the space in soft pulses before she settled beside Damien who had slid down the wall into a sitting position.

Neither spoke, and she didn't force conversation. The silence stretched on, interrupted only by the soft crackle of the low fire.

Damien's voice was so quiet she almost missed it. "I'm sorry."

For a moment, it was as if she had imagined it, but then he spoke again. "I don't know what happened."

Blair looked at him, her expression soft.

His eyes were locked on the flames, still unfocused. The fury was gone now, replaced by something else entirely.

"We had no idea it was coming. No one sensed anything," he continued, voice low. "There was nothing, and then they were everywhere." He shook his head. "I had to find you first but then I couldn't help them."

Blair didn't interrupt, she just placed her hand on his leg.

"I don't know if Rhea made it out. Or Adriel. Or Kael. Or… any of them." His voice cracked on the last word. "And I left them."

"You didn't leave them. You didn't have a choice," Blair said softly.

As she spoke, he finally looked at her. His eyes were rimmed red. It wasn't from tears, not exactly, but from

347

everything just short of them. All the fury that filled him, and the weight of failure that followed.

"They told us to run," she added.

Damien didn't answer, so she shifted a little closer to him. "We'll find them. We'll find out what happened."

A faint exhale escaped him as he leaned his head back against the wall, his eyes closing. "Are you okay?"

Blair didn't say anything, she only watched him until he met her eyes again. "I will be, once we find them."

After that, the silence came back. It was like that for a while, because neither would sleep, both counting the hours since they had arrived.

The sky shifted from black to steel blue, and with it came the first signs of morning. Blair sat quietly at the mouth of the cave, listening to the fire pop behind her. The light brought more information about the environment, and as she looked around, she realized they were in a mountain range. Her eyes followed the jagged lines of the peaks until they met a soft glow that stretched out in the east. In the light, something began to emerge.

She leaned forward, her pulse quickening.

There, across the distant ridge, a silhouette began to sharpen. A building, or more so, a castle, with spires and towers. A broken flag pole held fabric that was shredded, a diamond barely visible on the worn cloth. The material was pale against the rising dawn, yet stubbornly familiar. Too familiar.

Blair's stomach twisted.

She narrowed her eyes, trying to deny the way her memory clawed at her. It wasn't possible, it couldn't be, and yet there it stood, the Shadowborn kingdom, or what was left of it.

"Damien," she called over her shoulder, still staring at it.

When he appeared at her side, she pointed toward the horizon and the castle that stood against the creeping light. His eyes followed her gaze and narrowed immediately.

"That's it, isn't it?" he asked in a whisper, like he didn't believe it.

Blair didn't reply verbally, but her body responded. The mark on her thigh began to warm, a heat she knew. She exhaled sharply through her nose.

Damien glanced at her, and for the first time since they'd arrived here, the edge in his expression softened. There was something close to concern behind his eyes.

Blair took a deep breath, exhaling audibly. Pulling her eyes away from the castle, she looked at him. "We need to go there," she said.

She watched his face carefully to gauge his reaction but there was no shift, no visible emotion. The only confirmation he gave about the plan was when he turned silently and began to put out the fire.

With nothing to carry, they moved fast. It wasn't long until the air bit at Blair's cheeks, as the mountain wind howled through the ravine they found themselves in.

Damien descended a few steps ahead, his boots steady against the slick rock, his jaw set tight. Every movement radiated focus except for the low, irritated grumble that escaped him.

"Damn Blake," he muttered under his breath. "How in the hell did he even manage to shadowstep us this far?"

Blair scoffed, adjusting her footing on the uneven slope. "You say that like it's a surprise."

"It is," Damien shot back, not turning. "Last I checked, he could only do it within eyesight."

She clicked her tongue as her foot caught on a large rock. "You aren't the only one that's been training Damien. He figured it out."

Damien raised both eyebrows. "He what?"

"I said he figured it out," she repeated,. "Apparently, he was up to a few miles."

"He never practiced that in training, at least not with me." Damien's eyes flickered, confusion giving way to something else, something like disbelief, irritation, and admiration mixed together. "And then has the audacity to use it on me and throw us in the middle of nowhere?"

Blair gave a slight shrug, focusing on where her feet stepped. "Seems that way."

"If I'd known that idiot could manage it, I would've made him do this for our traveling months ago." Damien said dryly. He extended a hand behind him without looking, fingers brushing hers as they approached a stretch of jagged boulders. "Watch your footing here," he murmured, his tone softening. "The rocks look like they shift."

Blair took his hand without hesitation, letting him guide her. The air grew even colder as they descended, the scent of wet stone and shadow thickening around them. From below, the faint outline of the castle loomed larger, its silhouette like teeth against the horizon.

"Do you think there's a chance Blake and the others might be there?" Blair asked quietly.

Damien glanced at her, the corner of his mouth twitching. "Realisticaly? No. Hopefully? Yes. Just so I can kill him."

She chuckled under her breath as Damien stepped down onto the next ledge and reached up to steady her as she followed. "Understandable," she muttered as her boots hit solid ground beside him, and for a moment, their hands remained intertwined as they looked forward to a much smoother path.

They could see it clearer now, the dark castle that waited ahead. They kept their eyes on it as the terrain shifted slightly under their feet.

Blair summoned one of her marks as she moved, the shadow trailing behind her and Damien, never more than ten feet away. Sometimes she let it lead. Sometimes it preferred to be next to Damien.

By evening, the castle was in front of them.

It was carved from a dark gray stone, perched on the edge of a narrow cliff overlooking a dark ravine. The spires reached into the sky, covered in a silvery light that ran across the castle.

Blair's dagger mark suddenly exploded in warmth, the most intense wave she felt yet.

When they reached the gate, Blair was the first to notice the intricate black markings etched into the iron bars. Swirls of different sizes that seemed to shift if she looked at them too long.

Damien stepped up beside her, nudging her side. "Those were the symbols that covered your body when you woke up from the nightmare that one night."

Bair froze as she realized he was right. Pieces fell into place as she went through the last few weeks and every dream that had plagued her. She had already guessed at what it could be, but it all made sense now.

Could that have been her mark all along?
The mark of Fate.

Her thought was cut short as she noticed something, or *someone*. A young boy was standing just outside the gate and next to him, an older woman who sat in a chair. As the woman looked at them, a purple hue glinted in her brown eyes.

Damien and Blair walked toward them, stopping when they were just a few feet away. The boy stepped forward and his head tilted ever so slightly. His voice was low and strange, like he was reciting words he didn't fully understand.

"We fled when the veil whispered. We hid when the night cracked but the pattern still weaves, the thread still pulls."

Blair and Damien paused at the riddled phrase, both of them looking at each other as they replayed the words. Blair then turned her attention toward the woman, who gave her a slight smile.

A wave of deja-vu hit Blair. *She had seen her before, she knew it.* As she tried to figure out exactly how, the boy repeated himself, word for word.

Damien leaned in beside her. "It's like he's on a loop."

Blair watched his mouth run through the words again and again, finally pulling away with her brows together. Her dagger pulsed and she felt a charge beneath her skin, her shadow. "Veil whispered and Night cracked. He's talking about Lailah and the attack with Malrik. If the symbols from the castle were the ones I had during my dreams, I think that was the Mark of fate, my last power. I think this is a message from them. They fled, Damien." Ignoring the strange chill that crawled up her spine, Blair stepped forward toward the familiar woman.

The woman's voice was low as she spoke to Blair, asking for her hand. Other voices whispered around it, as if intertwined with hers. "Would you like your fortune told?"

Blair took a step forward. "Yes, please."

At her answer, the purple in the woman's eyes glistened and a memory came flooding in with a prophecy and stacked voices. Blair froze, her eyes widening with recognition as the woman took her hand.

Mark of the Fate.

The fortune teller was one of them.

Behind her, Damien stiffened as if he knew. "Blair" he muttered under his breath, in a warning tone.

Blair didn't answer. Instead, she straightened her shoulder and nodded at the woman in front of her. Heat flared instantly along her thigh and a sigil came to life. Geometric lines etched themselves across her skin, branching out like veins, forming elegant shapes that glowed faintly beneath her clothes. They pulsed once as the woman looked at them, and then stilled.

The old woman's expression changed then and a large toothless smile covered her face. Her eyes lit with a violet flame, not one of fire, but magic.

Damien stayed quiet, watching it unfold.

When the fortune teller spoke again, it was not her voice that left her lips, but the same one that had echoed in the market when they had first met.

"Stay within the castle walls. The roots run deeper than stone, and the blood that binds you here is not yet spilled. Those who are born shall fall, but not until the shadows gather and the sky cries in mourning. The gate will open and one name will be spoken. We shall be reborn."

The words seared into her mind, branding themselves in memory as surely as her mark had branded her skin. She wanted to ask what it meant, wanted to demand more, but the woman was already standing. Her

354

bright violet eyes that had seemed to burn, dimmed back down to a warm brown.

The young man took her arm, helping her walk down the path away from the castle. Neither of them looked back as they vanished between slabs of mountain.

Blair stood frozen as she watched the answers to everything walk in the opposite direction. Damien stepped forward slowly. Blair looked at him as her mind replayed the words like a song she couldn't forget.

Stay in the castle.

She knew it now, this was no ruin.

This was where everything began.

33

The walls of the castle groaned when they entered, as if waking from a long, bitter sleep.

Blair was the first to step inside. As she did so, she expected the air to be thick with dust that curled around her boots. She imagined how bad it would be, a whole castle pillaged, gutted, and abandoned by both man and memory.

Yet, that wasn't what she found at all.

The entryway in front of her was completely clean. New wallpaper hung on the walls, accompanying a tile floor that shined like it had just been scrubbed. There were no signs of ruin, it was almost the opposite, as if it had been restored for them.

She scoffed in disbelief as she pushed the door wider, sharing the view with Damien. He looked around, a look of shock crossing his features. "It's like someone was living here the whole time." he murmured under his breath as he followed Blair inside.

The room beyond the door was large and every inch of space was pristine. The gathering hall held long, maroon drapes that covered the windows. Different pieces of leather furniture were arranged neatly in the corners.

Blair turned slowly, taking it all in. "What does this mean?"

Damien stood in silence for a moment, then took another step. "I have no idea."

Blair continued to stare at the area around them and then turned back to him, with equal parts astonishment and excitement. As they ventured farther into the castle, they came across many hallways that led to different rooms.

The first was a bedroom, with soft pastels and rose-colored drapes. The bed inside was covered in a cream bedding embroidered with tiny gold leaves. Shelves lined the walls around it with varying decorative candles. A vanity sat in the corner, beneath a round mirror with glass bottles arranged neatly on its surface.

Damien's gaze flicked over the room, taking in the untouched sheets, the perfectly placed chair, the unlit candles that somehow still seemed fresh.

Blair walked over to the vanity. "It's like everything was set up for us."

Damien gave a small nod in agreement as they moved on.

The next door opened into something entirely different.

Deep red tapestries stood out against black wooden furniture. A massive four-poster bed stood in the middle, draped in heavy velvet that matched the same color of red. Weapons hung, lining one wall. From the smallest to the largest, they ranged from daggers and spears to a shield with a silver emblem.

Blair's eyes shot wide as they roamed over each weapon, each one seeming to be freshly polished. "This would definitely be your room."

Damien raised a brow. "I don't do decorations."

She looked over at him, a small smile tugging at her lips. "No, but if you did, this would be it."

He stepped inside quietly, studying the weapons but never touching them. His gaze lingered on the silver emblem, a diamond.

The next two hallways held more bedrooms, each one a completely different aesthetic.

At the end of the corridor, they stopped before a door darker than the rest.

Carved symbols wound over the wood like vines. Nothing like the pristine, symmetrical patterns they'd seen outside the castle.

Blair leaned in, as her fingers brushed over the design. "This one's different."

Damien stepped half in front of her, silent and instinctive. "Wait. You don't know what's behind it."

She lifted her eyes to him as she reached for the handle. "That's the fun part."

He didn't dignify that with a response, especially when she grinned and pushed open the door.

The room beyond expanded upward and outward. Shelves lined every wall, stacked neatly with different sized books. A warm, soft light filled the space, though Blair couldn't see the source.

"A library?" she breathed.

Damien followed her inside without a sound. His eyes swept the room in slow, calculating passes.

Blair drifted toward a shelf, fingertips skimming the spines until her hand stilled over one that was covered in bold letters. "Damien," she whispered. "Look at this."

He joined her, head lowering just enough to see the spine she pointed at.

"Veldusk," she murmured. "This is Veldusk." She slid the book free, opening it carefully. The pages were filled with black symbols she had once tried to decipher. "I've only ever seen this once," she whispered. "In that bookstore by the inn. The owner had said it was a lost language."

Damien moved closer. "I've heard of that before," he said quietly. "It's a language older than most." He then proceeded to pick up another book, the same writing scrawled on the pages within. He replaced it, choosing another and then another, all written in the same fading ink.

Blair swallowed. "But why would this castle have so many books written in it?"

His gaze traveled across the shelves, taking in the sheer number of books around them, hundreds, maybe thousands.

"This wasn't just a library," Damien said finally. "This was a collection. Someone preserved this."

Blair nodded slowly. "Like they wanted it safe."

Damien didn't answer, his eyes returning to the page she held open. He had just opened his mouth to reply, when a faint purple glow appeared beneath her hand. The glow moved as purple lines began unfurling beneath the Veldusk script, transforming the words into ones they could read. Stories unfolded of the Shadowborn history and the leaders.

The purple continued to curl outward, swirling in graceful, hypnotic patterns across the pages, and then the front, as Blair closed the book. They traced a shape and then finally settled, showcasing a large purple diamond across the cover.

Damien looked up at her then, as if in deep thought. "I think our world has been calling to you for a long time. You just couldn't hear it yet."

When he looked back down, the light had dimmed but the diamond remained. He smiled at Blair before softly taking the book from her and placing it back on the shelf. They walked a few more aisles before moving on to the next room.

The next being a grand dining hall, an area that was clearly set up to entertain. Each item in the area seemed new, including a long marble table. As they approached, there was something taped to the stone, a crisp white envelope. Blair's fingers shook as she picked it up and met Damien's gaze, both filled with apprehension.

She opened it, finding a hand-written message:

You're expecting company soon.
The castle and everything in it
is yours to use.

Blair's voice faded with the last word of the note. She turned to Damien to say more, but then something moved and a soft creak reached their ears. Not from the room they stood in, but from the doorway of the castle.

Both of them froze as their eyes moved together, scanning the hallway they just came from. Blair's hand went instinctively to her thigh. Damien was already turning. A shadowed sword manifested in his hand as he scanned the open doorway that led back into the front hall.

Another creak filled the room, louder than the last before a rustle followed, like footsteps.

They watched the door as four people walked in. Immediately, Blair jumped into the arms of one of them.

Blake.

He grunted from the impact, dropping the bags they had brought from Malriks. A sob tore from her throat as she looked him over for injuries. Pulling away, her eyes moved to the others, assessing them. Each one was covered in blood and black goo but they were here. All four.

There were supposed to be five.

Someone was missing.

Rhea spoke before Blair could ask, a tear sliding down her cheek. "Adriel didn't make it." Her voice broke on the last word and Blair watched as her body sagged in grief.

Blair immediately embraced her, apologizing in whispers as Rhea let her tears fall silently. Marrow made a whimpering sound and Blake pulled her into him, as if he could be her shield from the sadness. Damien rested his hand on Kael's shoulder who was staring at the ground, his eyes glossy.

It was only when Rhea finally pulled away that Blair knew they were utterly exhausted. She took Rhea's blood-covered hand and led them down the hallway.

Turning into one of the bedrooms they had found, she sat Rhea on the bed and collected items for them to shower. Like everything else in the house, it was out and ready for them. Clothes, soaps, and towels neatly placed in convenient spots.

They sat together as the Shadowborn took turns washing off the battle they had just come from. Blair watched them as they came out, one by one, with an ache in her chest. The death of Adriel had shattered them.

The night bled into the morning, as everyone just sat in silence. Blair and Damien kept them company, preparing makeshift beds and relighting the hearth that was in the room.

The fire provided an outlet, an area they stared into as the dancing flames moved.

Blair looked around at the group, their faces lit by firelight. Each of them seemed heavy, weighed by the same things she had seen in Damien only hours before.

Attempting to make conversation, she turned to Blake. "You said you'd been here. Did you know it looked like this inside?"

The question settled like a tremor through the room and yet, he didn't answer at first, his arms tight around

Marrow. "My travels never involved coming in. I had only ever seen the exterior."

Blair said nothing as she observed the pristine details surrounding them. When her eyes returned to them, she knew they needed more time.

She had been right, it was only when their bodies seemed to be giving out from exhaustion, that they began the attempt to get comfortable.

Rhea and Kael had settled with their backs to the wall in one of the corners. Blake had Marrow curled up in his lap with his head tilted back on the wall behind him.

Blair waited until their even breathing filled the room before she unpacked the bags they had brought. Folding clothes, she put them in dressers and then covered them all with blankets and laid next to Damien.

"You did good today. They needed that." he said, looking around the room at the others.

Blair nodded into him, as she pulled the blanket up and over them. Her exhaustion also taking over.

Blair had just closed her eyes when she was awakened by the light from the fire, or more so, the people moving in front of it. There were two forms, pacing back and forth in front of the flickering light. One stopped and turned, purple eyes gleaming. The elderly woman she had seen earlier. She was now in the room they were sleeping in, talking to someone outside of the doorway, but Blair couldn't see who. Blair looked around to find the others. As she did so, she realized the room was different. No one occupied it besides the elderly woman and a young boy who stood staring into the fire.

Blair moved up against the wall, realizing it was a dream. She took a moment to focus her mind and take in everything she was seeing. The decorations on the walls were the same as if it had been recently. The two people in the room seemed significant for many reasons. The third one, the one she spoke too, she still couldn't see, and the voice was almost distorted. She strained to hear it as the woman lifted her hand to her chest as if upset. She was physically shaking and a tear had fallen down her cheek. After a moment, she took something from the person in the doorway. A white letter, like the one that was left for them in the castle. The woman bowed her head as she accepted the letter and the conversation stopped. The woman then looked up, as if looking straight at Blair and then held out the letter to her. "He protected us and he'll protect you too." In the next blink, Blair now stood in the dining hall, staring at the same envelope on the counter.

Blair opened her eyes to find herself back in the room filled with her friends. Blinking into the darkness, she knew what she had just witnessed was confirmation from the mark of Fate. She silently thanked her mark before turning into Damien and settling.

34

The castle was still asleep when Damien stirred.

Ash-gray light filtered in through the high window of the room they had slept in. He sat up slowly, muscles stiff, the cold having settled deep into his bones.

Looking over next to him, his body immediately tensed. Blair's blanket was empty. He scanned the area and found no sign of her. The others were still asleep, curled in small heaps around the room. The fire had gone out sometime through the night, leaving only a soft glow of embers.

Damien stood, grabbing his boots from the stone shelf near the door, and moved into the hall.

The castle had a strange kind of silence, one that didn't feel abandoned, but rather watchful. He roamed until he found her, two levels above.

The door to the room she was in, was open, and light poured in from a stained-glass window on the wall. Blair stood at the center of the chamber.

This was one of the rooms they had not explored yet, a room that seemed to be set up for important meetings or collaborations.

A massive table was in the middle, dominating the space. It was crescent-shaped and carved from dark wood, warped slightly with age. Chairs surrounded it and within the surface, names were etched in different handwriting, each one weathered but deliberate.

Damien leaned into the doorframe as he watched Blair. She ran her fingers across one of the names, tracing the grooves with silence. After another minute, he stepped into the room, moving up beside her.

She continued to analyze the table in front of her as he cleared his throat. "I bet this is where they stood, where the Shadowborn shaped the world they wanted to build," she said without turning, her voice distant but certain.

He nodded in agreement, approaching the table. His eyes drifted over the names, reading what time hadn't erased. Some were simple. Others layered in older languages, glyphs and sigils barely visible now. His hand paused over one in particular.

Idris.

The name made him pause as he circled it with his finger. He then moved around the table, scanning each name. Then his eyes lifted to find Blair's.

Her eyes were rimmed red, not from tears but lack of sleep.

Blair exhaled, slow and deep, as if she was already aware of how she looked. She stood straighter, her fingers now tapping the edge of the table. She then traced two fingers along the wood as she walked toward him. "You said once that you felt like the dagger needed to be with me," she said, glancing up at him. "Why do you think that is?"

Damien hesitated. For a man who could command shadows and storms with a thought, he suddenly looked unsure of how to explain that question. "You have something this world needs," he explained, "I see it in the way you speak to children, the way you hug those who scream sadness. I needed to protect it, to protect you."

He stepped closer until she could see the beginning of the mark that bound him to her. "The way you fight," he continued. "You never surrender. You have a light that I love, the one that refuses to go out. I saw it a long time ago." He studied her in silence for a moment, then reached out, his hand brushing hers briefly before he pulled it back.

Blair exhaled slowly, her breath fogging the cold air. "What comes next? "

"Well," Damien said, looking down at the table, "The Shadowborn were never meant to act alone. This mark connects more than power, it binds us with purpose and if we're going to survive what's coming, we need everyone."

She nodded, her expression hardening with resolve. "Then we need them here too." Blair stepped back from the table, as a shadowed form appeared next to her. "Please go wake them. Be gentle, and help with anything they need. They're still mourning."

It wasn't long before it returned with all of them following. Each one a little less of a shell then they were previously. Some were freshly wrapped in healing cloth, and others had bruises starting to form. They entered one by one, looking over the room and gathering around the crescent table.

The Shadowborn sat silent, their eyes still hollow. Damien stood behind Blair with his arms crossed, eyes scanning every face. The room was still as she began, "Before I was marked, I met a fortune teller who told me a prophecy. It came true and I ended up here with this." She ran her hand over the dagger on her thigh. Her eyes then raised back those around her and she continued, her voice steady, but low.

"When Damien and I got here, I saw her again. She was here, in the outer ruins. She was waiting for us." Blair's fingers grazed the edge of the table as she spoke. "She said we had to stay in the castle. That the blood that binds us hadn't been spilled yet." Blair then repeated the second prophecy, word for word to the Shadowborn.

Kael leaned forward, frowning. "What do you think that means?"

"I think something is coming," Blair said. "And I think the Mark of Fate knew we needed to be here." Blair ran her hand over the names on the table as she walked around it. "I'm pretty sure the fortune teller I received the prophecies from was one of them." She then paused and looked at the group. "I've been thinking about a lot. I know we were brought together for a reason. I know that we will have to work together to go up against whatever this is but in order to do that, we have to completely trust each other." She looked over each of them and then her eyes landed on

Kael and Blake. "Why didn't we sense anything at Malrik's?"

"Are you accusing us?" Kael shot to his feet, his chair screeching backward, eyes burning with something between hurt and fury.

"You think I wanted this?" he snapped, chest rising and falling. "You think I wouldn't have torn the whole godsdamn mountain apart if I'd felt even a whisper of death near Adriel?"

Blair held her ground, but the silence around them tightened like a noose. "I'm not saying that Kael. I'm asking because I don't want us to suffer like that again. I'm trying to understand things."

Kael pointed at the table, at the carved names older than any of them. "We're Shadowborn. We don't get the luxury of excuses. If one of us fails, we all bleed for it. I would do anything to protect our kind. To make sure we stay safe."

He swallowed hard as his jaw trembled once and then twice, splitting his anger apart. Then, slowly, he sank to one knee.

Blair watched as he bowed his head. Shadows lifting off his shoulders in thin, trembling threads that swirled around. The shadows thickened, growing darker and radiating in a circle around him. His voice dropped low. "I make my oath now," Kael said. "To you, Blair. To the mark you carry. To the shadows that bind us."

Kael lifted his head just enough for her to see his eyes.

"I vow my senses to you," he whispered, his words sinking deep. "My nose, my instincts, my blood. All of it. If something comes for you, or for any of us, I will feel it before it breaches the damn wind."

The shadows surged upward, wrapping around him like armor.

"And if I fail again," His voice cracked, but he pushed through it. "May your void take my shadow before any Hunter ever does."

A pulse of shadow burst outward from him, not violent, but absolute. It then condensed and wrapped around Blair, moving to her wrist. It swirled there, replacing the star that had been Adriel's.

Blair took a slow breath, stepping forward. "Kael," she said softly, placing her hand on his shoulder.

He hesitated, chest heaving.

"I wasn't accusing you. I was just looking for answers."

Kael pushed to his feet, shadows settling back into him like a second heartbeat.

He met her eyes with his, a raw emotion etched in his expression."You have them," he said. "And now my oath, for as long as I breathe."

"Thank you, Kael." Blair swallowed and nodded before looking at the others. "So now you know why I've called you here," she began. Her voice was calm, but it carried. "The prophecy is closing in. Whatever's coming, it's not waiting for us to be ready." She looked at each of them, assessing their quiet strength. "We can't afford mistakes," she said firmly. "If we want to rebuild this, we have to pull together every ounce of will we have. One slip, one hesitation, and it all falls apart."

Rhea nodded, her eyes shining the brightest they had since she arrived. "Then we stand together," she said. "No doubts. Whatever this prophecy brings, we face it head-on."

For a moment, the room was silent, then Kael rose, resting one hand on the table. "You already have my oath. I intend to keep it."

One by one, the others followed.

Blake was the last to stand. His expression was earnest. "No mistakes," he said softly. He paused then, his eyes flicking toward Marrow. "Not unless they're worth making."

Blair straightened, drawing in a deep breath as she looked around the crescent table. "Then it's settled," she said. "From this moment on, every step we take is deliberate. Every choice has weight and no one falters."

Each one of them nodded again as Kael moved his piercing around with his fingers. "If the prophecy happens here, we may be at an advantage." he said, pointing toward the gates outside. "We can even add barriers."

Rhea nodded, her braid brushing her shoulder. "We will be able to see it coming. Plus, we have supplies here and we can learn the layout."

A proud smile formed on Blair's face. "Then that's what we'll focus on. Kael, you'll handle the fortifications.

Rhea, make sure anything we have that will give us an advantage, is out and ready."

Damien's voice rose next. "We need to tweak our training." His gaze swept the table. "If the prophecy unfolds the way we expect, brute strength won't save us. We'll need precision."

Blake leaned forward, his smirk faint but sharp. "Then let's make it count."

Blair met his eyes briefly, catching the spark of competitiveness.

Kael grinned. "We'll run drills so we can predict any type of situation."

Damien allowed himself a small smile as Blair straightened, her voice carrying through the chamber. "We may not have all the answers but we are not cowards, we were chosen because we endure."

The Shadowborn nodded and the meeting was adjourned with a scrape of chairs and the hum of boots against stone. One by one, the Shadowborn filtered out into the corridor, some already discussing battle formations, others silent with thought.

Damien looked Blair up and down, a proud light flickering behind his eyes. "You've given them hope," he murmured.

She exhaled slowly, the faintest smile tugging at her lips. "No," she said. "They already had that, I just reminded them what it feels like."

Damien stepped up next to Blair and put his arm around her shoulder, kissing the top of her head. They remained there for a moment longer until he glanced at the empty crescent table. "We'll be ready."

Blair nodded and took a step toward the corridor, the prophecy playing in her head.

Those who are born shall fall... but not until the shadows gather and the sky falls in mourning.

35

This time, it was Blair's turn to wake up to emptiness beside her. The spot where Damien had laid hours before, was still creased with the imprint of his body, but the warmth was long gone.

She sat up slowly, rubbing the sleep from her eyes as her gaze drifted to the faint light peeking through the rippled curtains. The dawn was gray, darker than normal.

Pushing herself out of bed, Blair padded across the room barefoot. She moved to the window and peered outside. In the courtyard below, Damien moved like his shadows, fluid and precise. Blake and Kael trained beside him, each of their movements synced with his. There was no laughter and no idle chatter, just the clash of shadows and the low grunt of exertion.

It had been this way for a two weeks, each of the Shadowborn settling into their duties and preparing for any type of danger. Every hour spent finding a different advantage, within the walls or themselves.

Blair watched them move, every face hardened with determination. Her hand moved to her thigh, her fingers lightly running over the mark.

Lifting her eyes to the sky, she scanned the clouds that churned above the courtyard. The weight in her chest thickened as she watched a storm approach from the east.

She turned to the dresser and opened it, searching for one specific outfit. It laid there folded at the bottom, waiting for the day she felt she would need it. Pulling it out of the drawer, she let it fall open. Black shadowcloth embroidered in purple thread, tailored perfectly to her body. There was power woven into its seams, thanks to Alessandra. Blair could feel it; protection, elegance, and something older. She tugged it on and braided her hair, a skill Rhea had helped her with recently.

As she stepped into the hall, she called to her shadow, asking it to stay in her room.

Once it was settled, she descended the stairs and passed by the dining hall, where Rhea and Marrow sat at the long table, eating. Rhea looked up, a piece of bread halfway to her mouth as the door slammed open, rattling the dishes on the table.

Blake burst into the room. "They're here!" he shouted. "We sense them coming through the eastern pass."

All at once, they moved in sync. Chairs scraped the floor, dishes shattered as they fell. The air filled with the rustle of motion as they all sprinted toward the door.

Outside, the sky had darkened more. A wave of black almost over them with angry rumbles in the distance.

Rhea stood tall underneath it, her armor already forming around her. Marrow stepped beside her, voice low and urgent as she looked at Blake. "How close?"

His answer came as he stepped in front of them, his hands balling into fists. "Close enough to know there's hundreds of them."

Kael had already moved to the gate. He knelt low, shadows spilling from his palms in long, fluid lines that slithered across the stone. They spread like veins, crawling up the iron gate and along the walls.

"What are you doing?" Rhea called, stepping closer.

"Setting the stage," Kael replied, his eyes focused on the floor. The shadow whips pulsed once, then vanished beneath the ground, invisible to all but Kael.

A single raindrop fell from above them.

She looked up as another fell, then another. They landed on her skin like ice, sharp and sudden. Just like that, the feeling of dread returned, as did the communication from her mark.

A sharp, sudden pain filled her thigh as if it demanded her full attention. She knelt forward, grabbing her leg as Damien moved to her and for one precious heartbeat, the courtyard held still. Blair could feel the quiet in her bones as she gritted her teeth through the pain in her leg.

There was an unnatural stillness in the air, even the breeze had stopped. A sword of pure black formed in Damien's grip as Kael stood frozen at his side, their eyes falling on movement in the distance.

Each face morphed into anger at what they recognized. Blair knew, without even having to lift her head. The mark on her thigh pulsed violently, like fire rushing through her veins, screaming against her skin.

Slowly and deliberately, she raised her gaze. Her eyes found him immediately, just beyond the open gate where he stood watching them.

The King.

He pushed forward. The ground seemed to vibrate with every step of his approach. Dark blue cloaks billowed in the wind around him, and behind him stretched a tide of people. Each one masked with their hoods drawn. *Hunters, Enforcers, and Phantoms waited for his command.*

Blair's shoulders stiffened as the King moved even closer. He held himself like someone who had never been denied a thing in his life, and wouldn't know how to comprehend the word no. His hair was blonde, touched with silver at the temples, and his eyes were locked on Blair.

The Hunters behind him remained silent, unbreaking in formation.

Their presence meant he was coming to *claim.*

"By the gods." Kael whispered behind her.

Blake didn't speak.

Neither did Damien.

Blair looked around at them, her family. The fire inside her surged again, the mark burning brighter than it ever had. The King's gaze hadn't left her, not even for a second and even from across the courtyard, his presence was aimed at her.

Rhea stepped forward beside Blake, her armor gleaming through the storm. "Hold your ground," she murmured.

Kael's fingers twitched as the King hovered above the hidden structure he had built. Just one more step and the King would activate the trap, ultimately being wrapped in shadowed whips. Just as his foot raised about the hidden webs, a figure appeared at the King's side.

The creature was tall and faceless, cloaked in shadow. *A Phantom.* Its head tilted, as it looked at the floor and raised a single hand. Swirling shadows gathered at its fingertips as he looked toward the ground. His hand slammed into the dirt below him, creating a shockwave that spread across the courtyard, exposing the lines Kael had hidden. Every thread of his trap flared white-hot, visible and useless.

Rhea cursed under her breath.

The King pulled his foot back, his lips curving into something cruel. "Clever," he said, his voice echoing across the yard. "But predictable."

Kael's teeth clenched as he ripped his shadows back, his whips returning to him.

"You set traps like children," the King declared.

The Phantom turned its head, the faint shimmer of his eyes meeting Kael's for an instant. Then, it dissolved into the others around it.

As if the sky was angry, thunder rumbled above them as raindrops began to fall around them, faster this time.

The King was too close now, his energy hitting them with full force. He was dressed in ceremonial black armor with a long silver mantle that trailed behind him like a stain. A crown sat atop his head, and his eyes gleamed with wicked intent. He stepped forward to the edge of the broken concrete that laid across from them. Taking his time, he looked down at them, amused, almost *pitying*.

"Well," the king said, his voice carrying with unnatural clarity across the ruined courtyard. "This is, *charming*."

No one moved.

"You all really thought this would be the end, didn't you? That all your little rebellion needed was a couple of chosen ones and a few tricks pulled from the dark corners of the world." He laughed, "*Pathetic.*"

The Shadowborn remained strong.

"You think I didn't see this coming?" The King spread his arms. "That I didn't prepare for it? I knew you would rise again and I knew I would have to be one step ahead." A smile spread across the King's face as his gaze landed on someone behind Blair. "Well done, Renner."

The words hit the Shadowborn like a ripple of ice, especially Blair, whose air was ripped from her lungs.

Renner.

Renner.

The King noticed her flinch, of course, smiling wider at the reaction, "And really, I'm quite offended none of you figured it out. He is a spitting image of me."

He lifted a hand toward them, "Come here, grandson."

Blair didn't dare to move, not even as someone stepped around her and moved toward the King. His green eyes catching hers as they passed.

His face then settled into stone as he stood in front of his grandfather. He didn't speak, but he also made no effort to deny the claim.

The only reaction he gave was when Marrow stepped toward him, her face contorted in pain. Blake's eyes narrowed as she tried to take another step, her mouth gaping in confusion. It was only a few more moments before she broke, screaming at him, "*No, NO!*"

She ran toward Blake, but a wall of shadow separated them as another Phantom stepped next to the King.

Marrow screamed louder, hitting the darkened wall as if she could break through.

Damien's posture stiffened as he watched her beg for Blake, his hand instinctively tightening around the hilt of his conjured blade. His eyes then roamed over the King. "You've got some nerve," he said, his tone low. "This kingdom isn't yours."

The King's smile was effortless and cruel. "Isn't it?" His gaze swept over the courtyard, and then lingered on each of them, before stopping on Blake. "I'd say it's more mine than you realize."

Blake didn't move.

Blair's thigh thrummed. "Why are you here?"

"To finish what I started," the King said. He then turned to Blake, "You've done well gathering them, by the way. As you always have for me. It sure saves me time."

Damien's eyes darkened as dark webs coiled across his body. "You're lying-"

But the King cut him off with a gesture, his gaze sliding back to Blake. "Tell them, Renner."

Blake's head turned toward them, but he remained silent, his eyes glazed over with a look none of them had ever seen.

Blair just stared, paralyzed by confusion and disbelief.

Kael spoke to his comrades, his voice low. "He smells of the truth."

The King's smile widened, as he reveled in their reactions. "Ah. So they never knew. How charming." He took another slow step forward, his boots echoing on the stone. "*Blake*, the loyal soldier with the sharp tongue and wandering eyes. But that's not who you are, is it? You're mine. You always were."

"Lies!" Blair snapped. Shadows forming on her skin, mimicking Damiens.

But still, Blake didn't deny it. He just stared at them, jaw locked, breathing shallow.

The silence broke when Rhea shouted across the courtyard. "What the hell Blake? Was Adriel because of you?!"

The King tilted his head, feigning pity. "Renner was my eyes in the dark. My shadow in your midst. That's the only thing he's good for. Each one I collected was because of him. Mark by mark, name by name. Every Shadowborn he found was brought to me. Some I killed. Some I kept." His smile turned vicious. "I do *so* enjoy keeping pets."

Blair's stomach twisted. She looked at Blake, *at Renner*, and for the first time, she saw it. The flicker of guilt behind his eyes, the heaviness he carried.

"Tell me he's lying," Blair said quietly as she took a step toward him, a purple glow fading into her shadows.

Blake's lips parted, but no sound came.

Damien's blade grew in size as his shadows convulsed, fed by his anger. "Say it, Blake."

The King chuckled. "He can't. Because even now, he knows his place and now that I have you, he's *worthless*."

Blair's voice was barely a whisper as she said his name. "Blake." A single tear fell from her blackened eyes.

Blake's eyes met hers, a raw type of pain filling them.

"Touching," the King said dryly. "But enough sentiment, I came to collect what's mine."

As the King moved, Damien's shadows burst outward, as did his wings, filling the edges of the yard in a dark surge. "You'll collect nothing."

The Mark of Void erupted on Blair's skin at the same time. A purple shadow encased her, twisting around her body and feeding on her emotions. Damien moved closer to her, and their shadows formed a wall, igniting together.

"Oh, how I'd love to get my hands on that kind of power." The king clapped joyfully as he watched their shadows rise. "I think I'll keep you."

Blair snarled and went to strike, but as she moved Marrow grabbed her wrist. In the next movement, Blake Shadowstepped to the other side of the King and swept a blade at the King's neck. A Phantom moved with blinding speed, forcing Blake to pierce the King's shoulder instead.

A scream tore from his mouth as he spat at his grandson, who glared at him with malice. The king grew more angry, spewing curses, as he watched Blake shadow-step next to Marrow. Once there, he intertwined his hand with hers.

From behind, Blair watched as a symbol formed on the side of their hands. Each side holding half a picture. Together, they formed a diamond that joined together as their fingers laced.

A shadow oath to each other.

Safety.

"My grandson," the king mocked, laughing maniacally, "the traitor to his family over *a woman.*"

Blake was shaking with anger. "*This* is my family, you fucking lunatic."

"One mark doesn't erase what I am to you, you will always be bound to me. Why don't I give you a little reminder."

He clapped twice.

From the shadows beyond the door, something dragged itself into the light.

As it emerged, Blair's stomach turned.

It was a man, but barely. His body was bloated and warped by shadow, muscles torn and reformed in loops that didn't obey human anatomy. Holes peppered his face, voids where eyes, nose, and jaw should have been. From those holes, black mist *leaked*, dripping down his throat. The man staggered with every step, but stood.

As he got closer, his features became more clear, and Blair *remembered*. The nightmare with his face, the voices apologizing over and over again. The scream that shattered her and woke her up. *Help me, help me, please...*

"Oh my god," she breathed. "He was real."

Blair tried to warn Blake but he had already seen him. She knew by the way his face had suddenly blanched, his hand falling from Marrows.

"R-Ronan?"

The king saw this and laughed with an exaggerated energy, "I always plan for everything Renner, including insurance policies. I thought you might have been pulling away, so I decided to change my tactic. The gas worked well, but I finally succeeded at stabilizing an experiment. It was quite a shame really. He had no one to protect him when I shoved shadows down his throat, when I was finally able to make the perfect weapon. This is on you Blake, you did this to him. *You* killed your brother."

Blake pulled away from Marrow as he took a staggering step forward, toward the mutilated man as a tear fell down his cheek.

Blair's dagger tattoo flared again violently, like it recognized the horror before her. Her skin seared with power, and for the first time, all four Marks surged to the surface urging her to fight. Fate spun silver rings around her spine. The Veil shimmered like broken glass across her collarbone. The Mark of Night throbbed, pulsing with grief and Void, the pure, jagged shadow, bled into her veins like acid. The shadow within her begged to be released.

"Blair!" Damien warned, but it was too late.

She raised her hand, power *roaring* through her as she moved like lightning. The sound of her boots against the soaked courtyard stone was lost beneath the thunder that cracked overhead, splitting the sky.

With the flick of his hand, the Hunters were released. Dozens of them, maybe more, poured toward them. They crawled over the stone walls, bursting through the iron gates, slinking from the shadows like assassins. Their bodies were barely human, twisting and sharpening into things designed only to tear, to shred.

Blair didn't hesitate as she raised her hands and sent multiple forms of her shadow to attack them. As she worked to slaughter the ones near her, a vortex manifested next to her, pulling shadows from the hunters into its swirling center.

The front line of Hunters screamed as the whirling cyclone consumed them. With every one that disappeared, more took their place.

Behind her, the Shadowborn followed her. Damien's shadow blade was already cutting down the first two Hunters that reached them. He spun low, and then flew high, dropping down to drive darkness through different hollow chests. His movements were ruthless, and efficient.

Kael moved beside him like a shadow, tendril whips of his magic snaking around his arms. He would expand them, wrapping them around the necks of the nearest Hunters and snapping them like dried branches. He said nothing as he did so, his silence its own kind of violence.

Rhea darted through the battlefield like a ghost, her armor glinting against the rain as she took out Hunter after Hunter, her breath coming fast but controlled.

And Blake? Blake unleashed. He carved through the second wave like a man possessed. Blades spun in both hands as silver flashed through blood and mist. His cloak was soaked through, his face streaked with crimson, but he didn't stop. Not when a Hunter lunged for Kael, not when three more closed in on Damien. He just kept moving faster, taking them out as if in retribution for his choices.

One shriek cut above the chaos. It was real, human, and wrong.

Blair's eyes snapped left just in time to see Marrow drop to one knee. A jagged gash was torn down her side and a Phantom held her up, with the King beside her.

Blair immediately knew she couldn't reach her in time, but she knew who could.

Her shadowed guardian ran through the Phantom, ensnaring it in shadows.

Marrow fell the rest of the way with a cry of pain as her blood spilled on the stone below her. The king laughed with a sharp, delighted sound, as if this was all a game to him.

That's when Blake really snapped.

He turned to the King, eyes flashing, and became a weapon of pure fury. He slammed one Hunter to the ground, twisted the next by the throat and broke it without a blade. A third, a fourth, a fifth, all fell in seconds. It was no longer a battle, it was a massacre as black blood splattered the courtyard, mixing with the rainwater.

Blair took that opportunity to move in his wake. The ground cracked beneath her feet, as the air turned thick with plumes of darkness. Shadows screamed around her, forming into long spears of night that were aimed at the king's heart. He didn't flinch but instead smiled, as *someone else* moved for him.

Blake's brother, or what remained of him, lunged with unnatural speed. In his hands was a *shadow-forged machete* raised high, twisting through the air toward Blair's throat. She had been so focused on revenge that she didn't see it coming. The cool metal had just touched the skin of her throat when she was thrust into the sky.

Damien's arms caged her in as she looked up into his eyes, which were completely silver now. His wings were entirely open, each feather shimmering with different runes.

They landed quickly, in a different place of battle away from the King and Marrow.

"Come then, Shadowborn," the King said as he loomed over Marrow again. His voice carried over the air as he lodged his knife into Marrow's injury. "Let me see what your bond has become."

Damien and Blake replied with a roar, each moving to battle a different darkness.

A crash shook the ground as Damien swooped down and slammed into the King, forcing him back a step. Rhea and Kael continued to fight through the hordes on the ground, slashing through them bit by bit.

For the first time, the ruler looked unsettled, but not afraid.

Behind them, a second battle erupted. Blake and his brother collided. Ronan moved with jagged precision, his body flickering between forms, solid one moment, shadow the next. Blake fought with fury, his eyes moving to Marrow frequently.

In a cunning move, he lured an attack near Damien. Once close enough, he grabbed him and Shadowstepped him to Marrow. Two rushed words was all he gave Damien as he returned to the fight. "Heal her!"

The chance of this angered the King who signaled more Phantoms.

More shadows ripped out of Damien's back, forming wings broader and sharper than before. Each feather-like blade shimmered between black and silver now, the runes along his arms igniting as if answering to his lineage. His entire form bent then, reshaping until horns curved upward through his hair. The first Phantom met him head-on, its blade of darkness slashing through air but Damien was faster. He caught the strike, crushed the weapon between clawed hands, and flung the creature aside as he turned to Marrow, healing her.

More Phantoms swarmed as Blair defended against them, each one pulling from a different form of shadow magic. There were dark whips, blades, arrows, all striking at once as rain poured on them. Blair tore through them, every movement a blur of black and purple shadow.

Still, for every phantom she tore apart, two more rose from the darkness. There was no slowing down, there was no giving up. Behind her, Blake gained ground, driving his brother back step by step. "You don't have to be this," he shouted. "We can end this," he yelled again, through clenched teeth, "together."

The malformed man only smiled, a hollow symbol void of emotion. His skin morphed and stretched, giving way to a black hole in his chest. From it, a spear burst out. A sleek, sharp weapon made to kill.

Instead of being aimed toward him, like he had expected, it was moving toward Blair who was unaware, her attention on the Hunter before her. On instinct, Blake shadowstepped, reappearing beside Blair and shoving her out of the way. As he stepped back into his darkness, the spear followed.

He reappeared as it made impact, breaking into multiple spears of darkness that tore through his body.

He froze, mouth parting in silent shock. His arms went slack first, then his body, as he collapsed backwards. Blair ran, falling to her knees in front of him as black blood bubbled from his mouth. His eyes found hers for a split second. "Take him down, P-princess." With that, the hue in his green eyes darkened and his body went limp in her arms.

The world went still as Marrow screamed behind her, a raw and gutting sound that tore open every single one of them.

"No. No, No!" Blair screamed, her body shaking. She held him tighter, willing everything in him to wake up but his body just continued to bleed out, seeping into her clothes.

Damien was shouting something at Blair as he leaned over Marrow, but she could no longer hear anything. Tears and blood blurred her vision as she fought the eruption inside of her.

She just sat there, cradling Blake.

Through the streaks in her vision Blair found the King watching her, smiling. "Oh look, you made me go and break my favorite toy."

Blair stopped rocking as a raw emotion filled her body, one of pure hatred. She gently laid Blake down and stood up. Fresh blood dripped off of her fingers as she looked down at her friend who lay lifeless.

For a moment, she waited, contemplating how exactly to rip the King into pieces. Her energy pulsed in waves, causing black ripples to spread from her. They moved, wider and wider, until they passed over Blake. Hovering above him, they settled for just a moment before they were pulled into his chest.

They expanded over his body, forming to his figure and then sinking into his limbs. His chest lifted off the ground as more waves poured in, and then swirled angrily above him as they twisted together.

As fast as they were stolen from the air, they stopped and everything stood still. A moment later a dark silhouette rose from Blake's body, a dark replica of the man who had just fallen.

His features were the same, even after death.

He turned toward Damien first, his eyes landing on Marrow who was now partially healed. Then, he stepped beside Blair.

Blair watched as he joined her side, her other guardian filling in the other space.

The dagger tattoo on Blair's thigh erupted, splitting in a burst of purple and black light. Shadows exploded around her, wrapping her in armor-like wisps, forming a mantle of twisting darkness that coiled and lashed in sync with her breath. As the violet inferno came to life around her, Damien's magic pulsed in response. Threads of black energy latching onto hers from where he stood on the other side of the yard. Damien fed every ounce of energy he could into her, and Marrow, who still lay beneath him.

Blair absorbed what he gave her with a cry as her glowing form trembled, and unraveled. Shadows roared around the Shadowborn, embodied by their leader's ascension. The Hunters were fast, vicious, and unrelenting but the Shadows were pissed now.

Blair and her two shadows struck like living nightmares, all across the battlefield. Blake's shadowed soul moved just as he had in life, gliding beside Blair as they faced the chaos together.

The air around them filled with dark pressure as Blake's brother began to flinch, his face suddenly twisting in rage and confusion. His limbs fighting against things that were not there.

The King and the surrounding Hunters were also affected. All of them holding their heads as they screamed in pain.

It was Marrow's influence, powered by her grief. Damien had healed her enough to activate it.

Nightmares curled around them all, like smoke, whispering lies, gnawing at the edges of their sanity.

Ronan staggered forward, snarling. He gripped his head with mutilated fingers as shadows invaded his twisted mind.

"Renner." he growled, the voice hollow and warped, as if coming from the bottom of a well. "Y- you left me."

Blake's shadow said nothing in return, he just stood and watched as his brother was ripped apart mentally by his worst fears. Blake's hollow shell was calm and unwavering, which only blended into the illusions.

Blair took that moment to strike. Her shadow-wrapped form blurred forward, a new dagger, one that glowed purple formed in her hand. With a cry of vengeance and mercy entwined, she drove it through Ronan's heart, as Blake and the other shadow held him still from behind. His scream echoed as he convulsed, shadows breaking through different parts of his skin. They poured from his mouth and eyes as Blair stabbed again. On the next strike, he crumbled into a dark pile of dust, immediately soaked by the storm.

Across the field, Damien took the opportunity to move away from Marrow and make his move as well. The King, who had been writhing in pain from the mental combat, stood exposed as he watched his creation disappear.

Damien's blade found its target with ruthless precision as he came up behind him and slit his throat.

The King gasped, a single breath hitching in his throat before he collapsed to his knees.

Damien stood over him, pushing him down with his foot and driving the shadowed sword into his chest. Blood bubbled from his mouth as Damien stared down at him and spat, "This is for *Blake*."

The King's eyes rolled and a final breath escaped his lips.

Marrow's ability had combined with Rhea and Kael's assaults, resulting in a downfall of Hunter's. One by one, the ones that were left began to leak shadows from their wounds. Slowly at first, and then faster as if the toxins were pouring out. Once empty, their bodies hit the ground like hollowed drums.

Blair dropped to her knees, chest heaving, her body marked by more than just the battle. All four marks still glowed across her skin.

She felt it then, how she was bound to all the previous leaders. She understood what Lailah had meant. The magic that others had wielded was running through her veins. She had been marked, chosen, cursed, *transformed.* The realization of this made tears fall freely down her cheeks as she looked at Blake's shadow soul. He still stood silently next to her, his presence flickering in the sunlight that was now fighting the clouds.

Then, slowly and deliberately, he stepped forward and sank into Blair's shadow.

Damien landed beside her then, quietly grabbing her hand. "He gave you his shadow."

Blair choked back a sob, closing her eyes as her shadows calmed.

Standing, she looked at the Shadowborn around her. Rhea and Kael stood, gashes on their bodies bleeding freely. Marrow lay unconscious on the floor, wounded, but breathing.

"It's over," she told them, her purple shadow fading. "It's over." she repeated to herself, as she looked at the shadow that Blake had just stepped into.

36

It had been one week since the battle. Seven days total since the sky had cried in mourning for Blake, and the King had fallen. Eighty-four hours that had been filled with grief.

It was only in the last two days that the Shadowborn had gained the ability to move and even then, it was out of necessity. The castle had been filled with silence as each person took their time to process everything that had happened.

The heaviest silence came from Marrow. She hadn't spoken since the night Blake had taken his last breath. She sat apart from the others, her back always to the fire, the light flickering against her unmoving form. The bowl of food left beside her each evening went untouched, the steam rising until it disappeared.

Kael had tried to help once, placing a hand on her shoulder, murmuring something about strength, about moving forward. Her body flinched as though struck. After that, no one tried again.

Blair watched from a distance, unable to decide whether to approach. Damien warned her not to. "Let her break in peace," he'd said.

So she did.

Each day bled into the next. A sunrise, and then a sunset, one after another.

But it was in that time, slowly and quietly, that the world around them began to shift.

The first to arrive was Grei.

It was a quiet morning, the air heavy but cool. Blair was half-asleep when the knock came. Damien answered the door with a shadowed blade tucked behind him, only to find Grei on the other side.

He stood tall as ever, lean and silent, with two thick slabs of wood slung over his back and a solemn look in his eyes. He didn't speak at first, just stared at Damien for a long breath before bowing his head. "I'm sorry for your fallen friends," he said quietly.

Damien nodded once, and stepped aside, inviting him in. He spent the day helping with what was needed around the castle, and even sat with those who just needed company.

That night, Grei and Damien worked together to carve caskets beneath the stars. No words were spoken between them, but it was as if Grei knew that's what Damien needed. Blair sat outside with them, watching them as they moved, as if each strike helped with the grief.

A few hours later, both of the men sat beside half-built coffins. Rubbing shaven wood from their hands,

Grei broke the silence. "I've been visiting them," he said, his voice barely above the wind. "In dreams. One by one, telling them the Shadowborn have risen."

Damien glanced up, his brow raised in question.

Grei gave a faint, tired smile. "They are on their way."

The next day, Grei was proven right when a large group, led by Shiloh, arrived. They approached quietly, the news of Adriel, weighing heavy.

Shiloh sought them out, bearing food and offerings from baskets that they carried. "I am sorry," was all he said, his eyes glossy. Blair hugged him and looked at the others behind him, most too young to have known Adriel well, but old enough to understand what he meant. Regardless, they had all come to pay their respects.

Blair stood by the edge of the courtyard as someone stepped through the crowd.

Alessandra.

She said nothing at first, just crossed the last few steps between them and wrapped Blair in her arms. There were no words between them as they held each other. That was what she offered, the firm, grounding embrace of someone who understood the pain.

On her back was a satchel, stuffed to the seams. She had brought clothes with her. Some black and soft, threaded for mourning. Others lighter and new, stitched with threads Blair didn't recognize at first. Alessandra only smiled as Blair looked over them, "Woven from hope."

Blair thanked her quietly and showed her to the space they would be staying in.

That night, she dreamed.

The veiled women stood around a fire, surrounded by columns. In the dark, their faces were hidden, their voices soft. They didn't offer any words of encouragement, only silence, and the brush of fingers through shadows as they whispered names over the Loom. *Adriel. Blake.*

Blair woke with their voices still echoing in her mind. Her hands shook as she ran her fingers over her mark.

The last to show was Malrik.

He arrived the next day at dusk, limping heavily, leaning on a cane that looked hand-carved from the obsidian rock that had covered his cavern. His cloak was worn, still stained from battle, and his eyes had been aged with sadness. Shadows no longer clung to him in groups but just a few reminders of the people he had.

He said nothing when he saw Blair. Just looked at her, and nodded once.

When Damien approached, Malrik let out a quiet grunt. "I didn't think I'd ever be walking into this castle."

"Welcome to our home," Damien replied.

Malrik stared at him, then at the growing amounts of people who roamed the halls.

"Yes, indeed, it is," he said as they helped him inside.

Blair noticed the way he winced when he moved, the fresh scars peeking through the fabric at his collar.

Whatever had happened there had left more than just wounds, it had stripped some of the darkness from him, too.

He didn't speak of the fallen, not aloud but that night, he placed a single stone on the edge of the garden where the two caskets would lay.

Blair stood by the window that night, watching the firelight flicker across the courtyard where so many had now gathered. The battle had ended, and she had lost a piece of her heart.

And yet, it felt like the Shadowborn were all coming home.

37

After a night of tossing and turning, morning came too soon.

Light gently bled in through the breaks in the curtain, casting pale stripes across the stone floor.

Blair was the first to wake, staring up at the ceiling until Damien rustled next to her. Still asleep, his arm rested loosely across her waist. His warmth was grounding, the familiar feeling of safety. For a moment, everything seemed normal but then she pictured Marrow, and then Blake, and her chest tightened. Her breath slowed, moving in and out, as if she needed to remember how.

Grief was funny in that way. The absence didn't come with screams, it came with a deep ache. Her chest seized before the tears even came. She turned her face into the pillow, trying to muffle the first broken sob that forced its way out, but the pain didn't care about silence.

Damien stirred beside her. "Blair?"

She couldn't answer.

His arms wrapped around her without hesitation, pulling her against him as the grief finally spilled from her in full. There were no words. Just raw, ragged weeping, the kind that scraped the throat and left everything hollow.

"I'm sorry," she gasped, though she wasn't sure why. "I'm sorry that I couldn't-"

"Don't," Damien whispered into her hair, holding her tighter. "Blair, *don't.*"

She gripped the fabric of his shirt, knuckles white. "I keep waiting for his dumb comments, his idiotic smile, *anything.*"

"I know," Damien said, his voice thick with his own grief.

They laid there in silence for a long time, the world outside beginning to move, slowly and softly, as the sun climbed higher. Birds called outside the castle window but inside, time stood still.

Blair sat up eventually, brushing her hair back with trembling fingers. Her eyes were swollen and red, her face pale and raw.

A soft knock sounded at the door and Damien rose to answer it. Opening it with caution, he found Marrow standing there, swaying slightly, her face pale like she too, had not stopped crying.

She was wrapped in fresh bandages that covered her torso, with one arm pressed tightly to her ribs. Even though Damien had managed to heal most of the larger wounds, there was still damage within. In her other hand, she held a small letter with trembling fingers.

"Blair," she rasped.

Damien stepped aside without a word, and Marrow limped through, her steps slow, each one etched with pain. Blair sat up in bed, startled, but not because of the wounds, because of the look on Marrow's face.

Marrow crossed the room without explanation and sat down beside Blair on the edge of the bed, exhaling through clenched teeth. She didn't speak right away, just stared forward, breathing shallowly. Then, finally, she spoke.

"Blake was many things," she said softly, her voice hoarse. "But you need to know that a *traitor was* not one of them."

Blair froze as her chest tightened. She didn't know what she'd expected, but it hadn't been that.

Marrow blinked, and a single tear traced down her bruised cheek. She didn't wipe it away, she just let it fall. "He came to me," she continued, "the night Adriel died, as we waited to come here." Her jaw clenched. "He was frazzled and I thought it was because of Adriel." Blair sat up straighter as Marrow turned to her, gaze wet but steady. "He made me take an oath. That no matter what happened, no matter what was said or what it looked like, I would believe in him and I would believe in you. I'm sorry it took me so long to remember that."

Blair's throat tightened. She tried to speak, but no words came.

Marrow looked down at her hand, where the mark that bound her to him shimmered faintly beneath the bandaged skin. "He said that you would change everything, and that you would need this when the time came." She stared at it for a long time before extending the letter. "He wrote it for you," she said, her voice quieter now, cracked.

Blair reached out, fingers numb, and took the envelope from her. Skimming her finger under the back, she opened it, and a small knife fell into her lap. Picking it up, she realized it was the one Damien had imbued for him.

Looking up, Damien's eyes were glued to it like he had immediately recognized it. She handed it to him as she turned back to the letter. The parchment was pure white, familiar in a way that made her chest ache. After flipping it over in her hands, she realized it was the same kind of paper from the letter they had found when they first arrived.

Marrow rose with a grunt of pain, limping toward the door. Before she left, she looked over her shoulder once more. "Whatever Blake was planning, it was never meant to hurt you," she said. "You really were his family." Then she was gone.

Damien stood by the bed, watching Blair closely. He didn't speak as she unfolded the parchment with trembling hands.

His handwriting, the handwriting written in black ink, was the exact same. The handwriting she had read before on the notes.

Blair,

If you're reading this, it means I couldn't change my fate. I'm sorry for that. Gods, I'm sorry for a lot of things. You deserve the whole truth and not just the pieces that were given.

I made choices to run from my family and I made them knowing that it would eventually cost me. I never thought I would have the chance to find everything, just for it all to be taken away.

I guess now is a good time to tell you I lied. I didn't grow up in a camp like the other Shadowborn and I wasn't trained by Hunters. I grew up on the edge of silence, in between different places, dragged from one dark corner to another. Raised by people who saw me not as a boy, but as a tool. My family used me and my gift of tracking, to hunt others like me. My mission was simple: find the ones with the strongest abilities, with the most hope.

I had no choice but to listen to them. As a form of retribution, I made myself watch it all. I witnessed each and every Shadowborn be broken and tortured, used until there was nothing left.

Every time I closed my eyes, I saw their faces. Eventually, that wasn't enough and they sent me out into the field, with my grandfather's eye on me like a chain around my throat. He called it my duty but it was a leash and I wore it for years.

The first time I fought back was when I found the Mark of Fate; Here, in the castle. My grandfather always thought they were just a legend but he was so incredibly wrong. I spent time with them, rebuilding the Shadowborn foundation.

They taught me that I could choose my own fate and I helped them stay in hiding. The goal was to keep this place safe, for you guys.

I visited often, to check on them, to make sure the future of the Shadowborn was still alive. When I realized how close we were to certain prophecies, I knew I was willing to do whatever it took.

It wasn't until I met you guys, that I knew I was okay with that. I don't even know the exact moment it happened. Maybe it was the first time we stood back-to-back in a fight and you trusted me. Maybe it was the night we all sat together and ate with Shiloh. I remember telling myself to just keep eating because then it wouldn't end. It might have even been when Damien gave me the knife. I almost broke down then and told him everything.

At some point, you guys made me feel like I wasn't just a shadow in the room anymore, I actually belonged somewhere.

So now that I'm gone, know this, I haven't left you. I won't leave you. I'm still with you, and I will be, to fight beside you, and to sit with you in the quiet moments between battles because that's what family does. We stay, even after death.

I have no regrets loving you guys, especially Marrow. Please tell her that. I was never good with words, not the soft ones anyway, you always knew that. Please protect her, keep her safe. She's going to need you. Don't let her grumpiness fool you, she has one of *the most fragile hearts I've ever come across, please don't let it shatter.*

I loved you guys more than I ever thought possible. You were the one thing I didn't think I could have, and the one thing I will do anything to protect.

I'm sorry for the things I couldn't tell you. I'm sorry if you ever doubted me but gods, I'm so damn proud of all of you. Keep going. Keep fighting. Keep each other alive and if you ever wonder if I loved you, The answer is always.

> *- Blake*

She looked down at the tears that littered her lap, her heart broken into a million pieces. She reread each word over and over again, until her eyes were so blurry that she had to close them.

After a few moments, she turned to Damien. "He knew-" She couldn't even finish the thought. She couldn't manage to form words.

"He knew how this would turn out." Damien said for her. "It seems like he had everything planned out, baby." Pain etched itself into his expression, tears shining that he didn't bother to hide.

Another long silence passed between them, as Blair took a moment to compose herself. She then stood, even though her limbs were stiff, and her movements were slow. She crossed the room and opened the shutters.

The sun was hidden behind a veil of clouds, casting the land in a muted, gentle gray.

It felt right.

In the center of the courtyard below, two caskets rested. The first was deep oak. A simple yet beautiful wood for the quiet, yet strong man it was meant to embody. The second was unlike any other. It was carved from midnight-dark wood imbued with shadow, it shimmered faintly from the sunlight.

The weight of Blake's loss, and the other fallen warrior who lay beside him, echoed through the small crowd of people who now surrounded the coffins.

Blair closed the shutter, moving to change her clothes. Damien followed closely behind and soon they joined the people below. Standing at the foot of Blake's casket was Marrow, her arms wrapped around herself.

Looking up, she caught Blair's eyes just as she hugged her tightly. Marrow laid her head on Blair's shoulder, sighing deeply. Damien stood behind them, anchoring them.

Blair's face was streaked with silent tears, her expression broken but strong. She leaned toward Marrow, making her meet her gaze. "Blake was never serious about anything except *you,* Marrow. He loved you," her voice broke, "so much."

Several tears fell from her eyes as they hugged again, Marrow nodding into Blair's hair, confirming she knew. As they pulled away, Blair gave her strength to Marrow in every way she could. With one hand, Blair held hers, with the other, she wrapped it around her bicep, almost as if she was steadying her.

The sermon began quietly, with Shiloh leading. He spoke of Adriel first and his bravery. He reminisced about stories from the camp and memories from when he watched Adriel grow into a leader. He then turned to the other coffin, and took a deep breath.

"Some people are born to lead, others to fight but there are a rare few who are born to light every shadow they walk through. Blake was one of them. He brought laughter like lanterns, even in the darkest places. It didn't matter if you'd known him for years or minutes, you felt it. He saw people and not just their strengths or flaws, but who they were, underneath."

Heads nodded slowly and Blair let out a quiet sob. "He gave everything and because of *him*, we rebuild."

Marrow pulled away from Blair slowly, her face red and wet. She took a few hesitant steps forward, then turned to face the room. The hush that fell was complete, even the torches seemed to dim for her.

Her voice shook as she began. "Blake…" Marrow sniffled. "Made a choice so the Shadowborn could live. He will forever deserve a place next to Idris and the others." Marrow's voice caved on the last word and with that sound, a shadow instantly formed at her back.

His form was ethereal. The edges were soft today and his expression showed the same light-hearted mischief that had defined him in life.

Marrow turned toward him instinctively and when she saw him, a large smile grew on her face. Blake's form lifted his hand and placed it on Marrow's cheek before dissolving. Trying to fight it, Marrow broke into a fresh wave of sobs as she stumbled down from the dais. Damien caught her and pulled her close and Blair stepped forward in her place.

"Because of Blake, we will have a different world. I promise to make this land the one he should have had. A land where laughter is not a rebellion, but a birthright. Where children don't have to live in solitude or know what sacrifice is." Her voice grew stronger. "I will build that world. For him. For all of us."

Blair returned to Damien and Marrow, a sense of strength forming between them. The casket was lowered and soil fell to seal the final resting place for both Shadowborn.

<u>38</u>

The castle was no longer a place of sorrow. The stones, which had once been slick with blood and silence, had begun to warm under the touch of returning life. The halls that had echoed with grief now hummed with the quiet sounds of rebuilding. Voices had begun to trade stories of Shadowborn's safety.

It had been months since the battle and the courtyard where Blake had fallen was no longer a grave, it had become a garden, looked after by Marrow. Each morning, she moved carefully among the blooms, holding her growing belly as it brushed against the rare blooms that lived there.

She had planted the purple ones, the flowers from SilverDawn that Blair had loved so much. But here, no matter where she put them, they grew laced with shadows. It was a unique combination, one that showcased how darkness can sometimes bring out the beauty in something.

This flower began to grow everywhere, clinging to the pathways and walls of the castle. Marrow would always clip a few to lay on the two graves, to honor them.

It wasn't just Marrow. All of the Shadowborn continued to honor them both in quiet ways, everyday.

It started after the funeral, when all Shadowborn had decided to stay. Instead of the groups returning to their separate hidden camps, they rebuilt together, extending the castle.

The walls were fortified by Grei and a rotating circle of Shadowborn who worked through blistered hands and aching bones. Every stone was laid with intention. Each bore different marks; sigils, names, memories carved into them like blessings. The central keep was divided and every wing was gifted to a different camp. Everyone had their own space, but the lines between them blurred quickly. They were not divided by discipline or power, they were held together by choice.

The meeting room, once dark and cold, was lit again. They reclaimed it, and its long crescent table bore new maps, hand-sketched with routes into old territories. The goal was clear, find the ones still lost to camps and in hiding. It was essential to bring all their people home.

An elite team was created to help run their kingdom, one that was directly under Blair and Damien. The members consisted of a council made up of different Shadowborn: Kael, Rhea, Marrow, and Malrik. Shiloh was unanimously chosen as the leader, due to his ability to find those who were in need.

As Blair became the heart of the kingdom and led the people through kindness, Damien became the backbone and often led the missions.

In just a short time, they had all changed. Damien stood taller now, not just as a warrior, but as someone with something to protect. Someone who had chosen this life, and chosen Blair beside him.

Blair had found her sense of belonging. She led not with orders, but with presence. With a hand on a child's shoulder during a lesson. With hours spent in the kitchens, listening to reports and managing rations. With her mark glowing faintly during the meetings, pulsing like a heartbeat that belonged to all of them.

Soon, Shadowborn began arriving in greater numbers.

Some came alone, drawn by dreams, whispers, or letters carried by silent couriers. Others arrived in groups, led from ruined camps, or rescued from underground cells. Some didn't know their names, some still bore brands, but every single one was met at the gates with open arms and none of them were turned away.

Soon, the castle was no longer just a home. It was a thriving kingdom.

The outer village rose in its own glory, stone cottages, winding streets, and lanterns that glowed with gentle magic. They called it Diamond Ridge, in honor of the ones who had started it all.

Soon, came the laughter. Not from warriors or council members that had been elected, but from children. They ran through the cobbled paths, chasing their own shadows, laughing as sparks jumped from their fingers or as illusions shimmered behind their eyes. They trained in open fields, watched over by old soldiers who had once bled for a world that told them they were cursed.

The people didn't forget the dead, they honored them, by living fully.

It was one random morning that Blair stared at all of the glory around her. Damien stepped beside her, fingers brushing hers.

"Look at what we created," he said, "they don't look afraid anymore."

She smiled, eyes stinging. "They aren't."

He looked at her for a long time, the kind of look that carried weight and memory.

"You were never chosen by chance Blair. You were always meant to be bound to me and to the Shadowborn."

Blair looked over at him and the mark that seemed to glow under his collar, the mark that bound her life to everything that mattered. She kissed him, and turned back to their world.

A world for the Shadowborn

<u>Epilogue</u>

The afternoon sun was high, causing light to stream through the thick pink curtains that hung in the room. Several patches of warm light scattered across the floor where two little girls played, surrounded by stuffed animals and dolls, their laughter filling the space around them.

One was older, her blonde curls framing her bright green eyes. The other, almost two years younger, had blue eyes, red hair, and freckles that sprinkled across her cheeks like delicate constellations.

They squealed together as their shadows moved, dancing across their arms and moving toward their fingers.

The door opened and Blair stepped inside, followed by Marrow.

"Mommy!" the blue-eyed girl said, lifting her arm to show the faint geometric patterns on her skin. "Look!"

Blair smiled brightly at her daughter, who was a perfect mixture of her and Damien. She bent down and traced the patterns, brushing a stray hair back from her daughter's face. "They're beautiful, Blakely. Just like you."

Across the room, the blonde girl ran to the door as well with a black shadow circling her wrist.

She was Blake's daughter in every way, from her wild blonde curls down to her defiant posture. Giggling, she raised it proudly to her mother as well.

Marrow clapped, a huge smile on her face. "Great job, GloomBug."

The praise only energized them. With matching squeals, the girls grabbed their dolls and tore down the hallway, stopping only when a small space of shadow opened onto the floor next to them. One by one, they dropped their dolls in and then squealed even louder.

"These two." Marrow whispered, casting a helpless shrug in Blair's direction. "At least she doesn't realize she's the one creating it yet."

Just then, Damien approached them, his body strapped with shadowed daggers as if he had just returned from training the new groups of Shadowborn.

"Hey, feisty," he murmured, his voice low and playful. He knelt, his hair falling forward just a fraction as he pressed a lingering kiss to Blair's rounded belly, where their son moved beneath her skin. As he stood, light caught the ice-blue of his eyes, making them almost luminescent. "The girls giving you guys trouble again?" He asked, his arm wrapping around her lower back. "Blake would be proud."

Acknowledgments

To everyone who has held my hand, lifted me up, or gently pried my laptop out of my grip when I refused to stop writing, thank you. This book wouldn't exist without you.

To my husband, Donnie. You are my emotional support human, my designer, my formatter, tech support, late-night brainstorming partner, and the one who reminds me to breathe when I'm buried under chapters and chaos. Thank you for believing in this world before I even let myself believe in it. You're my biggest cheerleader, my grounding force, and the reason this dream feels possible.

To my current readers, the early supporters, and the people who picked up *Marked* on a whim- thank you for every message, every TikTok, every "I can't stop thinking about this book" comment, and every review that made my entire week.

I still squeal every time someone tags me. I don't think that will ever stop.

To my team: who answered a million questions, helped spread the shadows, and pined with me over fictional men with wings, your patience deserves awards. Truly. Thank you for loving me through every plot hole, teaser, and energy drink.

To the incredible indie author community… what a wild, welcoming, slightly chaotic, unbelievably supportive corner of the universe you are. Thank you for answering my panicked questions, cheering for every win, and reminding me that we're all in this madness together.

And to Blake, Damien, Blair, and the rest of the Shadowborn, thank you for screaming in my head until I wrote you down. I hope I've done your story justice.

Stay tuned for my next series.